IAN RICHARDS

Ian Richards' first book, a collection of short stories *Everyday Life in Paradise* (Godwit Press), was a finalist in the 1991 Heinemann Reed Award for best book of fiction. His biography *To Bed at Noon: The Life and Art of Maurice Duggan* (Auckland University Press, 1997) was nominated for the Montana Best Book Award. Richards' stories have been broadcast on Radio New Zealand, published in several anthologies, and appeared in numerous magazines, including *Landfall*, the *NZ Listener* and *North and South*. Richards was born and raised in Palmerston North and is currently an Associate-Professor of English Literature at Osaka City University in Japan.

DRONGO

IAN RICHARDS

Atuanui Press

Published by Atuanui Press Ltd
1416 Kaiaua Road, Mangatangi RD3, Pokeno 2473
www.atuanuipress.co.nz

ISBN: 978-0-9941376-4-7

Cover Design: Ellen Portch

Printed in New Zealand

'Well, mash 'em.'
(A sea-cook to a tyro sailor who, having spewed into a bucket of boiled spuds destined for the crew's dinner, asked: 'What shall I do?')
Heinemann Dictionary of New Zealand Quotations

ONE

I left Palmerston North when I was eighteen years old...it was 1977... up until then I, Andrew Murray Ingle, was a blank canvas.

I'd spent five numbing years at Palmerston North Boys' High School, where every day began the same way with morning assembly...in the assembly hall we got ourselves started by unstacking our school benches...we pulled them from great sloping piles along the walls and dragged them by their tubular-steel legs, clattering and scraping, over the badly gouged varnish on the honey-coloured hardwood floor...the benches were spread into rows till the whole layout for assembly was complete and the whole school's population could be fitted into the auditorium. By now the toughest boys were already lounging on their own seats...the staff were gathering quietly up on the stage...we shuffled into our places as best we could and sat, and the boys who were late hurried in before all the doors were closed...we stared down to the front of the hall over the furniture, looking through the frame of the floor-to-ceiling roof-beams that lined the space...everything had a horrible predictability. Then we were given the signal to stand up again...it was when the head boy at the edge of the stage, his puffy face scrubbed clean and pink, shouted, 'School!'...it meant another day had really begun, and we stood on cue...the headmaster had been waiting just inside the rear door of the hall...the headmaster's name was Evan Blake, and we watched him now while he paced down the centre aisle amongst us for the stage up front... he strode past each row of us with his hard rubber shoe-heels clicking against the surface of the floor, marching with his shoulders stiffly back and his head kept high. Evan Blake's face was large and square and he had small intense eyes, and his heavy chin was always blue with stubble...he paraded by us dressed in a long black flowing academic gown, something which he, and he alone of the staff, was allowed to wear...it was his mark of rank...we all knew that, except for morning assemblies, his crappy gown mostly stayed hanging on a peg in his office...the gown had ungainly armholes through which the grey sleeves of his suit poked, as if desperate for a way out...the gown collected floor-dust in the folds of its frayed hem with every movement forwards that he made. But Evan Blake never seemed to notice...instead he glared about at us, row by row, as he trod on and on for the stairs up to the stage...we watched him start working his jaw as he went...he was thrusting it out at us with each arrogant step...we could tell he was grinding his teeth at us in a rough, sliding gnashing, with a scarcely suppressed fury. Having got up on stage, Evan Blake announced a song...it was always a hymn, because we sang a hymn each morning...the exception was the new 'God Defend New Zealand' on Mondays...we all had to continue standing and open our crumpled brown hymn-books to sing, because standing was the rule too...Evan Blake stood rigid to attention before us...behind his back, the staff looked as if they were trying their damnedest not to wilt. At the piano the music master struck up the tune...the piano was positioned away to the left of the group of staff...it was just up against the pleats of the red velvet curtain that was spread across the rear of the stage...the piano was old and smashed, and had its wooden veneer peeling off in strips that hung along the sides. But the music master was a tiny, energetic man...he stole the show...his feet stretched hard to reach and pump the pedals below him... he had long, wildly uncombed white hair, and he wore a permanently startled look on his little face...that look was beautiful to us, like an expression of divine panic...it was clear that he liked to pretend he was Beethoven. We sang, and watched the music master bouncing up and down on his stool...he hammered the slow chords from the stiff, wrecked keys...he pounded it all out...something like chalk dust, or maybe dandruff, flew up freely around his neck and excited shoulders...he appeared almost ready to dive into the piano's keyboard and be lost. But Evan Blake ignored the music and sang solemnly above it...he stood at the centre of the stage, feet planted, next to the massive wooden lectern...he braced himself with his solid, meaty hands clenched down at his sides and I thought he looked as if he could barely restrain himself...he looked as though he wanted to attack and mutilate every one of us...it was obvious, and we all knew it, we boys, all waiting down before him in our raggle-taggle rows...Evan Blake hated us with a fierce, fierce passion.

8

We slouched about, wailing up the song, sulky in our grey flannel uniforms and jerseys and shifty on our feet...our scratched and muddy knees stuck out from below our shorts...our V-necked, regulation jerseys stank of damp wool, stale and heavy across our backs, drying from the morning's rain...we were bored, and we were tired of being bored...we felt that growing up seemed to be taking forever...we were so bored that anything, even just a stray fart, a little fluff, something silent but violent, would have lifted our spirits. There was only one hymn we ever really looked forward to singing...we liked droning out 'Make Me a Captive, Lord, and Then I Shall be Free'...we enjoyed singing the line 'Force me to render *up* my sword' and making it sound sexy...then we all giggled together...it made those of us who were sad want to laugh...it made those of us who were already cheerful feel even happier. Sometimes, on purpose, we'd sing the wrong lyrics, or perhaps we'd sing a line too far ahead...sometimes we substituted another song altogether, but always we sang the words as loud as we could in an extra-religious tone...our favourite song as a substitution was 'The Teddy Bears' Picnic' and we loved to have a go at singing it...we'd try to get well through it before being stopped from the stage, and the line we always hoped to reach was, 'See them *gaily* dance about'...we nervously envied homosexuals because gay people, to be gay, must be getting some sex, or so we reasoned...for us, there seemed to be no sex to get and there seemed to be nowhere out in the world to go find it. And that was why more than anything, each day at school, I wanted to be off on my own and in private...I wanted to be away someplace else and masturbating...I was obsessed by the prospect of sex with a woman and by everything to do with it...I didn't really know much about it at all, but I could not keep my hands from myself for even a moment. It was tough to force my thoughts into forgetting about what sex must probably be like...I knew that to help me try there were all kinds of sports at school, healthy running, jumping, stretching, kicking, catching, open-air activities...but I'd never been able to work up any sort of saving enthusiasm for games...sport left me too tired for anything except thinking about sex...then, of course, the only way I could get myself some sex was to masturbate. Each morning before school I started going to the Lido, the town's public baths...I swam up and back freestyle in the chilly Olympic-length pool...I struggled along and gasped for a breath at every fourth stroke...my nostrils were chafed by the sour chlorine...my eyes were red as though from uncontrollable weeping...

but it just felt a lot like filling in time before more single-minded masturbating. I even tried paying proper attention in class, a last-ditch effort...I thought perhaps studying would teach me a few things that might prepare me for life...but more than learning in readiness for anything about parabolic equations, the accusative infinitive or the periodic table, I desired to prepare for sex...I was over-preparing for it...when I wasn't masturbating, I was wishing I could be...if I wasn't wishing I could be, it was because I'd just finished. Already I could scarcely believe there was a time when I'd never heard of masturbation, not even a rumour...in fact, I really heard of it by reading all about it in *The Little Red Schoolbook*...
The Little Red Schoolbook was actually published just before I started at Boys' High...it had only a few pages about sex, but it was from Denmark and scandalous, and the scandal went on for ages and ages...in my third-form year Evan Blake denounced it in a rage at assembly and said it was a communist book...it was already a confirmed bestseller. Its copies lay piled up for months on end in Wynyards Bookstore on Broadway...they were on the central display-stand inside the wide front entrance, a short distance from the street...they were visible, tantalisingly visible, from the footpath going by...but anyone could be seen who went in and paused at the display...anyone could be remembered if they fingered the book's sharp edges...anyone could be known and named if we tried even to get a peek inside the book's rough-cut, red cardboard cover. We'd heard stories that, after all, the book didn't have any pictures, but there was too much temptation to scare me off...Evan Blake's disapproval was like a personal recommendation...on a late-night Friday at closing, after an evening of eating chips from Gibb's Burger Bar over on the old railway land with some schoolmates, Simon, Neil, Tony and Peter, I did it...I left them, stole away alone and slipped past the long main front window of Wynyards...I ignored the window's arrangement of picture books and atlases, organised into casual stacks that showed off their titles and their clean white pages...I headed into the shop to buy pornography. The place was unfamiliar, and not least because I almost never went in there...it was suddenly interesting to see how semi-grand Wynyards looked from inside...it was another wide, high-ceilinged nondescript hall, shaped a lot like the auditorium at school, except that the floor space was filled with tables and islands and there were dark wooden shelves on the walls, and everywhere was crammed with the colourful covers and spines of books... I was surprised that the shelves ran so far up on the walls towards the roof

and by the unmistakable thick odour of mould...there weren't many customers, and those I could spot were standing still and stooped, bent over to ponder the books before them, and not looking at me...they seemed very peaceful in their lost, distracted way, and I rather envied them for it. I slid one of the fat copies of *The Little Red Schoolbook* from the top of the display pile and it fitted snugly into my palm as I passed on by...then I walked along an empty aisle directly to the nearest counter, feeling shameless...the blood was thumping in my ears and my knees were turning more and more wobbly with each step...but I'd had no idea, till now, that being shameless could be so easy...I glanced back and could see almost in detail my own determined-looking face on the dark windows of the shop, with the fluorescent lights shining down across my cheeks...I thought that buying a communist sex book had become the most ordinary, the most manageable thing in the entire world. I arrived at the counter...there were no other customers anywhere nearby, and I thrust the book out over the till at the cashier...she was a dumpy red-nosed woman in an ugly chintz floral smock and she'd been standing with her arms by her sides, pinching the seams of her clothes and watching me approach... she reached out to take the book and I stared at her, and she stared back hard...I went on staring at her even more, staring and staring...then I had to glance down while I fumbled for money in my pocket. To my dismay my pocket felt utterly empty, and it was incomprehensible...all I could understand was that my hand was sweating as I searched...still I could feel only coins in the soft lining, but then at last I touched some crinkled dollar notes and got them up onto the counter with a rush of relief...the book was more than worth the trouble...the book told me everything I needed to know, because its few vital pages had all the details...it was much better than my mother's description of sex a couple of years earlier. There'd been no indication from my mother that this would happen when I'd simply walked in on her one morning while she was in the dining-room...she was a small thin woman with pale skin and short, tightly permed brown hair, and she wore a pink cotton housecoat around the home...this morning she was leaning with one hand flat against the woodgrain-panelling on the wall, balancing her weight on her knobbly wrist as she dribbled water from a yellow plastic watering-can down onto a rubber plant positioned on the floor by the sideboard...I was in a hurry to get past to the kitchen and out of the back door...I mumbled a word or two, and at first my mother didn't hear...through her tortoiseshell horn-rimmed glasses she was squinting down almost into the dangling leaves, an air of concentration etched into each line of her gaunt features. I was close to being gone, but when my mother noticed me she suddenly straightened up and called me back...I stopped, and returned, and saw her put the watering-can down onto the veneered surface of the dining-table, where it would probably leave a mark...that meant something was a big deal, almost for sure...she told me to sit, and so I pulled out a chair and did what she asked...then she remained standing a little away from me, rather stiff-backed and formal, while she started in on talking. Her tone sounded important but tentative...I wondered if there was going to be a hassle...I wanted to listen, but there was a long list of possible troubles flashing through my head and I began squirming on the chair's vinyl seat...in any case I found my mother was talking to a space up somewhere near the ceiling. My mother was talking about beds...things happened in beds...a lot more could happen in a bed than you'd bargained for...she seemed to hesitate at this and abruptly, unaccountably, paused... I didn't know how to help...unsightly red patches were appearing here and there on her face. '"Intercourse," Andy. It's called "intercourse,"' she said. She stood still and blinked down at me for an instant through her glasses...her gaze refocused on my forehead, or possibly my eyebrows... she kept her hands pressed firmly against the fabric of the housecoat on the sides of her hips, arms akimbo. She added, 'You know, the man rolls over on top of the woman.' All at once whole new batches of agitated thoughts were filling up my mind...my mother liked to call the vacuum-cleaner 'the vaccy-c' and she called our summer nightclothes 'shortie pyjamas'...it was hard to assume that, really, she knew what she was on about with a subject like this...I watched my mother pause again and reach up to tug at a loose curl of her hair near the base of her neck...she took a moment to grapple with the difficult dry tuft...but soon, with her arm frozen in place by her head, she went on speaking once more as if she'd made a decision. My mother said, 'Then the man actually does it. Puts his thing in the woman. And afterwards he rolls off and usually goes to sleep.'

'I see,' I said.

'Do you have any questions?' she added.

I asked, 'Does it go all the way in?'

I couldn't stop myself from inquiring...I saw my mother give a distinct flinch. 'Just briefly,' she nodded. She relaxed her hold at last on the stray curl of hair. She asked, 'Anything else?'

'No,' I said. 'I'm good.'

I wasn't really good…I had no end of questions…but I thought it best to act as though the topic was all done…my mother had made intercourse sound like a makeshift cure for insomnia. But then I read *The Little Red Schoolbook*, and I just couldn't wait to get myself started…all day at school, each day, I'd imagine every part of having a good long fuck… in class the teacher might be talking about kings, the Tudors, whatever was in the syllabus, but I'd begin to feel myself rising majestically in my shorts…I didn't need a specific reason…the tip of my cock would brush itself up against the rough plywood bottom of the desk…that instant felt like springtime in my pants. Soon I had to grip at the sides of my seat, with my solid erection jammed up into the small space available under the school-desk…my eyes began to water from an exquisite pain…I held my breath with my head kept lowered to my chest, gritting my teeth… normally, at the next moment, I adjusted the chair…the brief thrusting movement was so terrific that I'd let out a gasp…I fought and strained not to forget myself, but still had to sit on, pretending to listen to the teacher while my underpants burned. At home, I loved the toilet…from the first it was my favourite place to masturbate…it was the only room in the house with a lock on the door…inside the free confines of the toilet I'd remove my pants and take out a handkerchief…then, gingerly, I'd lay myself face-down on the lino…there was never enough space to stretch out properly, and my knees had to be bent and my calves tucked with laborious effort up around each clammy, cold side of the bowl. At this point I was ready and wild in my excitement, and frequently I was even a bit more than ready…I'd reach down in a blind rush and grip myself with the handker-chief…next I fucked the floor…the rock-hard linoleum in the toilet had no give, but I thrust at it anyway, over and over…I humped and showed it a damn good time…before long I'd come onto the handkerchief, though occasionally I'd miss and have to clean up the lino afterwards. At night, in bed and in private, I soon started to get a little more adventurous…I lay on my stomach between the sheets, spread the handkerchief beneath me, and ran my fingers around myself…I was searching for what *The Little Red Schoolbook* termed 'erogenous zones'…I felt around pretty much everywhere, checking with delicacy…it seemed important to stay open-minded and thorough…I discovered that I was pretty much all erogenous. But by now my mind would be focusing on some woman…it was easier

13

to manage this in the comfort of the bed than in the clinical environment of the toilet...the woman had no special face but only a special body, all curves for caresses, and a rampant desire...she existed only for me...she was my nameless love-machine. Thanks to *The Little Red Schoolbook* I could bring this almost insatiable woman slowly to climax...so slowly, but so inevitably, it would happen, that she'd be my slave...I whispered 'yes' as I explored her erogenous zones...I could hear her steadily begging and groaning in my ears. *The Little Red Schoolbook* said it was important to be generous in bed, but I yearned more than anything to be quite the stud...I held myself back for as long as possible...I twitched and flopped about in the overheated sheets, aching with pleasure...the pair of us would reach the verge, or quite a way past the verge, and then I'd remember with frustration to fumble about for the handkerchief... usually it had shifted down in the throes of our passion and was somewhere off by my feet...there was a desperate scramble to reach along for it at the cooler bottom of the bed. This search delayed me for a few extra ecstatic seconds...sometimes I was turned topsy-turvy amidst all the confusion...my toes were wriggling against the pillow with pent-up anticipation and my face was shoved down at the foot of the bed into the gap between the mattress-edge and the fold of the sheets, till I could scarcely breathe...but finally, impatient, shaking, sweating, I'd sigh with relief, feel unbridled happiness and ejaculate. I was never especially cautious, since I was too preoccupied with stage-managing the fathomless depths of my own conquests...but soon afterwards I often wondered if I might have been heard...the uncomfortable idea of being discovered would grow in my mind, and I'd creep out of bed and stand, motionless, on the bristly carpet in the middle of my room...I was listening nervously for the sound of someone noticing...sometimes I sneaked as far as the bedroom's dark doorway and strained with my ears...I kept hoping to be the only person awake in the whole empty night. Then at last I would hear my father's snores sputtering from along the corridor...their raspy rhythms were long, calm and slow...when there were pauses, between extended gasps or exhalations of air, I'd try to make out any other noise behind them...occasionally there was the rumbling movement of a train crossing far off on the other side of town, going to new places...in the large quiet the sound was barely muffled by distance...but mostly there was no sound, nothing. I'd return to the bed...on many nights by this time the chill of the air was gathering across my back...I was still worried

14

that I might get caught and, with my fingers trembling, I'd bend to put the sweaty sheets in order…what would I say if anyone found me here?… what would it be like, now, if a sexy woman just came on in wearing only some revealing, skimpy negligee, something filmy and see-through, or even better, nothing at all?…I'd go and pry open the chest of drawers for another handkerchief, and I'd climb into bed again with the woman waiting, panting. Soon I had a new reason for swimming in the Lido's icy waters each morning, because the icy water relieved the raw, chafed skin on my cock…I was so sore that it was becoming difficult to walk without endlessly adjusting my trousers…also, my handkerchiefs were getting particularly cruddy…I'd take them along to the pool each morning as well, where I rinsed the hankies by swimming a few laps with them stuffed into my togs, and stretched them out in one of the open lockers for some minutes to dry…letting strangers see all this felt much better than explaining the state of my nose rags to my mother. Already I'd had a minor disaster, after I'd borrowed my mother's oven glove to experiment with in the toilet…*The Little Red Schoolbook* was in favour of putting spice into a relationship…I'd started out by gripping myself hard with the glove…finally I penetrated its insides for some glorious minutes and messed on the quilted interior…it was so bad that I had to throw the thing away in secret. My mother went around for days complaining because it seemed that she just couldn't find what she needed in the kitchen anymore…for weeks she was reduced to using an old tea-towel…after that I also resolved to make do, and I exploited only my handkerchiefs and the Lido, the mere essentials…I'd put the handkerchiefs damp into my pockets after swimming…next I'd bicycle off for another school assembly…I was a little perturbed that already my sex life was becoming a routine, but the memory of the oven glove lingered for quite some time.

For fun there was also Friday night in town…for a while I used to hang around with a few mates at the Record Hunter, a music store in the far end of the Stafford Arcade…the Record Hunter wasn't a large store… it didn't even have the best record selection…but the Record Hunter had cool rock-star posters pinned up on the walls and some were even Blu-tacked up across the ceiling…also, the music playing in the shop was loud, pounding and strange to me, so it was probably good. The Record Hunter's owner was a tall man who had long hair that drooped all the way down his skinny frame to his elbows…sometimes he'd remember my face and say 'hi'…I'd nod back with studied nonchalance as I shuffled through some bins, thrilled, or nudge a pal in the ribs to let him know I'd been noticed...but the Christian Centre was where the tough boys all started to gather...the tough boys mentioned it at school and declared that it was a hip place...the Record Hunter was finished. By then my parents had taken to insisting that I go out into town on Fridays in smart clothes...I didn't know why they wanted me to do so...why did they want me to wear stuff which only they would approve of when they weren't likely to be around?...why did they want me feel so utterly embarrassed each time I departed from the house?...I was never going to appear hard enough for the Christian Centre dressed up in my Sunday-best. I'd leave home on Friday evenings attired in my sissy clobber...refusing to return any goodbye waves, I'd ride off on my bike into the low twilight with my drawstring duffle-bag over one shoulder...inside my duffle-bag was a secret stash...there was a T-shirt, a pair of jeans and some sandshoes, which I thought of as my travelling clothes. After a while I'd stop at Milverton Park...in haste I'd drop my bike with a clatter on the grass at the edge of the deserted soccer pitches...I'd steal across the white-marked fields in the mingling shadows of the dusk...I was hoping to find the best available cover behind the distant, sickly-looking trees that bordered the rear of the park...but it often felt as if people, somewhere, were already watching me and knew who I was. I'd creep in among the trees and the insubstantial scrub as far from the road as seemed manageable...there was never a perfect spot and I always had to settle for some sort of compromise...then I'd strip down to my underwear, praying that no one would happen to come by and see any of me naked while I changed...it was foolish...it was quite possibly even unsafe to stumble about there, semi-exposed, with only one leg in or out of my own trousers...but I did it, the same rigmarole, every Friday night before going on to town. The Christian Centre was run by fanatics who were determined to save the world, starting with Palmerston North...they were renting a bankrupt shop in one corner of the Square, an unfashionable corner tucked in near Broadway, with no kind of sign or anything out front to advertise the place...when I waited outside the entrance in the evening dark with some friends the building always looked closed up and derelict, except to those of us who knew it wasn't...we always relished its pleasantly seedy feel as we pushed at the door and drifted in through the opening. After entering fresh from the night, we began by instinct to bunch up together just past the doorway...inside, the shop looked as though everything of any value

16

had been torn out by the previous owners and then the Christians had put nothing back in...the shop's empty, brightly lit space stretched back in plain view the entire width of the room to the rear...each time we came in, we saw again the damaged gib-board walls along the sides, unpainted and crisscrossed with filler...we saw the same old heap of broken fittings at the back, still lying half hidden under a rotten tarpaulin...we could smell the tarpaulin's sour odour of canvas and make out the dull stains of damp above the skirting boards. One of the youngest Christians was usually squatting on his haunches nearby us, in charge of an electric jug set up on a low pile of timber...he was clad in the nicely tatty but always somehow old-fashioned clothes, the nylon shirts and flannel trousers, that the Christians mostly preferred...it often made me question the wisdom of changing my own glad rags...the junior Christian waved us over to him, one by one, and gave us each a cup of 'steam'...steam was the Christians' term...but it just meant Raro instant orange, mixed from the packet with boiling water. We all stood about, drinking our steams, shuffling back and forth with nowhere to go...there were exposed copper wires hanging from among the harsh fluorescent lights in the ceiling above us...there was a lot of plaster powder everywhere, spread along the uneven concrete floor and crunching into a fine white grit beneath our feet...I guessed probably the Christians didn't think that cleanliness was next to godliness...they didn't seem to think much about cleanliness at all. At last we were allowed to advance, those of us who'd been collecting there, to the only furniture in the place...it was two long rows of flimsy plywood school-chairs extending across the width of the shop, with the rows lined up to face each other...about a dozen Christians sat waiting for us on the uncomfortable chairs, ready for the counselling part of the evening...they were all ranged together along one side...they leaned back and crossed and then uncrossed their legs...a few of them folded their arms and looked unnaturally satisfied. We came over and sat in some disorder on the chairs opposite...the chairs wobbled and creaked as we chose our spots, and we shifted a bit in our seats and felt embarrassed, trying hard not to stick out...next the Christians did their level best to convert us by argument...they spent most of the evening with us this way, locked in passionate dispute...the singsong rhythms of their voices struggled upwards and filled the bare room. We were supposed to pick a Christian each to talk with...the Christians concentrated on trying to convert us individually...they didn't like us interrupting the other disputes in

17

progress alongside them…they felt that interrupting was solely their own privilege…they did most of the talking anyway, and they were arrogant and immune to our counter-arguments…when they couldn't win by logic, they'd seek to wear us down. For us, it was a success if we made these would-be pastors confused…it was a success with the worst ones if we even made them pause…but nothing like that happened very often, and soon everyone was leaning forward in the same uneasy, tired posture… we hunched ourselves over with our elbows down on our knees while we listened…we lifted our heads only when it was time to speak. I had a favourite Christian to argue with…he was a big, extra-shabbily dressed German immigrant…mostly he sat stooped forward from the very beginning, as though ready to spring, with his shirtsleeves rolled up to show the thickly matted black hair on his heavy, pale forearms…he told me to call him Steve-oh and never volunteered anything else as a name. I always had time, as we talked, to marvel at the sharpness of Steve-oh's haggard, surly face, which looked as if someone had pared it back with a sheath knife…his long cheeks were hollow scoops and his nose was bent, badly askew, to one side…the sticky sandy fringe of his unkempt hair was brushed in the same direction as his nose…I thought it all seemed remarkably German…Steve-oh's favourite verse from the *Bible* was: 'And if thine eye offend thee, pluck it out, and cast it from thee,' and often he managed to quote it at unwelcome moments…his crooked features suggested he'd tried out the same idea on his own face, and his fierceness felt every bit as German as his looks. But I wondered that Steve-oh never displayed any trace of an accent as he spoke…he'd just go on leaning himself further and further forward while launching into his usual opening speech…he'd glare at me intensely…he'd stare out at me from under his half-lowered brow as he argued. 'I really believe that God is communicating through me tonight,' he liked to say. He liked to grind out the words through his teeth…Steve-oh shrugged his strong, rangy shoulders…he normally had dark rings forming under his smouldering eyes…he fixed me more and more deeply with his scary gaze. 'God's here in this room, communicating through me. He wants you to come into his ministry, eh,' Steve-oh snarled. 'That's what God wants—He wants to win the battle for your immortal soul.' By now I knew that any talk of what God wanted meant Steve-oh's argument was getting itself into gear… God always wanted a whole lot of stuff. 'God's asking you, eh—He's asking you to join his kingdom of light. He's looking for your redemption,'

18

Steve-oh warned me. 'It's so's that you'd go and take your part, yeah, in a paradise on earth. And it's a glorious paradise that's right here and now this minute, mate. Right now, right here, God wants you, *you*, to repent all the sins on your soul. Acknowledge them, eh, admit them tonight, and then you'd be one of the saved. God wants you to do that—He wants you know unlimited joy.'

'Well, that's nice,' I interrupted.

I had a pretty big mouth…I could think of lots of smart answers like that. 'Tonight,' Steve-oh hissed. He pressed on regardless…he shoved the topic across at me. 'In the midst of this cold dark night on earth,' Steve-oh said, 'with God bloody communicating through me in this room, right here under the celestial gates, why don't you accept the Lord Jesus Christ down into your heart, eh? Why not? Why the hell don't you? You should accept him into your heart as your saviour, eh, and renounce your aimless, wicked ways. You should read the good news in his book and rejoice. Rejoice in yourself with the truth of his word.'

'What makes you think I haven't already?' I asked.

Steve-oh took a moment to glare at me especially hard…I hoped the others would notice he'd stopped speaking…then he waggled a finger in front of his damaged nose. 'You don't look fucking saved to me,' Steve-oh growled.

'How do you know? How do you know anything? Are there merit badges?' I asked.

Steve-oh ignored me and went on talking…it was obvious to us that sarcasm was wasted on the fanatics…that was why they were so good to practice arguing with…he went right on bludgeoning me with my own salvation. But what I wanted to hear from Steve-oh was something else entirely…when God wasn't communicating through him, Steve-oh liked to relax and unburden himself…he liked to tell stories about his own past…he was in his thirties, though his waxy, broken-up face looked older…he often told me about how he'd been born in Hamburg…his family had moved to Manchester when he was only fourteen, but at school, in England, he was bullied constantly and called a Nazi pig. He'd run away from home…he'd lived on the streets by stealing what he could…it was great and he felt free, but every time he was caught by the police and brought back…at seventeen Steve-oh joined the army, where he was considered unusually tough in training…soon though, he was thrown out for almost killing a man in a chokehold. It was after that when he'd started

19

into drinking heavily...he'd made a lot of money selling drugs for the London mob...Steve-oh became consumed with bitterness, he said, till he reached the age of twenty five and then, at last, one fateful day, he saw the face of God...Steve-oh's eyes always brightened dangerously whenever he mentioned the face of God...but God's face turned up in his stories almost every week. I couldn't tell for sure if Steve-oh's tales were true, and sometimes I thought they were probably not...sometimes new and more remarkable things appeared in the latest version...his past always seemed to be getting busier and longer, and his stories didn't really explain anything about him...but the stories were the best part of listening to Steve-oh. The Christians had all had pretty tough lives...they liked to describe for us how thoroughly bad they'd been before being saved, but I had no intention of joining them and renouncing stuff in their screwy church... they'd seen a few things and done everything imaginable, but now they didn't want us to have a turn...it made me wonder why they'd bothered to go and get themselves saved in the first place...perhaps it allowed them to enjoy the past at a safe distance...perhaps being young hadn't really agreed with them. The second part of the evening happened after nine o'clock, and this was the part we all looked forward to, because it happened when the shops were shut and most of the town was dead...we got to accompany the Christians outside, to the clubrooms and the late-night cafes that still remained open...the idea was that we'd take along a few bunches of pamphlets praising the Lord and be a bit evangelical ourselves...we were aiming to seek people in those places who were in dire spiritual need...the visits felt like adventures, since spiritual need tended to flourish in some fairly rough territory...we'd never have got into such interesting after-hours clubs and cafes on our own. The Christians always split us into small groups and took charge of where we went...but there was a spot to visit that was, by far, the most favoured of all the places to try for...it was the billiard parlour upstairs in the Coleman Mall...there was a lot of jockeying for that particular opportunity, and only once did I manage to get myself into the group which would be going. It was on a night's visit which started much later in the evening than usual...we left the Centre in a hurry, clutching our literature...we spilled out into the sudden darkness on the street, and the hush outside and the seriousness of our mission killed off any chatter...soon we were marching in silence past streetlamps along the footpath on the edge of the Square. The town was all so different late at night...just a few yards from us the trimmed

20

blue grass of the Square plunged away into blackness and weird space...
across the road there were one or two mild gleams from shop lights that
had been left turned on, and I struggled to make out a shadowed figure
moving in front of a store...but the streets elsewhere were deserted and
we could hear our own isolated footsteps slithering off into the confusing
distances...each of the approaching streetlamps flooded us in a welcome
pale glare till we passed by below it...the lamps showed up our faces shining pink and greedy with excitement. I thought that I seemed to be the
only one in the group who was really nervous...I was pals with none of the
others walking beside me, and some of them were the meanest boys in
our school...I guessed that a few of them probably went to billiard par-
lours anyway...even worse, the Christian in charge was one of the biggest and most unpleasant at the Centre, and he was the only Christian
coming with us...I didn't know for sure what would happen, but I knew I
couldn't rely on anybody if there was trouble. We left the Square and
entered the Coleman Mall, wandering in the middle of the narrow, empty
road...in the dark the Mall looked shabby and somehow threatening...it
had cobbles underfoot that were loose and jiggled, and its broad verandas
loomed out at us across the roadway as we passed by...on the edges of
the footpaths, in the gloom, the kerbs were lined with ugly planters filled
with spiky, damaged shrubs and dead weeds...after a minute or so we
halted opposite an open stairway between some shop-fronts...it was a
simple, unlit flight of rising steps not even protected from the street by a
door or shutter, and I marvelled that I'd never noticed it or its importance
until now. The others paused for the briefest moment to gather everyone
together and headed across the footpath for the entranceway...then they
began to march up the steeply pitched stairs in front of us...I was left following at the back as best I could...each of the boards on the stairs
creaked crazily under our heavy footsteps and made a hell of a noise...
with my free hand I found a loose, clinking brass hand-rail up along one
wall...I grasped at it with gratitude. Next somebody was pushing open a
solid wooden door and we were crowding through...we entered a long
dim room, halting in a cluster...at the back I couldn't see well, and the air
around me felt dry and smelled badly of cigarettes...I heard a loud, distracting series of sounds...I guessed it was billiard balls, clicking and
banging in play from snooker and pool. The Christian got us to spread out
in a line...the darkness around us filled everywhere but the centre space
of the room and its lower portions...I discovered most of the billiard

21

parlour's strained yellow light was coming from shaded lamps, dangling on their cords from a high ceiling, with the lamps arranged regularly over several neat rows of grey-green tables that stretched off towards the rear...I could also make out thin white wisps of tobacco smoke rising far above the tables and lamps...the smoke was coiling up into the deep darkness overhead...I had to work hard at not letting myself cough and disturbing the people, the customers, all around us. Mainly the players were just standing about in the gloom, still as statues...they seemed engrossed in their own games...they were waiting quietly on the bare wooden floor, poised and relaxed, ready for their turns...they held cues in their hands taken from the racks along the walls, but I saw that some of the players had swung round to inspect us...their faces were tough and unwelcoming...they were definitely watching us and how we were behaving. But the Christian began to lead us forward in a single file, down between some tables...the billiard tables were sturdy, and heavily scored with scars and scratches around their corners...they looked dauntingly large as we passed them by...we didn't want to bump into anything, and we tried to stick together and move in our line...but often we had to wait, since there was just no choice, if a player was bending to make a shot... we straggled on and on in our clumsy, broken group, and soon we were scattered and pretty much alone. I tried not to catch anyone's eye directly as I shuffled about...I focused my gaze at the floor, or at things off in the distance...further down the room a lot of hefty men with their backs towards me were crowded along one side of a table, and the darkness from the ceiling appeared to collect as shadows on their necks and shoulders...I could see they had bunches of dollar notes clasped in their hands, and by turns the men were tossing down some of the money...it fell from their fists away somewhere, off onto the wide hidden bed of the table. Then one of the men, muttering to himself, lifted a very ordinary-looking plastic cup up high near his jaw...he shook the cup about, and it slapped and rattled...there were dice inside...the other men seemed to press forwards closer to each other, almost intimately, across the broad space... the cup-holder reached down again and their heads all followed his movement...he spilled a pair of dice out into the darkness, and I thought I heard them bounce on the slate of the tabletop. After a moment the men all reacted together with the same long, intense grunt...they began to consult amongst themselves...they looked satisfied, and one slapped another on the arm...they turned a little and commenced glancing about

22

them as if the room had just started to exist...I made a rapid effort to stare away at another table. So, I thought, this is a den of iniquity. Still, our Christian didn't appear in any screaming rush...I managed to get him in sight once more across the room, and I saw that he seemed to know several of the people in the place...he was lingering occasionally to chat with a player in a confidential way, and he'd glance back behind him as if to include other players in the conversation...but I wasn't close enough to hear them talk. I started watching some of the games instead...it was beginning to feel more than a bit awkward, what with all the waiting...my fingers were very damp and my pamphlets praising the Lord were wrinkling in my grip...I held one out towards a player, but he nimbly waved me off and hurried away for the far side of his table...the other player with him tapped his cue against his foot as though I simply wasn't there. I didn't feel disappointed...I'd never bothered with reading the handouts either...but now I was very aware of how crudely printed and silly they seemed on their cheap, water-absorbent paper...the games all around me looked much more interesting than anything written in a pamphlet. After a while I sensed somebody had come up by my shoulder and was hovering close to me...I turned, and saw that beside me a stocky, pot-bellied man stood, slowly shifting his weight from one foot to the other...he appeared elderly, but despite his age he was dressed in youthful-looking black-and-brown striped shorts and a red T-shirt...also he had a strong, solid neck and a good head of snowy-white hair, and his large face was half hidden by the sweeping curls of a white handlebar moustache. The man was up so near to me that I couldn't help taking a small step back...I noticed there was a money-satchel streaked with blue chalk slung on a belt under the low curve of his gut...the man kept his hands on his hips, elbows out, and was nodding while he rocked from side to side as if I'd already said something he agreed with...I watched the wide tips of his moustache splay out as his cheeks spread into a big grin...it occurred to me that sooner or later, as a real conversation opener, I'd better try saying a word or two.

'Excuse me,' I managed. 'But does that there make you the owner of this billiard hall?'

I pointed down at the satchel...I was pretty confident that I was right and he was the proprietor. 'Yeah, I reckon,' the man said. His voice was loud, but unusually high-pitched. He chirped, 'Would you be wanting yourself a game of snooker, eh, young fellow?' All at once he put his own arm out, letting it linger near me, and I saw he was gesturing towards a table...around us now I could tell people had begun to stare.

'Thank you,' I said. I was taking extra-special care to be polite. 'Unfortunately, the thing is—'

I glanced about to indicate the Christian and a few of the others who'd come with me...but the whole group of them was gone, the lot, vanished...not even a solitary one of them was left...they must have disappeared downstairs without my noticing, and I was surrounded by all these people. I started to blush...I couldn't stop myself...the man went on staring into my eyes with a cheerful air...I spoke up with the first thing that came to mind.

'I've never, ever played any snooker before,' I said.

The man let out a distinct chuckle and the colour came up into his face...he drew his arm in at last and slapped at his belly with a loud thump...perhaps he just wanted to confirm its solidity, but the rough movement made the small change rattle in the satchel. 'Well,' he said in his shrill, fluting voice. 'You must have a hell of a lot of money saved away, if you've never had a game of snooker.' I dry-swallowed and put on a smile...I was still taking the best possible care to be polite.

'Well, you can't spend it in heaven,' I agreed.

'Too right,' the man replied.

'You can't even spend it at the Christian Centre,' I said.

I wasn't at all sure what I was talking about, but then I saw the man's large eyes widen further and suddenly shine. He announced, 'You're smarter than you look, eh, young fellow. Smarter than you look.' I just could not prevent myself from beaming at this...my glee radiated from my face...the man let both of his large, weathered hands rest on his satchel, and turned slowly to the players nearby...most of them had put down their cues onto the beds of the tables to watch. 'But that's only because you look so fucking dumb!' the man shouted into the room. I didn't suppose the man meant me much harm, but I could feel my blood beating hard...my ears felt as if they were turning scarlet...I was aware that everyone at all of the tables around us was laughing...their laughter rang in my head like shame. I hurried off...nobody stopped me...that's the way I remember it.

I got myself an after-school job...it was during my seventh-form year...I worked each day at Wynyards, out in the dirty backrooms of the shop, where the floor was nothing but crumbling old concrete and there

24

was a dry sawdust smell in the corners...it was intriguing to see how the place actually operated from within...the store was a much bigger and more intricately ordered world than I'd expected. My job was to help out...I was an assistant to Bob Sykes every day after school until six...it was the sort of behind-the-scenes work that made me feel rather important. Bob was a small middle-aged Scotsman with a cheery, busy manner...he had a square, heavily wrinkled face and blunt features, with greying curls of ginger hair that lay thin on the top of his head but poked out lower around the sides...he had salt-and-pepper-coloured side-whiskers that only made his face seem even squarer...he always wore a neat white cotton shirt but with baggy khaki shorts and sandals, and long walk socks...Bob stood with his back held straight while he worked, showing off a vaguely military air. We both had to stand the whole time for the job, unpacking books on a table near the open entrance at the very rear of the store...the table in front of us was enormous, built of pale rough-hewn pine, and it was all ours, and only ours, to use... together and clumsily we'd haul up onto it the misshapen corrugated-cardboard boxes, filled with new titles, that were delivered to the shop several times a day...the boxes were brought by a postal van to the back entrance, and each parcel seemed to have a look and feel of its own...we dragged them inside into large wire storage bins behind our work area where they awaited our attention...they seemed to arrive filthy from their exotic travels...sometimes just picking one and getting it up onto the table left our noses and mouths harsh with dust. Bob would start to pry open the stiff flaps of a new box...he'd pull out the invoice papers and we'd see what books were tucked inside...the papers, once smoothed out flat on the table, usually required Bob's calculator...he always held the machine away at an arm's length and stared suspiciously at the liquid-crystal display...his side-whiskers would twitch on his face as he pursed and unpursed his lips and poked at the buttons. Meanwhile I'd finish with the unpacking of the books...I'd get them stacked up neatly along the tabletop...Bob would announce the currency conversion and the mark-up...then we pencilled the prices over and over into the flyleaves until Bob called for a break. Mostly we preferred boxes that were filled with only one title, to be all priced the same...what we liked best was a series of boxes with the same Hammond Innes or Alistair MacLean...but Palmerston North was a university town, and there were plenty of small packets with strange scholarly texts, and strange prices and mark-ups...

25

we worked only from the top of the bins and left these misfit parcels for later…that was another calculation of Bob's…small packets were trouble, and so we kept them waiting, mashed into the bottoms of the bins, for weeks. Sometimes Bob left me for long periods to go visit his fellow staff, offering me no other excuse than mere social exercise…he'd wink at me with a brief shake of his head and then stroll away into the store, going for a chat…I'd watch him depart, swinging his arms in a peculiar, off-kilter little saunter as he went…I thought he was very keen on spreading bonhomie. Also, every day at four-thirty Bob would disappear into the toilet…he'd vanish with a book and not be seen again until after five…he liked to call his habit a 'wee comfort-stop'…one day at afternoon tea in the staff room, Mr Knightly from technical books called him 'the navvy in the lavvy'…I supposed that this was the reason why Bob kept clear of the toilet for a fortnight. Soon Bob had me start to empty the mousetraps… there were usually a few mice living behind the storage bins where we kept the books, and they left bits of droppings…I'd throw the tiny corpses, curled up in death, into the rubbish sack every evening…I got into the routine of resetting the traps each night before leaving. Then Bob got me to do the banking…each afternoon, at four, I walked with the entire day's takings out of the shop…I carried the cash and cheques in a brown cardboard suitcase that was stencilled with 'Wynyards' on the side in white letters…I marched out through the front of the store and everyone, staff and customers, watched me go…for a few happy moments I was the centre of attention. I'd proceed across Broadway to the Bank of New Zealand, tapping the edge of the suitcase against one leg and feeling as though I was carrying contraband…but nothing ever happened, and there was never even the slightest trouble…only Bob sometimes theorised on the best way he might rob me…he finally settled for a tyre-iron to my arm, with a quick grab at the case and a run…he wanted an escape car on Broadway and a switch in Grey Street…I thought Bob's professionalism was pretty impressive. I decided I liked everything about working for a living…especially I liked holding aside the expensive art books that came into the back…that way I had something to look through during Bob's comfort-stops…I enjoyed the broad pages, slow to flip over, and the slick feel of the costly paper on my fingers…my favourites were the nineteenth-century painters…I relished the sexy pictures by Delacroix and Ingres as they shone at me under the backroom light, and I'd find myself feeling horny while staring at them, but Bob had the toilet completely sewn up. Despite his visits, Bob kept up bad blood with one of the salesladies out at the front of the store...the saleslady's name was Mrs McCreedy, and she was in charge of children's books...Mrs McCreedy was a massive woman with a fat lumpy face, a blocky build and a reputation for severity...to conceal her looks she wore straight, pink or green ankle-length dresses, decked out with rows of ruffles and frills that only left her seeming bigger, and she had short, violently blue-rinsed hair...she had a deep resonating voice and spoke with an intimidating, upper-class manner...if I was out in the front of the shop, I was always a bit apprehensive around her. The children's corner seemed a lot like Mrs McCreedy's private billet, with a 'no-trespassing' sign up in the middle...she'd pace back and forth along its aisle, round-shouldered and looking irritable...she'd comb her fingers through her appallingly coloured hair and review her piles of Little Golden Books and Puffins while keeping mothers away from anything not quite appropriate...a pair of reading-glasses always swayed with authority on a long silver chain round her brawny neck as she walked...Bob nicknamed her 'The Duchess'...he encouraged everyone to call her that, but we only dared use her nickname if she wasn't around. Usually I saw Mrs McCreedy up close at afternoon-tea breaks in the staff room, when it was half full of other people...if I rushed from school when the last period was over, which I always did, I could be at Wynyards just before afternoon tea was finished...the staff room was just off the narrow corridor that led through from the front to the back of the shop...it was entered down a small set of treacherous concrete steps that I'd leap in one bound to save time. I'd hurry across to the far side of the room, to a bench and sink with a Zip water-heater attached at one edge...getting there meant sliding past people already seated round an unsteady dining-table which took up most of the space...I bruised my thighs bumping against the table's corners as I went...I got myself a fast cup of something awful by dunking with a teabag, not caring if the teabag was used or not...finally I sat anywhere handy down along the bottom of the table and joined in...Mrs McCreedy had her own special chair, arranged at the table's head. 'Oh, Bernard,' I'd hear her intoning. She liked to say Bernard's name...she seemed to say it every few minutes. 'Oh, Bernard, is there a fresh cup still, over there, do you think? Something proper from a pot, or any such? Not something dredged through a horrible strainer.' She'd sigh and add, 'I'm in dire need of the cup which refreshes.' That was the sort of thing she mostly said...

27

she spoke in rich, implicit commands that sounded half-forgotten the moment she'd made them...then she seemed to ignore Bernard as he shambled over to make her another pot of tea. Bernard was Mrs McCreedy's sales assistant and he worked at Wynyards only in the afternoons...there was something a bit wrong with Bernard and Mrs McCreedy saw managing him as her personal duty...but I could never find out what was wrong with him exactly, beyond the expression 'handicapped'...no one else ever felt it was polite to say more...Bernard was in his twenties, affable and even sweet-natured, though with a permanently unfocused look in his grey-blue eyes...his mouth appeared too stiff to form his words well when they came out from his lips, and this was the first real hint that something was not right. 'Yei, Mia M-Ceedy,' Bernard would moan at whatever Mrs McCreedy told him. Physically Bernard was short, strong and noticeably bullnecked...his head always looked jammed down onto his shoulders at an awkward angle...his grey suit was always too tight around his hugely overdeveloped upper-body...when he approached Mrs McCreedy with a saucer and teacup gripped between the tips of his powerful fingers, his long face would tilt far over to one side, as if doing such a delicate task required special thought...it was a second hint that all was not well...I was mesmerised at how trapped Bernard appeared by whatever it was that had damaged his being, and at how much he struggled against it. But Mrs McCreedy would often scold Bernard, no matter what he did...she seemed convinced that he was always being clumsy...she never even thanked him each time he completed the job of bringing her a teacup... instead she liked to wait and watch, fingering the chain for the glasses on her neck, while Bernard shuffled round the table and back to his seat. Then, as he'd sit down, Mrs McCreedy would make an announcement like, 'Oh, Bernard, I seem to have no spoon here. Could you manage perchance to get me a small spoon from the drawer?' 'Yei, Mia M-Ceedy,' Bernard would say. He would rise automatically and do her bidding...but Bob would jump into action, and it was as though he only lived for these chances...once he lurched in front of Bernard, practically pushed him aside, and hurried over to the drawers below the bench...from a drawer Bob pulled a spoon out and dropped it, then picked it up and held it to his lips...he blew on the spoon, with plenty of spittle, and at last he put it down into the Duchess's cup. 'And as the Americans say: "you're welcome",' Bob declared. Next he smiled, playing to the whole of the room, and we watched him sit and settle himself in the awful silence...he folded his arms across his small chest and gazed about himself with an air of aggressive satisfaction...some days Bob used Mrs McCreedy's chair and some days, in her presence, he began animated conversations with others that made fun of her...one time he left a large dead mouse hidden in a packet she kept of digestive biscuits...Mrs McCreedy screamed when she found it and ran out of the staff room, and I thought she was crying as she fled...I told myself it was just like the pranks we played at school, but Bob never stopped, not even one bit, and all through my year at Wynyards he made Mrs McCreedy suffer.

Along with the job, during my seventh-form year I also got myself a girlfriend...her name was Chloe...she was the same age as me, and she was at the local Girls' High School...we met during the evening of the Girls' High annual social...it was the only time that boys and girls from our single-sex schools were ever likely to be together. I went to the social wearing my brand-new brown vinyl jacket and a pair of almost-new moccasins...my parents thought the outfit made me look spivvy and they kept on with their objections to it for over a week beforehand, but that was exactly how I wanted to look and confirming their disappointment meant a lot to me...at Boys' High the rule was that, at any function, a striped school tie had to be worn with plain black trousers and a plain white shirt, so the jacket and shoes were our only margin of latitude...for myself, I felt all wrong going to the Girls' High social with a tie around my neck because ties were uncomfortable and really meant for old people...I also suspected that a tie made me look somehow childish instead of grown-up...in any case, I tried hard to make sure my school tie and white shirt stayed hidden under the bulky cut of my spivvy jacket. Blind dates had been arranged for most of us...my partner was a girl who was somebody's sister's friend...I rendezvoused with her that evening in the lobby at the Girls' High assembly hall...that was where the social would be, and when we found each other and said hullo, a little shyly, we went in from the lobby together. The hall was long and rather grand in a familiar kind of way...I soon realised it had the same design, the same high, drab walls and sloping floor-to-ceiling roof-beams, as my own school's assembly hall...but above us I saw parts of the ceiling had been decorated with a vast number of fat, garishly coloured balloons which loomed thick and low in bunches, bobbing and squeaking in the air...there were banks of large black speakers positioned up on the stage and a long trestle table down in front for party food to be served on to us later...I could see where silver streamers made from milk-bottle-top cut-outs were strung, hanging across each of the room's corners...some of the streamers had fallen to the floor and a few guests were kicking them casually about. I felt buoyed up by everything around me and endlessly curious...we strutted over towards the centre of the freshly polished floor, watching some of the other couples nearby us to pass the time...more and more couples were coming in and I sensed that I knew most of the boys, but they seemed different, like adults, like people I'd never met before...some of the boy-girl pairs were already breaking up...a few of them, the real couples, were standing close together and holding hands. Then without any introduction a D.J. began playing a dance record...he'd appeared suddenly up on the far end of the stage next to the curtains, had put on some headphones and was now crouched intently over a console with twin turntables...the D.J. showed little interest in us, mere high-school students, all ranged below him across the floor of the room, and he concentrated instead on twiddling the buttons on his equipment...but nearly everyone in the hall started dancing as if on cue, and the confined air around us quickly turned warm and sticky...soon the upper-windows had to be opened by someone going about with a special pole. After a certain amount of bouncing and jiving over several interconnected songs, I saw Chloe not far off and my eyes lit up with greed...she was standing with a partner I didn't recognise, who was evidently taking a breather...almost all of the girls had made their own clothes, and she was wearing an ankle-length, blue crinkle-muslin dress wrapped tight around her like a sheath...she was very short but with a good figure, a pretty, square-jawed face and brown hair cut in layers that went down to her small shoulders...her shoulders were shaking as she laughed at something or other her partner had just said. The laughter was so effortless that for an instant it seemed to come out of her whole body...it left deep dimples in her cheeks where the corners of her mouth were drawn back...Chloe's hair was curled slightly at the ends and was falling against her neck, and I watched her hair brushing her neck while she moved...but within a moment or two she ceased laughing and started shuffling her feet, as if in anxious anticipation to dance once more...the thin, almost translucent material of her blue dress shifted a little up the edges of her prominent hips as she swung them, back and forth...I thought those hips looked wildly sexy. It wasn't long before I had my opportunity...everybody at the social changed partners a lot and the teachers preferred that we keep it that way...when a new song started I

30

simply nodded to my own partner, left her and went up and asked Chloe to dance...I hoped my calculations wouldn't be too obvious, but Chloe smiled and stepped forwards to join me...we hopped about together for a while in the middle of the dance floor...there were lots of other couples doing the same thing all around us so none of our actions seemed special or strange, but I couldn't take my gaze off Chloe, swaying and still shifting her lithe body in her dress at just an arm's length from me. No one was supposed to dance too close or too slow...some of the Boys' High staff had been recruited to keep an eye on things, and Mr Collins, our phys-ed teacher, was stalking about amongst the pairs...now and then he called in a high, angry voice, 'Break it up! Break it up!' like a referee at a boxing match... he was red in the face from the stuffy damp air...the spit seemed to fly in specks from his lips. I saw Chloe roll her eyes as Mr Collins's hysterical voice rose up nearby...I smiled back, and felt proud of myself for agreeing with her...in the safety of our numbers everyone who was dancing tried to ignore him, and ignoring him was fun...the song changed again and immediately I asked Chloe for another dance...she didn't refuse, and it never occurred to me that she might...we were delighted when Mr Collins came over to yell at us. At last the music stopped and the D.J. gave himself a break, marching with a surly glance at us away behind the curtains on the stage...by now a lot of the balloons on the ceiling had burst or withered, and some had been hauled down and stamped on...the floorboards under our feet were cluttered with torn bits of rubber and scraps of streamers...around me everyone's faces seemed to glow from excitement and the accumulated heat, and a group of us trooped out into the lobby together in pairs...the lobby was pleasantly cool, though we could still feel the humid air from inside the hall on our backs. I made sure that I kept standing next to Chloe in the crowd, and was pleased that she appeared to regard me as with her...everybody was trading funny stories and the boys were leading the charge, and there was a lot of hearty, self-conscious laughter...some of the boys in our group started to pull at the ties around their necks, loosening the knots and taking them off...I began removing mine too, since I didn't want to be outdone by the others... Chloe didn't like me taking off my tie but I kept on going, working at its narrow folds which had turned a bit stubborn...everybody seemed to be having such a fine time putting down everyone else that I didn't want to offer a target by being different. 'Good one,' I heard voices around me saying with more and more obvious aggression. A trio of the boys began to harp on in a chorus at everything that was said with, 'Good one. Yeah, good one.' I couldn't help comparing all this to the Christian Centre…this was a lot more enjoyable than arguing with fanatics…finally I got the tie off and left it dangling from my fingers…next I reached out and tried putting my arm around the back of Chloe's delicate shoulders…as I did so, tentatively, she looked up and didn't appear to mind…instead she wriggled a little closer under my arm and turned towards me. I heard her asking, 'Is there anything up in my nose?' I could tell she was serious…she'd stayed with her head lifted towards my gaze for me to check…she was even flaring her tiny nostrils so that I might get a better view…the very public laughter from the others was still chiming and barging in around us, but it had lost my attention…I'd no idea that a girl might ask such a question, one that felt so private, to a complete stranger…but then, I'd no idea what girls thought or talked about at all.

'Well,' I muttered, and tried peering hard.

It was difficult to see up inside her nostrils…there were only some blurry shadows that I could make out…but I felt her pink snub nose was definitely lovely.

'Not a thing,' I announced after a moment.

I hoped that was what she wanted…I winked at her gently for good measure. 'Fine,' Chloe replied. She lowered her head…then she even nodded a little, as if in satisfaction, but I thought maybe it was to stop me from going on staring any further…all the same, Chloe's face just seemed to capture my eyes because it was endlessly and beautifully fleshy, and it was real…there was so much more to it than the ecstatic features of my masturbation-women…I took a deep, fluttery breath…raw sexual desire was making me bold.

'Would you like to go to the pictures next Saturday?' I asked.

I was mumbling…I hoped she'd actually understood my words…but it was important to speak so quietly that the others couldn't hear.

'Together,' I added.

'Can't,' Chloe declared. 'I've got baby-sitting. I do baby-sitting all that evening, eh, for this family round in Awapuni.'

'Oh,' I said.

'Well, you could come along and help me,' Chloe offered. 'We could watch some TV or something.' I felt disappointed by the casual tone in her voice as she suggested it…but I started quickly to say yes and how that would be a pretty good idea, until at that exact instant all the other conversations around us suddenly died away...I stopped talking...from the darkness outside, Evan Blake was stepping up to the door and pushing it open to enter the lobby. He came in and I saw Mrs Blake was beside him too...she had on a long, formal salmon-coloured dress with complex arrangements of frilly seams and lacy edges that appeared rather artyfarty for a school social...she had a vacant look across her narrow face which told everyone there she was doing her duty...Evan Blake was wearing his usual threadbare suit from morning assemblies and school... I half expected to find his black gown trailing along somewhere behind him...as he caught sight of our group all that was left of our happiness, the remainder of the entire party atmosphere, just seemed to drain away. Evan Blake marched past some others and right on up to us...his gaze was fierce...he was working his jaw, which was displaying an extra-heavy evening stubble...he planted his feet stiffly in the centre of the lobby and arched his back and shoulders as he started speaking to us...Evan Blake even began hammering his fist into one hand to emphasise his words. We were not wearing ties, and we should be and he didn't care if it was only out in the lobby...he could not, he would never, allow this sort of thing to pass muster, and we were letting the side down...we seemed to be forgetting that we were here to represent our school...we were forgetting our duties and our principles and our self-respect and all sorts of other things...Evan Blake started to yell, and he went right on smacking at his palm with his hairy fist...it appeared that he was never going to forgive us for not matching his old-fashioned notions of fair dinkum British schoolboys. Watching him, our headmaster, and his stupid rant, I thought about how he had no off-button...a negative emotion never seemed to leave him once it had taken hold and was making fuel for itself...I stole a few seconds to observe Mrs Blake waiting patiently a little away to one side, and I felt sorry for her...Evan Blake was in the middle of asking us who we thought we were...just exactly who did we think we were?...it was a bloody stupid question, and he kept nagging at us about it and about what on earth we were doing. Then at last he paused and took a breath...his face was purple with accumulated rage...even Evan Blake seemed aware that he needed to round things off with a big finish...he told all of us in the lobby to go home, and at once, right now...he was throwing us all out and we should vanish from his sight if we knew what was good for us. It took a bit to sink in...we were actually, genuinely, being thrown out of the dance, and I was thrilled...I'd never really let the side down before, not like this…I couldn't think of a better way to impress Chloe. All of us wandered through the doors of the lobby into the dark in our pairs…it was suddenly chilly outside, and it was easy to clasp Chloe round the shoulders against the cold…there seemed to be a lot of us, and we felt more daring than ever…we gathered, after a few moments of indecision, in the middle of the dark asphalt playground…it was located just in front of the hall, and we were standing, milling about, among the complex white lines painted for athletic exercises and netball courts…the broad, flat view from the playground, tinted by the yellow glow from the lobby, stretched off beyond our gaze into the night. None of us wanted to go home…slowly our eyes grew more accustomed to the lack of light…I could start to see the shadowy outlines of classroom blocks and grass cover away in the near distance…there were cheery bunches of stars clustered up in the clear black sky above our heads. Then we decided to dance some more…somebody from one of the pairs began, and the rest of us all joined in…we couldn't hear any music from anywhere, but we tried dancing anyway, swaying slowly together as couples in silence…it was dancing of a sort…I let my arms drape around Chloe and she had her hands up along my back…she had her awfully real body pressed up tight against my chest. Chloe's belly was brushing on mine…I was worried that soon she might be able to feel my rampant erection…but there was nothing much I could do about it… her dress's lovely material was so thin, so sheer…finally I thought it best to bend and reposition myself a little to one side. Next I tried giving her a kiss…I was fairly sure how it was done…I twisted my face downwards as a hint until my mouth encountered the barrier of her skin…quickly I gave the dimple in the middle of her warm upper lip a hesitant slurp…Chloe's own actual mouth was somewhere lower, but I tried again a second time and managed to get my lips properly onto hers. By now sweat was running in tiny rivers down my back and my wet shirt was sticking into the lining of my jacket…I felt more or less certain that I was going to explode with excitement…it was almost a relief when Mrs Thorson appeared… Mrs Thorson was the Girls' High principal, and we became aware of her marching out through the doors of the hall, half in shadow and half illuminated by the lights behind her…she stood on the dark plaster step a little off from us, at the edge of the playground. Mrs Thorson called, 'You girls come away from there this minute!' Her voice was high and wheezy, a heavy smoker's voice, and lacked Evan Blake's menacing authority…but one by one the girls peeled off from their partners…slowly Chloe drew herself back from me...I wanted to say something but wasn't sure what, and it was too late because she was already disappearing with the others...Mrs Thorson fluttered her arms out protectively in the girls' direction as they all approached her...they drifted past her and inside the hall once more. Some of the boys were upset at being abandoned like this and some were just excited...we whispered to each other in agitated tones about what had happened...soon our voices rose, higher and almost girlish with pleasure, as we began to trudge off in a gang together into the night...I felt a peculiar sense of recklessness at being with everyone else in this group...our laughter was ringing loudly in each other's faces by the time we reached the main road...we all of us believed that our reputations as ladies' men were secure.

Next Saturday, I met Chloe for babysitting outside a house in Whikiriwhi Crescent...I arrived feeling flushed with anticipation...Chloe was already standing around, waiting, by the large metal letterbox at the gate...she was dressed in a loose white blouse and jeans, her hands resting on her hips, and looked casual, relaxed and desirable. I said hullo, glanced quickly past the gate and scrutinised the two-storey house, painted in an ordinary cream shade, with its wide windows and flimsy net curtains...it was positioned well back amongst an untidy lawn and garden on the good half of the street...it seemed too bright, too normal in the early-evening sunshine, to be the setting for our first date...but Chloe told me to come on and marched up the drive...I followed, almost competing with her now at acting unconcerned. The owners let us in, and Chloe and I slouched into the downstairs living-room...we ignored the easy-chairs and sat together on a soft, pastel-grey-coloured suede sofa opposite the TV...I watched the owners as they stood by the mantelpiece in their fancy clothes, ready for going out...they looked uncomfortable and nervous in their own home while they tried to assess me...Chloe and I listened to the wife explaining in tedious detail that the children were already in bed upstairs and they should be sleeping, and what numbers we could ring if there was trouble. When the woman finished her speech, Chloe just shrugged...but at the same time I did hear her promise that we'd keep a good weather eye on everything...maybe Chloe thought her show of indifference might make both of the owners feel calmer...I could tell she wanted them to hurry up and leave...she stayed beside me on the sofa as they headed, drifting a little, for the doorway and out into the corridor. As soon as the front door slammed shut and the owners were really gone, Chloe bent closer and got into my arms with a willing sigh…I took the hint and we started kissing frantically…right away I had my hands all over her…I ran them down around her coarse denim jeans…I could feel the curve of her buttocks encased and shifting in the tight material…with our mouths pushed together, I could hear the air gushing from Chloe's nose. After a few minutes we were leaning, with most of me locked around Chloe, pressed into the back of the sofa… one of my arms was trapped, but I worked the palm of my free hand up and over the slipping fabric of her blouse…I brushed my fingers round where I could feel the tantalising edges of Chloe's wide brassiere…then I struggled with my hand downwards over her jeans again…this routine, up and down, went on for quite a while, but gradually Chloe seemed to be getting bored…finally she paused for breath from our kissing. 'Aren't you going to be, you know, a bit more rough now?' she asked. I felt surprised, disconcerted…I felt more than a little bruised by my own inadequacy… but Chloe didn't even appear to notice…instead, she pulled up one side of her bulky blouse…it lay flapping and open around her bare waist, and she slid my hand in underneath. After that I didn't stop…I didn't even want to slow down…I slithered my damp palm all along Chloe's skin, up under her bra onto her breasts, and she let me…a few minutes or more later, I had no real idea when, we fell sideways across the sofa and I was lying half on top of her…even in that position I started putting my hand down into the front of her jeans…I pushed my fingertips in as hard as I could beneath the high, tight waistband. Chloe reached up from under me… she obligingly unzipped her fly…it made a lovely, promising noise…I was trembling so much I could scarcely breathe…I didn't care if I never breathed again…in a fever I began to pull the top of her jeans down. But Chloe suddenly tried grabbing for my arm…she held my wrist tight with both of her small hands, pushing it away from her…it took me a moment to realise what she meant…we were each of us panting hard. I could see Chloe staring up at me with an intense look on her face…I gazed around us and saw that, sometime ago, she'd kicked off her shoes…her stocking feet were completely up on the cushions of the sofa with her toes dug in against the plush armrest…I wriggled myself out into a more comfortable posture alongside her…there wasn't a lot of room for my own legs… the sweat was already cooling on my neck, but I was happy with developments. I noticed Chloe hadn't actually moved to do up her jeans…for several lengthy seconds what seemed an acute, wordless negotiation went on between us...it was about how far she'd let me manoeuvre my hand downwards with my wrist in her grip...at last, my fingers were allowed to stay inside her underwear. I held Chloe tight against me and felt around in her cotton briefs...I was gazing over her shoulder into nothing but the smooth grey cushioned panels of the sofa's backrest...but I could sense it was warm, it was hairy and a little squishy down there. So, I thought, this is sex. I tried to remember what *The Little Red Schoolbook* had told me I'd find...but to remember any reading at all was difficult at a time like this...in the end I just came into my own pants. The next day my fingers smelled with a faint persistence...I supposed, in delight, that it was the smell of Chloe...playing with her vagina was certainly a lot more fun than masturbation...I began to think that I was outgrowing masturbation now anyway, a bit like Picasso outgrowing his blue period...soon we were baby-sitting somewhere almost every Saturday night. Baby-sitting was an ideal arrangement...I was planning to lose my virginity, and Chloe was making a lot of pocket money...my underpants were getting so cruddy that I had to begin washing them with my handkerchiefs at the Lido...I couldn't believe my luck.

During the seventh-form year at school, in the last term, we discovered our futures had to be decided on...that was because from the next year our futures were finally going to start...it meant having jobs and being settled and sorted out like adults...before now, we didn't need a future because we were too busy getting an education. But I had no idea at all what to do with my life, and I felt that no one else knew anything about the details of my personal world either...I felt the adults just thought I should hurry and get the deciding part over with, as if I was a minor mess to be tidied up...they wanted to make me exactly like them so that they could go on back to whatever they were doing...but with their fuddy-duddy ways none of the adults ever seemed to be doing anything very interesting. Because of all this, the school had a vocational-guidance councillor to help get us suitably settled...the councillor's name was Mr Booth...mostly he taught geography, and vocational guidance was only a sideline for him between teaching and stuff, but it meant he got an office... one day he sent a third-former to fetch me there from the middle of class...I heard the third-former's squeaky voice saying to the teacher would I please come see Mr Booth at the Vocational-Guidance Office now, so I had to stand in front of everybody and leave the room feeling as though I was already in some kind of trouble...I supposed my name had popped up on a list somewhere. I trotted from Prefab E across a worn asphalt path for the centre of the school, taking care to break the rules and step on the grass whenever I could, and soon I was heading past a couple of long two-storey rows of featureless Nelson Block classrooms...I could hear sounds, the soft droning of teacher talk and the loud buzz of pupils, dropping from the windows, and it was all so humdrum that I couldn't think why I'd even bothered to get out of bed that morning... after some time I reached the old brick Main Building, a hideous leftover from the early days of the school at the beginning of the century, and I tramped up a set of awkwardly made concrete steps to its back entrance... inside, the bare wooden floor thudded and creaked with my footsteps and with those of one or two other shamefaced boys who were going some-where...the corridors were poorly lined and, to me, only suggested pov-erty...their walls had high casement windows that were always left open to the cold and the rest of the space was filled with rows of photographs of forgotten sports teams, pictures stained and curling in cheap black frames. At last I knocked on Mr Booth's office door...a deep, muffled voice on the other side called for me to enter...I tried turning the brass door handle but it merely came off in my grip...there was a difficult moment spent reinserting the handle before I could push my way for-wards, and I wondered if this nonsense happened to everyone who came here...I'd never been into a Vocational-Guidance Office before. I entered and found myself standing in a very small, very bland room...it had a bare wood floor, just like the corridor outside, and thin plaster walls that were covered in an uneven shade of light yellow paint...it felt crowded, mostly because of a large jutting grey metal bookshelf, attached to a wall along one side, that ran all the way up to the ceiling...the shelves were empty except for a few dusty rolls of what looked like builders' blueprints. Mr Booth was opposite me, sitting behind his desk...he was a compact, mid-dle-aged man wearing his sparse dark hair in a comb-over, and his severe face and ruddy wrinkled features showed the weight he was starting to put on...he was reclining far back in a battered brown leather chair with his legs stretched out somewhere below the desktop, and he'd sunk down, half slumped, among the chair's pleated cushions...there wasn't much space left for visitors to the office and Mr Booth waved for me to come and wait a bit further in, just past the doorway...while I shuffled forwards he pushed his heavy arms up behind his head and flexed them, and the movement showed off the fatty wads of muscle in his biceps...his whole attitude appeared to say, I've *got* a job. I stopped, waiting where I'd been told...Mr Booth had already begun speaking in a blithe sort of tone...his guttural, lazy voice was echoing from the closeness of the walls as he talked, and it was only gradually that I realised what he was going on about...it was an arrangement to do with an apprenticeship...he was trying to convince me to become a panel beater. I failed to react and held myself very still...I kept standing in a position something like at-ease, with my hands clasped behind my back...it seemed the best way to let Mr Booth continue without noticing me...I started thinking of how badly cracked the small office window was up behind his head...I thought about how somebody really ought to invent a special type of putty or caulking for repairing glass, and I considered that perhaps somebody already had...Mr Booth went on talking about the advantages of a career in panel beating. Finally he paused, and finished up, 'Well, it's an option.' I failed to react some more...I was still pondering whether a big crack in a small window produced much of a draught...Mr Booth gave up with a sigh of exasperation and waved me out of the room...I hoped that meant my name was off the list. But meanwhile, at home, my parents had been hinting over and over about varsity...I was pretty sure that the idea was to prevent me from leaving them and going out flatting...I could imagine them boasting to the neighbours about their eldest boy at Massey...but my school marks were mostly erratic, and my only constant interest was down in Chloe's vagina. I was tired of being told what to do for my own good...I was tired of going to school every day in my clammy grey shorts...I was tired of washing up the dishes in tepid, oily water after dinner, and I was tired of making my bed, of mopping out the shower, of mowing the lawns...I just wished that other people could see my tiredness...if they could only see how unusual it was, this being so fed up, then they might understand that life was all a big have...I hoped they might recognise me in the end as a special case. I'd got rebellious, and I could tell that everyone else thought so too, but mostly I was just short of an answer to everyone's questions...besides, I was distracted by sex...thinking of the future only made me go and lock myself away in the toilet...in fact, thinking of almost anything finished up by sending me away to the toilet in a frantic mood...but I was even getting tired of that as well, the toilet, the handkerchief, my jerking off...was this what the future really meant, me holding myself and crooning 'darling' into the lino? Then at last I had an inspiration...the thing happened all in a flash...it happened

39

at an ordinary dinnertime, on a normal day, while I was seated at the dining-room table...everyone in the family was there around me...we were working away at eating a typical sort of meal, a meal that my mother had dished up, as usual, on some slippery brown stoneware plates...we were tucking into soapy-tasting chops and twin heaps of boiled vegetables mixed in with a sludge of mashed potato. I was listening to the stainless-steel cutlery scrape back and forth and the sounds of chewing...it was hot, and that might have been a factor...I'd never had a flash of inspiration before...but I recognised it immediately when it came. In an instant my mind felt full and very calm...everything around me, everything else, seemed to stop, suspended, no longer existing...I put down my knife and fork on the edges of my plate to concentrate...I put my elbows up on the table and my hands deep under my chin, with my teeth clenched in anticipation...it was as if a marvellous idea had been waiting patiently, somewhere just beyond the border of my psyche, to come in for me and be discovered. I stared outwards at the room but focused on nothing, with an inward gaze, while the whole world was arranging itself in place around the solution to my problem...it was neat, thorough, even perfect...I realised what I was going to be in my future...I was going to be a writer. It meant I'd write books, books that I could enjoy...but I'd write the most enjoyable sort of books that everyone else would appreciate and adore as well...then everyone, appreciating and adoring them, would make me famous...best of all, I already had the equipment...I had a portable grey typewriter, kept in my bedroom for schoolwork...I'd never actually tried to use it until now, but in my mind's eye I could see myself sitting over it, inspired, writing. I was writing hard, hunched slightly forwards, with the typewriter balanced on my lap...I was typing out all those words with a steady sense of wonderment at my own genius...I couldn't believe that up till now I'd never even thought of this...already I felt warm, a little weary, from the efforts of my creative fever...but being a writer seemed much more important than being stuck at the boring old dinner-table. At the dinner-table there were always the same people around me...I always sat in my same creaky dining-room chair, with my bottom nestled into the comfortable, hollowed cushions on the seat...I was always staring before me, past my brother opposite, at the same stultifying brown-woodgrain wall...a bit self-consciously I turned my head...I gazed with new yearning in the direction of the windows...what could I see in the world outside as a writer? I saw the flat, freshly mowed, freshly watered green turf of the front lawn…I saw some decrepit red and purple roses on bushes trained against the diamond-patterned wire of the property's fence…beyond the camber of the berm I saw a long, dicky-looking yellow car creeping past on the way back from the river…it had its boot open and something like a piece of two-by-four, marked with a white rag, was poking out under the tied-down, bouncing lid…views didn't come much more ordinary, much more disappointing, than this. Suddenly I heard my father growling from over at the head of the table…I realised, a bit late, that it was already the second time he'd spoken to me. He was asking, 'Why aren't you eating anything? Eh?' I turned my full attention back to the room and observed his large, muscular, aging face staring at me with annoyance…his head was bald and round and he held it very upright, and he'd already begun arching his bushy eyebrows…I knew exactly what that look meant, his scrunching those splayed brows into two sharp curves while staring down his nose at me…it showed he was primed to explode. 'What on earth's the matter with you, eh?' he added in another growl. 'Eh? You're not sick or something?' These both sounded like pertinent questions, but still I risked not condescending to him with any reply…it was because, from this point on, I was a man apart…I wanted to return in my own fecund mind to imagining myself writing words. My father had lifted his fork in his fist…he was looking away from me now to my mother, but stealing a glance at me on and off…he put a ragged portion of cut-up grey meat into his mouth and swallowed without chewing…a little greasy mint sauce dripped from his trembling lower lip at one edge, but he said nothing more and went on with his food…I saw a drop of the sauce slipping slowly down across his solid pink chin, ignored by him in his frustration. He probably thought I was being obstinate, and I considered it best to leave him safe in this middle-aged illusion…I'd just decided on my unlimited, idealistic devotion to literature, but at the same moment I'd also decided more practically not to tell my parents…they would only say I was watching too much TV again…TV was how they explained whatever I did that bothered them…but from now on, no doubt about it, I was offering no more concessions, and I'd shoulder my patent irresponsibilities as an artist…it just seemed strange to me that my father couldn't see how I'd been visited by the muse. But I did tell Chloe all about this…I didn't wait for her to waste any precious time on guessing…besides, these days I told Chloe everything…it was because she always wanted to know, although, more than that, it was because I was always busting to tell her.

41

'I'm going to be bigger than Shakespeare,' I said.

Shakespeare was the only big name I was sure of...we'd suffered him every year in school, so I knew he was meant to be good...we'd done a lot of that *Twelfth Nightly* stuff, and I'd decided it would impress Chloe if I started by aiming fairly high. I told her this on one of our meandering walks...we were heading around the rose garden in the Esplanade... the garden was extensive, flat and boring, just numerous circles of regular spaded beds of flowers, but they were the type of walks that Chloe liked...we were holding hands, slowly following a cement path on the grass between the flowerbeds, and the languid pink and white rose petals kept brushing against our legs as we passed...the full, syrupy fragrance of the blooms drifted up about us and made me want to sneeze. After I'd told Chloe my idea, she went on treading carefully along the path beside the muddy earth in the flowerbeds...I watched her looking down at her feet as though she was hoping to avoid a particularly bad crack in the cement...I felt surprised that she'd made no response to my big moment of news...but she merely continued swinging my hand back and forth in hers. 'What are you going to do about money?' she said at last. Chloe had her own future all worked out...she was off to the Training College to get herself qualified...she was going to become a primary-school teacher and she wanted me to enrol too, along with her...we'd end up being teachers together. But hell, I was no brainy bastard of any type...over the past few years I'd put my energy good and hard into learning nothing at all...the notion of me teaching, actually teaching somebody else, seemed bizarre, and I guessed the staff at the T. Coll would probably agree, though I'd said none of this to Chloe...she wanted us to be teachers and get married...she wanted us to stay in Palmerston North and start a family...she wanted us to live like grown-ups, do without things and save our incomes and plan for old age. I hadn't held any opinion on this sort of this stuff till now...the start-a-family part on her list stood out and got my interest... it sounded nice in a quaint kind of way...I loved crushing Chloe's child-bearing hips against me on baby-sitting nights.

'Writers make money,' I said.

Chloe said nothing...she led us away from the rose garden and off towards the rest of the park, pulling me gently behind her...I wasn't sure if she'd heard me or not. We went by a set of wrought-iron gates at the garden's entrance...they were swung grandly but pointlessly back against a mostly ornamental red-brick fence, since they were far too heavy to move and shut…we began to cross a narrow road that was still within the confines of the Esplanade, and my jandals flapped against the smooth, warm bitumen…there were no cars coming from anywhere, and we were heading towards a long row of thick, scaly palm trees on the other side of the road…as we reached the trees, I took the time to gaze at their tufts of saggy, stringy fronds and to observe how the bases of their trunks were missing any cover of leafstalks…still Chloe said nothing and we shambled onwards. There was a broad fountain bubbling in a blue concrete pool before us…there was an old aviary just beyond that, a bit niminy-piminy now and down-at-heel, but charming all the same…I reflected that this whole area had been laid out long ago to make people happy, to give locals like us someplace to be…I could see the loose, heavily painted black wire on the birdcages, and somewhere I could even hear the indignant squawk of a peacock.

'What you have to do is publish,' I added at last, thinking I needed something to say. 'Those genius guys make tons of money, eh. And when they become rich and famous, they get streets named after them in their hometowns.'

We drew to a halt next to the concrete pool and its busy, chugging fountain…I could smell the chlorine from the water spilling into the air… still holding Chloe's hand, I glanced back over my shoulder at the road we'd crossed…there was a reassuring vision in my mind of Andrew Ingle Street…I was getting very chuffed with my own imagination and its powers. Then my imagination even changed the street name, practicing its sound and putting it on show…I started thinking of Andrew Ingle Drive… I considered the beautiful possibility of Andy Ingle Avenue. 'Well, what are you going to write about?' Chloe asked beside me. Andrew M. Ingle Boulevard vanished from my inner gaze…it felt as if something cold and nasty had been tipped all over my head…I turned back to Chloe, wondering why she had to spoil my brilliantly conjured world with such a question.

'Oh, I don't really know for sure yet,' I said.

'Well,' she announced, 'sooner or later, you have to come up with a kind of topic, sort of thing, eh.'

'So why are you so concerned with all the details and that?' I asked. 'You're not the one who's going to do the actual writing—'

'Because it's just like you, eh, you've got no scheme,' Chloe cut in. 'You know, you're just being selfish and childish—that's what you are, always. There's just no point to this.' Chloe's voice had kept rising as she launched herself into this complaint, but suddenly she stopped, stood very still and frowned in silence at something she was thinking of...it was as if she'd become worried, deep inside her, about giving vent to her true feelings. After a moment she said with heavy emphasis, 'It's all a kind of silly dream to you, eh.'

'Listen,' I said.

I let go of Chloe's hand...she needed to know I was being candid, and I thought it might look more like being candid if I spoke to her from a little distance...but my mind went blank, and I just said the next thing that came into my head.

I asked, 'If I'd told you about me going into forestry, yeah, would you want me to start out by naming the trees I'd cut down?'

It turned out that this wasn't the right thing to say at all...Chloe swung round on one foot and marched off...she left me waiting alone near the shallow, sour-smelling pool...I supposed this meant the end of our walk, and I watched her stamping away through the Esplanade over a neatly trimmed expanse of grass, going somewhere but mainly away from me... her head was up and she took small, angry, determined steps...I felt surprised at how unpleasant she looked. Chloe was moving steadily towards a bend in the road...at last near the kerb she skirted round a decorative park bench made of thick slabs of rough-hewn wood...I took a moment to reflect that it was the sort of uncomfortable bench that only the elderly or infirm could ever be bothered with...then I wondered if Chloe might turn and glance back...she kept on going. It wasn't our first fight...we'd been fighting about little things, and I was unhappy...mostly I was unhappy about our limited progress with sex...I kept hoping we could maybe continue with getting a bit more rough. Already I'd put in several months of exacting work at being gradually rougher...I'd succeeded at getting one, and then two, fingers inside Chloe...but she wasn't going to let me go any further inside her, not on someone else's living-room sofa...I still hadn't lost my virginity...I still hadn't even started to find out about literature. One afternoon I mentioned my writing to Mrs McCreedy...it was an impulsive thing to do, perhaps foolish, but I was too excited to withhold my new secret from the world for long...it was at the end of November, and the final breakup of school was approaching fast...I'd just wagged the last class of the day and arrived at Wynyards early...missing some class time felt so good that it had put me in a pretty conceited mood.

But when I came into the staff room only Mrs McCreedy and Bernard were there…Bernard looked busy with making another of his fresh pots of tea…the Duchess was installed in her own chair and had her broad back to me as I trotted down the steps…she was sitting hunched forward, propped with her strong elbows on the table, leaning towards Bernard… she had an odd air of intensity about her, as if in the midst of some kind of conference. But despite this, all I heard the Duchess growling was, 'Oh, you can just pour it out there at the sink.' I sidled along one edge of the table, scuffing my shoes…I felt that, this afternoon, each of the empty chairs was in my way. Next the Duchess added, 'Oh and Bernard, don't forget the saucer.' 'Yei, Mia M-Ceedy,' Bernard responded. Mrs McCreedy glared at me while I selected a place opposite her and sat… she knew I was the one who worked with Bob, but I sensed that she had nothing special against me and that her attitude was an extension of her foul behaviour towards Bernard…the Duchess was fiddling with her reading-glasses absent-mindedly in her stubby hands…the chain for the glasses was off her neck and spread loose on the tabletop…she looked like a newsreader ready to announce a shipwreck or a downed plane. But next Mrs McCreedy turned from me back to Bernard, acting as though I wasn't even there…he reached out and put a cup down beside her, and then stood waiting at her shoulder…Mrs McCreedy started talking to him about books…she was explaining something quietly about their care and handling…Bernard still hovered beside her, bent over a little, listening intently, and finally he said something respectful in reply. I couldn't quite catch Bernard's raspy words…I always had to concentrate hard to manage making out his speech, but it sounded as if he was grateful and didn't want to miss the least thing…Bernard was getting advice on how to sell books…it occurred to me that, for Bernard, this might be a lot like a quick visit from the muse. The Duchess went right on explaining and fiddling with her glasses…I began to listen too, nodding, as Mrs McCreedy talked…at last she stopped and stared at me across the table…her gaze seemed to ask what the hell I was doing, and it took me a long moment to understand that I'd interrupted her.

'Suppose,' I asked her, and paused to dry-swallow a little. 'So, suppose you were going to be a writer, eh,' I said. 'Just suppose.'

I smiled and nodded my head once again…it was amazing how I'd put such a cleverly hypothetical note into my speech…I knew I'd made a signal that Mrs McCreedy should go ahead and answer, and so I waited in anticipation of her response…but nothing happened, and the Duchess continued glowering at me…the remains of my earlier excitement and composure appeared to have fled.

I pressed on, and added, 'Well, for a writer, sort of thing, what do you think that you would actually write about?'

Mrs McCreedy offered up a tired sigh. She rumbled, 'What are you driving at?' But I was confused that she didn't understand my question…all I could think of was that her voice sounded much, much deeper than mine. 'What is it, do you mean poetry?' Mrs McCreedy prompted. She slipped her large hands apart in a brief gesture of query and clasped her glasses on the tabletop again…but I didn't mean poetry at all…I was imagining something much more manly…I wanted to write novels of the kind that came in hard covers and took up a lot of space in the box when they were delivered to the rear of a bookshop…my novels would have stiff, bulky bindings and they would have the weight of authority when they got unpacked…Bob would have to grunt as he lifted each masterpiece from the cardboard box to pencil in the price.

'More sort of fiction,' I managed to reply.

Already I was wishing I hadn't broached the subject with Mrs McCreedy…why on earth had I interfered?…why had I left Bernard standing there, useless beside her, with her tea getting cold?

'Stuff like that,' I said. 'The illustrious stuff.'

I grinned hard to hide my embarrassment…my grin was meant to double as a sign of ingratiation, but already I was beaming so broadly that even I knew it couldn't be working…what would be the best way now to escape?…I felt as though I'd fallen in with the wrong people in a barbarous land, and I was so immersed in myself that I nearly missed Mrs McCreedy's suggestion. She'd dropped her glasses and picked up her cup…she was fixing her severe gaze on me over the white china rim…it was as if she wanted to create a larger distance between us than silence and the table might provide. But after a long wait, in a low growl Mrs McCreedy intoned, 'Write what you know.' That sounded plausible…I stood up.

'I see,' I answered quickly. 'Thank you.'

But I didn't fancy writing what I knew…that was because I didn't know anything…it was like some sort of stupid hitch in the system, and I left the staff room more rattled by the problem than when I'd come in… what did other writers know about if they wrote fiction?…there wasn't much left in the world these days to protest over or proclaim…where did they forage for the topic when there wasn't one to find? I lay awake in bed at night, preoccupied with the whole business…I stretched my legs out in frustration and stared up at the pale Pinex ceiling and thought… it meant I'd become serious…I became impressed at how deadly serious I was. I arched my head back on the warm spongy pillow, straining my eyes for some pattern in the stippled Pinex…but the ceiling was too far away to take in any of its detail…I wondered if this in itself might be an insight. Summer was coming up fast…in the stationery area at Wynyards I bought myself a ream of long, floppy foolscap…but I didn't bother opening the packet and I put it in a drawer…even the greatest writers could go through the odd dry spell.

Of all the friends I used to hang around with at school, probably the one I most wanted to be like was Philip Bream…he didn't trouble himself with the Christian Centre or even spend much time at the Record Hunter, and he often seemed to go his own way which, paradoxically, made me want to copy him…I thought he was a lot more worldly-wise than I was… that was because he appeared to lead a life far more remarkable than mine, richer in adventure and filled with more people. One day, Philip was approached by the teacher in charge of the choir at school, although Philip had showed no interest in the choir or in singing before…the choirmaster was a delicately built man with a mop of brown hair, a fine-boned, birdlike face and soft, searching eyes…he invited Philip to join him and some other boys who were going away camping on the weekend…Philip thought about it for a bit and declined…but after the weekend the boys were all expelled, suddenly, with no explanation or warning given to the rest of the school…the choirmaster was never mentioned to us again. 'Well, he had a ring on each finger. Both hands,' Philip explained to me later and held up his palms. Philip looked at his own upraised fingers, letting them hover before his gaze…then he nodded his head gravely…he seemed to be persuading himself of his own perceptiveness. Philip's parents were divorced, which was unusual and exciting, and he lived with just his mother and younger sister…he told me his father had remarried and was selling antiques from a house out in Masterton, and Philip wanted to head into the business himself when he was finished with school… Philip knew all about curios and old furniture, and once in a while when bargain hunting he took me along with him…we'd comb through the ancient op shops that spread down George Street behind the Square…

the shops were in close-packed, two-storey buildings put up during the early days of the city, brightly painted now and bohemian, and they filled the street in a ramshackle row...they were the coolest places around, where the varsity students went. I always thought Philip looked very grown-up on these expeditions...over his small frame he wore a blue roll-necked skivvy and a light-brown corduroy jacket, and I really wished I had a jacket just like it...we drove the length of George Street in Philip's mother's car, an Austin Westminster, and then parallel-parked...in the shops, we both behaved as sophisticates...we liked to display a casual prissiness amongst the stock, moving with deliberate caution through the cluttered, narrow aisles...we kept our elbows in tight to avoid brushing up against anything grimy, while smelling the enveloping mustiness in the store's air. Occasionally, Philip halted and gazed at an object with something resembling intense interest...he would lean back as he stared for a long, long time, frowning...he wrinkled his broad forehead...he rubbed his jaw, then ran his hand through his hair and then applied the hand thoughtfully to his chin again...each time I waited alongside him and observed his movements...I was trying to guess what it might be that Philip was thinking. Usually at last I grew impatient...I'd interrupt his mysterious plans...I'd point out a nicely patterned oriental vase or a really neat sort of art nouveau lamp...but Philip would only smile with an indul-gent air...he'd go on looking at the dull boring object of his attention, perhaps a soiled red fire-bucket or some other piece of bric-a-brac...once it was a scratched-up black-and-brown giant tortoiseshell, lying on its back in a corner with nothing inside but dust. 'I can get a hundred and forty dollars for that, you know,' Philip told me quietly and gestured at the tortoiseshell. He liked to speak in a confidential tone...it emphasised the Englishness of his somewhat plummy voice...I bent down to look for a price on the ugly, bumpy thing...Philip swivelled away on one heel. 'Up north,' he added. 'Collectors, sort of style.' Philip knew all about how to haggle over prices...he dealt with the shop staff, handled negotiations and arranged for everything to be comme il faut...my job was to haul the heavy stuff out to the car and find a way of fitting it into the back seat... the rear of Philip's mother's fibrolite-clad double garage in Marne Cres-cent was jammed to the ceiling with strange objects...Philip restored them with tremendous care and sent them, crated up, to his contacts in Auckland...there in the big smoke they sold his renovated knickknacks as decorative accessories. Our last week of classes finally arrived, though

48

it had seemed far off until almost the last moment...none of us, and certainly neither Philip nor I, could wait for school to end and be out of our lives...I nursed my secret plans for bringing more literature into the world...Philip was spending more and more time on his restoration projects. The breakup ceremony was scheduled for the night of 6 December...we handed in our textbooks at one of the science labs that same afternoon, stacking them in untidy piles and crossing our names off on a complicated list...for the school, getting back its tattered, dog-eared property was something that really seemed to matter...the process took ages and we were checked and double-checked...afterwards the teachers appeared to lose all interest in anything else and we were let off home early to cool our heels before the breakup. The ceremony was held each year at the Regent Theatre...we pupils had to arrive there ahead of time, and my father drove me up and dropped me off...the Regent was an old movie palace near the middle of town...it was in a gorgeous state of neglect, having suffered every kind of damage and second-rate repair imaginable, and each time I entered its draughty, fussy-looking foyer I noticed evidence of the slovenly way that the place had been treated...I stepped onto scruffy carpet and saw the chipped edges of the pillars in the lobby before me, the gouged and discoloured areas on the shoddy marble walls, the cracked moulding across the vaulted ceiling and, over almost every possible surface, the heavy brown-and-gold paint that had been applied repeatedly to hide the blemishes. There were a lot of people milling about in the foyer and chatting before the ceremony started, mostly pupils but also a few parents...I drifted further in amongst them, passed the grand staircase, ducked a little under the low mezzanine and headed through the entrance to the auditorium...inside the theatre was broad, chilly and unheated, and stocked with close-packed seats...the seats were spread out in sloping rows all along our floor and there was another tier upstairs...they were real leather, red and cracked, and everywhere they were creaking as people folded them out and sat on their rock-hard cushions. I got myself squared away amongst all the other seventh formers... we were perched on some rows near the back...we were jiggling around on our bottoms and scraping our feet a bit, mostly busy trying to keep ourselves warm...the parents had begun occupying the more comfortable dress circle out of sight above us...we could hear the impatience in their chatter and, like us, the restless sounds they made shifting and sitting down...no one could wait for the whole potty business to be over.

Up on the high stage before us the movie screen was gone...instead the entire stage area was open, fitted with seats, and lit with a glare that hurt everyone's eyes...a sombre black banner with the school's name stitched onto it was draped down from the theatre-flies at the rear...at the very front and centre of the stage, in everybody's view, had been placed the wooden lectern from school assemblies...it had been specially transported, hauled in and set up. After a while there was a flurry as Evan Blake crossed the stage from the wings in his pompous manner, which meant the ceremony was beginning at last...he strode up and sat on a fancy wooden chair just beside the lectern...the staff and prominent guests commenced trooping in and taking their seats behind him...as he waited for the others to arrange themselves, Evan Blake lounged under the warm stage-lights...he sat enfolded in his gown, facing us all, gripping the ornate carved arms of his chair with both hands...he looked grim and in control of everything, which was the nearest he ever seemed to come to satisfaction. Once everyone on stage was properly settled and some announcements had been made, the guest-speaker was introduced and stood up...he was a portly, florid-faced barrister wearing a double-breasted grey suit with a gaudy lime-green tie...he leaned on the lectern, picked at a scab on the edge of his nose for a moment, and soon began giving us a lengthy speech...it was a speech that managed to digress all over his own achievements, though it came out at us mostly as fuzzy crackling through the sound system overhead...we had to strain just to gather up some sense from the words. Gradually the man kept coming back to something about the importance, the vital value, of teamwork... by the time he was onto not letting the side down, none of us, not me nor anyone else in the rows around me, was paying any real attention...somebody in a seat nearby opened up his mouth and yawned hard, hard enough, we hoped, for the man to hear...we were united in our contempt for him. Next Evan Blake made a brief speech of thanks and there came the doling out of awards...in advance a line had been formed close to the front of well-heeled, top pupils, each of them excellent at something or another, and they commenced filing one by one up some steps onto the stage to receive honours and trophies...this went on for a good while, but then I heard my own name being called aloud...it was being announced again in confirmation, right there, Andrew Ingle, through the fuzzy speakers...I was the winner of the Bruce Irvine Memorial Essay Prize, though my name wasn't listed for anything in the programme and I hadn't been told beforehand to join the line of recipients...other classmates nearby were staring at me. The whole theatre appeared to fidget as everyone hesitated, until finally I stood up and let my seat fold back with a squeak... the end of the row was far, far off, and I had to work my way charily along past a series of knees...at last I started hurrying across the worn beige carpet up the aisle in the direction of the stage...it was a relief just to move freely, heading somewhere, under the gaze of so many people...I was beginning to feel my heart beat faster with each stride...I was also beginning to wonder who Bruce Irvine might be, that they should be giving me a prize in his memory. When I arrived at the bottom of the steps to the stage, a teacher stopped me...I thought he looked tired and harassed as he reached out and took my arm...a long sinuous blue vein was standing up across one of his temples...he bent close and spoke into my ear in an anxious whisper...the school had forgotten to get any essays, but the bloody prize had to be awarded anyway. The teacher let go of my arm and pushed me forwards...I trotted up the steps...there was some confused applause...a stout, solemn woman in a big wide-brimmed straw hat gave me five dollars. The next morning was the seventh form's absolutely final assembly at school...we shuffled in small groups into the hall, just the seventh formers and no one else, since nobody except us was going to be at school that day...we stood in a few rows, unsure what to do and feeling a little ashamed at being in the large hall entirely on our own... Mr Booth came round and gave us our seventh-form certificates...the deputy-head, Mr Cantlon, sat us down and made a short speech from the stage. Then we went up to him one by one when our names were called and received our testimonials...Mr Cantlon handed them to us sealed tight in manilla envelopes with our details printed on the front in block capitals...these were the personal testimonials that the headmaster had written for each of us, affirming our good character...our testimonials were supposed to secure our futures, and for five years Evan Blake had been threatening to withhold them if we didn't toe the line. Afterwards, we straggled off from the hall with the day over...there was nothing else that we were required to do, and already the school seemed to have forgotten all about us...we'd reckoned on being around till the end of the last period as usual but our educations had finished just before lunchtime...I sat in the quad to eat lunch with Philip, Neil and Simon and some of the others, and we pulled out our packs of carefully made sandwiches...I had thin slices of white bread with cheese and vegemite...there was a strong feeling of anticlimax. At last, Philip and I got onto our bicycles and dawdled down the school's main drive until we stopped just outside the wide school gates...I stared back at the barren front lawn, a lawn that was watered and mowed each day and that we'd never been allowed even once to walk across...I waved a goodbye to it and to the nasty, shabby brick ruin of the Main Building beyond it...next, still sitting on my bicycle saddle, I reached round into my bag and took out the envelope containing my testimonial...I tore the envelope open, casual as I could be and feeling very daring. Philip sat up straight beside me on his bike...he had his arms folded across his chest...he was affecting an air of exaggerated amusement...I drew forth the single sheet of flimsy paper from inside the envelope and unfolded the testimonial to read it aloud...Philip swayed on his bike a little, pushing one foot for balance into the rough, galvanised wire of the front fence...I thought that he, too, was daring anybody in the school to come out and tell us off. Evan Blake had once told me that I contributed to school life only by keeping down the averages for everyone else...I was interested to see if he'd repeat it on paper and so I scanned the page...but instead he'd merely written that I was an articulate young man who lacked discipline...if I ever found discipline, he wrote, I might learn to make something better of myself...his tone suggested he didn't fancy my chances. I recited the testimonial in a big voice with all the hauteur I could muster...I leaned back on the bike's saddle...I kept my head up and declaimed every flaming word on the paper...but I thought that if only discipline was waiting for me, out there in the world, I'd be better off learning sweet fuck-all. After finishing, I refolded the paper and put it into the envelope once more...I weighed up the idea of going back inside the school and sharing with Evan Blake a little of my opinion...I even considered flinging the testimonial away onto the lawn...but I decided my parents might enjoy having something from the school to keep...they also thought I lacked discipline...they'd be pleased to see it made official. We still had a whole half-day left that was free...I didn't want to go straight home to Albert Street, so I bicycled with Philip over to his house...on arriving we immediately changed out of our clothes and got ourselves into swimming togs and sunglasses...we weren't going to need school uniforms anymore. Next we opened all the windows of the living-room onto the back yard and shifted the stereo...we set up its impressively large speakers on tables by the window frames, facing them outside...we got some music going and cranked up the volume...then we sat ourselves down out in the back yard on a couple of rigid plastic patio chairs...we reclined as comfortably as possible on the wobbly, hard-backed seats, stretching our legs and striking poses of languid abandon. It was far too overcast to be hot, but the summer warmth radiated off the cement paving and from the corrugated-iron fence around the section...we tapped our feet energetically to the songs...after a bit we began to feel as relaxed as we were trying to look. Every once in a while we'd sneak into the house to turn up the music even a little further...then after we'd hurried back to our chairs, in what quickly became a game, Mrs Preslin would lean her small wrinkled head out of one window...Mrs Preslin was Philip's mother, and though she worked in the offices out at Massey she was home that day...she'd poke her face past a speaker-box with her hands on the sill, always with a cigarette poised in her fingers...she had bushy, untrimmed grey hair which stuck out at odd angles as she twisted to get us in sight... ragged bits of hair pushed through the wisps of cigarette smoke rising up beside her. Each time she called, 'I'm going to turn down this awful, devil-worshipping cacophony!'

'I know what "cacophony" means, Mrs Preslin,' I'd call back to her, enjoying myself. 'I'm an articulate young man.'

Mrs Preslin never failed to laugh at this...we'd left our testimonials with her to read when we'd come in from school that afternoon, and she'd told us they were nothing but a trashy joke...so now I really didn't mind going along with whatever she asked. Several times Philip's younger sister, wearing a white halter top and some skimpy denim shorts, marched into the yard on platform sandals...she never stopped speaking in rapid French, a string of sentences...she was back from six months in New Caledonia, where she'd developed in the most startling ways...now with each entrance she appeared to have been preening herself further for our benefit, and I could see that Philip's sister had strikingly good legs to preen with...I liked watching her strut past saying, 'Il n'y a pas de piscine,' or some other new phrase...finally Philip asked, 'Qu'est-ce que c'est the hell you doing?'...fortunately, this didn't put her off. Sometime later Mrs Preslin came out of the back door with afternoon tea for us...she had cups, a pot and a new tin of biscuits on a tray...she gripped the tray by its sides and bore everything cheerfully down the narrow back steps towards us, and as she approached I stood up and fetched another chair for her. Mrs Preslin made grateful noises and sat down in the patio chair with a grunt...she was wearing a very plain, ankle-length rust-coloured dress, practically a caftan, and she had to brace her knees beneath its thick and slippery fabric to balance the tray in her lap...all of the tea things rattled with her movements. 'So, Andy,' she said to me after a moment as she picked up the pot and commenced pouring out a cup. Mrs Preslin usually took a little breath, a sort of pause and hesitation, before saying something important...I watched her gulp a small mouthful of air now and ask, 'Well, are you thinking of doing any papers at Massey next year?'

'No,' I said.

More than anything, I was thinking about Philip's sister...she was off somewhere, hidden away back in the house...what on earth could she being doing there in those tiny shorts, or even out of them?...but Mrs Preslin was offering me the freshly-made cup and I reached forward with both hands to take it.

Then I added, 'I'm going to be a writer.'

'A what?' Philip asked. 'Wait a minute, where did this come from?' He lowered his sunglasses on his nose and stared...he was peering at me over the rims, and I could tell it was an imitation of one of our teachers. 'You never mentioned this before, laddie,' he barked in his most culti-vated manner.

'No sir,' I said. I grinned for him, extra-hard, to show that I'd got the joke. Next I said, 'It's basically stop-press stuff. I'm going to write a whole entire novel, from go to finish. But the thing is, it's still in a state of flux, because I'm kind of having some trouble getting started.'

I wondered what Philip's sister might make of this. But instead I heard Mrs Preslin say, 'Ah.' Her eyes had widened. She took another hesitant breath and said, 'Well, to write, you want to write.' She'd finished pouring a second cup, and she craned forward and gave it to Philip...but even as she did so, she leaned to one side and gazed severely at me. She said, 'Then first you have to live, eh. Really, you have to *live*.' The skin on Mrs Preslin's face was worn, discoloured...her features were rough, but her harsh look softened and was replaced by a definite twinkle in her rheumy eyes...for an instant I could guess where Philip's sister got her charm.

'That's fine by me,' I said.

'Oh yes,' Mrs Preslin grunted. She put the tray down onto the ground by her side...she seemed too excited to pour herself a cup. 'But I mean real living,' she went on. She reached down for the biscuit tin and picked

54

it up with her bony fingers...agitatedly she began scratching at the Sello-tape around the lid. 'I mean,' she asked, 'you know, why does the sun come up in the morning?'

'Because somebody's pulling the strings?' I asked back.

But I saw Mrs Preslin had been serious...she looked disappointed, as though she suddenly didn't approve of me...she gave up on the bis-cuit tin and took out a packet of cigarettes and a lighter from a pocket in her dress instead...I remembered that my parents had made some unpleasant remarks about her...they'd hinted that she'd done a lot of liv-ing herself, had Mrs Preslin...they said she was twice divorced, not once, that woman, but twice. 'Anyhow, writing sounds a hell of a lot better than going to varsity,' Mrs Preslin declared. She lit her cigarette, drew back on it hard and let the lighter fall onto the paving with a careless clatter... for a moment she sat up in her chair and stretched a little tension from her back, supporting herself with one hand tucked behind on her hip. 'You'd think I should know,' she said, 'I have to fucking go out to the fucking place every day.' Despite my own love of the word, I still wasn't very used to hearing adults saying 'fuck' in front of me...proper adults were supposed to talk in a grown-up manner with measured, grown-up language...even Philip looked embarrassed for a second or two by his mother's outburst...I watched his jaw quiver slightly while he searched for something to respond with. 'So,' he managed at last. Then he said, 'Why don't you bring this new novel of yours on over to Masterton?' The notion appeared to cheer him even as he suggested it. 'Bring it over to Stokewood, eh,' he added.

'Why, what's Stokewood?' I asked.

'Oh well, it's the house. That great big homestead just out of town—it's where Dad lives,' Philip said airily. He sounded surprised that I didn't already know, and I thought that probably he'd told me sometime and I'd forgotten. 'The whole deal, the house kind of thing, it's like his shop,' Philip went on. 'You know, for antiques. And he's got the living quar-ters right there upstairs, right above the entire shooting match. I'm going to head out to Masterton tomorrow, but you could come over any old time you like, eh. And you can stay as long as you want, because there's loads of room. Stacks.' 'That's true,' Mrs Preslin said. She'd leaned back-wards into her chair once more and I thought her tone had become a little wistful.

'Well, it's fine by me,' I said.

Up until now I'd never considered the idea of staying at an antiques shop, but before I could say anything further, I was distracted...Philip's sister had emerged from the back door...she was sashaying towards us on her nicely tapered legs again. It took me a moment to realise that the place everyone was talking about would be perfect...I'd just been invited to come and write in an old country house, to get my literary career started and sorted out in the midst of a gracious, rural retreat...it was the type of thing authors did when they needed to have their muse flourish undisturbed...suddenly I remembered to be more polite.

'I'd certainly be very glad if you could put me up there, at least for a bit,' I said.

I wasn't sure who to say this to, whether to Philip or Mrs Preslin, so I glanced at them one after the other, and again at Philip's sister approaching...somehow I felt confident that, over in Masterton, I'd have no problem finding a topic to write about...I might actually get my whole novel knocked off and ready for a publisher. I even began to imagine asking Chloe to come with me for the first few days...Chloe had bought herself a second-hand Morris Minor recently, and the Morris had proved handy for taking trips into and around town...I'd grown pretty used to cadging lifts in it...I imagined that I could easily get my writing things and stuff across to Masterton with the help of Chloe's car...I also imagined that, at Stokewood, I could lose my virginity at last. 'Stay as long as you want and get yourself set up,' Philip was saying once more. I saw him smile grandly at his mother and at me...it was as if he was divining all my thoughts.

But Chloe was not happy...she hated my exploratory suggestion about Stokewood, when finally I asked her...she had plans for us to spend the summer together...Chloe's 'us' always meant just the two of us. She wailed that I didn't seem to understand her at all...it would be our last real free time together, time over the summer, before enrolling and going to Teachers' College...but what I really couldn't understand at all was why she kept on with her ridiculous talk about me becoming a teacher...I just went ahead and made arrangements for Stokewood...I guessed that Chloe would come along if I was definitely going...I felt that, sooner or later, she'd realise the value to a writer of having an assistant with some decent transport. The day before leaving, Chloe phoned me at home... telephoning me was something she seldom did...she liked us both to talk face-to-face...she didn't like asking my parents if I was there and whether she could speak to me. But on the phone Chloe didn't mention one word about Masterton…there was nothing about the fact that my departure was tomorrow…in turn, I didn't mention the importance of her providing me with a ride…instead, Chloe said that she was going to take a drive out of town that afternoon…she invited me to come with her for a while over to Bulls.

'To Bulls?' I asked.

'Yes,' she said.

'What for?' I asked.

'Do you want to come or don't you?' she snapped.

'All right,' I mumbled, and I added, 'Why not?'

For someone who'd just said yes, I hoped I'd been as noncommittal as possible…Chloe had been tetchy for days…I liked to think it was frustration over the state of our love life. In the afternoon we headed out of town in Chloe's snug little car…plonked in the passenger seat I sat, as usual, with my legs cramped up and the front window near my face…today it all felt especially uncomfortable…beyond the city limits we passed several well-ordered-looking stud farms, with horses wandering up to the fences, and we continued on into grazing country…Chloe drove us in a steady fashion across the gently rolling grey-green landscape. The Morris had only something like a sewing-machine engine, but it ran easily along the narrow open road…Chloe kept both hands up on the wheel…she was a relentlessly careful driver…she'd taken all her driving lessons very much to heart…I didn't speak to her as we went on, and I tried to amuse myself by watching the roadside power poles flitting by…I began focusing on the rough, lichen-spotted timber in some of the poles, but soon my gaze, no matter what, kept getting dragged off towards the increasingly threatening weather in the distance. Over in the paddocks, the shadows among the windbreaks were turning sombre and chilly…from the far edges of the hills long grey layers of Rangitikei rain-cloud were coming in across the sky, hanging almost low enough to collapse out of the air…I thought the wind was picking up, and at length I felt it starting to push and shove the side of the car…I hoped we weren't going for some sort of picnic. We reached the central intersection at Bulls, with nobody around…I had a brief instant to wonder yet again what we were doing here…but next, not stopping or saying a word to me, Chloe drove us right on through the crossroads…she kept gripping the wheel with her lips stiffened and her jaw set tight, and she stared forwards at the street that was taking us away out of the township again…she looked far too determined on wherever she was going to explain anything...I didn't feel it would be good to ask. After a few minutes more we reached Lake Alice, and I thought we might be heading for Turakina...but all at once Chloe pulled off the highway... she swung us hastily into a small approach road...the car didn't like the sudden change of direction and slipped into a short skid on the loose gravel...Chloe halted us without trouble. 'Shit,' she said. For a moment we sat still in the quiet of the empty turnoff...I concentrated on saying nothing...finally, with stubborn movements Chloe put the engine back in gear and we pulled away, but this time she drove on more cautiously, as if the car had made its point. The tiny road took us across low-lying, spacious ground...there were no stock that I could see anywhere on the paddocks, but the weather was deteriorating even further...the view around us was almost smothered now in the closeness of the sinking clouds... as we went on and on, I began to wonder if anything was really out there amongst the bleary, soggy scenery. But then we arrived at our destination...I could tell that we'd arrived, though I'd no idea where, because the road had abruptly ceased at a wide square of asphalt laid out in parking spaces...Chloe slowed us almost to a stop and I saw that the entire parking area was completely deserted...its white lines had recently been repainted and several of them were in different positions from the older, faded marks...Chloe spent a few minutes carefully manoeuvring us into a space. Beyond the asphalt square I could see broad and uneven parkland around us through the poor light, its uncut, fluffy grass planted here and there with ornamental birch trees...there was nobody about, not a soul... but far off I could discern some two-storey yellow villas looking isolated in the grim and empty distance...at last I guessed where we were...I'd heard of what Lake Alice was. So, I thought, this is a mental hospital. Chloe was already getting out of the car...she slammed the door behind her in a tremendous hurry and the Morris rocked on its chassis under the impact...she stood still beside the car for a moment, evidently making up her mind...next she marched without me towards a narrow concrete path at the edge of the parking area...the path looked half overgrown with unsightly weeds, but Chloe started heading off along it...it was taking her in the direction of the nearest villa. I hopped out of the car and tried to follow...I was already some way behind...as we walked on, far apart but moving faster and faster, there was no sound but our own rushing footsteps and the steady rumble of the rising wind...I thought the whole place was eerily quiet...I wondered if maybe it was nap time for the inmates, and thinking this gave me an urge to giggle...but I felt ashamed and managed to suppress any more stupid ideas. When we got closer to the villa, I saw the building had a plain, almost jerrybuilt look...it had a flat, stuccoed front, a flimsy concrete porch in the very middle with a door that was painted the same yellow as everything else, and big square windows... after another few moments Chloe reached the steps to the entrance, still several paces ahead of me...I caught up and watched her standing on the porch...she was rattling the door handle with an impatient growl...then she succeeded at shoving her way in, and I followed after her over the steps. Inside, Chloe led me from the hallway off to our right and along a passage...the villa's interior was dim and a bit bare, but it looked tidy... the thin purple carpet underfoot was faded and didn't reach all the way to the walls, and everything smelled a little musty and sad. We passed a broad staircase where I saw somebody at last, a shrunken, elderly man who was halfway up the stairs, heading for the landing...he was wearing red slippers and had a dirty grey-tartan dressing-gown hanging on his frail frame, and his shoulders were hunched in the effort of hauling himself up each step...when the man heard us behind him, he paused. 'I got to stay in shape, eh,' he croaked, still with his back to us. With one hand he was grabbing at the banister beside him...his pale wrist, poking out of his dressing-gown, was trembling from the strain of his grip...the man twisted himself to look over his shoulder and stared straight into my eyes...there were blue bruises along one side of his pallid face...he started mumbling again in his ruined voice. 'Got to. I got to stay in shape, you know,' he repeated. Finally he turned away and recommenced struggling up the stairs. 'Thing is,' he continued to say between gasps, keeping his head down and his back to us while he worked to lever himself forwards, 'thing is, in the baseline game—better for maintaining the rally, eh. That's what it is, sort of deal. You—you don't want to get any older in the baseline game.' I assumed it was me, or perhaps Chloe, that the man was talking to...after all, there was nobody else around.

'I see,' I said.

The old man moaned in reply, 'No time for my bath.' I wondered if maybe I should try going up the staircase and helping him...automatically I glanced at Chloe, but she made no movement...we waited until the man had climbed safely to the landing...then Chloe turned and led us further into the villa. At the far end of the passage she pushed open a solid wooden door...it had the word 'lounge' stencilled on it in rough white letters and there was a small ragged hole on one side where the handle had been removed...over Chloe's shoulder, as we entered, I could see a grossly fat woman seated at a dining-table in a cramped room...she was leaning forward with her spectacular bulk hung awkwardly between her chair and the table's edge, bracing herself on her elbows. The woman was middle-aged, dark-haired, and was wearing a shapeless white T-shirt and a pair of black track-suit pants that were stretched hard across her tubby thighs...she had a round red face with huge, bloated-looking cheeks which dominated her features...she was squinting through thick horn-rimmed glasses at something down on the table...it was several jumbled piles of torn-up magazines. I drew in closer behind Chloe...along with the magazines there appeared to be a clutter of stuff, paper and pens, a Sellotape dispenser and some scissors, spread across the dining-table's Formica top...the woman went on staring at the pages in front of her and finally glanced up at us both with a busy air, her eyes weirdly magnified by her glasses...we'd been waiting inside the doorway for several seconds already but the woman only reacted to our presence now, startled, as if she'd just been interrupted...she opened her small mouth, which was almost hidden among the folds of skin along her jaw, and moved her lips, though no words came out...I could tell she was badly sunburned across her face and neck. 'Hullo,' Chloe said at last. The woman beamed in response. Suddenly she said in a loud voice, 'Look at all the specials.' She manoeuvred herself back from the table with a snort that made the baggy cheeks flap in her face...next she sat up very straight and pulled the glasses from her nose...they fell down onto the pages on the table with an echoing clatter, and the hollow sound made me look about us properly. I took in the bare brown hardboard walls in the sparsely fur-nished room...there were windows opposite without any curtains and below them three other chairs for the table were arranged in a line... crammed into a corner nearby there was a cheaply-made bench with a set of drawers and a stainless-steel sink, and that was the lot...I tried to imagine what kind of jiggery-pokery we'd got ourselves into. The woman was picking up a long pair of scissors from where they lay near her arm, holding them by the blades in one hand...she scrutinised the scissors for a moment and then waved them in front of her. 'Sending off for samples,' she announced. I felt a touch of concern and shuffled out a little from my position behind Chloe...I wondered if the woman might be about to use the scissors to hurt herself, but she gazed at me with satisfaction, as

60

though she'd understood the question in my eyes. 'I'm not borrowing these. They're mine,' she said. 'Well,' she continued, 'I just can't get over the number of specials. So many—I mean, here, eh. Look at these.' Still clasping the scissors in her gigantic grip, she gestured at a small heap of brown envelopes...they were gathered in a loose stack at the far end of the table, all addressed in a large, round hand.

'That's a good idea,' I said.

'I know,' the woman answered. 'There's lots of stuff, eh, and some of it's even for free. You should—' 'Mum, this is Andy,' Chloe interrupted. 'I *know*,' the woman said. The strange, childish lady who was Chloe's mother looked up at me from her seat and grinned...I tried grinning back. 'Are you going to stay here?' she asked brightly.

'No,' I said. 'I'm visiting you.'

'Why are you so sunburned, mum? What did you do?' Chloe asked, cutting in on us. She reached out and deftly took the scissors from her mother...at almost the same time, with her other hand, Chloe picked up a chair from among the row by the wall...she drew the chair to the table beside her mother and sat, and gestured for me to bring one too...I followed and sat myself down as best I could, opposite them both. 'Oh, we went out to Himatangi on the bus the other day,' Chloe's mother was saying in an odd tone of indifference. 'We saw the sea, eh. We saw the sand, and driftwood, the whole scheme, it was a very beachy beach.' I wriggled on my chair to try and make myself comfortable...then I watched the woman sweep a hand over the shredded magazines. 'Just see how I'm getting on!' she said triumphantly. But Chloe ignored all the paper in front of us...she stood up again from the table with a weary look in her eyes. She said, 'You'd like a cup of tea, wouldn't you, mum?' 'Oh yes, but I can't have a biscuit,' Chloe's mother replied. 'They've put me on the diet again. For the weight, eh. They're always going on about it. Watch your weight, drop some weight. I swear it's the last bloody thing I'll ever hear in this world. These people are just a teeny-weeny bit obsessive, you know. But I look all right, don't I?' Chloe's mother was addressing me...she started leaning forward hard across the table with her blubbery face up surprisingly close. She asked, 'I've still got my figure, haven't I?' She grinned once more...I grinned back with all the force I could muster...I was beginning to get the hang of this.

'Don't see any change,' I said.

Chloe's mother straightened up again and sat quiet and satisfied...

but at the same time Chloe herself was banging about through the drawers and cupboards under the bench, almost ready to bust a gut...she couldn't seem to find what she wanted in them for the tea-making...the clanking noises went on and on...I thought that either the drawers fitted badly or she was turning a cuppa into terribly hard work. 'Your fingers are puffy, mum,' Chloe announced out of nowhere, even though she had her back to us. She said it while plugging in an electric jug she'd finally found. 'Must be the medication,' she added. But now I could tell Chloe was right...even on such a bulging body with such lumpy arms, her mother's hands and fingers were definitely swollen. 'It's just the sunburn,' her mother said. 'It's the medication,' Chloe insisted, still with her back to us. 'Well, take a peek at that silver birch,' her mother exclaimed. She pushed herself away from the table with an effort that made her chair squeal... she began pointing with one heavy arm for me out of the windows at a tree close-by...Chloe's mother kept her arm up and stiffly out, as if directing me to be fascinated, while I twisted a little on my seat and looked properly...my eyes travelled to where the tree's old gnarled branches were heavy with leaves. 'All tough and gravelly and solid inside,' Chloe's mother was declaring in a rush, 'and not really silver there, yeah, but patchy white and bright and black and stippled, sort of, and the branches, oh, the branches sticking, licking, up, up, and pointy at those ends all beckoning to the sky—but with those stringy twigs, foliage, the leaves, all curled and furled round bunches of air, big fuzzy green bunches of it and hanging down, down, at the ground and swinging from it, from the breeze, and dangling every which how.' She halted, and I heard her arm slap on the tabletop as she finally lowered it. Then I heard her say, 'I've been admiring the thing the whole day, eh.' I gazed at the tree a bit longer, feeling something like respect...I wanted to see further into the details of what Chloe's mother had been describing...as I turned back, I saw her watching me looking. Next she whispered, 'Are you sure you're not going to stay here?'

'Well, what's it like in this place?' I asked.

Chloe's mother raised her eyes to think. 'The TV's good,' she said. 'Sit up at the table, mum,' Chloe said in a firm tone. Her mother shifted her bulk forwards, and we sat quietly once more...Chloe finished boiling the jug, slopped the hot water into a teapot and, after not much of a pause to let anything draw, poured the brew into some cups...but by now her mother appeared to have forgotten all about what was happening...

62

she just looked surprised when the tea was placed in front of her…she reminded Chloe again that she couldn't have a biscuit. Over the cups we sat and chatted about the weather and admired the magazines…we even admired the birch tree some more…Chloe and I did most of the talking, since it was as if Chloe's mother didn't want to be included, and so the time seemed to pass by peacefully. But as soon as the tea was finished Chloe started to act as though she was restless and uncomfortable…she kept glancing away towards the door in an obvious manner…I thought perhaps I should make some noises about leaving, but I did nothing until at last Chloe said that it was time to be gone…Chloe's mother appeared distracted from the moment we stood up…she didn't even attempt to raise herself from her chair and made only a casual waving gesture with her hand after we said bye-bye…it was as though she believed we might return in a minute. I lingered, and looked back at her over my shoulder as we were departing through the doorway…Chloe's mother was absorbed again by the magazines on the table…in front of me, Chloe was already striding ahead up the passageway…she didn't look back even once. 'She's a manic-depressive,' Chloe said a few minutes later, as we stood outside on the villa's porch. Without waiting for my reply, she began heading off briskly again on the weed-choked path…I hurried after her…the gusting breeze tugged through the grass at our ankles. Chloe kept marching a little way ahead with a kind of fierce confidence…I guessed it was this confidence that I'd been following all day and felt as if I'd met a whole new Chloe…I was almost trotting along on the untidy path behind her.

'Will your mother be here for a while?' I managed to ask.

'No, that's the trouble,' Chloe said. She spoke in a loud, bitter voice, not once looking round at me. She added, 'They keep letting her out, but she never gets any better at home. She just goes on a high, eh, and then we have to ring them up some more. It's bloody hopeless.'

'She's going to get a lot of free samples,' I observed.

We were making rapid progress along the path…I was staring at the base of Chloe's tiny, bent back as we tramped onwards…her shoes were landing with sharp, hard thumps against the broken cement. 'No she won't,' Chloe said. 'She won't get even one of them. The hospital intercepts all non-family mail. Anyway, she'll be too bloody depressed by tomorrow to remember anything about it.'

'I'm sorry,' I said.

I meant it, but the words seemed to disappear into the windy space between us...it made me feel how inadequate they were...Chloe hurried on.

'I really am sorry to hear that,' I said.

Chloe halted...she swung round on the path...the wind was whipping her hair into her eyes...she reached up and pushed the strands of it angrily away from her with her fingers, as if it was the cause of all her troubles. 'I showed you this,' she snapped. 'This, this—' I'd stopped too, and I waited for her to collect her thoughts...she waved past me, gesturing towards the villa. 'It's because I love you,' she announced. Chloe still looked furious as she said it...but next she said the exact same words again...she was bent forward into the buffeting wind, shielding her eyes and accusing me of being someone she loved...for a moment I watched her staring straight at me...she'd paused, tensely, expecting my reply.

'I love you too,' I said.

'Well, if you really, really loved me, you wouldn't talk about going off to bloody Masterton and writing a book,' she shouted. 'You'd spend your time in Palmy with the person you really care about.'

'But you're coming with me,' I said.

I couldn't understand why Chloe had revealed all this about herself to me...for an instant or two, keeping a safe distance from her on the path, I pondered what the whole business could signify...did she really believe in her heart that she loved me?...did she really think that presenting me with her mother would somehow prove anything?...nothing seemed to explain even the tiniest fraction of what had happened. But then I started thinking of my plans for literature, and then of my brand-new plans for sex...I just couldn't help it...I started thinking about how wonderful it would be to get away from all this...I thought of how marvellous it was sure to be when everything was up and ticking. I heard Chloe say, 'I'm only going there for a few days, eh. You know what I mean.'

'Well, you can't mess with art,' I said. 'I have to be there. I've got an artistic destiny to keep in perspective.'

Chloe sighed from deep down in her throat...she squirmed a little, swinging her hips, and turned her back on me again...then she stamped off for the car in the nearby parking area as if she didn't care whether I was following or not.

TWO

The Morris Minor struggled for the entire journey up over the Pahia-tua Track...the whole thing was sad, pitiful...at each new rise the engine was within a moment of giving out and dying...somehow it managed to hold on. We inched forwards up the road into the ranges, on and on past paddocks and the sodden bush...we proceeded by winding our way between steep, bulging spurs, always climbing...Chloe stayed in the low gears and she pumped at the accelerator...she had her hands gripped tight on the steering wheel. Here and there we saw old horizontal patterns of sheep ruts scoured down in layers into the soil, but there was scarcely an animal anyplace in sight...finally all around us the grim slopes were covered with nothing but patches of grey withered grass...it looked as though everything good had been blown or washed off the hillsides long ago. Chloe kept her gaze fixed on our route...she stayed silent with the effort of her driving...in front of us the road continued twisting away, up and up...it seemed to be endlessly scurrying out of view around the next bare shoulder of rock...not even a white centre-line marked the brief, straight stretches, and past each bend I thought the sky before us had grown bigger and even more jammed with cloud. I was sitting in the passenger seat yet again, uncomfortable and cold...mostly I was thinking literary thoughts...my typewriter I held a little primly in the narrow space on my lap, and I drummed my fingers on its thick plastic cover...eventually Chloe told me to stop, without even lifting her eyes from the road...I wondered when I'd begun to need her permission for things. Already I'd shown Chloe the typewriter...that was while helping prepare the car for our trip, when I'd dropped my duffle-bag, with a change of clothes and the still-untouched ream of foolscap inside, into the tiny boot...almost at once I'd had to take the duffle-bag out again, because Chloe had appeared dragging a heavy travel-suitcase...she said to fit it in and waited for me to do the job. First I'd crammed the suitcase into the boot with an old blanket, to stop anything from shifting around, and repositioned my bag in a corner...then I had the idea, a good one, that the typewriter could just go up front with me...I'd never carried it anywhere before...but Chloe objected that she didn't want us to start out with stuff all over the seats...I thought I might help my chances by demonstrating my typing for her a little.

'This here is the machine,' I said, placing it gently on the bonnet.

I popped open the cover with a sense of pride...I tapped on a rattling key or two...I ran my index finger along the row of typebars for her to observe...then I nudged up to the edge of the grimy red-and-black ribbon.

'The literature is all waiting in here,' I said.

Chloe craned her neck to see past what I was doing and checked the bonnet instead...perhaps she was worried I'd scratch her car...she seemed to give my typewriter no more than a glance. But after a moment she said in a perfunctory tone, 'That what-do-you-call-it, the scoop round the typebars on the top, eh. It looks like half an arsehole.' She was trying her best to be mean, but I was overjoyed at this comment...it really did look like half an arsehole...it was perfect...I dubbed my typewriter 'Half-Arse' on the spot. The nickname only appeared to annoy Chloe further, though I wouldn't be put off...I won the short, sharp argument that followed about bringing the typewriter in the car...it felt somehow safer to have the machine close at hand, perched on my lap...while we drove, I kept imagining how Half-Arse would get me a good strong start on my novel. For some time as we continued I patted my feet for warmth against the worn-out floor carpet of the car...but beyond the top of the ranges we lost the cloud and the weather improved dramatically...the foothills below turned bright, and we descended through a much more summery afternoon onto the Wairarapa plains...the newly warm sunlight began to settle on my arms through the windows...we headed south along the highway, and soon it was even hot...at length I saw a heat-haze shimmering dreamily on the asphalt, and couldn't recall the last occasion I'd seen one in Palmerston North. I decided I liked the Wairarapa...I liked everything about it...I liked its dry, solid heat and the way the yellow pasture, the trees and the scrub all looked dusted with fine grains of windblown dirt... I liked the straight, flat, uninterrupted highway. We drove faster now, past rows of thick wild grass spread along the roadsides and clumped up before the wrinkled battens in the fence-lines...in the paddocks beyond, I could sometimes glimpse stock chewing at the hard, parched cover... at last I understood what people meant when they said it was a good day to sell a farm. The minutes slipped by until finally we started to approach Masterton...I'd never bothered to think of what we'd do when we actually got there...Philip had told me that we'd find the house without trouble if we turned off from some sort of street...he said just to inquire about Upper Plain Road and Stokewood...I'd nodded my head in response because it didn't sound like a real address, and then I'd forgotten all the details. But Chloe seemed to have done her homework...she made a few turns that were more or less decisive, and once we drove up and down for a while when we got lost...but after a bit we were chugging at an easy pace down a smooth flat straight on the outskirts of the town...there didn't appear to be any other choices, so I felt pretty sure that we were on the right road. I saw a large square sign coming up, at the edge of some empty paddocks in the near distance...the sign had quaint red letters and an arrow indicating a small turnoff...it got easier to read the words as we drew closer, and I squinted and made out: 'Traditional 18th and 19th century furniture from England and other countries. Also decorative accessories'...I knew then that we'd found the place. After a few minutes we drew level with the turnoff...there was a large bed of red dahlias and a new tubular-metal mailbox by the gate...a long unsealed track stretched away through some untidy scrub and disappeared round a belt of shaggy grey poplars...Chloe swung us in, and bumped the car into and out of the ruts on the approach road...even with all the dry warmth the wheels beneath us splashed through a few muddy puddles. Next we came past the end of the poplars and the scenery changed...I saw that we'd suddenly entered a sparsely metalled driveway bordered by white stones...it skirted a pale-green unmowed lawn and ran up to a grand Victorian homestead. That homestead, coming ever closer into sight, was complicated-looking and two storeys high...I strained my eyes to get myself a better view... there were rooms protruding on the near side, and they had small gabled windows upstairs and a much larger flat bank of windowpanes below... then the remainder of the house, the frontage, was overshadowed on the ground floor by a long veranda and a porch, with a neat but flimsy-looking row of dormers above, set into a sharply sloping iron roof...an enormous elm tree with a wide grey trunk and a canopy of glowing yellow leaves stood just before the house near the front steps. Behind the tree I noticed the veranda seemed badly lopsided, and the porch's shadows were keeping a pair of old, tatty armchairs and a number of other jumbled objects partly obscured...but elsewhere along the sides of the house I could easily make out unpruned roses and creepers that had begun to attach themselves to the exterior walls...the mottled, flaking paint on most of the weatherboards was gone from long neglect and the grey-blue grain of the wood was showing clear through.

'Gosh,' I said.

Chloe said nothing...we were drawing up to the homestead at last, and she slowed the car down...she seemed to be thinking about somewhere to park...we pulled up right underneath the elm, and I could tell that it was planted much too near the house...it was threatening the veranda with its bulky branches...its twigs and leaves were littered everywhere on the uneven driveway around us. Chloe stopped the car and switched off the engine...still she said nothing...the motor's noise ceased, and we heard the busy sound of cicadas enjoying the heat of the day...I sat staring out of my passenger's window and understood now why the veranda was out of true, since the whole homestead appeared to be sinking on its piles...the far end was sagging so freakishly that it seemed almost ready to break off from the house...I felt sure that I was going to love staying here. Philip had come outside...he stood waiting for us on the porch, deep in the shade, but next he appeared to change his mind and stepped self-consciously down into the sunlight...with one hand he protected his face from the glare as he approached the car...I saw he was dressed in the natty corduroy jacket from his shopping expeditions in Palmy. 'Good to see you both,' Philip called. I thought that here, amidst all this, Philip's posh and jovial voice seemed to make perfect sense...Stokewood was a setting designed for him...or perhaps, I reflected, Stokewood was a setting that he'd been designing himself for, in a way that Mr Booth in the Vocational-Guidance Office would advocate...Chloe and I opened the creaking doors of the car and stretched a little as we slid ourselves out from the seats. 'So, did you two have a good trip over?' Philip asked, and smiled.

'Piece of piss,' I said.

I trotted round to the rear of the car, holding Half-Arse...I got the boot open, took out my duffle-bag and walked ahead of the others to the magnificent house...I couldn't wait to see the inside and dismissed all thoughts of anything else...but with my first step up onto the porch the long boards beneath my sandshoes let out a despairing groan...I paused and examined my footing, making even more noise with each new movement. 'Don't worry yourself one bit about that,' Philip said from just behind me. 'It's all like that, all over.' I supposed he was trying to be reassuring, but I didn't care anyway and was already getting distracted by other noises...now I could hear stately classical music, perhaps a string quartet or something...the music was coming faintly through the windows nearby. Above the sounds Philip was explaining, 'This whole place, you know, it was built far back in the 1870s.'

'What's up with the tune?' I asked.

'Handel's Sarabande, from Suite number eleven,' Philip announced. He spoke automatically, as if he'd answered the question before. He added, 'We have the gramophone on, oh, I'd say basically all the time. For the punters.' I turned away and saw Chloe was standing well apart from us, waiting by the open boot...she had both her arms akimbo and a strong pout set on her lips, and I thought it best to take the hint...I went back to the car, still holding my own gear, to haul out her luggage and bring it in. As I moved aside the blanket and fished up Chloe's suitcase, she hissed quietly near my shoulder, 'This *place* is falling to pieces.' But I didn't bother to answer...I kept myself preoccupied with hustling all the bags back towards the porch...Chloe started coming along close behind me, silent but still in a mood...Philip led us inside into a wide entrance hall. After sitting cooped up in the car, the spaciousness of the hallway felt airy and cool...everywhere around us, from the floor up to the ceiling, was lined with dark-grained wooden panels that were attractively old...a beautifully carved staircase was in front of us, with a broad floral carpet runner along the centre of the steps...the carpet looked as if it was slipping dangerously loose, bulging in weird spots out of its worn brass rails...I gazed up and saw an ornamental light dangling from the ceiling, its cut-glass cover so coated with dust that the slightest disturbance would probably bring a fine shower of grit down onto our heads...this house just kept on getting better and better. Chloe seemed to shrink a little closer to my side, but I ignored her stupid reaction and moved away...I put our bags down in a corner next to some dirty-yellow porcelain doorknobs that had been tossed into a heap along the skirting board...when I straightened up, I saw Philip's father, Mrs Preslin's ex-husband, was coming into the hall. Philip introduced us...Mr Bream was a heavily built, thick-necked man wearing a loose white shirt and dull-coloured slacks, and for an instant he stood before us rocking a little from one foot to the other...he carried himself with a certain middle-aged vigour, though I couldn't help noticing his extra weight and the wavy strands of grey amongst his thin ginger hair...then Mr Bream leaned forward and shook my hand while looking carefully into my eyes, and the large pouches of skin hanging on his cheeks deepened into an approving smile...he greeted us both in a hearty, rich base voice...he started apologising, saying that his wife was busy with a customer, and I supposed that by his wife he meant the new Mrs Bream. To my surprise, Chloe let Mr Bream greet her with a brief, easy hug...finally he stepped back and nodded for several seconds, as though taking us in again...I thought he was going to say something more...instead he proceeded to duck quickly past us and headed away into another room...we heard his footsteps moving off and some muffled distant talk, and in the empty moment that followed his hasty departure Philip offered us a tour of the shop downstairs. 'Come on and start making yourselves at home,' he insisted. 'Come. Come on.' He began by leading us through the door from which his father had appeared and into an expansive drawing-room, crowded with furniture...there was a random jumble of cabinets, sideboards and chests of drawers pushed back against its beige-painted, match-lined walls...at the very centre was a huge dinner-table with a number of lumpy red easy-chairs positioned in the places where dining-chairs should have been...the classical music had grown louder and I spied a record-player set up in a corner...even amongst all this furniture the room was still large enough for the trilling sounds from the small speakers to echo...thick swirls of dust motes were gathered in the sunbeams coming through the broad front windows near us. I caught a faint aroma of mildew, and I glanced up and could see white spots of fungus along one edge of the high ceiling...I looked down again and saw Philip was frozen in expectation beside us...I gave him an ingratiating grin of appreciation...Chloe wrinkled her nose...in a huffy manner she began leading us on round a coffee-table that blocked our way. Then I saw that we were not really alone...just past a gaudy folding Japanese screen, almost motionless, stood a man in a tight black suit...he was reaching out and fingering the old glass dome of an ornamental clock on top of a chest of drawers...the man seemed busy looking thoughtful, and he was probably one of the punters...we came towards him with the grimy floor creaking and cracking under our feet, but he continued to disregard us as we passed. Philip was gesturing about us with an air of proud ownership, offering a few comments on things...I tried my best to stay close to him while we walked and listened...it appeared the safest way to indicate to the punter that we were guests and not just customers. Everything in sight had yellow-tinted price stickers attached, and I saw the sideboards and glazed cabinets around the walls were cluttered with decorative accessories that also had price-tags showing...we passed a low table piled with rows of twisted and bent iron curtain-rails, candle-holders and coat hooks, and my eyes lit on a really neat plaster bust lying amongst all the mess on its face...I wondered if it might be a bust of somebody famous, somebody a little like the artist that I was going to be.

70

Philip moved us on into a smaller back room which was every bit as cluttered as where we'd just been…I started admiring a large square oil painting in an ornate gilt frame propped up against a chair, but Philip directed my attention away towards another picture hanging above the mantelpiece…it looked early century, Philip explained, with possible elements of Goldie, so it had to be worth a bob. I contemplated the picture for a while…it was a grey-haired old Maori man smoking a pipe…I twisted my head to see better past the streaky glazing but what I appreciated more and more was my blank lack of engagement, and I decided that this connoisseurship of art was a tricky business. A squat little dog wobbled up and interrupted us…it had a fat brown trunk and neck, with a narrow head topped by floppy ears…its wide gait made me think it might be a corgi, but with possible elements of dachshund…the dog was beginning to sniff at Chloe's shoe…Chloe shook her foot back and forth to get rid of it. 'That's Humphrey,' Philip said. Humphrey was gazing up at us with his mouth open…there was a loopy look in his beady eyes…he started to follow after Chloe as we moved away…I still had Half-Arse with me, and so I tried manoeuvring the typewriter between Humphrey and Chloe's calves. 'Don't mind him,' Philip said, 'Humphrey here, he comes with the house.' I watched the dog cocking his head in an effort to understand us…he had his tongue out and he was panting, drooling…then with rapid little steps he tottered after us again as we entered another small room. The new room was crammed with older, even shabbier furniture…its only window had a pane of glass that didn't fit and a strip of cardboard Sellotaped along one edge to cover the gap…up against one wall nearby was a waist-high bookcase of dark red wood…it was loaded with books. I leaned closer to take the books in…Humphrey nuzzled against my leg but I paid no attention to him…I was staring at old, used copies of *Landfall*…I remembered that *Landfall* was a famous literary journal…I'd never seen a literary journal up close before. 'Solid mahogany,' Philip said. Perhaps he thought I was admiring the bookshelf…I reached down and, seeing that the magazines were arranged by year, pulled out an early copy…a film of brown dirt came off the top onto my fingers…I examined the faded paper cover…the black type of the title had an authoritative air. Philip and Chloe were going on ahead, but I stayed and started flipping through the brittle pages of *Landfall* with my one free hand…my other hand was gripping Half-Arse's carrier strap tight in enthusiasm…I tried not to crack the hard line of glue in the magazine's spine….Humphrey pressed his bulk into me with his furry, flabby shoulders...he began to slobber on my sandshoes...he seemed intent on sharing my moment of discovery. But I was busy imagining the day when I'd be published...I'd be in there, on the pages, amid the wide, neatly-spaced rows of print before my eyes...I felt sure that day couldn't be so far off...there wasn't a price anywhere inside the magazine's cover and I wondered if maybe the copies came with the bookshelf...finally I put the journal back and gave Humphrey a comradely pat. Sometime later, Chloe and I took our bags upstairs...Philip had said to use the bedroom at the far end of the left-hand corridor...it was exciting to mount the staircase and manage the slippery carpet...it was even more exciting to step over the 'Staff Only' sign, strung on a low rope across the upper landing...nevertheless, all this surging passion might mostly have been sexual anticipation...I was feeling as sexy as all hell. But the upstairs corridor, when we got there, had no lights in the ceiling...the passage was narrow and crooked, with the dim, varnished wooden walls sloping weirdly to one side...it was as though the whole upper storey had been deformed by the sinking piles beneath the house...the bare uneven boards under our feet seemed even grimier than the ones downstairs. I trod with caution, leading the way... Chloe struggled silently at my back, even though I'd taken her bag again when we'd paused on the landing...everything was a surprise, but every-thing felt so thrilling in its eccentricity...I tried not to scratch her suitcase on the protruding walls and four-panelled doors as we went. The door to our own room, once we found it, was badly out of plumb...it wouldn't budge when I used the handle and I needed two solid shoves with my shoulder to get it open...as I stepped inside, my shin straightaway hit the corner of an ancient double-bed...the bed took up most of the space in the room, along with a tall carved wardrobe and a lengthy sheet of mirror glass, without any frame, that was leaning up against one wall...the cramped conditions made me wonder how on earth they'd managed to get everything in here. Still holding the bags, I wedged myself sideways, manoeuvring into the tight gap between the bed and wall and thinking that this was where it was all going to happen with Chloe, the hanky-panky...the mattress was awkwardly low, well below the level of my knees...it was covered with a musty orange bedspread that didn't even reach down to the floor...after a moment I hauled Chloe's suitcase up onto the mattress, and the springs around the case shivered and groaned with the sudden load...then her bag sank deep into the mattress's centre, down almost to the floorboards. I checked back over my shoulder… Chloe was still peering in around the doorway…she looked reluctant about entering our room…she kept her eyes on the suitcase, which was more or less enveloped by the sagging double-bed. 'Don't you go getting any big ideas,' she said. Chloe didn't spare me even a glance as she said it…country living didn't seem to agree with her.

At six o'clock Mrs Bream appeared…she was a small stumpy woman in an old plain blue sundress that had broad, over-padded shoulders… she had a bumptious manner which I thought rather high-strung…in a peremptory fashion she rounded us all up, Philip, Chloe and me, from the upstairs rooms where she insisted that we'd been hiding…then without further ado she led us away, trailing behind her…we struggled to keep up as she hurried down the staircase and along a corridor towards the kitchen. Mrs Bream wore her straight black hair cut in a short sticky bob…I watched it drooping and swinging against her sallow cheeks as she strode on ahead…above her shoulders, as she went, she kept gesturing back to us in nervous excitement with big red masculine hands… she kept telling us in a breathless tone that she'd been very clever… she'd been terribly, terribly clever to find some time…she'd actually got a whole bally roast prepared and into the oven. The old-fashioned kitchen at Stokewood, once we'd entered it, seemed uncomfortable and small with all of us crowded inside…it was dominated by pots and saucepans hanging from the walls and ceiling, and a huge copper range hood was jutting out over the stove…Mrs Bream immediately commenced pacing back and forth on the blue-checked lino between a long wood-topped bench near the stove and a row of badly painted cupboards…I felt she enjoyed giving the impression that there was too much to do…shooing us away from her, she seized a gravy boat from a cupboard and bustled across to the oven. 'Those plates, no, try over there. I told you, those plates. Over *there*,' she suddenly began announcing to the three of us. But we stood by and managed to respond only with a few useless gestures…Mrs Bream seemed far too rushed to wait for anyone to follow her instructions…she scooped some thin, fancily patterned china plates down from a nearby shelf with her free hand and then she tipped them with an anxious clatter into the oven's warming drawer…I reflected that, though Mrs Bream wasn't Philip's natural parent, her commanding, British sort of voice made it easy to think so. Several times Mrs Bream kept moving us back so that she could open and close the oven door…an oily smell of mutton soon lay heavy on the air...next we were supplied with tea towels and were actually able to help, at last, by pulling out the large iron roasting-pan...Mrs Bream directed its delivery from the oven with a series of rapid, incoherent orders while waving an old bone-handled carving knife at us. As we got the pan's bulk successfully up onto the bench, I noticed Mr Bream had appeared from somewhere behind us...he stood waiting near the doorway, hesitating, and all of a sudden declared that the dining-table was sold. 'Just been taking the entire thing apart,' he said in a cheerful tone that sounded a little rehearsed. He added, 'The new owner, you know, he's lugging it off as we speak, completely loaded and roped down on his mate's truck. Nice mate. Quite a job, eh. There wasn't a skerrick of space left on the tray.' Then he said with a glance at Mrs Bream, 'Not too sure where this leaves us for dinner, though.' I thought this news was outstandingly funny...I couldn't stop myself from laughing aloud...Mr Bream grinned nervously. But Mrs Bream said only, 'Damn. Damn!' She threw the carving knife down into the sink...Philip and Chloe united in giving me a look. Finally, when all the preparation had been suffered through by Mrs Bream, we had dinner on the easy-chairs in the drawing-room...we ate leaning back into the cushions, careful of the wide armrests, with the plates tilted and poised in our laps...the record-player was off and the whole sleepy quiet of the house struck me as very peaceful...with daylight saving it wouldn't be dark for a while yet, but the temperature was dropping...there was a mild chill above and around us in the cavernous, high-ceilinged room. I'd given Philip a hand earlier to get a little fire ready, but it was just something, mainly, that was supposed to look good for the customers...the few logs we'd managed to get smouldering were lost in the wide brick fireplace...Humphrey was even able to lie comfortably up against the brass fender...his ears were flopped half across his eyes as he slept, and a shallow lake of drool was collecting around his mouth on the floor. I was sitting off in one corner next to Mr Bream, with the padded arm of my easy-chair up beside a tall display-case...the case contained butterfly collections, and its fragile glass door felt dangerously close to my elbow...I worried about breaking one of the glass panels if I worked too hastily with my knife, and it occurred to me that probably the sensible thing was to move the chair...but I just wanted dinner to be finished and out of the way...I wanted only to think about having sex with Chloe a few hours from now. I didn't much like it when Mr Bream leaned across from his seat nearby me to talk...he started

74

to tell me how he restored turn-of-the-century costume jewellery…I'd no interest in learning about it and offered him nothing more than an occasional nod of my head…even so, that was too much encouragement because he kept up his chatter…he seemed to think that I merely didn't understand and gave me more details. But after some minutes of his jewellery monologue Mr Bream broke in on himself and said to me in a wistful tone, 'You know, I used to be one of the professors of Soil Science, over there. Back in the old days. Over at Massey, that was.' He went on, 'So it's quite a jump, if you will, to having this place. And I mean, it really was just such a bastard trying to run a department out there, and a major department at that.' Mr Bream glanced briefly downwards… his hands were hovering over his plate, gripping his knife and fork… he looked up once again and announced to the whole room, 'Academics are such children.' He grunted, and continued in a loud voice, 'Do you know, we couldn't spend more than a hundred dollars out of our annual budget on any one item? Not without getting written permission from the Vice-Chancellor. Can you bloody believe that? A hundred bucks. That's nothing out there in this day and age, eh. Plus, if you didn't spend what was allocated, you'd lose it.' There was bitterness in his tone…he seemed to be running through a familiar and well-worn story…on the far side of the room I could hear Mrs Bream had started muttering something in response. Mr Bream spoke above her and said, 'You use it or you lose it, eh,' and his voice rose even further in agitation. He declared, 'That's what it is. I mean, I once had a greenhouse crammed up to the tits with the entire next year's-worth of pots and fertilisers, and all so that idiot Veale couldn't take it away from us. Plus a department's-worth of scientists who wouldn't know what to do with a single bloody bit of it.' Mr Bream had begun pressing down hard on his plate with his forearms as he spoke… he still gripped his knife and fork in his fists, but now the cutlery stuck up into the air in front of him, forgotten…then he twisted violently towards me. 'You know, Chairman Mao was right,' he growled. He fixed me with a fierce look. 'Chairman Mao was absolutely bloody right. The elite classes, they ought to be sent out into the wop-wops for a while and given a rough time. That way those supposed-to-be soil scientists would get to know what real bloody soil's like.'

'It's the dirty stuff stuck under the cow pats,' I said across the small space between us.

Mr Bream merely smiled at this, though I saw his tired red eyes remained serious…next I heard Mrs Bream speak up more clearly. She was saying in a calm voice, 'Really, it didn't do much for the department that you and Jack Fry had to be in such a lot of competition as bedroom operators.' I was baffled…I looked about for help at interpreting some of this from Philip, and even from Chloe, but they were seated too far off… also, they were keeping their eyes directed onto their plates. 'This is true, we were indeed,' said Mr Bream, without flinching at what he'd heard. He glared back across the room at Mrs Bream and said, 'We fucked anything that moved.' Then he rested back into the cushions of his chair in what seemed like a daze…his plate almost slipped from his lap…I wondered, sitting next to him, if perhaps he was lost in reminiscing…perhaps Mr Bream was thinking about something that moved which he'd fucked particularly well, and I rather doubted it was Mrs Bream…she appeared too old for that sort of thing. 'But it's just, I couldn't live in a city,' Mr Bream suddenly burst out, 'not any longer, not after all that was happening.' He started twisting round in his chair towards me once more, leaning with an elbow up over the armrest. Mr Bream glowered at me and announced, 'All that bloody noise and traffic, you know? I was over in Wanganui one day, eh. I was only taking samples, if you will, out in the field. That's the whole sort of deal, taking samples, but my colleagues never did it. Never out in the field. Never. They were mostly about theory—theories of anything. They just thought themselves too good for it, the lot of them. And when I drove back in the evening I came down Mt. Stewart and what did I see? There I could see Palmerston North, all spread out on the plain. All of it there, eh. Like Sodom or Gomorrah without any of the fun. And it just looked like shit, literally. Covered with a layer of deep brown crap, the whole city. Probably smog from the chimneys. Well, I mean, that decided me right then and there. I thought, I don't want this shitty town to have the power to do me any more harm—' His voice had begun trailing off, but Mrs Bream interrupted. She said, 'The university, they invited you to leave.' But as his only answer Mr Bream seemed to insist on holding my gaze through the now gradually fading light of the room…it left me afraid to look about, or even to look away. I could hear the haughty tone in Mrs Bream's voice as she added, 'They all reckoned that Jack Fry had the better research record, and he did. He did, too. So they chose him to stay on.' 'And the water,' Mr Bream almost whispered to me. 'We've got ourselves a town supply here, but we can get it straight off the roof.' He paused, breathing noisily through his nose, and I could tell he was waiting for me to give him some kind of response to this hugger-mugger, some flourish of sympathy…possibly he wanted something like my witty comment about the cow pats…from his chair far off I sensed Philip was trying to cough in an obtrusive way…I supposed he was meaning for me to keep quiet, but I went ahead in any case.

'Obviously Stokewood does seem like a good place to do your own thing,' I offered. 'You know, I was thinking of writing my—'

'It is. It's a damn good place,' Mrs Bream cut in from across the room. She spoke as if I'd been suggesting the opposite, but she'd caught my attention…I saw the colour was up in her face. 'Damn good,' she went on, 'we have everything here. I can even make my own yoghurt.' 'Well, it is a very fine base for an antiques showroom,' Philip spoke up and said quickly. But Mrs Bream was continuing, 'I do most of my own baking as well. Even pies. And I'm thinking that, out the back, it might be jolly good to try putting in some kind of beehive.' 'Also, you know, there are lots of buying opportunities and wee oddments all over the district,' Philip persisted, 'at least if you can get stuff from the right type of person, if you can stay away from the hoarders.' 'I'm going to make my own honey,' Mrs Bream interrupted him. I saw her turn a little towards Philip and ask, 'What would you think of some home-made clover white on your toast every morning?' 'Well, I'm sure that would be very nice,' Philip replied with a lofty air. There was a confused, uncomfortable silence that followed…I wondered if perhaps this was the moment when someone might need to apologise, but I wasn't sure who should do so, or even why…above the mantelpiece a fat grey moth kept banging its body along a mirror with a fluttery sound that seemed loud and disconcerting in the artificial stillness. At last Mr Bream said, 'Bringing up Jack Fry was a bit bloody uncalled for.' 'Of course it was called for,' Mrs Bream hissed back, 'I was insulting you.' All at once Chloe stood up and thrust her plate out in front of her. 'Do you think I could have a little more of this delicious roast?' she inquired. I watched her take a few steps across the creaking floor in no particular direction…it was as though she was thinking of stretching her legs as much as getting a second helping…I thought that, as an attempt to smooth things over, Chloe's action was transparently clumsy…it seemed so clumsy that I felt almost ashamed, and in my mind I could imagine a vivid scene between us later with me saying to her, 'Are you satisfied?' But Mrs Bream got up and took the plate from Chloe's hand…she laid it on top of her own plate and motioned for

77

Chloe to sit once more...next Mrs Bream bustled out of the room, and some considerable time passed...eventually it became clear that she wasn't going to return...quite a long while after that Chloe left the room as well. At the end of the evening I went off upstairs for a bath...I'd put everything behind me...I was eager to prepare for losing my virginity. I reached the bathroom in a nervous hurry...I barely noticed how much the floor sloped as I crouched over the stained enamel tub and turned on an ancient brass tap for some hot water...but the water simply dribbled out of the tap's nozzle and was warm at best...it didn't seem capable of filling up the bottom of the tub...instead, it collected slowly in a small tepid pool around the plug at one end. After a time I lost patience...I got undressed and sat my buttocks down in the deepest part of the water available, which was just a few inches...it was hard work cleaning myself by splashing, and my feet stayed mostly dry so that I had to turn around in the tub when I tried to wash them...the novelty of it all made me laugh out loud...I thought of this as the start of a funny story, but I could think of no one to tell it to, and certainly not to Chloe. I stared down at my cock above the shallow, soapy water...my cock was difficult to miss...it was already hard and red and sticking up at me, and I resisted the urge to play with it a little...the sight of it made me try to think responsibly about birth control...I had two Durex, both of which I'd got way back in the fifth form, waiting for me inside their purple wrappers in my wallet...I wondered if two might be enough, but then I told myself not to be greedy. I got out of the bath, dried myself and put on my jeans again... zipping them up was no easy business with a hard-on...it felt massive as I tried cramming it into the crotch...my erection just wouldn't go away, and so I made an effort to distract my attention and calm down. I pictured a tramp I'd been on recently...I'd tramped with some schoolmates, Neil and Simon, up through the bush in the Kahuterawa Valley...I focused for a moment on the bush, on the slippery supplejack and frothy ferns underfoot, the clumps of kawakawa, ngaio and tea trees, and the stands of kahikatea...but that didn't really manage to relax me, and I couldn't seem to concentrate properly...there was something now about the Kahuterawa Valley that was unaccountably sexy. After a few more minutes I trotted along the corridor to the bedroom...my bare feet padded on the dusty floorboards and I was bent half over to disguise the painful bulge in my pants...I had to hope that no one would appear suddenly from anywhere and see me. Chloe was already in the bedroom when I entered, standing

78

in the narrow space by the wardrobe…she was trying to examine herself in the mirror…she was leaning back a little and brushing her hair away from one shoulder with her hand…I saw she'd changed into a simple green, ankle-length cotton nightgown, and I supposed she wasn't going to bother with the irksome bath…the nightgown was smooth and loose on her figure but lay close along her hips…it reminded me of the dress she'd worn when we first met. Chloe turned towards me as I came in, and I went up and kissed her happily…she put her small warm arms around my neck, and with ease I pulled up the nightgown almost to her shoulders…I took my mouth away from her lips and glanced down…she had nothing else on, and it was the first time I'd ever really looked at her naked…usually we were half clothed and busy on somebody's couch… in the sharp yellow light from the ceiling I recognised the wide brown nipples on her breasts, pushed up against me…those nipples were old friends. I took a step away and gazed lower, past her belly…I'd spent a lot of time imagining it but I'd never actually seen a vagina up close before… it was hairier than I'd expected…I was delighted. I reached forward and wrapped my arms around Chloe again…I felt a feverish rush of anticipation and my knees began to shiver…I pushed Chloe, with the nightgown still hoisted up around her shoulders, down with me towards the bed… she let me and we fell sideways onto the mattress…it sagged troublesomely under our weight, but I didn't care. In a moment I was rolling about on top of Chloe in excitement…the bedspread's coarse chenille rubbed and burned against my forearms…I hoped Chloe's back wouldn't get hurt from her being crushed beneath me…it was all I could do to stop myself from finishing, then and there, in my underwear as usual. I rolled off…I got up onto my knees beside her…I thought it was about time to pull down my jeans…it was a battle just to start getting the fly open with my trembling fingers, but I needed to make my intentions towards her clear. 'What are you doing?' Chloe asked. Suddenly everything seemed to be interrupted…I found that I'd already paused, with the blood pounding loudly in my head…it appeared such an idiotic question for her to ask… but I knew that, above all else, I shouldn't give her the wrong answer…I pondered for what felt like a painfully drawn-out instant to think of something approaching the right line to take.

'I thought you wanted to,' I said.

The words gave me a renewed burst of confidence…they left me feeling pretty proud of myself…it was a formulation worthy of an author.

But Chloe asked, 'Wanted to what?'

'Do it,' I said.

I was flustered...my skin was prickling with sweat...I hadn't reckoned on all this.

'Fuck,' I added.

Chloe looked up at me and spoke in a shrill tone. 'Oh no,' she said. 'No!' She spoke as though struggling to control her voice...at the same time she squirmed away from me along the ugly marmalade-coloured bedspread...then she sat up and began to pull her nightdress down again...she kept on at it, tugging and shoving parts of the material, until she was wedging the hem all the way down near her ankles and aiming for her toes.

'I've got a Frenchie,' I said. 'I've got two.'

'That doesn't matter. I'm not doing it, eh,' she said.

'What?' I asked.

'I am not doing it,' Chloe repeated slowly, as if the real problem was that I hadn't properly heard.

'But—' I began.

'Not until we're married,' she said.

'What?' I asked.

Chloe wailed, 'I told you not to go expecting any big ideas.'

'This is the seventies!' I screamed.

Chloe flinched and started to cry...she drew her knees up towards her chest and put one hand over her face, as though to get rid of me... the thin cotton nightgown was stretched beautifully along her thighs... but absolutely nothing was going to plan. 'You don't understand,' Chloe moaned. She lowered her head and her voice became muffled...her shoulders were gently shaking as she sobbed. She whimpered, 'You never listen. You never, ever listen. I just want to lead a happy life. I want to have a nice house one day, eh, and some children, and you just don't understand. But that's what I want. That's what I want. And it takes a husband to do all of it.'

'How are you going to have children if you won't fuck?' I asked.

At this, Chloe started crying a whole lot harder...even without being able to see her face I could imagine her swollen eyes drowning in tears... evidently I'd said the wrong thing again...she raised both of her little fists and began bunching them up into her eye sockets...she was weeping in a lonely, bitter way. After a while I said I was sorry...I felt a powerful urge to propose marriage right there on the spot, but I also felt another powerful urge never to say one more word to her...at the same moment I noticed Chloe had commenced talking again...she was still curled up, almost into a ball, but she was speaking half to herself in a small voice...I tried to listen, and to ignore the sweat sticking to my T-shirt in the hollow of my back. I heard Chloe say, 'You don't see what I think and how important it is to make a life for the future.' I wriggled around a little, hoping to get myself more comfortable...this was probably going to take a while. Chloe said, 'I don't know what goes on through your head. It's always so complicated with you, eh. You keep acting as if this writing business was some sort of stupid cure for everything. Well, it's not. It's not real. And I want to have a real life. You just don't see that.' As she went on speaking, I marvelled at how much Chloe loved talking...she loved a nice talk, a proper talk, a one-on-one communication where somebody else was there and just taking it all in...she'd already forgotten the several months she'd spent talking to me about our lives together...we'd had some of our roughest sessions on the sofa after she'd talked herself out. Chloe was describing her schoolteacher's job...she kept on saying that it was very important to make a contribution...there were these sweet little children whom she'd see every day...they'd write letters and numbers on the classroom blackboard with her help, and there would be games of Punchinello and four square in the playground...there would be cheery sing-alongs of 'Old Macdonald had a farm'...there was going to be a lot of cutting things out from coloured paper. At any rate, it had stopped her crying...bit by bit Chloe uncurled herself and lay stretched out on the bedspread...she was looking up at me once more...she was scrutinising me with such intensity that I felt I should at least try to concentrate on her words. 'I'd use the other car, a smaller one, for getting to school,' she was saying, 'and I could use it to stop off for groceries on the way home. It's important to shop at several supermarkets, eh. And the meals would have to be proper, not always mince on toast. And you could help with the washing up, and the cleaning and vacuuming—properly, not just on weekends.' Chloe pushed her legs out together...she reached up along her ribcage and adjusted her nightgown...there was a compelling glow in her eyes that reminded me in a crazy fashion of Steve-oh...gently I moved to sprawl out a bit beside her, propping myself up on one elbow... my hard-on was aching a little in my pants and still feeling fairly urgent, and I tried unobtrusively to shift and free the cling of my underwear...it

81

was gathering too far up into my damp buttocks. I envied Chloe for the strength of her imagination...I really didn't want to distract or upset her, but I also didn't understand why, for her, things couldn't just happen... finally Chloe seemed to run out of vision to describe.

'Okay,' I said.

I smiled at her, with a face I hoped was well prepared...it was a smile meant to reassure her that I'd understood everything.

Then I said tentatively, 'So let's just, maybe, fool around a bit like normal.'

Chloe rolled away from me with a low growl, and I was left staring at the back of her head and into her hair...for a minute or so I stayed still, not moving a muscle, and after that I decided to risk craning my neck and sneaking a look at Chloe over her small shoulder...I held my breath, trying to be delicate, as I arched my back and inched my face up...her eyes were clamped together unnaturally tight...her pink cheeks twitched a little as she breathed...I'd killed the goose that laid the golden eggs. I lay down again on the bedspread and tried to relax...I was staring up at the unpleasantly bright ceiling light burning above us...I didn't want to shift, to get up and turn the bloody thing off...I went on lying quietly, and my hard-on took a long, long time to wilt. Once or twice I attempted to say something, a few words...I thought I just might manage to start Chloe talking again...but she ignored me each time, and at last I thought she must really be asleep.

The next morning I awoke still dressed in all my clothes...Chloe was sleeping on the far side of the mattress...like me, she was lying on top of the bedspread, but she'd found a sheet somewhere and had it wrapped tight around her...she was still facing away from me towards the wall. I coughed and tried shifting about...my movements made the springs in the mattress dip and rise in waves...Chloe didn't react...I shifted about some more, on purpose, and tried another experimental, louder cough... despite all this, she did nothing...after a while I got up and left the room. I met no one as I passed along the corridor, and the doors to the upstairs rooms were all closed...I took good care not to make too much noise as I trod down the staircase, stepping warily on the floppy carpet...it seemed that I was the first one awake in the whole house. In the kitchen Humphrey was dozing...he was lying across a woolly blanket on the lino... when he saw me, he rolled over and peed upwards in a happy little fountain like a puppy...I rubbed Humphrey's warm head and his now damp belly, and then plugged in an electric jug on the bench to fix myself some coffee. Once the coffee was made, I opened the back door and went outside with my cup...I wandered past a poorly tended vegie patch bordered with fragments of brown brick...the cloudless sky above was a dazzle of blue colour, and the air was refreshing though it was dry and stung my throat...I stared off at a view of empty, rambling paddocks which stretched away so still and quiet in the morning that the fields looked serene, and next I took a leak into a clump of lilies by a fence...afterwards a lot of the coffee went over the flowers to cover the evidence. As I was zipping myself up, I spied an old black bicycle leaning against one wall of the house...suddenly I thought it might be good to borrow the bike and get away from Stokewood for a while, and the more I considered it, the more it appealed to me...perhaps this was unused sexual energy, but I was beginning to feel mighty restless...I went back into the kitchen and gave Humphrey another pat...after a few moments' hesitation I left him my empty cup on the floor to lick at...then I grabbed hold of the bike and shook it, as if this might help me judge whether it was up to snuff, and I wheeled it round the homestead to the driveway at the front. When I climbed onto the bike and started to ride, its rear tyre bulged out under my weight... every bump on the metalled road came up at me through the seat as I wobbled along away from the house...but by the time I got myself out to the turnoff, I was enjoying things. On the main road I tried riding mostly in the smoothly paved gutter for some comfort...there were only a few cows around me in the nearby paddocks, all standing about with their heads down to the grass cover, chewing lazily...I felt as if I was the last person living on earth and moving through an abandoned landscape, but after a long while of pedalling the edge of town came up into view...I was puffing a little, though still feeling energetic...I crossed a couple of deserted intersections, among houses now, and eventually made a turning for variety's sake. I passed a bend, and in the distance I could see a small row of shops along one side of the road, huddled next to some residential sections...there was a black-and-white sign up on the veranda above the nearest store saying: 'Laird's Books'...I rode on towards the shop and slowed to a halt outside its narrow frontage...my arse felt a bit bruised when finally I put my feet down on the asphalt...the shop had beige stuccoed walls with a poky display window mostly covered by some venetian blinds and stacks of boxes, but its door was ajar, and I saw the lights were on within and the place was open. It occurred to me, gazing at the store from the roadside, that I knew very little about literature despite all my hours of work at Wynyards...but I'd need to shanghai me some kind of idea for my novel fairly soon, that much was certain...I thought I might get inspired by checking through a few books...it couldn't hurt to find out what some of the other gun writers had been doing with the time they'd put in ahead of me. There was a grey tubular-steel bike rail at the kerb by the footpath and I propped my ride up carefully against it...it took a couple of tries to turn the handle and get the bike's frame leaning in against the bar...then I stamped my feet on the footpath and entered the shop. I thought a doorbell or something similar would clink in a welcoming fashion as I pushed my way in, but there was nothing, no sound... inside the shop was as narrow as its frontage had first suggested, though it was darker and more cramped than I'd imagined, with a long centre island...half the strip lights in the ceiling were off...for an instant I wasn't sure if the place was really open after all. I strolled up one aisle past the island, peering at its shelves and how they were pleasantly cluttered with magazines and bags of snacks...the magazines in particular were all leaning out at me over the wires that held them into their racks, as if ready to drop to the floor...up on the walls alongside me were shelves with items of stationery, and more with board-games and boxes of model kitsets... but I couldn't see anything like the books I was hunting for, even though the shop seemed to be brimming with everything else. Far at the back of the store, behind a counter and under the only patch of strong light, sat a small, stocky-looking, elderly man...I started to approach him, and saw that he was reading a newspaper open before him on the counter and was lost in concentration...I was pretty sure he hadn't moved a muscle since I'd come in...his stubby arms were spread out wide, and he was using his large hands to hold the pages down flat...the man was scanning the newsprint with his back kept very straight and his head up. The man's face was square-shaped, wrinkled and podgy, and he had thin silver hair...he was wearing a fusty olive-green cardigan and he was stout around the belly, so that the lower half of the cardigan appeared badly stretched across his protruding stomach...he squinted severely down his nose at the pages, as though reading from a great height...his fleshy jowls quivered a little as he mouthed some of the words he was getting through...when I stopped just in front of him at the counter, the man's eyes finally flicked up and took in my existence, giving me a hostile look.

'Good morning,' I said.

The man said nothing in reply...he merely arched his neck and gazed upwards briefly in the direction of the ceiling lights...he seemed to be examining the colourful rows of cigarette cartons stored in wire holders far above his head...then he went right back to the paper before him.

'Do you have any books?' I asked.

Without looking at me, the man lifted one arm a bit in a suggestion of annoyance and shook it...I heard the newsprint rustle...whatever he was reading, that news was certainly absorbing...next with the same raised arm he waved to somewhere behind me in the shop. 'What you see is what we've got, eh,' he said. His voice had a desiccated, grating sound... with his hand he now wiped away a few loose strands of white hair at the side of his head...he was using a thumb to place the stray hair securely at the back of his ear.

'I wanted to check some books,' I said. 'I'm a writer.'

That did the trick...the man stopped his fidgeting and stared straight at me. 'Well, try the library, mate,' he said after a moment. 'We don't stock much of that type of deal here.'

'Why not?' I asked.

The man fingered his paper once more, but then abandoned it...he took in a deep, resigned breath that made his heavy cheeks shudder...at last he puffed out his chest. 'Don't stock anything there's no money in,' he snapped. He appeared satisfied with his own answer...I gave his words a few second's thought, and this did seem to chime in with what I'd heard about making a living from books...before their fame the truest artists always happened to subsist in the direst poverty.

'So, what is the money in?' I asked.

The man grinned fiercely at this. 'Are you blind or something?' he said. He nodded his head towards the dim walls behind me again, and added, 'What do you think all those bloody toys are for?' This time it was my turn to say nothing in reply, but I glanced quickly back to where he'd indicated at the toys...there really were boxes and boxes of them lined up on some of the shelves exactly as he'd hinted, guns, dolls and games wrapped in cellophane...when I turned round again, I saw the man's expression had relaxed...perhaps it was because he'd just finished insulting me...he was eyeing me up as though deciding whether I was trustworthy. Finally he announced, 'There's an eighty percent mark-up on kids' stuff, eh. I mean, that's if you can get them cheap enough from a wholesaler. All you've got to do is guess what's popular. And you know what's the best days to sell, don't you?' I shook my head...the man grinned again even harder at my ignorance. 'Tuesdays and Wednesdays,' he said. He added triumphantly, 'The benefit days.'

'Well,' I said, 'I'm not on the benefit.'

The man grunted...with an effort he tugged a blue-and-white packet of cigarettes and a plastic lighter from a pocket in his cardigan...he peeled open the square top of the packet and I could see all the cigarettes loosely lined up inside...he took one out and lit it with an unsteady hand. After a slow, lengthy puff the man put the cigarette down on the countertop with the lit end poking out a little over the edge...now I noticed rows of burn marks in the wood along the counter from where he must have done this before...suddenly the man pushed his lower denture half out of his mouth and pulled it back in again lazily with his tongue. He announced, 'You say you're a writer fellow?' I nodded.

'Can I have one of those?' I asked.

I was pointing at the cigarette packet, still cradled in the palm of the man's left hand...I didn't actually smoke, but this seemed like a good time to start. 'You're not going to steal from me, are you?' the man asked, though he'd fallen into a confidential, teasing tone. He said, 'You bohemian types can be real buggers for nicking things.'

'Not me,' I said. 'I'm living for art.'

The man reached out and handed over his packet...I borrowed the man's lighter and quickly lit up a cigarette...the first draw, thick and hot, didn't seem any worse than the few smokes I'd tried at school...I surprised myself pleasantly by not gagging, but that was mostly because I'd exhaled everything straightaway through my nose...all the same, I felt very grown-up. 'Intermediate-school kids are the worst,' the man was saying with a philosophical air. He paused to cough and bring up some phlegm...clearly he was a student of human nature. 'The little bastards in first year are trying to get into gangs run by the second years, eh,' he went on. 'Primary-school kids are buggers too, but they're usually too scared. And high-school kids have got into trouble somewhere else, so they mostly know about the consequences.' I took another puff, and reflected on how it was probably true that high-school kids knew the score...I fingered the cigarette and thought smoking wasn't too foul...it might just work out, provided I kept the actual smoke out of my lungs.

'So do you reckon you can spot the criminal type?' I asked. 'I mean, if they come wandering in here?'

All this was starting to seem useful…the man's talk sounded like good background information for my own writing and for an instant I was disappointed that I had nothing with me on which to make notes. 'No,' the man was saying hoarsely, 'even the angelic, well-dressed kids can be bad, I reckon. You just can't tell, eh. And their parents nick things too.'

'Do you have an ashtray?' I asked.

'Just flick it on the floor,' the man said. He leaned back and stretched his square shoulders inside his cardigan…the small plastic buttons in the wool along the front were pulled impressively tight. 'Crime's about it for excitement around here,' he said. He rubbed his belly, and then sat up again with a brisk movement. 'Now if I was you, young fellow,' he declared, 'I'd write about something interesting, eh. Like the war.'

'What war?' I asked.

'World War Two, you nong,' the man said. He pretended to look surprised at my foolishness, but I could tell that he was pleased I didn't know. 'The western desert, fighting the Krauts sort of thing,' he said. 'Somebody had to do it, go save the world and all that. Turns out it was me. You know, I was on detachment to the British army for a good while out there. We were training their machine-gunners.' The man was looking away from me now…he'd picked up his cigarette but didn't appear in any hurry to smoke it, and he was staring off across the shop without any special focus…I could see he'd adopted the manner of someone settling into a yarn. 'My mate out there, he was this pom named Dicky Dixon,' the man said. 'Well, Dicky was the ex-heavyweight boxing champ for the British army, eh, he was a handy bloke to have for a pal.' The man chuckled, so I chuckled too. Then he coughed again briefly and said, 'Poor Dicky, he joined the army in England during the depression, and he signs up for twelve years. They'd all been posted to the West Indies for the first five years and, after that, coming back to England, there was this mutiny. So they all got punished. They got sent straight on to Egypt instead of home. Then, after about five or six more years of that rubbish, the bloody war broke out, just when they were finally about to go home again, sort of style. So for Dicky, it was a bit like being stuck in an endless bloody loop of the same thing—and by the time we palled up, I felt pretty much the same way too. Anyway, we were both sergeants and we hated our colonel, eh, who was a right little prick, I can tell you. So one day, we get the order to parade next morning in full kit. All cleaned and polished and with webbing blancoed. Well, Dicky and I had just been to Cairo together the day before on leave, see, and what you did on leave was, you always put on swimming togs to escape feeling part of the army and then you just walked around in them all day. So this stupid order really got to us. Anyway, I said that I'd refuse to parade in a polished uniform because it was against New Zealand army orders on active service. And I was still technically part of the New Zealand army.' The man glanced across the counter at me…it was as if he'd just remembered that I was still there. 'Being polished up so shiny makes you a target,' he explained. He grinned…I nodded my head. 'So I got off cleaning, eh,' the man continued. 'And I reckon that just made Dicky even more pissed off. He said he wouldn't clean and polish either. So the next morning we appeared on parade like this, and we discover it's an inspection by the Deputy-Chief of the Imperial General Staff. Jesus! I mean, we were really in the shit. And the D.C.I.G.S., when he arrived he was walking along the ranks, and he was asking soldiers if they were pleased to be in Egypt. Fucking stupid question. And of course they were all saying "Yes, sir!" and every time they did, Dicky beside me mumbles, "Liar!" So the head scone gets to Dicky, right, and he says, "Hmm, Northumberland Fusiliers. Fine regiment. Are you happy to be here, sergeant?" "No, sir!" Dicky barks. "What, you don't want to be in Egypt?" "No, sir!" "Well, where do you want to be then?" "I want to go home, sir!" So the D.C.I.G.S., he asks, "Just how long have you been in the army, sergeant?" "Fifteen years, sir!" And the D.C.I.G.S. turns to some poodle-type beside him and he says, "Take his name." Then he looks at me—and you know, I was dead set on having my share of trouble now too. "Ah, a New Zealander!" the arsehole says, "one of our fine colonial blah, blah, blah. Are you happy to be here, sergeant?" "No, sir!" I shouts. He says, "Well, why not, man?" I says, "I don't like the way the place is run, sir!" Jesus, our colonel nearly had a stroke on the spot.' The man's cigarette, still held forgotten in front of him, suddenly dropped a long trail of grey ash onto the counter…the man brushed it away from himself absent-mindedly…the ash fell to the red lino at my feet. 'Well,' he said slowly, 'it turned out afterwards that the D.C.I.G.S. went back to the mess and roared with laughter about the whole thing. But I didn't know that. And my name had got taken and I was really deep in it, up to my neck. Anyway, the next day Dicky got an order to go to Cairo for immediate repatriation, and yours truly, I get put under open arrest for insubordination. I also got called up before that little fucking colonel and bawled out, twice. And I was due to get called up a third time and be flat-straight court-martialled when I met this New Zealand major out there. So

I asked him, what does he reckon I should do, eh. This bloke, he told me that, as a New Zealander, the thing was, I was entitled to be interviewed and have my case reviewed by the New Zealand commanding officer. Well, that there was General Freyberg.' The man spluttered, and his body rocked back and forth as he broke into his own story…I could guess he'd said something meant to be absurd, so I smiled in a show of amazement… the man stifled a laugh and went on talking in his rough voice. 'So anyway, I says to this guy, "But Tiny Freyberg's in Italy, and he's not going to come all the way out over here just for someone like me." And this major told me, "That's the whole point. It'd be just too much bother to follow up." So, you know, I tried it, and the bloody colonel nearly had *another* stroke. But it worked, eh, and I got off.' There was an abrupt silence, which soon became lengthy…I understood at last that the man had finished…I smiled again in appreciation, and thought that the world had been pretty lucky to get itself saved…I wondered why the man troubled himself with keeping this old memory alive, but perhaps it was so that he could tell it, one way or another, to people who came in…we continued being silent for a moment or two longer…we were savouring the tale. But the silence went on and on until it was uncomfortable, and finally I knew that I was expected to make some sort of comment…I supposed it was an outright remarkable thing to have happened, being almost court-martialled for a mate…even so, I wasn't sure if I should actually say this.

'The army sounds like a dangerous place,' I said in the end.

'War is hell,' the man said. He nodded his head…he seemed happy with my remark…I was glad I'd managed to come out with it for him. 'Months and months of boredom followed by several hours of sheer terror,' the man added. 'You better stick to literature, young fellow.'

'That's good advice,' I agreed. 'Thank you.'

I waited for another few seconds or so…the man said nothing further…since there were no books for me to see, I started to turn away, but I was still hoping that there might be some more story left…I made only hesitant motions at walking out of the shop…while heading past the centre island I turned round to the man again and waved with the remainder of my cigarette…I'd almost finished puffing on it and exhaling through my nose.

'Well, thanks for the smoke,' I said.

But the man had gone back to his newspaper…now he was craned forward over the pages, and I watched him straining to read. 'Just throw the fag-end out on the street,' the man called, 'not in the entranceway.' I moved off, genuinely this time…on the footpath outside I tossed away the cigarette-end and blinked for a moment in the light…there were a few people on the street now walking near me, and a car passed…I could see the red sign for a small Wales bank painted on a window further down among the shops and I remembered my bankbook was with me, snug in my back pocket, so I began to stroll in the direction of the sign…I thought it would be nice to get some money to buy a few smokes…maybe I'd even get some money for a notepad. I entered the bank and found its compact interior looked very new and spruce…the vivid blue commercial carpet underfoot made the place appear cheerful, and I let my eyes run along the silvery patterns in the weave as I trod on them…only one teller, a young woman, was working at the counters, with two people waiting there in a queue…I headed over to the smart wooden stands set up across the rear wall, and noticed they were so new that there wasn't a single blemish anywhere in their woodgrain veneer…for a while I fiddled with a ballpoint pen fixed to a short, shiny brass chain at one of the stands and filled out a withdrawal form arranged in thin lines of red ink. After that I joined the queue…I peered around the backs of the other customers towards the high counter, trying to guess how many minutes I'd have to wait…the teller's long ash-blonde hair caught my eye, and I thought it was wonderfully crimped…it fell bulkily about her large, angular face and along the shoulders of her stiff brown uniform…it stirred whenever she shifted forward on her seat, working mechanically, to get money from a drawer. The teller looked to be a girl only a little older than me…I thought she was probably tall and leggy…then somebody left the counter and I was able to shuffle a lot closer, but to my disappointment I could still see the teller only from the waist up, with her brown jacket and her blouse buttoned tight to the top, and with a wide pink bow fluffed up around her neck…even so, I decided that despite the billowing, ugly bow the girl was sexy…I also reflected that, almost for sure, I felt this way because she was nothing like Chloe. The last customer before me turned and started to walk off out of the bank…I stepped forwards and got myself right in front of the sexy teller…she scribbled something down on a small piece of paper at her desktop below the counter and then looked up…she was smiling at me with her broad mouth partially open…I saw that mouth was full of strong, healthy, sexy-looking teeth. 'Can I help you?' she asked. I said nothing in reply, and she repeated her question…I was in a fluster but I was also beginning to feel daring…I felt curiously awake and alive… I decided that this was a good moment to try at being a bit flirty.

'You know, you've got lovely eyes,' I said.

I could see that my compliment was right, too…I could see they were almond-shaped eyes…they were large, and almost as blue as the bright blue carpet. 'Well, you've got a cute little arse,' the girl growled back. 'Why don't you just twirl about and show it to me properly?' This seemed reasonable…I turned around slowly on the spot before the counter… no one had ever praised me for my arse before…it was a pity there was nobody else waiting behind me who might also be impressed…I found there was no one even waiting at the stands along the far rear wall…there was only me and the teller when I'd finished turning and showing my arse and was facing her again. 'You're a nut,' she said. But I saw she was amused…I had to speak now and keep up the momentum…I thought of injecting a little humour into my voice, something suave…it needed to be something that contained just the right glass-and-a-half of charm.

'So, darling, what time do you get off from work?' I asked.

'Oh hell, not till practically tomorrow,' the girl replied with a groan. She flicked her head in annoyance at my inquiry and her hair shook. She said, 'But at least from tomorrow I'm getting out and away from this bloody job for all of a whole week, eh.' She was speaking in a tone that sounded flat, even final, and I thought maybe it meant for me to mind my own business. But next she added, 'Yeah, I'm taking my summer entitlement, you know what I mean? Man, it'll be great. Going to hitchhike and get myself down to Christchurch.'

'What about if I come with you?' I asked suddenly.

I tried opening my eyes wide to seem more like a nut, since I needed to seem as appealing as all hell and that felt like the best method…but I realised I'd just asked a serious question…it was because I also realised that I'd had enough of Chloe and, though Stokewood was nice, I didn't really enjoy the place's weird disruptions. 'Why? What do you want to come for?' the girl was asking in response. For an instant she furrowed her brows. She said, 'What would you want to do down Christchurch way?' The girl tightened her lips in suspicion and examined me up and down…I felt confused…I'd forgotten about momentum and being suave. But when I didn't answer, she simply went on again and offered, 'Some friends of mine—well, they're kind of friends of mine, they're putting on a Heads' Ball, eh, and I'm planning to be there for it.'

'Really?' I said, aware of how my voice was shooting up in delight. 'That sounds great.'

Actually, a Heads' Ball wasn't anything I'd ever heard of...but it did definitely sound like something great...it even sounded like the sort of something you might go halfway down the country for.

I added, 'I'd love to see it. You know, I'm a writer.'

'You're a what?' the girl asked.

'A writer,' I said.

The girl examined me all over again. Then she mumbled, 'What—so, do you mean kind of poetry and shit?'

'No, novels and shit,' I corrected her. 'I want to write a novel.'

I thought the girl still looked surprised, so I spread my arms out far apart, the whole way, to show her that the size of the novel concerned was big...but in reaction the girl's eyebrows merely arched up for a moment into beautifully tweezed-and-tapered curves...I supposed that literary people didn't come into the bank very often...it seemed best to drop my arms to my sides again, so I did, though I went on admiring the wide brown tips of the girl's eyebrows and her face in general. She was saying, 'You mean, like *Little Women*?'

'Exactly,' I said.

I'd no idea about *Little Women*...I had no more idea what *Little Women* was about than I did of the Heads' Ball, but I'd heard that title somewhere...now I thought it was sexy...now it sounded like the title of a super-duper new novel forming on the edge of my imagination. The novel grew, pushing out branches here and there in my mind around the name... I thought that it just might happen...a book like that could get itself written if I hitchhiked down south with this sexy girl...she struck me as someone who'd already had a bit of valuable experience in life.

'So, what time do we start?' I asked.

The girl breathed in sharply...then she sat up and rubbed at the nape of her neck with one hand...it moved her thick lovely hair about once more in all sorts of interesting arrangements. 'Well, er—tell you what,' she said at last. 'You meet me on State Highway 2 by the river, at eight o'clock tomorrow morning. That's if you're for real.' I told her I was very for real...I insisted on how for real I was...then to show her, I went back to the stands, tore up the old withdrawal form and filled out another one...it was for taking half my savings out of the bank, the earnings from my after-school job...I'd need the money for the trip. With a faint air of embarrassment the girl told me her name was Penny as I passed the new form to her across the counter...I told Penny my own name back... she began reaching into her cash drawer and pulled out a wad of notes wrapped in a rubber band. 'As it comes?' she asked. She held the money in her long pale fingers.

'Is there any other way?' I growled.

I put on a maniacal grin...I was good at being witty. 'You're a real nut,' Penny said again. Afterwards I bicycled back to Stokewood...the bike wobbled, bumped and rattled on the road, but it didn't matter anymore... I was thinking that I'd managed to make some important decisions...but I was also wondering just how on earth I could talk about them to Chloe.

Chloe didn't come downstairs until lunchtime...I was in the drawing-room when she appeared, chatting cheerfully with Mrs Bream and sharing the story the man had told me in the bookshop...Chloe stood just beyond the door and gazed in sullenly at us...I could see her hair was wet from some sort of attempt at the bath...her hands were thrust into the pockets at the front of her jeans...I broke off my story in the middle, and Mrs Bream and I both said good morning, but Chloe merely turned and walked away. I thought this was rather rude...I thought she wasn't behaving at all like a good guest...partly I felt responsible, but it was disappointing that Chloe couldn't make more of an effort to get along with people herself. Lunch was cold cuts from the previous night's roast...Mrs Bream had packed it all into Tupperware containers suitable for a picnic, so Philip, Chloe and I took some fiddly, flapping canvas deck chairs outside to find a spot...but there was basically nothing except farmland nearby, and so in the end we just shifted Chloe's car a little and set up the chairs under the elm tree at the front of the house...both Mr and Mrs Bream were too busy with customers to join us. During the lunch we didn't fuss very much with cutlery other than for scooping up bits of cold vegie...we used our fingers to peel the slippery slices of roast from their coverings of Glad Wrap and ate with our hands, slapping away the midges and sandflies that tried to settle on us...through the shade of the yellow leaves, the sunlight fell around us in little rings that burned our skins, and there were a number of cicadas buzzing nearby...after a while I'd eaten sufficient and became very sleepy. For comfort I reclined further back in my deck chair, which was slung so low that my bottom scraped on the ground each time I moved...I tried listening to Philip's complicated plans for a setting up croquet court somewhere out there on the lawn right in front of us...Chloe seemed restless and kept playing with her food…it just felt a lot easier not to bother making conversation with her. Later that afternoon I helped Philip to restore some things for the shop…we worked in a small, overcrowded storeroom at the very back of the house…for a long time we used a rubbing compound to clean the grainy, discoloured wood on a grandfather clock which had come in for sale…Philip said that the compound was really meant for cars but it was the best stuff and did the job…next we applied boot polish to darken up the wood, using pieces of cloth made from Mr Bream's old underwear. I was excited to see a few tricks of the trade…it took us several hours to work away diligently at the sides of the tall clock, turning it into even more of an antique than it already was…occasionally I saw Chloe through the doorway, mooching about…at last I managed to convince her to come in and help us, but she only complained that the polishing made her wrists ache and she soon gave up…I still hadn't figured out how I was going to break my big news to her. We had dinner once more in the drawing-room, rather late, where we all ate together with everything balanced on our laps, mostly in silence…it was the first time since the previous evening that we'd all of us been in the same place, and I couldn't help wondering what might happen…but Chloe's sullenness appeared to have infected the entire atmosphere of the house and no one said any more than a word or two…finally, after the meal, Mrs Bream put her dinner things down beside her on the floor and got up, nervously muttering to herself…she stretched a little, ran her fingers through her hair and started across the room in a shy fashion, as though giving way to an overweening impulse…I saw she was making for an upright piano at the opposite end of the room that was pushed into the corner against the wall. I wasn't even sure if the piano had been there yesterday…I could see that it looked worn and broken down… it was suffering from a combination of overuse and neglect…the piano's panels were heavily marked with cracks and stains in definite need of a lot of rubbing compound and boot polish. Mrs Bream pulled the piano stool out from under the keyboard…she sat on the stool hesitantly, not offering a word of explanation, and one of its legs squeaked a bit as she shifted about to settle…next she raised the piano's lid…I watched her spread her large hands across the yellowed keyboard and survey it without making a sound. Then, quick and tense, Mrs Bream bent forward over the keys and her face disappeared into the short, falling curls of her dark hair… after a pause for the tiniest instant, she hunched her shoulders and began to play…she hit the keys with power and confidence…the tune from the very start sounded complex…it began with a brief introduction and moved on into a lilting, delicately recurring run amid trills of notes. Mrs Bream seemed to concentrate more and more on her playing…it was only a few times that she faltered, and it was in particularly intricate passages…each time she started up immediately from a few bars back…once or twice she failed yet again when she reached the same place…she rocked back and forth…her fingers skipped and sank among the keys. The complicated tune appeared on occasions to get lost within its odd, quieter diversions and in stately moments of greater loudness, but it always returned again to the same delicate run of notes…Mrs Bream tapped with one hand and then let the other swing hard towards it down the keyboard…some moments later the song was done and, as she finished, the echoes from the closing trills faded off in a slow fall…afterwards Mrs Bream remained stock still and bent over the keys…I saw she was gazing at the music-sheet rack before her, which was empty. 'Scarlatti's F Minor,' she said at last softly, as though to herself. She straightened and turned to us… she began swinging one leg self-consciously beneath the stool. 'One never really gets it quite right,' she added, looking at us across the room.

'That was wonderful, absolutely the bee's knees,' I said.

The words gushed out of me…I had the feeling I was jumping in ahead of everyone else with my praise, though I also felt impressed at the sincerity of my own reaction…twilight was rapidly descending and it was getting hard to see, but a little to my relief I heard murmurs of agreement from the others chiming in around me…I decided to press on.

I asked, 'Do you play very often?'

'Well, whenever I can get an instrument,' Mrs Bream replied. She gestured at the top of the piano's upper panel…the shop's price sticker was already attached. She said, 'Ah, you should hear someone who can really, really play. Do you know, Martin Smail comes out here whenever he's in town?'

'Ah,' I said.

Mrs Bream didn't show the least displeasure at my ignorance. She added, 'He's an accompanist. He's one of the best. Martin plays with touring violinists and singers all up and down the North Island.' Amid the growing darkness, which seemed greater off in her corner of the room, she smoothed a fold from her dress with one hand and smiled. She said, 'Martin always tells me that, in the old days, they used to have some awfully tiny concerts out in the backblock towns. Just three or four people turning up—and they'd leave the local hall and go and listen to him play in the vicar's parlour, that sort of thing. But Martin, well, he always kept on touring. He says people offered him such polite excuses. You know, the numbers are down because of a P.T.A. meeting. Or a big-time Scouts camp, or something. And they'd always say, "If only you'd come on another night."' Mrs Bream chuckled dreamily to herself. From somewhere nearby me I heard Mr Bream say quietly, 'Why don't you play some more? Make up a wee bit of a concert, just for us.' At this Mrs Bream stood up, looking delighted... she started marching across the room with a distinct bounce in her compact frame, and I remembered all the problems of the previous evening and felt like congratulating Mr Bream on finding exactly the right thing to say...but Mrs Bream had already begun declaring that before any further kind of music she wanted every last one of the dishes cleared away first... she fussed at Philip to get a fire lit...she was insisting that Chloe and I go out and gather up some lamps...but her bustle only appeared to increase everyone's sense of anticipation. It took quite a while to make everything ready...we sat at last in our chairs once more with the curtains drawn and the room prepared, feeling all set, when suddenly Mr Bream came in with some bottles and announced he'd got fruit wine...he sat in his easy-chair with the bottles spread around his feet and went contentedly to work at pulling the corks...to my surprise Mrs Bream offered up a little shriek of pleasure at this, and rushed away...a few minutes later she brought in some fancy-looking cut-glass goblets for us with an air of triumph. Mr Bream filled the goblets with wine and gave one to each of us, acting like a waiter...as he went about, he switched off all but a pair of the lamps we'd hauled in, which left us with a comforting sense of semi-darkness and the languid glow from Philip's freshly kindled fire...we glanced at each other, almost surreptitiously, and saw that everyone else was feeling the same way...it was perfect. Mrs Bream played several short pieces in succession, and after that she attempted something a lot longer and more ambitious... she paused from playing only occasionally, to reach down for her goblet at the side of her stool and take a drink...the sweet fruit wine soon made us all drowsy...gradually the notes from the piano sounded charming but distant amongst the heavy, vaguely-defined shadows in the room. Even Chloe looked relaxed...she sat with her legs drawn up under her in a large wing-back chair that she'd taken over...she nodded at me, and I watched her waving away an insect from the glass goblet cradled in her hand. I began to reconsider leaving Stokewood...I thought perhaps I didn't really need to run off with Penny in such a rush…perhaps, tonight, I might even finally get to be a bedroom operator with Chloe…it was marvellous to feel the thrill of expectation well up within me once more. Sometime much later, there was a sudden noise outside in the night…it was a solid, rhythmic banging…it interrupted Mrs Bream's playing and she broke off, startled… the sound continued, full of its own drama, outside in the darkness…away somewhere in another room Humphrey responded by breaking into a frantic yipping. Mr Bream got up from his chair and he turned on the ceiling lights in a hurry…we blinked, stunned, in the glare…already he was hastening off out of the room…the banging had developed into an even louder tattoo…I guessed it was the front door being pounded on hard. In the entrance hall we heard voices raised in anger…then Mr Bream backed towards us into the room again…everywhere was still dazzlingly bright, but we could see that Mr Bream's arms were up high above his head… another man was quickly following him in through the doorway. The man wore a rubber gas mask strapped over his face…he was dressed in what looked to be an oversized, floppy white nylon bodysuit…the bodysuit was ballooned up around the man, with folds and wrinkles, and it covered him from his neck down to some gloves on his hands and a pair of large black gumboots on his feet…the gumboots flapped and the cumbersome material in the suit crackled, but the man kept on striding towards us. 'It's all right,' Mr Bream started saying. He was still retreating…the other man was breathing noisily through his gas mask…I could see that a long grey oxygen cylinder was slung on his back…he was stooped from its weight, labouring, as he marched in past Mr Bream and stood among us…Mr Bream continued moving away and bumped his hip on the side of a chair, and his arms, still above his head, were swaying and waving. 'It's all right,' he kept declaring. 'It's all right, it's all right.' We ignored him…our eyes were fixed on the man before us in the bodysuit…the man was working his gloved hands up and along his own face…he seemed to be wrestling at pulling off his mask, but the straps were tight and the gloves were awkward… the man's features looked red with frustration, until finally he dragged the goggles and mask down below his chin. 'Everybody has to get out,' he shouted at us. 'Now!' The man was wheezing…he was puffing for breath… he started making violent gestures at us with the hand that was not clutching his mask around his throat…nobody moved. 'Now!' he repeated in a gasp. We began getting to our feet…Humphrey scampered in. 'Well really, what on earth's the matter?' Mrs Bream exclaimed. Humphrey made a

97

spirited assault on the man's gumboots...the man tried to shove the dog off with the edge of one heel...somewhere back behind the man through the doorway I could spy several other men in the same sort of bodysuits and gas masks...they were out in the entrance hall, crowding inside now from the dark...the men were getting in each other's way and clanking clumsily around...I craned my neck a little to watch better, and saw that all of them were carrying heavy-looking tin buckets. One of the men came and put his head round the drawing-room's door...he held his bucket up high in front of him and it swung in his grip...dry sand was beginning to dribble from its rim. 'Upstairs,' the man who was with us growled over his shoulder. 'It's upstairs,' he repeated. He half turned and watched until the other man had gone back to consult with his mates...next the man turned to us again, but we'd still barely moved...I saw that Mr Bream had finally lowered his arms...Humphrey was barking from a safer distance. The man shouted above all the noise, 'Look, look, you've got a bloody chemicals leak!' I heard Mrs Bream squawk, and she slammed her piano lid shut...then the man began struggling forwards around the room...it was as though he wanted to shepherd us...he was flailing out with his bulky, scrunching, slippery-suited arms, and the floorboards groaned under his weight...Mr Bream had a go at trying to assist him...the rest of us just shuffled to get away from the man's reach. 'Who rang? Who rang up the Fire Brigade?' I heard Mr Bream calling in a fluster.

'We're on fire too?' I asked.

'Jesus Christ!' exclaimed Philip. The man kept pushing his arms crazily into our faces. I heard Chloe saying, 'I think it was—I think it was me that rang them, eh.' But her words were partly drowned out by a tremendous thudding...the other men in the entrance hall seemed at long last to be stamping up the staircase in a group. 'I just found these big cans up top there labelled "sodium cyanide",' Chloe persisted above the racket, 'and the bottom one, the can, it was a little bit corroded.' 'Jesus Christ!' Philip exclaimed again. 'Will you come *the fuck* on!' the fireman bellowed at us. I followed Philip and Chloe out through the doorway, with Philip's parents still somewhere behind us in the drawing-room...the fireman accompanied the three of us into the hall, lurching along close at our backs...he was fumbling to pull up his mask and goggles onto his face once more. He managed to rasp, 'If that bloody stuff finds any water, then this old dump'll be shit full of poison gas.' 'This is not an old dump!' Philip turned and shouted. But the man shoved Philip away with a large gloved hand...at the same time someone upstairs fell down heavily and let out an appalling scream...Humphrey skittered out into the entrance hall and past us, escaping the hurly-burly, and looked to be heading for the rear of the house. I heard Mr Bream hollering, 'Mind the floorboards where it's loose.' A muffled, resigned cursing followed from upstairs...Mrs Bream appeared from the drawing-room with a few goblets gathered in her arms...at the same moment Mr Bream pushed his way past her and then past me...he was making eagerly for Chloe...I saw her start edging up against a panelled wall in the entrance area at his approach...Mr Bream's eyes were flushed from the wine and his cheeks were quivering in fury. 'You rang them, you bitch!' he began roaring at Chloe. He howled the words close into her face a second time...Chloe lowered her head, and I could tell she was working hard not to cry...actually I thought it was a very fetching look for her. 'That was hours ago,' she tried protesting. Next she whimpered, 'They just said they'd check into it. That was ages ago.' Mr Bream swung away from her and rounded on a fireman who was trudging back to us downstairs. Mr Bream snarled, 'You people took your sweet time getting here, eh.' The new fireman began yelling something in reply through his gas mask... it was incomprehensible, and he tried repeating his words with care...I watched the goggles fog up around his enraged eyes...perhaps he just wanted us to get the fuck outside, but Philip was blocking the front door... he was insisting on trying to quiz his father about insurance.

'You guys should all go on ahead,' I called to the others.

I didn't say it to anybody in particular, but next I pushed past the fireman and made for the stairs...he was in a panic to try and stop me...I ducked away from his swinging arm without difficulty.

'The dog!' I bawled at him, hoping that might help.

I sprinted, all harum-scarum, up the creaky staircase...I reached the landing at the top and saw two more burly white-suited firemen, and I headed towards them...they were standing in the corridor with their backs to me, gazing off together through a doorway into a room. Neither of the men noticed my approach...the oxygen cylinder of one fireman was blocking my path along the corridor, scratching up against the varnish on the wall behind him...I drew up next to the man and tapped on his shoulder...he twisted his masked face around towards me, and I could see his eyes widen in surprise at me standing there. I gestured that I was in kind of a hurry...the fireman hesitated...I gestured some more in a form that could mean anything, simply poking the air with my fingers...to my relief he shifted sideways and let me shuffle by. In a few instants I reached the end of the passage and with a single shove forced open the door to the bedroom that Chloe and I were using...I stepped inside, grabbed Half-Arse and my duffle-bag from the wardrobe, and stepped out once more...on my way back along the corridor the fireman watched me returning to him...he waved a determined arm at me, and shouted something into my face from his mask when I got close...I kept nodding as if he was absolutely correct while I slid past him against the wall. I could see over the fireman's shoulder into the room behind him as I went by...there were several other firemen bent or crouching inside, intent on their work...they were painstakingly patting down a broad yellow sand-pile, like children playing on a beach...the sand was spread in a ring over most of the floor. At the bottom of the stairs I found everyone was gone from the hallway, and I thought perhaps they were gathered out at the front by the porch...I turned with my things and headed for the rear of the house...in the kitchen Humphrey was cowering against the fridge beside a small pool of his own saliva...I whistled to him as I trotted by, but he didn't follow me...then I hustled myself out through the back door. Beyond the homestead the darkness around me was immediate and almost total...I stumbled in haste past the brick edge of the vegie garden and kept right on going...in the dark everything seemed to become an obstacle...everything wanted to bump into my legs or reach down and scratch at my shoulders...but soon I began circling the already distant lights of Stokewood, looking for the main road in the featureless night.

THREE

I tramped hard across a series of paddocks in the nearly solid darkness...my feet kept scuffing against lumpy swads of grass, and I was afraid I'd trip and fall and then hurt myself...every few hundred yards in the dark an aspect of all that was around me became changed...smooth ground became stony...level land became sloping, hollow land...clumps of bushes turned into rows of high trees. As I walked, I could hear almost nothing above the noise of my own laboured breathing, and again and again my approach startled groups of drowsy livestock...I seemed to come up to

100

them in a hurry, but I could scarcely perceive their outlines until I was right on top of them…they were mostly sheep, and they jumped and went off, heavy-footed with fright, into the dark…they bleated and moaned and tumbled against each other in terror, heading away from me towards the fence-lines. I had to climb each one of the paddocks' fences amid nothing I could see, and I grew accustomed to the shaky feel of the wire beneath me…sometimes I sensed the dry old wood in the fence posts splitting as I clambered over with Half-Arse in my hand…each time I hopped down into yet more farmland and heard more panicked animals running…here and there I passed windbreaks with the ragged mass of the treetops silhouetted in the sky…getting across the bars of a gate, I slipped and ended up in the dirt, hard on my elbow…it stung along the edges of the bone's joint, and I hoped it was only from skinning myself a little. But finally all my energy left me…I sat down against one of the loose battens in a fence… where I was I didn't know, though most likely still out in some back paddock somewhere…I thought it might just be possible to doze…for a long while I contemplated the airy quiet around me, and then fell into a kind of dog-sleep. At last I roused myself, unsure of whether I'd been asleep for minutes or hours, and I began heading sluggishly off once more across the paddocks…my aim was to get to where I hoped a road might be…but I came upon a river instead, barring my path…in the darkness the river water looked black and intimidating, and I thought it best just to try following alongside it. I struggled with Half-Arse and my duffle-bag on the difficult and uncertain ground near the river's edge…it was impossible to keep my sandshoes dry…they sank down into the oozy softness of the marshy banks…I had to work, in places, to get past massive clumps of toetoe that grew down to the waterline and hindered my progress…the going was slow…there was time for me to wonder if I might be walking the whole way to Wellington. After a long, long while I saw some glowing orange lights in the distance…the lights were ranged in a neat row, spaced across the top of an old iron railway bridge…I kept heading for them, still tramping along the boggy riverbank, and it seemed to take forever to get any closer. By now a thick dew was forming on the ground…the dawn had started to come up without my noticing it, not at first, and the moisture all around was keeping the blue air cold…finally the bridge was just above me…I clambered up a loose, shingled slope alongside it…I had to reach out and grab where I could at damp bunches of stringy weeds…then I stepped warily over the train tracks and to my delight saw a road nearby.

I made for it, supposing it was just possible that I'd arrived at State High-way 2 and, without bothering to think too much, I felt sure my luck was in…at the roadside I stood staring all about me, and found the highway's actual number on a heart-shaped sign on a power-pole a short distance ahead…along the far-off edge of the horizon a slim, broad hint of yellow sky was spreading, with its glow illuminating the underbellies of fleecy clouds…in front of me I could see where the highway went out onto a road-bridge over the river I'd been following…I supposed this could be the exact one, the bridge that Penny had meant…in any case I thought it was worth taking the chance. I approached one edge of the thing, put down my gear and sat myself cross-legged on the cold gravel…it was right where the shoulder of the road ended, and I could rest my back up against the curled start of the bridge's metal safety rail…somewhere a few birds had commenced their singing…with my tired gaze I saw the pale rocky tops of the ranges begin to brighten far away…slowly the light flittered, and next it began to drift and to cast long, slanting shadows over the mountains. I pondered the scene for some time while the light and the shadows crept across the wide upper-bush cover, making it all come into view, and then slipped down over the pastureland on the slopes…finally I watched the dark patches fade on the shining foothills below, and I felt how much the air smelled clean…I let myself bask sleepily in the sun's growing warmth… I tried not to think about how, by this stage, the gravel was starting to tin-gle and cut into my bum…but after my night in the open a faint and pleas-ant sense of self-pity was creeping over me. I thought to examine the state of my clothes, wondering if I should change them…they were stained with streaks of dirt and there were a few spots of blood smeared from my elbow…with my fingers I felt a small growth of beard prickling along the bottom of my chin…I guessed this all gave me the look of a real traveller, and I liked it. After a considerable period I heard some engine noise off at the far end of the bridge…I turned a bit and craned my neck…there was a little ute coming up towards me…something like farming equipment was stacked, rattling, on the tray in the back…I waved as casually as I could manage while the ute drew nearer and nearer, but the cockie who was driving ignored me…I could even stare up into his mud-caked wheel rims when he passed close-by. Soon more cars and trucks, the traffic of the morning, began to turn up on the other side of the road and pass me in a monotonous way, coming, I guessed, from out of town…then after a very long time a taxi appeared far off, approaching from the same direction…

I tried to stop myself thinking that this just might be Penny arriving, but for the life of me I couldn't imagine how it might be anyone else. The taxi seemed to advance only little by little...it cruised along as if drifting between the rows of low white marker-posts that bordered the highway...I didn't move to get up but just watched and listened to it droning towards me...the car slowed down almost to a crawl as it neared the bridge... finally it pulled to a halt on the far side of the road and waited, idling. The back door opened and I saw that it was indeed Penny inside, sitting in the rear, but she didn't bother even to glance at me...instead she started reaching forwards to the front to pass the driver some money...with the door open I could see she appeared awfully well dressed...she was wearing a thin, sleeveless gingham blouse of blue-and-white plaid and a long, brightly-coloured peasant skirt...after a moment or so she lifted the skirt's lace-trimmed hem and stepped carefully out from the car. Penny's feet were in simple, low-heeled sandals, with her ankles looking strong above the straps...she was as tall and willowy as I'd imagined her yesterday, sitting behind her counter in the bank, but now when she stood and reached back into the car her bottom was rather bigger than I'd expected...she hauled out a large orange string bag and slung low it over one shoulder. 'So, you made it,' she called, with her back still towards me. She slammed the taxi door shut and stared at it for an instant. Next she turned, and asked more hesitantly, 'You been hanging around here long?' I shook my head, not knowing why I was lying, but once again Penny wasn't paying me any sort of heed...she'd started flexing her shoulders and was stretching herself, waving her arms from side to side as if she was the one who'd been sitting out here and waiting for ages...several golden bangles glinted along her wrists and I heard them jingle from her movements...at last she ceased her exercises and began reaching up and brushing back her wavy hair. By now I'd got to my feet, and with my gear I stepped briskly across the road towards her...the taxi was already reversing as part of a complicated three-point turn, so that when I drew near to Penny it began cruising off again in the direction it had come...within a moment or two we were alone, and after my rough night and all the sitting around I was feeling excited about our trip.

'You travel light,' I said.

I gestured at Penny's sagging string bag. 'Oh, I'm not so into material possessions, eh,' Penny mumbled in a careless manner. 'Besides, you know, you can always borrow off other people.' Then she asked, 'What's that?' She was pointing down at Half-Arse, gripped in my hand.

'My typewriter,' I said.

'Oh yeah?' she said. 'Just in case the mood comes over you, eh?'

I nodded and grinned.

I said, 'The typewriter's named Half-Arse. Want to borrow it for a while?'

Now I was being sarky too...I liked this little bantering back and forth between us. 'Shit no,' Penny replied.

'Oh,' I said.

I shrugged, and couldn't manage another response...that really seemed to be about it for repartee...instead, I gazed off across the bridge at the long, gently curving stretch of black-tarred road before us.

'Well, let's get a ride,' I said.

'Yeah, I suppose,' Penny mumbled. But she didn't sound too keen...I watched her lift one hand to shade her eyes and then glance all around, taking in the highway, the bridge, the river, even the paddocks nearby... meanwhile, back from the direction of town, a solitary truck was coming up the road towards us. At last Penny seemed to acknowledge the approach of the truck and she took a deep, slow breath...but she didn't move, or even seem about to, and I thought maybe I'd better get us started off...I plopped down my gear and stepped up to the white line along the road's edge...the truck rumbled nearer, and I raised my arm with my thumb sticking out...it felt just a smidgeon silly. I tried searching hard for the driver's face in the window of the approaching cab...I thought maybe eye contact would be important...but even as the truck drew up close, I could see nothing of the person inside...the wide front window was covered with dust, and grey exhaust fumes were tumbling out among the large, rolling tyres...the truck changed gear with a fierce growl when it reached the bridge...then it drove on past. I had plenty of time to watch it go, and so I stayed there standing at the roadside...after a short while a few cars came by, driving in a slow file...for each of them I put my thumb out...each one coasted past me. A bit later some more cars went smoothly by...the sun seemed to be growing a little higher in the sky...I felt I was beginning to get quite comfortable with hitching. 'Why the hell isn't anyone ever going to stop?' I heard Penny grumble behind me. I'd not been paying her much attention, so I turned to ask whether she'd like to have a go...it would be wrong of me to keep hogging all the action...I could see she was standing a little off from the highway's shoulder in some rough dry grass, with the yellow stalks up around her skirt...she had her arms folded, and there was an expression on her face that suggested she was already doing all the work. But at that moment, while I was half distracted, I more or less failed to notice a large, old black boat of a car approaching nearby and changing down to a slower speed...it floated past us on its massive, rocking chassis and within an instant I gave up on it stopping...but the car continued to get slower as we watched, and next it appeared to halt altogether, not too far off, on the road in the middle of the bridge...we both of us stared at the car...it definitely wasn't moving...it was definitely waiting for us. 'Gosh,' Penny said. I grabbed Half-Arse and my bag up from where they were lying at the edge of the highway...I started to trot with them clumsily out across the bridge...the car carried on staying put in front of me. As I bounced along to it with my stuff, I could see that the car was very, very old, a real jalopy, and rested high off the ground with its protruding front fenders low and its back panels up...from the roof downwards the rounded, dull black bodywork showed terrible streaks of dark red rust...I drew level with the wide boot, which looked like a rump stuck out under the car's small rear windshield, and I could spy a maker's mark saying 'Vauxhall'...I thought the whole thing seemed like a little piece of history. Sitting up in the front seats were two men...I came round the side of the car into the road and noticed the driver was dangling a podgy, muscular arm out of the window...he was Maori, thick-necked, and had a square, heavy face...he was wearing wraparound sunglasses that hid his eyes, and he was staring someplace ahead into the distance away from me...when I drew up beside him, I could see the front door of the car had rear hinges and its handle was forwards, near the long slope of the bonnet...it was that old...the Maori driver was picking at the discoloured chrome handle lightly with his hefty fingers. So, I thought, this is hitching.

'Hey, can you guys give us a lift?' I asked.

The driver raised his head...I saw he was wearing a grey tank top, and his hair was bushed up into a large, frizzy afro that had collapsed from the middle into two parts...also I could sense, rather than tell, that he was gazing at me through his sunglasses with something like surprise...I was still a little breathless from my running on the bridge. I tried to sneak a look past him at the other man over in the shade of the passenger seat...the other man was also Maori and in some sort of loose orange T-shirt, but he seemed altogether smaller and wirier...his thin face had long golden-brown wisps of moustache and beard poking out of it in a haphazard way...there wasn't much else of him in view, so I turned my attention back to the driver...I found the driver was sliding his solid jaw from side to side, as though considering me. At last he said, 'Hop in, bro.' That sounded companionable...I stepped back and dragged open the weighty rear door...Penny had come up just behind me, and so I clambered in quickly across the enormous seat in the rear of the car to give her room...the seat's sticky vinyl upholstery was warm to the touch. 'Hey thanks, man,' I heard Penny say to the Maoris. I was a bit busy trying to arrange myself along with Half-Arse and my duffle-bag, but I thought her voice sounded nervous...I looked up and watched the driver raise one brawny arm in a gesture to us...his gesture seemed somewhere between a greeting and lack of interest. Penny had dropped her string-bag beside her on the seat...she hauled the door shut with an effort, using her shoulder...next I heard the driver push at the clutch, and the gears graunched...the car trundled forwards but its engine mostly made a lot of disappointing noise and we had difficulty getting up any kind of pace...I supposed the old dear must be feeling the extra load. My feet were hot, and I glanced down and noticed all the carpets underfoot were gone...our shoes were resting on the bare metal of the floor pan, and I hoped this would be all right...then I looked up again and tried to focus on the road before us, but it was hard to see properly through the windscreen over the top of the high front seats. 'Where you guys headed, eh?' the Maori sitting on the passenger side was asking. He was looking at his mate and bobbing his head up and down as if that might help us go a bit faster, and the car was in fact jiggling along more and more...the Maori half turned and poked his hairy face close towards us round the gap in the seats. 'Whereabouts, eh?' he asked once again. He sounded very polite.

'Wellington's good,' I replied.

We were at last picking up some genuine speed, but we were also sway-ing...the increasing movement from side to side was becoming dramatic...I found I had to grip at the door's armrest in order to stay upright...ahead of us, on the road, I caught glimpses of the white centre-line swimming in and out of view.

'Actually, we're really off to Christchurch, for a Heads' Ball,' I man-aged to say. I added, 'I'm going to write about it, sort of thing.'

The Maori in the passenger seat pursed his thin lips...he turned away and muttered something to the driver...but I couldn't catch what he said above the shrill whine from the engine. We were swaying ever

106

more violently…the driver was wrestling with the steering wheel, sitting hunched over and tensing his shoulders, but the steering wheel seemed very loose on its column and he swung it this way and that in his powerful grip, working just to keep us at going straight…I watched his forearms bulging from all the effort…they were covered in smudged blue tattoos, and he was grunting now and then as if tired from his exertions…I felt a little queasy as we yawed about but I said nothing…after all, it was their car. Beside me, Penny was attempting to roll down her window…the air around us was stuffy and difficult to breathe…but the old chrome window-handle wouldn't catch and she laboured at it, cranking it with her fist…after a minute or two she gave up and just sat back, staring out at the view through the glass, with the firm set of her jaw looking frustrated and grim. The road seemed to be rising steadily, though the yellow farmland around us still appeared flat and arid…it was broken by shelterbelts of wilted macrocarpas and scruffy pines, and the stock were grazing the dead brown grass near the boundary-fences…the animals ignored us, despite the revving noises from our engine as we reeled uneasily past. I saw that now the Maori in the passenger seat had got his head down and was bent over double…I strained to gaze at him from where I was in the seat behind, and to guess what he was doing…his face was almost pushed between his knees…first I thought perhaps he was going to be sick, but then I saw he was scrabbling about…at last he appeared to find what he was searching for and pulled something upwards, holding it close to his sparsely whiskered cheek with a triumphal air…it was a large, crumpled brown paper-bag. Penny stiffened and seemed interested…next the Maori was fumbling to open the glove compartment…he reached in and took a small object out with his free hand, clutching it between his fingers…I could see it was a dirty-looking glass pipe with a wide bowl and a short, untapered stem. I glanced in Penny's direction for some sort of confirmation of how strange this was…her eyes were wide and fixed with attention on the pipe…the Maori was already stuffing pinches of dried leaves into the bowl from the bag, forcing them down with his thumb…after a minute he produced some matches, lit the bowl and took a long, smoky puff. He turned round to us again…he draped one thin arm back over his seat, still gripping the pipe, which was bleeding smoke…casually, using the edge of his other hand, he started to brush away stray bits of his moustache and beard…Penny was craning forward and almost getting in front of me as we went on bounding along in the car…a harsh grassy smell had filled the vehicle...the Maori took another steady draw and held his breath for what seemed an interminable period of time. Finally the Maori gasped and exhaled with a raspy sigh of satisfaction...then he held the pipe out to me, shaking his head a little in an embarrassed way...it was as if he was asking me not to take all this paltry business too seriously...by now, I was pretty certain this stuff was maybe marijuana. I told myself a writer should never pass up a chance like this, and I braced myself against the bouncing arm-rest as I reached for the pipe...it took a moment to get the right end of the thing up towards my mouth...hot green flakes of burning cannabis were dropping in a hotchpotch out of the top...I paused for a second, before putting the pipe to my lips.

'Thanks a lot,' I said to the Maori.

I hoped saying that might be the right etiquette for someone who was a regular at this type of deal...then I put my lips round the glass rim of the pipe-stem and drew back hard...getting everything down wasn't much worse than it had been with the cigarette I'd cadged in the bookshop, but this time my chest felt packed with searing smoke...I had to work to keep the brutal heat in my lungs, though I guessed it was the proper thing to do and struggled...my cheeks bloated up from the effort. I started to hand the pipe back, but the Maori gestured that I should give it to Penny...I turned, still holding my breath, and saw in Penny's eyes a stinging look of indignation that I hadn't already passed her a little weed...she seized the pipe from me and immediately took several deep puffs...the rear of the car clouded up for a moment with gritty white smoke...she handed the pipe forwards to the driver, and he accepted it cheerfully and started smoking too. An airy feeling was coming over me and I couldn't keep my breath held down anymore...finally I retched and cleared my lungs...my brain started to throb in my skull until my whole head felt fizzy, as though it was expanding...my mind and its perceptions were all floating mysteri-ously outwards and beyond me.

After what seemed a good while I managed to say, 'Well, this is fun—'

I said it to no one in particular, but I could hear Penny chuckling beside me. 'Oh,' she groaned. 'Oh, I'm ripped.' I had no idea what 'ripped' meant, but I was sure this was the funniest thing...it was the funniest, funniest, most hilarious thing I'd ever heard...it was probably the reason why every-one else in the car was laughing so hard out loud too...it was because everything around us now was so incredibly wonderful. The space inside the car felt enormous and the view outside was near and huge, though

I was far, far off…I was beautifully removed from it all…I couldn't help giggling about this over and over…I was looking at the whole world from the far edge of the moon. The car passed through a wonderful, crumbling brown cutting…there the cutting was, up alongside us and passing us by, with its fat loose layers of dirt slipping and even tumbling onto each other…then a few instants later came some blobs of lazy, fluffy white sheep grazing the long acre and I was enthralled by the lightness, the wonder, of my own thoughts about them…at one end of a paddock nearby was an old abandoned sheep yard and race, its wooden boards twisted and splintered and furry with pale-green moss, and wonderful…my eyes appeared to have become damp and heavy in rapture…just breathing in and out seemed like a wonderfully fresh idea. Suddenly from the tarseal on the highway before us a large grey hawk rose up…it had jumped, startled, off the road surface, and was clutching something red in one of its talons…the hawk began pushing its powerful dappled wings downwards to climb into the sky, almost wrestling with the air…I gazed at it in long stunned awe…the hawk commenced flapping more casually above us and was gone. Next the Maori in the passenger seat was back again, holding out the pipe…he offered it to me with an obliging grin, dangling the end of the glass tube just in front of my fingers…but Penny grabbed at the pipe with a determined leer on her face and took it away…I could see her wide teeth as she arched open her mouth to wrap her lips around the stem. She inhaled and coughed…she smoked at the thing greedily in huge, sucking rasps…I thought she was definitely taking her time to finish…finally I was able smoke a little more myself. 'I am so, so out of it, I am so ripped,' Penny was mumbling. She was leaning back on the seat…she sighed with a tone of massive contentment. 'I am *so* really ripped,' she announced. I saw the Maoris glancing at each other, though I couldn't make out the expressions on their faces, but in a flash, right there, I began to lose my nerve… it occurred to me that this might all be part of an elaborate plan to do us harm…I couldn't help wriggling about on the clammy seat…I felt panic rising and my blood racing, and for a moment it was impossible to take a breath. But then nothing happened…the car went on swinging wildly from side to side while we cruised forwards…the driver went on grappling with the wheel…he stayed focused and kept grunting and snorting…nobody listened as Penny went on insisting that she was really, really fucked. Once in a while as we continued we passed through a small town, never stopping or even slowing much, but mostly we were just busy with climbing…

we were heading ever upwards on a series of switchback roads along the edges of heavily eroded hills...there were raw patches of wet sandstone on one side of us and scrubby grey-green bush cover was dropping down in long vistas on the other...collections of fallen boulders seemed to line the route, and sometimes loose rocks nipped at our tyres. The car began struggling on some of the slow, drawn-out rises...after a time I noticed tiny white wisps of steam were drifting up in front of us and they appeared to be coming from under the broad, V-shaped bonnet of the car...the steam got fluffier and thicker...the Maoris hurried to turn on the heater...its warm, humid air started roaring and rumbling through the car into the back seat, and we could feel the solid rough blast of it blowing against our faces... within minutes sweat was dripping off our chins onto our laps, but still we felt far too wonderful to care. At length the engine seemed to settle and the steam was gone...we were no longer climbing...gradually the number of downhill sections of road increased and the car started to enjoy itself...we careened faster and faster on every declining bend, with the white wooden fences at the side of each turn coming up closer and closer to the edge of the fender...soon I had to hope that the brakes would hold out. But some-time later we reached the outskirts of Upper Hutt...the driver had to drop all our speed with the sudden arrival of the city streets and we crawled at an unnatural pace, as if we'd been snagged on a rope...the marijuana had worn off, and finally the driver pulled the car over to the kerb...the engine shuddered and idled, and no one said a word, but we appeared to be at the end of the ride. We were halted somewhere just past a nondescript inter-section, and it looked like the sort of place that might be near the middle of town...Penny and I got one of the doors open, and we both climbed out on the same side into the road with our bags...I started coming up to the front window to thank the driver...but before I could draw near, he waved a heavy brown arm out at me in his easy, noncommittal manner. 'Hooray, bro,' he called. Then he leaned away from me back into the car... he cranked the engine up with a mighty crunch of the gears and the sound of stripping metal...the whole jalopy shunted off in little bumbling bursts... I stood gazing in silence and admiration as it puttered away around a corner and was gone from sight. Afterwards, Penny and I ambled off the bitumen towards the kerb...I thought she looked as tired and washed out as I was... we squatted down together on the smooth edge of the concrete gutter... it was easy, it was even fun, to ignore the pedestrians and the cars mov-ing by around us...I was sitting beside a Give Way sign, and I propped my shoulder against the painted steel pole and stretched out my legs as far into the road as I dared. Penny and I held hands, and we stared up at the open blue sky...we could see the swollen spurs of the ranges that we'd come from glinting in the distance...some calm white clouds were drifting in lazy bunches above us. At last Penny said, 'That was really some amazing shit.' I thought I could already hear a strong nostalgic tone in her voice.

'You're telling me,' I said.

'I mean, that really was some amazing bloody shit, eh,' Penny said.

'I'd say it was amazing,' I agreed.

I thought perhaps I was beginning to understand why writers were often attracted to drugs and general dissipation...it was because drugs and general dissipation were so enjoyable...Penny was continuing to stare off, bleary-eyed, into the landscape...she sighed comfortably. Next, as if having guessed my thoughts, she said with the air of someone announcing a great truth, 'Yeah, drugs won't solve your problems. But they'll make you a lot happier about being all fucked up, eh.' Penny turned sideways, a bit closer towards me...I felt buoyant and very aware that she was still holding onto my hand...I felt that life, living, was an exquisite gift, and though I understood none of it, I didn't mind. Penny said, 'You know, we could catch the unit into town from here.' She added, 'And let's get some grub. I'm bloody hungry.'

'Fine by me,' I said.

We soon found a nearby takeaway bar...it was a small, boxy-looking shop that had its counter facing out onto the street, with the counter painted in orange stripes and set up so high that we could hardly see over the top...a young, moon-faced man in denim overalls took our order...we got ourselves hamburgers and pots of chips. Penny asked the man who was serving us about where the unit came in...he said the railway station was only a few blocks off and gestured with one hand in its direction while dangling the brown bags for the hamburgers from his fingers... we thanked him, and when the burgers were ready we carried our food away to eat at the station. On the platform we sat on a bench and gently pulled the dry, toasted buns out of their bags...we ate, and greasy slices of sweet fried onion from the burgers slipped down across our chins... the platform's sun-baked asphalt cover felt as though it was burning the undersides of our legs...there were birds singing in the warmth somewhere and I heard the occasional rumble of passing cars behind us... we both munched ravenously, stuffing our fingers in amongst the chips and tomato sauce in the pots, and afterwards I had to fight off the urge to fall asleep…it was a long time before the railcar rolled towards us up the rust-stained tracks. When it arrived, Penny and I climbed into the nearest carriage…our feet clomped on the grooved metal steps as we got in…we chose our seats, feeling just like ordinary people once more, and as we sat I was bothered by a dim sense of disappointment.

In Wellington, after leaving the station, Penny named each of the streets that we were on as we walked along them…it was as if she wanted to show off her local knowledge…soon we were dawdling on a busy foot-path between shop-fronts and the lanes of a road crammed with buses, trucks and other traffic…I could smell exhaust fumes, and there was a lot of disorienting noise from the cars heading past…more than once Penny bored me by insisting that this bit here was called Lambton Quay. The wind kept coming up in uncomfortable gusts and pushing us in the face, and at times I had to watch where I placed each footstep…Penny would often halt to point out expensive-looking clothes in the windows of some of the stores we were passing…but I only noticed how low above us the endless series of coloured shop-signs seemed to hang from the verandas. I saw a businessman strolling just in front of us with his small change, or perhaps his keys, bulging and jiggling in both of his pockets…he was trying to speak to an overweight woman next to him who was dressed in a puffy blue blouse, a black skirt and some high heels which gave her a slight limp, as though her shoes were pinching her…another busi-nessman shoved past us and then between the couple, moving with one shoulder down into the wind…we overtook a pair of Malaysian-looking women wearing headscarves…a small group alongside us met someone they knew and they all halted to start talking, almost blocking our path… I slipped my duffle-bag down off my shoulder as we moved on and tried swinging it back and forth to make myself appear more casual, because the road was turning and narrowing and the high-rise buildings around us were beginning to feel oppressively tall. 'And this is Willis Street,' Penny announced. We encountered an untidy queue of people waiting to board a bus…a man in a charcoal-grey suit was pushing hard against my elbow from behind, trying to wedge himself by…I gave the man a good decent shove back into his ribs…he looked me up and down in extreme annoy-ance, but he hurried on with his red necktie flipping up onto his shoulder in the breeze…I grinned and decided that I could rather like this bus-tling, thrusting, go-as-you-please city atmosphere…after all, the big city was usually where writers thrived. Penny had walked ahead and was wandering to the edge of the footpath...she stepped down over the gutter and glanced about her...carefully she avoided a manhole cover marked with a yellow circle in the asphalt...then, with the heels of her sandals briskly clacking, she began to stride away across the road. I watched Penny proceed in a long diagonal up to the street's white centre-line and next drift sideways, almost skipping a little, while some cars passed...it gave me a useful chance to admire her legs...they were swaying nicely in the dress below her heavy buttocks as she moved...perhaps she sensed me staring at her because she turned back and waved me towards her with a small, bossy swing of one arm...I hesitated, and found a gap in the traffic. When I finally got across the road, Penny was already waiting on the other side... she stood with her hands on her hips and seemed to display a wholly new sense of determination. She barked at me, 'We need to haul arse.'

'Okay,' I said. I wanted to be obliging, but I couldn't resist asking, 'What's all the big hurry?'

Penny said it was her friend...she said how it would be much better if we hooked up with him...but she began walking quickly away from me even while she was explaining everything, and I had to follow just to listen...I gathered that her friend was called B.J. Lamborghini...we were going to meet B.J. Lamborghini in the Cuba Mall. Penny marched along ahead as if she was worried...maybe she thought B.J. Lamborghini might escape from the Mall and flee from us before we got there...I wondered why, now, he could be so vastly important.

'So—what, are we suddenly on a schedule?' I said to Penny's back as I trotted to keep close behind her.

'Hey,' Penny replied without looking round. She sounded strangely testy. A few moments later she said to me over one shoulder, 'I just really want to go up to the Cuba Mall and see him, all right?'

'How do you know that's where he is?' I asked, a little out of breath.

'Look, hey,' Penny said again. From behind her, I watched Penny arch her neck and give a long sigh...next she shook the fingers of her hands while she hustled onwards, as if ridding herself of something...I wondered if that something might just be me. Finally she half shouted back above the traffic, 'Because he's always hanging around there, eh, at midday. The Mall, right, that's his happening place.' We hauled arse...we were almost running along the noisy streets...we were twisting and weaving amongst the crowds...Penny kept in front of me all the way. At last we scampered across a little sharply curving road, dodging some cars…on the other side, we skirted a low graffiti-covered wall and some large concrete planters filled with flax and ugly shrubs…then we entered the precincts of a narrow area lined with bright stores, a closed-off street, and I guessed this was the Mall we were seeking…it was bustling with shoppers and cyclists, and people were sitting on wrought-iron benches, talking and smoking… the ground underfoot was laid out in red paving-slabs that were ruined by mould and felt slippery…Penny headed beneath the verandas on one side where the paving was better, keeping us away from the clutter of some sandwich boards propped up outside the stores. Soon I spied a high, funny-looking cage bedecked with a long stack of yellow buckets rising into our view, far off near the entrance to a Farmers'…the buckets twitched a bit up in the breezy air and appeared as badly out of sorts as Penny was… something about this grisly object made me guess that it was the centre of the Mall and had to be our goal. As we drew nearer, I heard a shriek and had time to see one of the buckets in the cage had tipped a big load of water…the water was exploding down across other buckets which were now dumping more water everywhere in a random series…people scurried to get back out of the spray, and even from far off shoppers clutched at their bags and stared…only one harassed-looking woman, wheeling a baby in a pushchair into the path of the splatter, did her best to ignore it… after that, Penny and I approached the bucket-cage a little more slowly… I could see two low concrete pools at its base where the water should have gone, though instead there was spillage all over the paving. Some tough, shabbily dressed street kids, a whole gang of them, were sitting in a line along the nearest edge of one pool…they'd positioned themselves on the cement rim as far upwind from the splashing as possible, though the youngest, unable to fit onto the end of the row, was sitting on his heels as best he could…they were only in bare feet or jandals and looked cold… one had a red-yellow-and-green woollen rasta cap pulled down over his head…I watched how they were all calling out aggressively at the passers-by, putting up their little hands to beg for coins…apart from the water, they were the sole excitement to be seen. I advanced close to the bucket-cage-sculpture, dangerously close…but nobody appeared and announced himself as B.J. Lamborghini…nobody was doing anything except keeping far from the spilled water on the ground and the annoying street kids… I supposed that, as happening places go, this one was quiet. Penny was standing away from the pool and trying to gaze about…she had a look of

114

increasing hopelessness on her face, and she made no attempt to hide her anxiety...maybe she believed that just staring about harder, hither and yon, might make her friend actually arrive...her eyes were bulging, full and heavy in their sockets, as if she was ready to cry...she looked a bit like a startled animal and I began to feel sorry for her. After a minute or so I approached the group of beggar kids alongside the pool...I chose the kid who appeared to be the oldest...he had dirty curly black hair and was sitting hunched over in a khaki army-surplus jacket that went down almost to his knees...the kid had both of his hands pushed deep into the jacket's pockets...when he noticed me come up to him, he started rocking back and forth as if nervous.

'So, hey, do you know B.J. Lamborghini?' I asked.

The kid glanced up at me suspiciously...he seemed very aware that everyone in his gang was watching us...he hunched himself a lot deeper into his jacket...then he stared off away from me, letting me know that I simply wasn't there, until even I felt a little that I'd ceased to exist.

'B.J. Lamborghini,' I repeated.

A smaller boy sitting next to the kid was picking with his teeth at some red scabs on the back of his hand...he raised his head a bit and squinted up at me. Still keeping his hand close to his mouth, he mumbled, 'You got fifty cents, mister?' I'd never been called 'mister' by anyone before...I shrugged.

'Well, I asked you a question first,' I said.

The smaller boy didn't reply...he gazed at me in surprise before finally stealing a look at the bigger kid...it was as though he needed advice about this...but the bigger kid was silent too and offered him no help...I thought that, for city types, neither of them seemed much good for any sassy comeback in the face of my ruthless logic...perhaps the whole gang of them were just getting started in their careers as beggars...but then the bigger kid spoke up. He said with a tone of authority, 'B.J., yeah, B.J. went down the end of Courtenay Place, eh.' I nodded and gave the kid fifty cents...he put the coin quickly into his pocket, as if afraid I might ask for it back. 'Thanks, mister,' the smaller boy piped up beside him. I felt a rash impulse to give everyone else in the gang fifty cents...but instead, I stepped over the damp paving to Penny and told her what I'd just heard...immediately we commenced hauling arse again, and I was pretty sure it was for Courtenay Place. We crossed a couple of streets and soon we were tramping on a busy footpath past a series of narrow storefronts...

the shops looked dim under the shade of their wide verandas and a lot of traffic seemed to be roaring by very near us along the road, coming and going in all sorts of directions, competing for space...I had time to consider whether telling Penny about Courtenay Place might have been a mistake...we went past a Chinese greengrocer's that had wooden crates of broccoli and whole grey pumpkins stacked out in front of the shop, and I could catch the ripe smell of cabbages coming from inside...parallel rows of trolley-bus cables were strung overhead and through the matting of the cables, almost with a sense of gratitude, I noticed the dull green hills in the distance had grown steadily nearer. We passed by a long line of red-and-white buses parked at the kerb, each with their grimy, square fronts hard up against one another's taillights, and then Penny finally spotted her friend and reached forward to point him out...he was a fellow stamping around under the long, jutting veranda of a building across the intersection at the end of the street...it was a big movie-theatre with an imposing brownish-coloured facade...Penny hurried onwards even faster, ignoring me dilly-dallying behind her. I struggled to keep up and at the same time tried to get myself a better view...I could make out a short, slightly built man by the theatre's shadowed lobby who was pacing on the footpath before a row of glass entrance-doors...he trod restlessly back and forth, again and again, moving up and down...B.J. Lamborghini looked swarthy and narrow shouldered, and he was wearing a black leather motorcycle jacket which swung awkwardly each time he took a step...as we drew up to the edge of the intersection I could tell that he had a gaunt and thinly bearded face, and that the arms of his jacket were far too long for him. B.J. Lamborghini turned his back to pace away from us once more...Penny had started crossing the street towards him...she was paying only minimal attention to the cars. I heard her call out, 'Hey, B.J.!' from the middle of the road. She called it again above the noise of the traffic when she drew nearer...I was still following as quickly as I could with Half-Arse in my grip...B.J. swung around and Penny threw her arms out...then I watched them both disappear into a hug...I couldn't help noticing that B.J. had to reach up to hold her. 'Amazing—this is amazing!' B.J. was saying in a muffled voice. His face was half wrapped in some of the long folds of Penny's hair...he stepped back and dropped his hands to his hips...loose strands of Penny's blonde hair were still peeling away from his cheeks. 'Yeah, it's really amazing,' Penny started to agree happily. I pretended to be absorbed by what kind of movies were on...there were a few red-framed stills of

116

something-or-other pinned up in a glass display-case outside the theatre…
it did look as if some interesting stuff might be coming up. 'Amazing,'
B.J. was repeating. I saw him beginning to shuffle a little back and forth
again…he'd raised his hands once more…he seemed unsure whether to
reach up for another hug or not. 'Can we stay at your flat tonight?' Penny
blurted out. Finally she waved across at me. She said, 'This here's Andy.'
B.J. gave me a quick, intense stare…he'd settled into an itchy swaying on
one foot and his dark eyes flicked about…after a moment he shrugged
and put on a poor approximation of a sheepish grin for Penny. 'Hey, okay,'
he said. Then he turned directly to me. 'But you've both got to come on
somewhere with me first, eh,' he announced. B.J. jerked with his neck as
if to indicate going up the street…I could see puffy red acne scars on the
skin beneath his wispy beard. 'Yeah, come on with me,' he said again. He
began immediately to stride off ahead of us, walking in a rapid, bow-legged
gait with the stiff hem of his oversized jacket sticking out and swinging
behind him…there was no time to inquire about what might be further
up on the long, straight street…we followed…we were hauling arse once
more…Wellington struck me as a city in a blind hurry. B.J. glanced back
over his shoulder, checking that we were still there with him. He called,
'You know, I do this just about every day now, eh.' There was a lot of traffic barrelling past us down the lanes of the road…the cars were buzzing
by only a few feet away from the regularly spaced parking meters beside
us…Penny soon managed to march out in front of me next to B.J.…her
bag flipped about loose on her shoulder as she went…I kept shambling
along at the rear…after all our exertions I felt uncomfortably hot, and Half-
Arse's carrier strap was cutting into my fingers…I reflected that, despite
being named after a car, B.J. Lamborghini was awfully keen on walking.
At length we reached a gradual bend in the road and across the street I
could see a long, curving, creosoted wooden fence, with the high back of a
covered grandstand half hidden beyond it…I wondered what all this might
be, but Penny seemed to have given up on any kind of explaining…we
began heading gently uphill, feeling the effort…we passed a small row of
three-storey stuccoed houses, crammed tightly together, and finally I saw
we were approaching an old, elaborately constructed brick wall that ran
on around the next bend in the road…the dark brickwork had a bruised
colour and there was an abundance of dense scrub spilling up from behind
the wall and almost smothering it along the top…B.J. was quickening
his steps. We drew closer…in a corner of the wall near us was a pair of

massive brick posts crowned with ornamental lanterns, and between the posts some fancy wrought-iron gates stood open...I saw B.J. was pointing vaguely at the gates and at the short turnoff up to them, and he kept heading in their direction...fixed to the curled iron tracery of their bars on one side was an official-looking coat of arms.

'Well, I guess you must have to be someone pretty famous to live in there,' I said.

But B.J. made a rapid gesture with his hands to be quiet...I couldn't fathom why, since we were the only people about on the street...but we'd come to a dead stop right in front of the entrance...beyond the gate was a thinly gravelled drive, with a red-and-white barrier-arm down across it to halt cars...a flagpole was set into the path a little further inside...I saw that the driveway briefly skirted the flagpole and entered some shrubbery, and I tried to tell where the route went, following it with my eyes, but it ran along a ribbon of palm trees until disappearing from sight. 'The Governor-General's residence,' Penny whispered to me. I nodded in my sagest manner, to show I'd been all too right about this being a place for someone famous...then I realised that B.J. had begun to stroll up into the driveway...he was ducking casually round the barrier-arm...he was heading towards a wooden guardhouse nearby. The guardhouse looked tiny and quaint and had a peaked tile roof...it was tucked away off the drive, but it was close enough for me to see a man inside, standing over a counter at its open window...the man was bent low and leaning forwards onto his elbows...he was dressed in white shirtsleeves and a necktie...I peered harder, and I could distinctly make out a policeman's blue patches on his broad, hunched shoulders. The coarse gravel kept crackling under B.J.'s boots...the policeman half stood up, but I saw it was only to turn the page of a newspaper spread before him on the counter...B.J. trod coolly past the guardhouse up the drive...the policeman merely appeared to tut-tut over something in the news. Suddenly Penny began to follow after B.J....I was left standing about on my own...I thought it better to be in as well and started tentatively onto the driveway...the gravel crunched in little explosions under my sandshoes with each step I took...I couldn't help trying to imagine what excuses we might offer if we got ourselves caught...still the policemen went on keeping up with current events. It seemed an agony just getting along the drive, step after step, but at last we all reached the cover of the trees...next we continued more freely up the sloping curve of the path and walked in quick, excited strides...several times Penny and I couldn't avoid glancing at each other...we were unable to believe what we'd gone and done...B.J. didn't look interested. Instead he led us onwards, treading well ahead of us amongst the cool shadows in the ever-denser shrubbery... I could smell woodsmoke coming from somewhere, perhaps from a burn-up of garden rubbish, and I thought it was high time that the staff attended to a few of all these overgrown plants...the noise of cars on the street had dropped far away behind us, and still there wasn't a soul about...I jogged forwards a little, approaching B.J. to strike up a conversation.

'So, how do you know Penny?' I asked him.

'I used to be a wool scourer,' B.J. said. I wasn't sure if this was a reply to my question or not...but in any case I was feeling distracted now by the sight of something through the gaps in the foliage...past the trees was a substantial sweep of lawn, and I could catch glimpses a very long, two-storey white building laid out at the far end. In a minute or two we left the thicket of trees behind and I could see the whole of the massive old building more clearly...its walls, faced with brown beams, had a gleaming whiteness in the sun, and under its pitched red roof it appeared strikingly symmetrical...there were large gables set in its central portion and at each end of its wings, and on both sides between there were showy banks of windows...along the ground floor it had porches shading pretty glass French-doors. We went on striding towards the fancy, prim-looking building...I guessed this had to be the actual residence part of the Governor-General's residence...I noticed several tall chimneys were sticking up out of the roof...well above them, a squat flag-tower was perched proudly right in the middle...the flag-tower was something Philip could have sold in Auckland as a decorative accessory...the entire place's prissiness reminded me more than a little of pictures of English cricket pavilions. 'Okay, is it?' B.J. asked loudly. He seemed aware of my discriminative interest...behind us Penny hissed at him to be quiet...we were rapidly nearing one side of the residence, and as we wandered past a small conservatory attached to one corner the glare of reflected sunlight from the windows was almost blinding. 'Yeah, I like to be here when I can,' B.J. said. He looked pleased with himself and made no attempt to lower his voice...he swung his arms and walked us still faster...I gazed up at the side of the building...no one was staring at us from any of the multitude of windows, but it all felt disconcertingly empty and quiet...there was no longer even the sound of birds. B.J. asked, 'Want to take a look inside?' By now we were marching around to the heavily shaded back of the residence…simple gardens of ferns, with most of the leaves ruddy and a bit dried out, were planted under each of the ground-floor rear windows…we could see a trim, modestly covered entranceway not far off. 'Here you go,' B.J. said in a confident tone. He hurried forward along the drive in the direction of the entrance…he was even humming some kind of tune…Penny waved vehemently for him to stop, but it was too late… B.J. was almost skipping ahead.

'Let's just pop our heads in,' I suggested.

B.J.'s bravado was becoming infectious…we continued to follow him, and I turned towards Penny as we went.

I asked, 'So exactly who is the jolly old Governor-General these days?'

'Probably some ho-hum guy done up in an Elvis Presley cape,' Penny muttered. We walked under the portico at the entrance, and in a moment we'd passed through the doorway behind B.J.…our shoes clicked on the solid floor-tiles…then Penny and I stepped gingerly onto an expanse of deep red carpet that came up before us, and I hoped my filthy soles weren't dirtying it too much…no one arrived to stop or challenge us, but we paused to look about and admire the place. We were in a high and airy entrance hall…the panelled walls around us were of a golden timber, perhaps kauri or something similar, and they were marvellously carved…a pale chandelier hung and twinkled with irregular flashes of reflected light above our heads…there was a grand wooden staircase just in front of us that I felt was inviting me to try it…I reached out to touch the rounded rail of the nearest banister, but B.J. began leading us away once again. He headed us off on a tour down a corridor…both Penny and I tramped along after him with a little reluctance, but conscious that we should try not to show it…the place still appeared to be quiet everywhere except for the muffled sound of our own footsteps…the corridor we headed down was brightly lit, even though it was daytime…there were chairs and cabinets cluttered in bunches up against the creamy-coloured walls, and I wondered if people had been pushing things out of their offices to save space. I saw that paintings were hanging above some of the furniture…I inspected a few as we passed by, though there weren't any that I could recognise from the books at Wynyards…B.J. noticed me staring and waved a hand at a picture without stopping. 'Yeah, we've got all the famous ones,' he said. I wasn't sure how to respond, but I thought that B.J. was most likely right… after all, he did come here a lot. The corridors seemed interminable… within a short while we grew tired of walking along and examining stuff, and so when we saw a half-open door we were happy to halt for a moment before it...B.J. eased the door further back a smidgeon and the whole thing creaked on its hinges...he tried peering into the room beyond... there was nobody inside, but he and Penny started whispering with new excitement...then I opened another door in the passage at random and called 'Peekaboo.' After that we checked all the rooms we came across more thoroughly, but everywhere we entered was deserted...soon, thanks to a handy old brass sign fixed to the wall outside, we found the office for the Governor-General himself...as B.J. opened the office door he rattled its handle...the knob seemed loose in his grip. 'Someone needs to fetch a screwdriver, eh,' he said. He sighed and added, 'They never get round to these things.' The Governor-General's office was empty too, so we crept in and took a break...the room before us was dim and had pale panelled walls with a lot of classy moulding and wide, ruched beige curtains drawn over the windows...there was a large, important-looking dark-wooden desk to one side, and a coat rack, bare but with many branches, stood next to it in the corner. Penny and I dropped our bags onto the floor...I reached for the light switch, and as some lamps flickered on above us I sat down with Penny on the plush visitors' sofa near the doorway...glass-fronted bookcases were lining two of the walls around us, almost to the ceiling, with their shelves filled by a mishmash of leather-bound sets showing gold or silver-embossed lettering on the spines...I thought that the books probably had to be famous, like the paintings, and it might be useful to give them the once-over a bit later on. B.J. went and threw himself into a red leather chair behind the desk...it tilted back for him slightly, and he stretched his legs out and swivelled contentedly from side to side, leaning on the armrests...I decided that, next time, I'd get myself a swivel-seat too. But Penny had stiffened a little beside me and began asking us, 'Listen, what's that? What's that noise?' We concentrated...somewhere far off we could hear orchestral music being played...B.J. sat up and stretched forward over his broad desk...he craned his neck to peer at a printed list alongside the blotter. 'Friends of the City Opera,' he announced, reading aloud off the list. 'Rehearsing for a ballroom function at eight.' Then he nodded his head in approval.

'Maybe it's a rock opera,' I said, and grinned. '*Tommy*,' I added.

B.J. ignored this, as though its vulgarity was beneath him...I felt a sudden moment of deflation, of only getting nowhere, despite our success at sneaking about...to distract myself I leaned back and looked at the walls where their complex strips of moulding met the ceiling...I examined the velvet of the curtains on the windows and all the nicely dusted corners.

'The seat of government is a big place,' I said at last.

'Shit yeah,' B.J. agreed. He was lolling in his chair. He said, 'They don't let just anyone in to see the G.G. It's pretty easy to get lost, eh, if you're not round here very much.' B.J. smiled briefly...he appeared to have forgiven me my tiny faux pas...he pointed at the grey telephone on the desk, and the long sleeve of his leather jacket slipped half over his hand. 'When you're not sure, mate, if you get in a room,' B.J. said to me, 'check the phone-extension page there by the blower. That way you can wind up all oriented again, eh. Because you know,' he added with a shrug, 'it's always going to be about who's who, when you're knocking around in here.'

'Do you ever see Mr Muldoon?' I asked.

B.J. shook his head. 'That little bastard never gets any invites to the G.G.'s house,' he said. He sighed, as if from the burdens of office...I decided to assist him by changing the topic.

'Do you have a souvenir shop?' I inquired.

B.J. waved the query away...he looked all business. 'It's against the protocol,' he explained. But Penny broke in on our tete-a-tete. She said, 'Well I reckon, you know, we shouldn't even be here, eh. Not for much longer.' I realised she'd been glancing repeatedly over at the door...it was almost as though she hoped someone would come in and prove her right...B.J. responded with another sigh and put his hands flat on the desk...then he pushed himself up from his chair. 'Yeah, haven't got all day,' he declared. We gathered our bags...we trooped out into the corridor once more, and B.J. started leading us onwards into the cavernous building...around a corner I noticed a tea tray on the floor...it was sitting abandoned on the carpet, pushed up beside the skirting board and piled high with dirty cups and saucers. All of a sudden, just ahead of us, someone came stepping backwards into our view out of a room...he was a thin, baby-faced young man, staring away from us and still talking to someone inside the room through the doorway...the man went on standing before us in profile, dressed in what looked like a well-tailored pinstripe suit...I could see his fair hair was short but stylish, cut just long enough at the back to nudge the top of his collar...with a casual movement the man began leaning up against the doorframe, using one bony wrist for support. B.J., Penny and I, the three of us, had come to a halt...it was hard to believe what was happening...the man was just staying there, ignoring us, smack in our path. 'And they should finalize those numbers pronto for the Christmas party,' the man said clearly. 'Because he won't want such a large crowd prior to heading away to Kinloch. Chop-chop. All right?' The man shifted and reached out with one hand into the room... next he pulled the door closed in front of him with an air of having got a good job done...at that instant the man turned and finally saw us in the corridor, and I noticed his mouth set into a grimace of surprise...before me, B.J. was hunching his shoulders...he stepped forwards to try getting past the guy, and I thought it best to follow. 'Hold on a minute,' the man said. The man's Adam's apple was beginning to poke out...it was rising and falling above the fussy wide knot of his tie...everything about his gaze showed that he didn't think we belonged here. I hesitated, and could feel the same hesitation in the others...in the stillness I could even hear Penny moving behind me...I glanced round and saw that she was backing away, clutching her string bag against her chest...all of the bangles had fallen to collect on the crooks of her arms...her eyes were bulging in their sockets again, just as they had in the Cuba Mall, and she gave off the look of a child being picked on. 'What are you lot up to?' I heard the man asking. I turned towards him once more, and I saw that B.J. was answering him with nothing but a shrug...quickly I swung myself up flat against the nearest wall.

'This is so bloody tiring,' I announced.

I tried hard to make it appear that I was resting...I waved vaguely towards the man, and paused...but mostly I was wondering what on earth I was going to say next.

'You know,' I suggested to B.J. after a moment, 'we should just ask this bloke. Ask him. Go on.'

B.J. looked lost...I pushed myself off from the wall, back onto my own two feet...it was maybe a bit fast for somebody who was being exhausted, but all at once I stepped up very close in front of the man...I stared at him sternly, peering into his pale-brown eyes, which were only inches from me...I could tell he was wearing a great deal of spicy aftershave.

'We been wandering around here for twenty minutes, eh,' I growled. Then I asked, 'Bloody which way is it to the kitchens, mate?'

The man said, 'Kitchens?' He was so near I could watch the pupils of his eyes moving...his gaze was slithering up and down as he tried to take me in.

'This place is a fucking rabbit warren,' I said.

It was fun to say 'fuck' into the man's face…I held his gaze…I thought I'd try saying it again.

'Yous fellows ought to put some fucking signs up,' I added.

'Why do you want to go to the kitchens?' the man asked. I paused once more…it was a good question.

I said, 'Don't you know?'

I tried hard not to look down at my own feet…I was jiggling my dufflebag vacantly on my shoulder…but I'd got nothing more to tell him. 'We have to get ready for that ballroom function,' I heard Penny say behind me. 'At eight,' she offered. 'Oh, right,' the man agreed. He seemed to relax…quickly he took a step back away from me, as though very happy to do it.

'Maybe they didn't bother to invite you, eh,' I said.

The man glanced down and brushed a non-existent speck of dust from his immaculate jacket…but in a huffy manner he started to provide detailed directions to the kitchens…I pretended not to understand…he sighed, and repeated the directions with obvious exasperation…I couldn't resist asking him if he was sure. At last, we headed back down the corridor the way we'd come…we were armed with lots of instructions…over my shoulder I waved at the man as he watched us go.

'Hooray, bro,' I said.

By now, I didn't want to leave…I kept suggesting we go into the kitchens and cook something, but B.J. was leading us away, walking us past a row of French windows that gave a clear view of the main grounds…presently I realised we were looking out across one of the porches I'd seen as we'd approached the house…a beautiful, low white railing broke our gaze, and then the lawn stretched vast beyond it…the grass had been mowed and rolled into long, regular stripes, and the whole lawn was wide enough to show the shadows from clouds moving above. I thought the residence seemed much better from the inside, staring out, but I appeared to be the only one interested…Penny treated everything around us as an annoyance…B.J. acted as if he'd simply seen it all before. We left the house at a fast pace…we didn't even try heading back the way we'd come…B.J. said security at the gate was a lot fussier about people going out than getting in…instead he marched us off across the rear of the grounds and we entered a rough, untended garden area, with thick scrub and clumps of ferns…we were heading in single file along flattened grass on a winding track…the grass cover changed to a yellow and muddy slush, and it was difficult for Penny to walk in her sandals. After several minutes we saw a high, chain-link fence rising up above the bushes before us…we drew nearer, and as the scrub fell away I could see what looked like a school's playing fields, with hockey pitches and changing sheds, on the far side of the intricate wire…Penny and I halted for a instant, and Penny began scraping some mud off the bottom of one shoe against the edge of a large stone…but B.J. just strode on up to the fence…he pushed the sleeves of his jacket back from his wrist and took a grip on the wire…immediately he started to climb, and the links rattled and shook each time he made a new handhold, dragging himself up. Penny and I watched B.J. and hesitated…then, reluctantly, we threw our bags up over the top of the fence so as to follow him…I'd forgotten the packet of foolscap I was carrying and heard my duffle-bag land on the far side with a hefty thump…that made me decide it might be better just to carry Half-Arse over with me… after a further moment's pause Penny slipped off her sandals and hiffed them over too. B.J. had already finished climbing when Penny started and he stood waiting on the other side, holding the wire…before I came up after Penny, I took time to watch her kicking in annoyance at the long hem of her skirt as she tried to place her feet…I admired the pleasant, rounded shape of her bare calves as she swung over the wire at the top… then I became very aware of being the last and that it wouldn't do to be left behind. I scrambled upwards in an ungainly fashion, gripping Half-Arse's strap with a few fingers as best I could, and slung myself over the top…finally, on the way down, I grew tired of hanging and swinging about awkwardly…I glanced down to where Penny and B.J. were waiting…B.J. was standing, looking patient, and Penny was bent forward, resting her hands on her knees and puffing…I thought I'd risk a jump. It was from still well up on the fence, so I kept Half-Arse cradled in my arms and dropped…the fall was the comfortable part…it was the landing that hurt, but the ground turned out to be softish and my ankles absorbed most of the shock…I straightened up, and discovered that Penny had remained bent over and was still puffing in her crouch. 'That was amazing,' she managed to say to us between slow breaths. B.J. said, 'Yeah, I like to get involved in things.' Penny's fingers looked red and sore from clinging to the wire…she raised her head…I could see that she was gazing at B.J. with her cheeks shining and with her eyes wide and bright from their own inner heat.

It was really quite a trek to B.J.'s flat...after just a few minutes of walking Penny started complaining about blisters on her feet...several times we stopped, waiting to let her pull off her sandals and rub her soles...later we halted to buy takeaways, and we sat for a good while on a park bench to eat them...it meant that we were all three of us tired and a little irritable well before we arrived. When we finally turned into B.J.'s long straight street, he pointed expectantly off in the direction of his flat, still far in the distance...it was up near the top of a rising slope that looked surrounded by bush-clad hills behind...the three of us commenced walking towards where he'd indicated, and we headed past a collection of ugly construction sites...we walked and walked until the road tapered off into a bottleneck and grew steep. By now we were trudging upwards among shops and industrial buildings and then past rows of rag-tag wooden villas lining each side of the street...the ancient houses were set hard up against the narrow, uneven footpath and I felt as if they were almost leaning forwards and down on us...I saw that some had concrete garages beneath with alleys off beside them, and with small, odd steps up to their gates, and bent wooden railings...they had ramshackle, up-and-down bay windows and balconies jutting out in places...all of the villas were in poor shape, and their cramped frontages, several storeys high, were covered with zany, random combinations of Dayglo-coloured paint that had already begun flaking off. We arrived, at last, at B.J.'s flat and paused on the footpath as he said, 'This is it.' I looked up and could see that his building was also tall and in crummy condition...the weird purples and greens painted across its weatherboards were faded even worse than the colours on the villas hugging it at either side...I didn't know why I was so disappointed, though I was...but next to me a moment later I heard Penny let loose a long sigh of contentment. 'This is Abel Smith Street,' she told me. We approached the porch and the dirty-brown, panelled front door of the house, and I wondered how often Penny had been here at other times...the door was unlocked and we filed without ceremony into the entrance hall...the sun was just beginning to droop in the sky outside, so the high walls of the passage appeared dim and half hidden in the shadows. B.J. led us down some dangerously steep stairs into a dark basement...he switched on the lights and revealed a large, low-ceilinged living-room before us...it was cheaply furnished, except for an expensive-looking stack of stereo components arranged on a cabinet beside a single massive black speaker over in the farthest corner. Penny and I stood self-consciously at the bottom of the stairs, setting down

126

our things…Penny seemed to be feeling as much a guest as I did…but B.J., as though from habit, started mooching towards a breakfast bar built into one wall nearby, with a small, jumbled kitchen area back behind the counter…his footsteps echoed up from the bare planks of the floor. Penny left me and wandered away, but I stayed put and gazed about…a drab, badly-worn brown sofa and a pair of dowdy wooden chairs were grouped in the centre of the room…there was a flimsy, baize-topped card table set up alongside the chairs, and a number of large purple cushions had been scattered about on the floor near the sofa…I took in a sheet with a blue starburst pattern pinned across the far wall. So, I thought, this is a flat. B.J. had gone and leaned far across the grease-stained counter of the breakfast bar with his back to us…he stood on tiptoe and kept glancing carefully about at something on the other side of the counter…I heard him grunt in an unhappy way, and with his head half out of view he announced to us that probably everyone else in the flat was going to be coming in sort of late, like usual. 'Get yourselves some coffee,' B.J. muttered. He straightened up and made a brusque wave at the kitchen area…then he turned towards the pile of cushions spread on the floor and with a comfortable sigh threw himself down on one and rolled onto his back. Penny was well away from me now across the room…I headed past the edge of the breakfast bar and into the kitchen to make us all a cup of something…the sink and the rows of cupboards and drawers in the walls around me smelled of fatty, boiled meat…I tried searching for an instant-coffee jar but found only the stainless-steel electric jug instead…it was pushed deep into a drawer, squeezed in beside a loose stack of red-and-black *Rip It Up* magazines. I hauled out the jug to fill it, and as I did so I took a moment to examine the magazine covers…they were all copies of the same issue, with the same large cartoon of a busty woman below the title…the picture was only a drawing, but it made me start thinking whether Penny would look that good naked…I hoped so, and started to think of Penny naked in quite a lot of detail. From his position down on the floor B.J. had begun explaining to me about his job with a bakery in Manners Street…he spoke in a loud, steady voice, as if I'd just inquired about what he did…perhaps he thought I wanted to know his life story instead of making some coffee…in the far corner, at the edge of my vision, I saw that Penny was rummaging back and forth through a dog-eared row of albums by the stereo. I tracked down the coffee-jar at last…the only cups available were a few dirty ones that were lying piled in front of me in the sink…for a moment I thought about washing them, but decided not to bother...this didn't really seem like that sort of place. B.J. went right on talking while I busied myself...he lay on his cushion, stretched out, with his hands up behind his head for extra comfort...over by the record-player I could see Penny was tapping a copy of *Born to Run* out of its black-and-white sleeve...she was smiling with a distinct air of satisfaction, as if pleased at her own good taste...she flipped the glossy record around between her fingers before putting it onto the turntable... when the first song began to boom out of the single speaker, B.J. sat up and tried to continue his explaining about the bakery business above the music. 'Yeah, the job's always going on for pretty much the whole night,' he called to me. He scratched with his fingers along the edge of his beard. He said, 'But I'm usually done and on the street by lunchtime, though. Earlier than that, it's not going to happen, because eight varieties, that's a hell of a lot of different types of bread. I mean along with rolls, eh.' Next B.J. began telling me how bloody important it was not to leave the dough in the mix for too long, so I leaned my elbows on the sticky top of the breakfast bar, flexed my arms and struck up a fake attitude of attention...I had nothing else to do while waiting for the jug to boil...across from us, Penny stood playing with the album sleeve and beating one foot in time to the music, and didn't appear even to notice us talking...I wondered to myself how old B.J. was, since he looked older than me...I wondered how long he'd been living here in this flat...it must have been quite a long time that he'd been working at his job, but I thought perhaps he only looked older than me because he'd been knocked around a little by life. 'Hey, hey, listen to this,' Penny was announcing. She waved at B.J. to be quiet...she crouched over the turntable and started fiddling with the stylus. 'Springs-teen, you know, he put my name in here on this bit,' she called. The music jumped about as Penny tried to find a place on the record...then she stood up and we took in a few bars.

'That's "Wendy",' I said. 'He's singing, "Wendy, let me in, I want to be your friend, I want to guard your dreams—"'

'It's not! It's "Penny" if you listen right,' Penny insisted. She reached out and jerked the stylus up from the track with her long fingers...there was a terribly shrill sound through the speaker and I hoped to goodness she hadn't scratched the record. 'Yeah, Penny used to think Mick Jag-ger was singing, "Gimmie shoulders",' B.J. said to me, still in a cheerful tone. He rolled his eyes for good measure. 'I did not!' Penny yelled back with delight. She turned up the volume...I watched her begin dancing on the spot in her corner of the room...she'd closed her eyes and appeared doing her best to act as though lost in listening to the song. 'Yeah, the worst is Easter,' B.J. called out to me above the music. 'You know, hot cross buns for three days, eh. And sometimes we get these bloody farmers come in ordering fifty loaves. Their big visit to town, sort of style.'

'What's the most popular type of bread?' I managed to ask over everything.

I hoped answering this question would keep B.J. busy, because the jug was shaking and boiling with a load of steam...I reached around to the wall to unplug it. 'Oh, that'd be doughnuts,' I heard B.J. shouting. I poured out three coffees, using the filthy teacups, and put the two cups for the others along the edge of the breakfast bar...I took a sip from my own cup and thought the coffee tasted bitter, even nasty, and it scalded my tongue...Penny was turning down the volume...she put the stylus back to the beginning of the record to let us hear her favourite track once more...then she approached me across the room. As she passed B.J., she glanced down at him and said, 'Why don't you ask Andy what he does, eh?' I watched Penny reach out and take a cup from the counter...she held the cup in both hands near her mouth and moved over a little towards B.J. once more...she wriggled her hips slightly as she tried drinking the coffee. 'He's writing a novel,' she added between sips. B.J. had lain back on his cushion again and propped himself up on one elbow...he gazed at me without blinking, not saying a single word, and his new silence left me feeling rather shy...I supposed it had never occurred to him that someone might write an entire actual book. 'What's it about?' he asked finally.

'I'm not too sure,' I mumbled, and took a second, larger gulp at my scalding coffee. I swallowed it down and over the sting in my throat I started to say, 'There's a process. See, I'm still really just trying to figure out a means of easing into things.'

I didn't like making this type of admission and could feel both my cheeks were hot from blushing...I guessed B.J. would probably ask me why I was always carrying around Half-Arse, and maybe he'd want to take a look at it...next would come a whole lot of bantering...I felt I needed to get ready a writer's sort of snappy replies. But instead, B.J. forced his mouth wide open and yawned...he got up with an effort from the floor and scratched lazily at his back...he seemed to have exhausted his fledgling interest in literature...I heard him say something about hitting the sack upstairs because he had to head off for work again soon in the wee small hours...B.J. stretched his arms high above his head and lowered them slowly. 'Yeah, there's a spare bedroom right up the top floor at the rear,' he said. His dark eyes drifted from Penny to me and then back...I watched him begin gradually shuffling sideways to leave the living-room. 'Well, you know,' he muttered, and his boots scraped across a rough patch in the floorboards. I felt sure that he was hoping one of us might delay him...but Penny didn't utter a word, and I took care to do nothing. B.J. grumbled, 'Reckon this job plays hell on my social life, eh.' After another moment or two he vanished up the stairs and we could hear his footsteps padding steadily off somewhere above us...for a while Penny and I waited together, listening in silence to the next song on the Springsteen album...Penny appeared in no particular hurry to move, but my heartbeat had quickened into a small storm at the thought of what we'd most likely be doing soon...I supposed that going to bed with someone, having sex, wasn't as unfamiliar to her as it was to me, but I felt this would be the fulfilment of an implicit bargain between us...it was a bargain that had been struck when she'd agreed for me to come hitchhiking with her. At the end of the song Penny began hinting about how nice things would be if we had ourselves a cold bottle of Blenheimer...but I didn't offer to go out and get us one...I had the idea that I shouldn't leave her side even for a few minutes...if I did, our bargain might be broken, and she'd be in bed with B.J. when I got back. Instead we went right on with our waiting... we both went on listening to some more music which Penny chose... she thumbed through the row of albums again and selected a few tracks here and there from some other records. At last the front door slammed violently above us, and we heard several people, probably the flatmates, heading in a rather raucous bunch upstairs...Penny suggested we should go hunt for the spare room while there was still a decent chance of us having it...she was already returning the stylus to its rest and shutting off the stereo...I didn't need any kind of persuading. Together we went softly out of the basement with our gear, hoping not to be discovered, and we started climbing the house's wooden staircase...it was narrow and creaky, and with the noise every footstep felt precarious...we crept along by the walls in a half crouch, as if this might be quieter, but at each corner our efforts only left us feeling more and more excited...we made gestures to be silent that were really like encouragements to be livelier...Penny grabbed at my shoulders from behind and giggled, and her touch just aroused me even further. Nobody seemed to notice us, but it was a relief

130

to find the back room on the top floor was empty…we entered without trouble and switched on the light, still in a silly mood, pushing and patting at one another…the bedroom was cramped and smelled of mould…I saw the walls were raw plaster and the only window was boarded up, with a row of old beer bottles lined across the sill…there were marks all over the plaster from where posters had been hastily pulled off. I bent to put my things down in one corner of the room while at the same time I inspected the bed…it was merely a simple wood-and-wire frame with a mattress, lying directly on the floor…there was an untidy bunch of rough grey woollen blankets piled on top and I stooped lower to unfold them. 'There you go,' I heard Penny say quietly at my back. 'You're showing me that nice little arse again.' I turned and straightened up…now I was completely inflamed by desire…I stepped over to Penny and put my hand behind her neck and kissed her…her billowy yellow hair fell round my face as I clasped her nearer. Penny moaned a little…she kept kissing me back but moaned again…I thought perhaps I was squeezing her too hard and let her go. But Penny only shuffled away from me, dropped her bag to the floor and started slipping off her sandals…I watched her using the toes of each foot for leverage on the sandals' heels…then she bent and began unwrapping her skirt…gradually she let it slide away from her onto the floor by her feet…it was an excellent, excellent sign. I took the hint and started to pull off my own shoes and clothes…I stripped quickly, got down onto the bed in my underwear and slithered beneath some of the blankets…at once the harsh wool in the bedcovers commenced scratching against my skin, but I ignored it…instead I noticed how my erection was sticking up uncomfortably past my underwear's elastic waistband, and it felt best to allow a bit more helpful freedom for my cock…below the blankets, using them as a screen, I struggled and hauled my grundies off. Afterwards, I wriggled about to watch Penny again…she was standing with her long bare back to me…she'd already taken off her gauzy blouse and removed the bunch of bangles from her wrists, and now she was patiently folding the blouse up…I thought how this was all going to be so much better than masturbation…it was hard to believe I could be this excited and not actually having sex yet. Penny hadn't been wearing a bra…when she turned around towards me, I saw with mild disappointment that her chest was almost flat, but as she bent forward once again I thought her blonde hair fell beautifully across her nipples…now she was stepping out of her panties…I caught my breath as Penny crouched down naked amongst the bristly blankets...she pushed them all aside and then sat cross-legged, brazen, before me. I shifted and sat up straight on the bed opposite her...we were showing everything of ourselves to each other...I let my gaze settle on Penny's dark pubic hair and saw how it was thin and wispy over her skin...I simply couldn't get my thoughts away from it...I felt fluttery with pleasure. 'You know, don't you, that B.J. and I used to go out,' Penny declared quietly. 'That was, oh, back when he was living in Masterton, eh.' It seemed a very poor time to mention this sort of stuff...I dragged my eyes from Penny's pubic region to look up into her wide face...she was evidently waiting for me say the right thing.

'Were you—' I strained to think of a word. 'Were you lovers?' I tried.

Penny grinned. She said, 'We used to fuck like rabbits, if that's what you mean.'

'Is it a problem?' I asked.

I certainly felt that, for me, it wasn't a problem...I didn't care how many people Penny fucked like a rabbit, so long as I was one of them... she'd paused, and so I waited too...I wanted her to know that I was taking her seriously. 'No problem,' she said at last. I leaned over towards her and started kissing her again...with one hand I tried a little exploratory play across her tiny breasts...I had to restrain myself from leaping on top of her, but after a moment Penny put her own hand up to mine and pushed it off...she pulled her mouth away and stopped us once more. Into my ear she whispered, 'This just has to be, like, a very spiritual thing.' She placed both my hands firmly by my sides...now we'd returned to sitting together, with a gap between us...I nodded my head to hide my dissatisfaction at halting.

'I see,' I said.

Penny uncrossed her long legs and got up...she stepped off the bed... she went to her bag, stooped down and began delving into it...this gave me a very generous view of her own naked arse...I was mesmerised by the pink flesh in her buttocks, shifting about, and by her confidence...I decided that it was a safe bet somebody so sure of herself would be on the pill and that I didn't need to ask. Penny took out a small fat scarlet candle and positioned it with care in the middle of the floor...finally she lit it, moved to the doorway and switched off the light...I heard her stumbling back to the bed in the sudden darkness...with a rustle of blankets she sat down opposite me once more as the candle's faint reddish glow expanded...it was beginning to shine and glide across our skins, leaving a backdrop of shadows. 'Fucking, see, is like an expression of cosmic consciousness,' Penny murmured through the gloom. 'Everything has to feel just right and ready, eh.' I thought that all this talk sounded wildly sexy…but then I thought that I'd been feeling just right and ready for years.

'I see,' I said.

'I want you to make me come,' Penny whispered. She paused, and next she added, 'I want you to do it with just, like, an idea in your mind that's so special. It'll be completely like—' she halted again '—it'll put me away totally in the zone. I want you to try and make me come without touching me, eh. Like, you know, just by the power of all the mental cosmic forces you'll unleash.' The rosy candlelight continued flickering gently about us…for a moment I searched through my eager memories of *The Little Red Schoolbook*…everything that I'd read about coming seemed to involve a lot of touching. But I didn't say a single word of reply…I thought of ignoring what Penny had said and just grabbing her anyway…all the same she sounded as if she'd genuinely decided on this, on me using no more than my mind to touch her body and do a bit of caressing. 'Close your eyes,' Penny was intoning, still in a quiet voice, 'and reach out to me in a really, really Tantric, a really beautiful kind of way. What we have to manage, see, is we have to get beyond the plane of individual sexual existence.' I thought that sounded like a pity…but I went ahead and closed my eyes as she asked…I wondered if B.J. had gone through all this hocus-pocus…I definitely wanted to make Penny happy, but I marvelled that B.J. had got to fuck her like a rabbit…even so, I didn't want to think any further about him, asleep, somewhere in the flat below us. Instead I tried reaching out to Penny hard in my mind as I was supposed to…but this didn't seem nearly as much fun as what we'd been doing a few minutes ago…in spite of myself, I started to imagine actually playing with her breasts once again…after a while I was wrinkling my forehead from resisting the urge to peek…I took a deep breath and struggled to unleash an extra-big burst of cosmic forces, but nothing appeared to be happening, and Penny was silent…we were still stuck on the plane of individual sexual existence. Next something moist and warm seemed to cover the top of my cock…I opened my eyes and saw that Penny's head was face-down in my lap…her heavy, crimped hair lay all about over my knees and I watched her head bob…then she sucked, and suddenly I saw stars. It took everything I could do to stop buckling into a ball…my entire body was centred on my swollen penis…I let out a groan of sheer, delicious excitement. But at the sound Penny ceased...she lifted her head and detached herself from me...finally she shifted back a bit, leaned quickly over sideways and blew out the candle...in the new pitch-dark space all around us Penny's legs brushed by me to stretch out on the mattress...I felt her pulling up the blankets away from me and around her...presently I could tell that she'd rolled over and was going to sleep. I sat stock still for a while, unsure if I was going to ejaculate everywhere onto the blankets or not...at long last I didn't, and lay myself down over the remaining part of the mattress available...Penny hadn't left much space for sleeping on...but there beside me she was already breathing regularly. My balls felt hot...they hurt with a raw, nauseating ache...the blood went on throbbing fast in the back of my ears...every so often my penis would start to calm down, but it would touch against the merest something and spring back up into life...I was sick of it, and I didn't feel spiritual. While I was lying quietly and trying to get comfortable, there was plenty of time for me to ponder what had gone wrong...at least, I supposed that the thing really had gone wrong, which meant there'd been a problem...I supposed that Penny must have been somehow disappointed with my performance...my sex life was turning out to be a lot more complicated than I'd planned.

In the morning I awoke with another hard-on...it was poking itself up, bold and insistent, toward my navel...Penny was asleep and I was feeling chilly...I found she still had most of the blankets. Elsewhere I could hear other people moving in the house...they were shifting about and using the toilet...after a minute or so I put my arms up over the back of Penny's smooth, wide shoulders...I began to nuzzle behind the base of her long neck...with an erection wobbling between us, this seemed fairly natural. Penny stirred and woke, and she turned around sleepily... she appeared surprised to find me so close...I saw her pull her head back away from mine with a jerk. She muttered, 'Hey, I don't like any more than just a cuddle in the mornings.' We cuddled for a while, and I didn't try anything else...Penny remained uninterested. 'Just a cuddle, eh,' she hissed at me unnecessarily. I thought her tone suggested a larger store of anger...soon I was only nuzzling at her to be polite...my balls were starting to ache again...finally we got up and dressed. We came down the stairs of the house, both of us feeling more than a little irritated... we moved without making the least effort to be quiet, but we met no one else until we tramped to the bottom of the awkward, steep steps in the

134

basement living-room…a man with a thin, pale face and a prominent moustache, and with lank brown hair down to his shoulders, was sitting on the sofa…he was smartly dressed in a dark-purple jacket and some well-ironed jeans, and he was stretching his legs out before him, flexing his ankles to admire the neat black tips of his own calf-high boots. When the man glanced up and spied us both, he stopped shifting his feet about and said, 'Ho.' I saw the man held a coffee mug that looked empty cradled against his stomach…he didn't bother to move further or say another word, except to start fiddling with the chunky ceramic mug with his fingers…it was as if he was hoping to coax something more from it to drink.

'Good morning,' I said. Then I hesitated, and added, 'B.J. Lamborghini told us we could stay here. Is that all right?'

'Yeah, and where the fuck's the coffee?' Penny growled from just beside me. She pointed past my elbow at the man's cup…but the man just seemed nonplussed by this…his moustache twitched gently as he wrinkled his lips…he drew up his legs close to the sofa and nodded in the direction of the breakfast bar. 'There's no milk,' he said after a moment. The man put his mug down on the wooden floor in front of him…with deliberate care he got to his feet and ambled past us. 'No milk,' he repeated with something like satisfaction. I turned, and watched him as he reached the staircase…he commenced plodding his way upwards and his back disappeared into the shadows…after I was certain he'd gone, I went to over the breakfast bar and began making us some coffee. Penny went and perched on the edge of one of the wide cushions B.J. had been using yesterday… she sat up straight-backed with her legs tucked alongside her…I watched her arranging the folds of her skirt, waiting while I worked. When finally I brought Penny a cup, she suggested that we should shove off a bit later into town…she seemed to have forgotten all about last night…she also seemed to have forgotten about the Heads' Ball happening in Christchurch…she held her steaming cup in both hands below her chin and stared away at the wall as she spoke. 'I reckon that today we can probably get B.J. to score us some dope,' she said. There was a wistful, resigned tone in her voice…I thought Penny's today sounded a lot like the one we'd just been through, but on this day I wanted to go to Christchurch…I remembered that I did, in fact, have a friend there, a friend from school, whose name was Struan Callow. I mostly remembered Struan as another fellow who went at things in his own way, and that he had big plans to study law down at Canterbury University…during high school he talked about it on and off for a good couple of years in a dreamy kind of fashion…it was as if his entire life, his real life, the nitty-gritty, was all waiting to happen in some place and time that was far removed from the here and now…he was very eager to get out of Palmerston. I'd liked Struan…I knew he quite often took extended trips down south…not so long before school broke up, he even told me he'd already got a flat sorted out down there…we were hanging around on the dank asphalt playground beside one patched-up brick wall at the back of the Main Building…Struan had looked me in the eye and repeated the address with care. The flat was somewhere in Salisbury Street…I felt rather proud of myself for remembering it…I thought that going south to catch up with Struan seemed like an excellent idea.

'Tell you what,' I said to Penny. 'Why don't I try getting us some milk from a dairy?'

Penny managed a distracted smile…I wasn't even sure that she was listening.

'My money's up top,' I said.

I went off without waiting for her answer…I hurried up the stairs and through the house, moving faster and faster…the whole place appeared to be deserted now…up in the bedroom I plucked my bag and Half-Arse from where they lay on the floor…then I stole with them quickly back down all the steps to the entrance hall while hoping my feet weren't thudding about too loudly…I had no idea how carrying things in secret might sound to other people. At the very last moment I was possessed by a powerful sense that I shouldn't go…for someone who'd never actually had sex I was getting quite well practised at running out on women…this sort of leaving in such an unhealthy hurry made me feel a bit guilty about the concept of personal freedom. But by now I was outside on the porch once more…the sharp click of the front door closing behind me was a relief… it was a hopeful sound that brought me back wholly to myself…I scampered off the porch and down into the sloping street. Soon I was trotting along in the centre of the roadway…I was breathing in great, soothing lungfuls of the morning's cool air…my footsteps gathered pace on the asphalt's easy descent, and everything felt fresh and good and clean… even my balls felt better for the exercise.

FOUR

I kept heading for the harbour…I was pretty sure the sea was far off, away in the distance across town, and so to find the harbour it seemed right just to follow one of the straight, important-looking streets…there were plenty of streets available, all running down in something like rows alongside the nearby hills…after a good while I left the central city behind and was walking amongst a cluster of grim industrial buildings…I passed what appeared to be sheds and warehouses, and soon their rough raw-concrete and brick walls were shimmering a little before me in the low morning sunlight. Next the city wharves came into view…the road I was on drew me closer to them, and there were watersiders already out at work…I could see their activities through the gaps in the railings of a high wrought-iron fence beside me…they were driving forklifts across wide storage areas crammed with rusting containers…they were up in the cabs of tall cranes, shouting to each other…a fat man in grey overalls was marching past some containers laid in a row and banging against each of their doors with a stick, but whether he was doing it for fun or for a genuine reason I couldn't tell. I began to feel cheered by all this, and lucky…I wandered past a noisy lumberyard with still more people at work…now there were hopeful blue flashes of the sea appearing almost everywhere I looked…at length I saw a sign tied up on a pole with some wire, directing me to the interisland ferry. The access to the ferry terminal was off beneath a long overpass in the Wellington motorway, almost hidden amidst the dark cement piles below…it was difficult to approach on foot…it was down between sloping ramps and service lanes for vehicles…I struggled on towards the terminal amid the damp, ribbed-concrete pillars for the motorway above, hearing the booming echoes from traffic noise, then ducked around some road signs and finally reached the building's entrance…all this hubbub made me feel as if I, too, was going to work. The terminal, when I got inside, looked large and newish, crowded with passengers and busy…everybody was bustling across the grey lino floor between counters, and there was shouting, banging machinery and the constant grumble of the cars passing on the motorway close overhead…by the time I'd lined up and bought a ticket at a counter from an officious-looking man with a wart on his nose, and who had swollen veins in his hands, I was feeling comfortably tired…I searched all about for somewhere to sit, but in the end I had to stay standing…other people were loading their baggage onto freight wagons over in one corner and it was a pity I had nothing to put on the wagons too, but I kept my duffle-bag on my shoulder and Half-Arse in my grip…I consoled myself with the thought that I was a real traveller. An announcement came over a loudspeaker at the far end of the terminal and turned out to be totally incomprehensible…even so, I saw everyone near me was now making off for the wharf and I drifted along with the group…there was a strong smell of slime and mud as we went through some doors, and then we could see the wide pale-green hull of the ferry suddenly up close and rising above us…it extended almost out of sight, looking oil-stained and worn, and not only real but far more real, somehow, than I was ready for…there were long braided mooring lines sloping up beside it…the ropes shifted slightly up and down as the ship moved on its haunches in the water. All of us on the shaded dockside, I realised, had paused together in an expectant body to gaze at the ferry… but I noticed the boarding ramp was away at the other end of the wharf, covered, and with a glassed-in entrance which looked shut and barred… the ramp snaked up alongside the hull of the ferry like some rickety appendage, ending at a protruding gangplank…I returned my attention to the crowd standing about in limbo around me and to the dirty seawater slapping casually against the dock near our feet. Even though I hadn't asked a question, someone next to me announced with a knowledgeable air that the ferry was called the *Aramoana*…this made me think of trying to find the name on the ship's side and I moved off a little to locate it…the word was tucked away back in a sort of corner, and while I was staring up at the white letters with satisfaction the boarding ramp must have opened, because suddenly I turned round and saw everyone else was gone…they were all gathered into a hasty queue by the glass doorway. It was far too late to claim a good place…I was one of the very last to tread up the ramp's steep passage…the gangplank rattled and jolted as I marched across the gap onto the ship, able to observe nothing more than the backs of the people in front. Once on board I tapped my foot several times against the smooth, sealed deck…I wanted to check that it was genuine and solid beneath me…I'd never been on a boat before…I'd been in a canoe on the Centennial Lagoon in Palmerston North, but I suspected now that it didn't really count. I saw there were puffy orange life-buoys fixed in a row to a riveted cabin wall beside me and broad drainage holes were spread at intervals along the bottom of the gunwales opposite…not far off I could hear the gangplank being withdrawn to a clattering of chains…

there were yells and whistles from the shore, and more bustle…I felt like a traveller again…then I could see that the wharf had begun creeping away…we'd already cast off, without further to-do or fanfare. For a time I amused myself by wandering amongst the other passengers on the covered decks…I opened some doors and stuck my nose into a few rooms, trying to take in everything at once, but I gave up at last and settled for leaning over the white-painted rail…I stared down at the bubbly whoosh of the water rushing past…far behind us the pale wake was spreading off towards the city in the distance…some gulls swooped about and squawked with enthusiasm overhead. We began churning in a lazy manner round some steep, bush-clad land at the edge of the harbour…the sunlight and its shadows played over the tree-lined slopes…there were lithe little bags of cloud drifting in a row across the hills…past the Heads, in the open sea, the wind freshened and the ferry's movement grew stronger, rougher… soon the boat was pitching and smacking into swells…a few people at the rail beside me started to look nervous, but the steady motion only left me feeling exhilarated. I decided that I must be a good sailor and felt like a successor to Caesar or Alexander…I was heading off to conquer some bright new world…I wondered what the South Island might look like when we actually got there. After a while I went up to the top deck and observation area…for a quarter-hour or so I tried sleeping across an empty row of red plastic chairs, but they were hard and uncomfortable, and the sight of the funnel was too distracting for me to keep my eyes closed…I got up at last, feeling suddenly very bored…there was a hand-lettered sign nearby with an arrow underneath, indicating hot food downstairs, and so I followed its direction below decks…at first the sign didn't seem to lead anywhere, but after a few minutes I found a large cold cafeteria filled with passengers…the room was ringing with noise and activity, and everything in the entire place was sliding about in the swell. At the counter I queued holding a tray, but I was stuck in the line for ages amongst pushy parents and their toddlers…from a warmer I got myself a pie, and next some sandwiches from a clear plastic case…the oily aroma of the pie made me hungry as I waited for the till and cashier…there was only a bare wooden bench against the back wall at which to stand and eat, because the whole dining-area was already hogged by other passengers…at the seats and tables they looked taciturn and remote as they pushed their food into their mouths…the lino on the floor beneath our feet was wet with puddles of salt-water and the bench I ate at smelled of disinfectant. Afterwards, I didn't know what to do…I roamed about in the ship's narrow and mostly empty corridors, marvelling that below decks there was such a maze of places…finally I turned a corner and could hear a lot of muffled talk and laughter…the noise was coming from just beyond a varnished wooden door which had a metal pad on it instead of a handle…the door swung lightly with the motion of the boat, opening and shutting on the sound from within. I pushed against the pad's slick surface and immediately entered a very large, very crowded room, where I was bunched up amongst a group of hearty-looking people who were standing with glasses of beer in their hands…they were all talking at once and had flushed, animated faces, and the air was sticky with warmth and smoke…I could see that further off most of the room was furnished with a muddle of low white Formica-topped tables which had yellow vinyl-covered chairs spread around them…all of the chairs were occupied by people…they were leaning in close together over the messy tabletops' collections of ashtrays and crumpled-up newspapers, chattering in a convivial manner and holding drinks and cigarettes clutched near their mouths…in the spaces behind them still other people were standing, hovering, also with beer glasses in their hands…everyone was acting as if nowhere else in the world could be better than this. Off along the opposite end of the room there was a brightly polished wooden bar that was even more crowded with drinkers…the bar seemed like a good place to make for, and I started shuffling towards it in an unobtrusive but determined way…I sidled around the backs of people…the customers who were standing nearby me were swaying from the boat's motion or perhaps from their beers, and a low lampshade dangled perilously close to my head…but still nobody noticed me, and no one stopped me to ask my age. Then, best of all, I spied an empty spot…it was an unoccupied stool with a threadbare cloth cover, along at one end of the bar near some dirty red curtains…I got to the stool and sat on it quickly, rocking a little on its unsteady top and putting down my things…I propped my foot against a heavy brass rail at the base of the bar and found the counter up before me was cluttered with small towels, glasses and beer mats. So, I thought, this is a pub. I imagined only an airplane could beat a ship for this sort of comfort…I swivelled round a bit on my wobbly seat and still nobody paid me the slightest attention…even the chubby barman in his wrinkled white business shirt was well away from me, off down the counter…he was bent far across the taps, talking to someone…I leaned past the customers sitting alongside me to see just who might be so absorbing for him…the barman was chatting to a buxom, blonde-haired woman with her sunglasses hoisted up snug on her forehead. 'Hell, that's what I reckon,' said a large man who was sitting on the stool right next to me. He swung around in my direction…he was bald-headed and wearing a wide-collared blue shirt…I thought he wore the shirt deliberately pulled open to show off his bull neck and broad, hairy chest…the man had been talking to the fellow next to him on his other side, but he spoke to me now as if we were continuing a conversation. 'Anyone can swim Cook Strait,' he announced. 'It's not all that fucking much of a distance.' Using one elbow as a prop, the man rested his back against the bar…he twisted a little on his stool so that the fellow on the other side could still hear him. He growled, 'I mean, what do they even need a ferry for? Let them bloody swim, eh.' The man nodded his big brawny head at me, and winked…I tried winking back.

'Just kick the bastards off the end of the wharf and point them in the right direction,' I said.

In response the man looked me slowly up and down…then he swung away again, showing me his back and the long slope of his shoulders, and went on having his discussion with the fellow on his other side. But the barman had appeared at my end of the counter…he gave me a quick, professional smile across the taps…I asked him straight out for a handle, and immediately he began to pour it.

'And throw in a packet of fags as well,' I added. 'With some matches, eh.'

I tried to sound as indifferent as possible, thinking it was best just to go for the whole hog…but the barman said nothing, not a word, and stayed bent forwards over the taps…he was working with short, practised movements…he gave me my glass and slapped a packet of Rothmans and a box of matches onto the counter…I made sure I had my money all set so there'd be no argument. I sipped a little at the cool top of my beer…I was already a man who knew his way around a shandy, because I'd had a few at Christmas dinners at home, and there was a time at school when a bunch of us had whipped up black Russians out of some Coke and the remains of a bottle of vodka, and got pretty woozy…but I'd never simply had a beer in a bar before…I unwrapped the cigarette packet and, after a bit of fiddling, managed to get a smoke lit…this gave a nice impression to the room of me being wholly occupied, and I used it to examine what was going on around me. I could hear that several of the people sitting at the tables nearby were racing drivers...they were talking of bringing their cars on down to Wigram...they turned and leaned over the backs of their chairs to chat to people standing, or to people at tables behind them, as if they'd known everyone in the bar for yonks...they laughed hard at everything that was said. I laughed as well...I tapped the ash from my cigarette into an ashtray at my elbow like a pro...I even wondered if I, too, might look a lot like a racing-driver...my beer tasted fine, and the condensation was gathering thick on my glass when I'd finished the drink down to the bottom...I got the bartender's attention and ordered myself another...in the end I had several beers, because they just seemed to keep on getting better and better. I was feeling nice and loose by the time we finally docked at Picton...in the bar everyone else around me appeared to understand within a moment that we'd arrived and what they should do, and the mood changed...everyone got up and the room started to empty out fast...I decided that, for me too, it would be a good idea to disembark from the ship in a hurry...that way I could hitch myself a quick ride from among the racing people who'd come with their cars on board. I headed along the airless, crowded corridors below decks, looking to get up top, following a few punters...I was clutching Half-Arse and felt excited by the genius of my plan...but the exit for upstairs was difficult to find...it seemed to keep switching to somewhere else...it was always someplace further off, not here, not close, but down yet another bloody corridor...at last it dawned on me that one reason for this just might be because I was drunk. I wasn't woozy, I was very drunk...I was shit-faced drunk...but everybody else was sober, and everybody else was striding off in different directions with the same expression of confidence and solemn determination in their eyes...that didn't help. Within me the luscious glow from the alcohol went on becoming stronger and stronger, a sort of slippery barrier between my mind and my coordination...what was worse, someone must have shifted the entire fucking floor when I wasn't looking...I'd started sliding and bumping against people wherever I went, but nobody would keep still for even an instant...it was incredibly provoking...soon I couldn't stop giggling at the strangeness of the whole idea. Finally I managed to get to the upper decks...by now I was conscious of appearing like a crazy person, a person who was reeling into other passengers and apologising for giving them trouble...it was an effort just to get across to the gunwale with my bag and Half-Arse and lean on the rail...my knees were going and it felt a lot like being thrown about in open water, even though

I was really alongside a dock and gazing down at some insipid, blue-roofed ferry buildings…I thought of taking one of the life-buoys and leaping over the side in a dramatic gesture, but by a piece of luck the gang-plank came up on the edge of my sight, maybe because I'd turned my head…I staggered in its direction before the thing could get away. Down in the terminal I went on a long, shamefaced trek to find a place to pee… my condition was wretched…I got myself outside through the front doors at last and shambled off from the low terminal building, trying to ske-daddle for somewhere in the distance…occasionally I glanced back, but the ferry and the building itself were already turning into a stupid blur…I wandered past some corrugated-iron storage sheds, a stretch of rail tracks and some shunting yards with battered wagons and containers, and found my way to the shoulder of a small, tidy-looking asphalt road… there I caught up to the vehicles from the boat. A steady convoy of cars and campervans with families sitting them was filing past alongside me, but nothing else, and I guessed that by now perhaps all the racing drivers had gone…a good spot for hitching was up ahead, an area of muddy grass by a large, square-shaped white traffic-sign…I made for it and stood with my things piled at my feet, leaning into the road with my thumb cocked out…the cars were passing close to me and through the windows I could discern the passengers' faces, the dads, the mums and kids…everybody appeared tanned and fresh, and very happy to be released from inside the ship…everybody was already on their way, and since they were all headed in my direction I decided that I wouldn't really mind too much just cadg-ing a lift with a family…but the vehicles were driving right on past me one by one, and I could turn and watch them cruise up the narrow, straight road towards the nearby hills, growing smaller until they faded into the bends and curves of the terrain. I turned back and focused on what was still approaching…a loaded-up blue Austin Mini was drawing slowly closer with a fat, motherly woman in the front passenger seat, and as the Mini got even nearer I felt sure she was smiling broadly at me…she had a round, double-chinned face and old-fashioned, bouffant hair, and there were chunky glasses pressed into her plump cheeks…the woman said something to the man who was driving and then struggled in her seat…I saw she was trying to put her large head out of the car's window… I started crouching to grab for my bag and Half-Arse, wondering if I'd be able to squeeze into the back of such a crowded-looking little ride. 'Get a job!' the woman suddenly screamed at me through the gap she'd got open above the window-glass. She yelled it again...the Mini accelerated by with a sputtering sound, and I could hear the woman and the driver shrieking with laughter...but it rather cheered me up that I might appear like someone so footloose, so fancy-free...I thought that this had to be the proper type of image for an active young writer. The last cars from the ferry continued to dribble past...they left me behind until there was nothing coming at all...I'd no choice but to start walking along the road on my own without a ride, and I set off...after quite a time the houses lining the street came to an end and were replaced by rough grass...only the power-lines in the sky above were keeping me company...I kept on tramping along, footstep after footstep, but the nearby hills were no nearer. Instead, the heat around me began to well up against my face...the dazzling sunlight seemed trapped amongst the low-sloping, sparsely timbered countryside all about...I was sweating in the sun-baked air and finally sat down, buggered, on the loose gravel shoulder to rest...I wished I'd walked far enough for the scenery to change a bit more...I'd heard that the South Island was a big place...this part certainly was. After a while I got up and forced myself to make some progress once again...I no longer felt so badly drunk but I was ready to give up on the whole concept of hitching, and I was still wondering what to do when a car went past and then started to slow down...it was a smart white Holden station-wagon, gleaming so much that it could have been straight out of the factory...it had drawn to a complete stop on the empty road, not far up ahead of me. I jogged clumsily towards the shiny car with my bag and Half-Arse clasped in my hands...the possibility of this ride flitting away before I got there disturbed me and so I kept my eyes focused on the rear of the vehicle and willed it not to escape...I could see a brown jacket on a hanger swinging gently at the back window as I approached...I came round into the road on the driver's side, feeling more than a bit seedy and out of breath...it was hard to remember if I'd actually put my thumb out when the car had gone past. The driver was sitting alone and had his window open...I moved up alongside the vehicle and stared down at him...he was dressed in an open-necked, striped business shirt, and I thought that he must be a commercial traveller...he was wiry and looked in his thirties, with a rugged, reddish square face...there was something not quite right about his hair...it was short, but flat and rather too nifty, and I wondered if the hair might be a rental and couldn't help grinning at my own shrewdness. The man was gripping the smooth rubber-lining on the top of the steering

144

wheel with one hand…he twisted his head to one side and leaned to gaze up at me…his shirt was so new and clean that I could make out the creases along the arms. 'You a student?' the man was asking. His milky blue eyes twinkled a little as he spoke.

'No,' I said. 'Listen, can you give me a lift down towards Christchurch?'

'That's where I'm headed,' the man responded. He raised his hand from the steering wheel…there was a flashy gold signet ring poking up on one of his fingers…the man motioned me towards the other side of the car. 'Reckon all your problems are solved, eh,' he said. I went round to the passenger's side and climbed in…I closed the door and dropped my bag by my feet, gathering Half-Arse in my lap…we took off almost immediately and began moving at a fast clip…the man kept his gaze fixed forwards on the road as he drove. 'You're not a student?' he asked me again after a while. He had a gruff, rumbling voice…I could see his heavily-lined face only in profile…he was concentrating on the narrow highway and on keeping up our speed.

'Not me, no. But I am actually going to visit a student friend of mine,' I offered.

This appeared to satisfy the man for ten minutes or so…we drove on in the powerful car through trim green farm country…we were passing easily among rolling hills, a series of them, and across long shallow valleys…at each bend the landscape seemed lusher and the paddocks more alive with growth…when the man opened his mouth to speak again, he continued as if there'd been no break at all in the conversation. 'Because some of yous students lead pretty wild lives, eh,' he said. The man still didn't take his eyes off the winding road…I wasn't really sure how to reply to this, not being a student. 'Parties, girls, boozing. You do much drinking, do you?' the man asked me. Even now I could feel the beer from the ship's bar sloshing about in my stomach.

'Not much,' I replied truthfully.

We drove on in silence once more…the highway was broadening and so the man managed to increase our speed…we passed through a tiny township, just a few houses, which was clustered all along one side of the road…I was beginning to feel sleepy and my eyelids were dragging themselves downwards…my thoughts drifted pleasantly off into the back of my head and I felt settled and comfortable…but without warning the man started talking again. 'What about dope?' he said. 'You ever smoke any dope, eh?'

'Oh yes,' I said.

I was surprised to hear him mention it...I wondered if my magical experience with Penny was going to be repeated...I wondered whether the kind of driver who picked up hitchhikers usually got them all amazingly ripped. 'Reckon I could use a good smoke about now,' the man was growling.

'Yeah, that'd be great,' I agreed, with my eyes half closed.

'Yeah,' the man said.

'Oh yeah,' I echoed him.

'So—what, have you got any?' the man cut in. I started to notice that something was going on, and became properly awake...we were driving so fast that the steering wheel was jiggling a little in the man's grip, but the man kept his hands tight along its top...he went on adjusting the steering wheel with firm movements, staring straight ahead. I supposed that back at the roadside I'd probably looked the type...I'd looked like somebody who might have a bit of marijuana on him...the thought made me suddenly self-conscious about my appearance...I put a hand up to my hair, and felt how stiff and matted it was...tufts of it were pushing in odd directions from my head...next I saw the man had stuck his jaw out, as if anticipating an answer he wouldn't like.

'Well, you know, I wish I did have some dope, sorry,' I replied for him in a rush. Then I added, 'There's some cigarettes, if you want one.'

The man ignored this...he flexed his lean and taut shoulders while his hands stayed on the wheel...he continued to drive without giving me so much as a glance. He was saying softly under his breath, 'A beautiful day. On a beautiful, sunny day.' I spied a yellow AA sign up ahead through the window and tried focusing my attention on it...the sign came up too quickly to make it all out, flashing past the car, but I felt fairly certain it suggested that the Wairau River was getting near. 'Yeah,' the man said aloud after a few more bends. His voice was low, measured. He said, 'A smoke'd be real beaut about now.' We swept through a long, sandstone-layered cutting...in spots the limp, grassy soil at the top of the bank was slipping over onto the brown strata of rock, threatening to cascade onto the highway beside us...I licked my lips, and thought how the man's incessant talk of marijuana had made me want a smoke as well. Just past the cutting, the man put his foot on the brakes...abruptly he pulled us over...the tyres scattered some roadside gravel and everything in the Holden was thrown forward...neither of us was wearing a seatbelt and I

146

had to put one hand out flat against the dashboard while with the other I wrestled to keep Half-Arse safe, pinned in my lap. But we were halted... the man had already switched off the engine...he gazed across at me and slapped his palms on the steering wheel...deep, dark grey creases were starting to furrow around the sides of his mouth. He asked, 'You bloody sure you haven't got any dope?'

'I'm sorry,' I said.

I shrugged my shoulders in confusion...I thought it might be best to come across with a cheerful look on my face...I tried for a smile, but didn't have much success. 'You just broke rule number one,' the man snarled. He turned away from me for the door...he began fumbling agitatedly with the handle, as if it wouldn't behave in his grip, but soon he got out of the car and onto the road in a series of jerky, flurried movements... the man was busy muttering to himself...I could see his lips working but couldn't tell what he was saying...I watched him stamp stiff-legged around the front of the car to my side. When he arrived, the man hauled open the passenger door with violent energy...he bent down and pushed his square face forwards into the vehicle to stare at me up close...a faint smirk was beginning to play along the edges of his mouth. 'You don't know what rule number one is, do you,' he said.

'Don't touch my car?' I ventured.

The man reached in...he grabbed me round the back of the neck by a handful of hair. 'It means you don't fuck me around!' he yelled. The man yanked me by the hair from my seat...he got me half out of the car, twisted my head sideways and banged it into the door...I groaned, and he wrenched me further out and threw me down onto the edge of the road... Half-Arse had come flying with me from my lap...it skidded up alongside my face on the gravel and I felt its plastic case clip my ear...from the ground I could observe the man tossing my duffle-bag away into a nearby paddock. I started to get up, but my knees were wobbling...the man swivelled on one heel and kicked me in the stomach...then he did it a second time...I supposed that getting up must be breaking his kind of rules as well. I was on the ground again, and winded and gasping...I rolled myself with difficulty onto my side...the man was staring down at me with both of his feet planted far apart...he had his fists clenched and was looking as if he wanted to hit or kick me again, but next he seemed to change his mind and turned away...for me it was a relief...it made two of us who didn't want me being kicked in the stomach anymore, and I even felt glad

147

when I saw him reach out and slam the passenger door shut. The man strode off around to the other side of the car...he climbed in and got the engine started with a wild roar...almost at once the tyres began rolling away from me across the sparkling asphalt...I lay and watched the back of the vehicle disappear rapidly up the road. Not moving much, not even letting myself think, I waited quietly on the tarseal for some good while till I'd well and truly got my breathing sorted out...finally I picked myself up and felt around the sides of my head...my scalp was hurting, and one arm had lost a little skin, but in all fairness I'd had worse experiences at school...that was the advantage of getting of an education in Palmerston North. I examined Half-Arse and discovered there were only a few ugly scratches on the case...I could make out the edge of my duffle-bag in the paddock, not too far off, lying in a grassy hollow near the end of a slope... I started a weak and unsteady struggle to climb up over the slack wire of the boundary-fence and fetch it. But by the time I got back to the road, I'd decided to go on hitching...it wasn't like there was a lot of choice, out in the middle of nowhere...anyway, I didn't think that running into a bad apple should spoil things, but I told myself to be a lot more careful about rule number one in future. For half an hour I tried putting out my thumb and had no joy...despite my desire to keep going at hitching, it was all getting to be a gigantic bore...then a large articulated truck passed me and slowed in a harsh rumble until I saw it pull over to the edge of the road with its air brakes still hissing...quickly I ran up towards the back of the truck, and as I did so I could feel puffs of smoky heat from the exhaust on my face...it took a few moments to trot the whole way past the long, grimy blue-and-white panels of the trailer. The truckie poked his head out from the window of the cab as I drew near...I guessed he wanted to get a look at me and check on what he'd stopped for...he was youngish, maybe in his late twenties, and wearing a floppy, white terry-towelling hat...I could see his tubby, rather appealing face with its small features beneath the hat's low brim, and how his babyish pink cheeks were framed by a pair of thick red sideburns...the sideburns extended to his jaw-line and stretched towards his mouth, as though almost ready to become a beard. The truckie had put one plump forearm out onto the window-edge, still surveying me...he took his arm nervously in again but soon thrust it out once more, perhaps unsure of how to get himself comfortable...I had time to see he was dressed in an old green woollen jersey and seemed to have no shirt on beneath it...God alone knew when he'd first bothered

148

to put the jersey on, since its neckband was frayed and ragged and hung loose on his small chest. 'You a traffic cop?' the truckie barked at last.

'No,' I called back above the grumble of the idling engine.

I'd halted a short distance from the driver's door high up in the cab, clutching my gear. The truckie stared down at me and I heard him asking, 'You related to a traffic cop?'

'No,' I answered again, and shook my head. I said, 'I've never even met a traffic cop.'

'Well, you bloody have now,' the truckie called down. He wrinkled his blunt little nose with satisfaction. He said, 'I used to be one, eh, and even I can't stand the bastards.' I shook my head again as vaguely as I could, trying to indicate whatever of yes or no might be the best answer to all this… but the truckie just told me to hurry up and get the fuck in…he said his name was Stunt. I bustled around the big square front of the throbbing artic…then I began clambering up onto the narrow step on the passenger's side, uncertain about how to manage things…I was holding Half-Arse and my duffle-bag in one hand and trying to shove them on ahead of me past the pitted rubber rim of the tyre…with a final effort I swung myself and my baggage up, opened the door and got into the cab. Inside there was no proper space for my feet…the floor in front of me was crammed with what looked like C.B. equipment, along with a litter of paper milkshake cups, soft-drink cans and an empty, sauce-stained chip punnet…I had to manoeuvre myself over it all onto the slippery, dirty passenger seat…I rested the soles of my shoes on some bits and pieces of electronic stuff and kept my knees up high…next I leaned out again to reach for the door and slammed it shut…at once the noise of the engine all but disappeared. Stunt had started fiddling with a long gear lever in the console beside him…then slowly the truck began to move and we were bobbing forward onto the highway…I could feel the weight of the load dragging and shoving behind us…the whole warm cab gave off a sticky smell of grease, and there were oily marks smeared everywhere across the wide dashboard in front of us. But it seemed to be taking Stunt a lot of work, more and more, to make the artic pick up any speed…I watched him keep pushing one of his short stumpy legs down hard to thump his steel-toe-capped boot on the accelerator…each time he moved to change gear, his bottom left the old grime-stained red cushion on his seat and his other boot pummelled the clutch pedal…with both hands he hauled at the low steering wheel, one way and then back…it was as if he was forcing the artic onwards through the restless efforts of his entire body. All the while Stunt kept telling me things…he spoke in a loud, distracted voice with a lot of heat in it…at first I didn't listen but he went on anyway, repeating himself…Stunt said that he was headed for Port Lyttelton, and he didn't have even a minute to spare…he said the boss had given him the whole fucking consignment at the last moment, but sometimes a man just had to do the job and bloody get on with it, because that was the way things were. Finally the artic started to proceed at a good pace…I was glad to put some distance between myself and the spot where I'd got knocked around for not having any dope…we were seated so high up that we could watch the road down in front of us slipping in under the cab…Stunt ceased his disturbing activity with the gears…but by now he'd launched seamlessly into a loud monologue on how he used to be traffic cop. 'See, I couldn't stand all the hassles, eh,' he was announcing. Stunt's small frame stayed bent awkwardly over the steering wheel, and his eyes were flicking constantly between the dashboard and the road…his hat kept jiggling down onto his brow and occasionally he thrust it up again, but he carried on talking all the time while he drove. He shouted, 'Just out of town we used to wait, sitting on some useless bloody intersection for hours and hours, seemed like forever. Always out in the boondocks, eh. And you catch some joker speeding, there's yards of paperwork. Bloody waiting for some dumb-arse cow cocky to come by. Hours. I mean, bloody hours.' Stunt paused for an instant and compressed his lips together…I didn't even bother trying to say something in reply, but next he nodded his head as if acknowledging my opinion in a fair-minded sort of way. 'I mean, it's a good uniform and everything, eh,' he said, 'but the whole flaming world hates you if you're a traffic cop, and that's no lie. I mean, every-fucking-body. And the things you get yelled out in your face, mate, when you drag some blokes over. One fellow, he kept calling me a jumped-up little meter-maid, I'll never forget it. It was out in—oh, I don't know where it was. But I mean, your own next-door neighbours won't speak to you, eh. And now, right—thing is, even I can't handle the nasty buggers. They just fucking sit there, eh, waiting for a man to come by. And I mean, fair doos, it's not like I'm ever up to nothing, or any kind of shit like that.' Stunt went on and on in this way…it was for some good while…he was a man haunted by his past…he turned out to have had other jobs too, as a storeman and as something in a glass factory…it was on his mind to discuss them all, but I couldn't work up the enthusiasm to pay proper attention. At last Stunt began to call out, 'Hey, listen. Hey!' I thought perhaps he was going to complain but he twisted round instead, skewing the cushion on his seat, and fixed me with his gaze. He said, 'You know what, mate? You've got to fucking speak to me if I start looking sleepy. All right? Talk to me. I mean, I've been driving all the way down from Auckland since bloody last night, eh. She's a fair hike, boy, I can tell you, and I don't want to get this shit into Christchurch any later than tea-time.' But I had no need at all to help keep Stunt awake...he was the worst man for yackety-yak I'd ever met...I got the impression that long-haul trucking must be a one-sided, lonesome business...also my head was starting to feel badly bruised after its accident with the door of the Holden...it felt easier just to sit, trying to ignore the motion of the cab...I went on staring quietly at the highway sliding towards us and thought we were making good time. We were following a flat, narrow thread of road along a rocky coastline...a set of rusted rail tracks ran steadily beside us to our left, and beyond lay the restless blue shallows of the sea and a smooth horizon that seemed very close...to our right, steep shadowy escarpments were hard against the road, all covered in a jumble of windblown bush...here and there a stray tree or a branch poked out and menaced us as we went by. We approached a town which consisted only of some small timber shacks, a few telephone poles and a row of high streetlights...a welcome-sign at the edge of the place declared it was Kaikoura...Stunt didn't even bother to slow down...once we'd passed through I rolled open my window for a bit of air, and a deep briny smell fell into the cab...I'd got used to the bobbing rhythm of the rumbling truck...I imagined we'd be in Christchurch in no time. But suddenly we rounded a bend and Stunt drew us up to a fast stop...the brakes wheezed as we halted, and the whole cab shook and swayed a little...we were at the far end of a long trail of traffic that went stretching up round another bend, but none of the cars before us was moving, and none looked as if they had for some while. Stunt cursed and let the engine idle...the artic immediately began to rattle from the effort of staying still...in the side mirror I could see other vehicles stopping and falling into line behind us...for several minutes nothing else happened, and we stared forward into the traffic and at the temptation of the yellow no-passing line...after a bit Stunt told me that it might be a fucking shifted fucking load up there. Gradually a string of cars started to appear coming from the other direction...they filed past us without much speed...through their windscreens I could make out the faces of the drivers, and they all of them looked tired or tetchy...the string of approaching cars ended, but still our line wasn't able to move forward an inch. Stunt had commenced drumming his podgy fingers on the steering wheel...he kept on announcing how it could probably be an accident that was bloody holding everybody up...each time he said this, he spoke as if the idea had newly occurred to him...he said that it might also just be a flock of sheep, but it might be a really fucking big one...I saw he wasn't even trying to control his impatience. At last Stunt snorted and groaned as though he'd had enough, and he pushed open the creaking door on his side of the cab...I watched him climb down to the road with twitchy, angry motions and simply march off...he was stamping forwards along the highway, at the fastest pace his unwieldy boots would allow, in the direction of whatever was blocking the traffic...his driver's door stayed flung wide open where he'd left it. I waited...I wasn't sure what else to do...I sat alone in the truck while nothing amid the scenery moved or made a sound...after fifteen minutes or so I spied Stunt's head in its towelling hat up above the cars and realised he was wandering back...it was a relief to see him...he arrived at the cab, and clambered up and onto his seat without giving me a glance. 'Struth,' he said finally as he settled himself, wriggling about. Stunt took a deep breath...he reached over for the door and slammed it shut...then he started muttering to himself about some buggers and scratched at his hairline up under his hat. 'That's a new one on me,' he said more clearly. I waited for him to tell me what was happening, but Stunt only gazed off in silence out of the grimy window of the cab...once or twice he nodded with a severe expression on his rounded face.

'What is it?' I asked in the end.

Stunt appeared startled by my question, but he soon launched into explaining...he told me there was some dumb, bloody, fucking fire across the highway...it was a sort of fucking gorse fire spread out all over on the flatlands up ahead...the fire service was out there with hoses and they were dampening stuff along both sides of the road. 'It's bloody hot over there too,' Stunt said, as though clinching an argument. But even from our position high in the cab I couldn't see anything special...there was still just the traffic, stalled in front of us, and I wondered if this was maybe some type of hairy story that Stunt was making up...I let my gaze run along the line of waiting cars extending away to the next bend, and I searched in the distance for any signs of fire...there were some small, ineffectual-looking tea trees around us and ordinary farmland, and a far-off border of more trees...from the other side of the highway a steady

152

column of vehicles was coming by us once again, and ours was still the wrong side of the road to be on...that was about it. For what seemed a good long time we went on waiting...Stunt didn't say a word, and I wished now that he'd speak up and come out with something worth listening to, but finally, and with no warning, the body of traffic far before us started filing onwards in a loose shuffle...at last we were moving too, though only at a crawl, bumper to bumper with everyone else...beside me Stunt had to keep tapping alternately on the accelerator and the brake...we jerked about uneasily between the cars immediately before and behind us. After a few bends at this slow pace we entered a lengthy straight...I saw a cluster of wide-bonneted white police vehicles and a pair of fire trucks parked up ahead on one of the shoulders of the road...just next to the fire trucks an official-looking man in an orange safety-vest was waving a red flag without much enthusiasm...but away in the near distance, on the edge of a low paddock, long clouds of grey smoke were swelling up into dark twisting plumes. Gradually we passed the police cars and trucks and drew closer to the smoke, and there was more of it, a lot more...it was rising everywhere in an extended sheet on both sides of the road and covering the view...it was bulging, heaving itself into the air, and it was getting worse, but we crawled on towards it amid the line of traffic and I felt an ache of worry tightening in my chest...I noticed that battered old yellow signs had been propped up at odd intervals against the fence-lines, warning us with 'Slow Down' and 'Hazard'...perhaps they were in case anyone had failed to notice that there was a fire going on everywhere we looked. We crept further along, until soon we could see where the grassy edges of the road beside us had been scorched black and the pasture away in the paddocks was burned down to stubble...the pall of smoke was still ahead of us, spread across a ragged front in shapeless layers that were darker at the base and whiter at the top, but next a blaze somewhere amidst it all seemed to flare up and release a sharp, crackling sound... that was followed by a massive burst of heat and I felt my cheeks being seared...almost immediately flakes of hot ash started dropping onto the cab, and I hurried to get my window rolled up tight. As I worked the handle, I glanced off into the sky above us and saw the sun had become a fat peach-coloured ball...it was effortless and felt weird to stare directly into the sun's bloated glow...around us in the cab the air was hard to breathe, and I could tell now that there were definite red flecks of fire outside, licking along the tops of the blackened pasture not far from us...

we drew ever closer…it occurred to me that no one had checked whether Stunt's load might be flammable…then the smoke blew over us and there was nothing else to see. The smoke's fine-grained dust was like a blanket pushing up against all the windows of the cab…suddenly even thicker, darker patches of soot began attaching themselves to the glass before our gaze…Stunt switched on the lights…their beams bored into the mist, but it was a struggle just to make out the car in front. 'Struth,' Stunt was grumbling. 'Bloody struth. Fucking bloody struth.' The artic ground forwards in low gear and Stunt leaned up hard over the steering wheel, peering at the grubby windows…in his worried features I could still see traces of his former excitement, and it surprised me to think that I also must look the same way…the pair of us were sweating from the intense heat…some of the hot smoke was getting into the cab and Stunt tried running the fan, but soon he gave up…he squirted water on the windows and used the wipers…both of us had started to cough. But all at once, as if parting a curtain, we were through…we were moving upwind with the other cars still around us, and the road and even the fence-lines came back into view again…the sunlight was falling fresh and bright and welcoming in our eyes. I opened my window to get some air and saw that we were passing more fire trucks…there was even the van for a TV One news crew, parked at the roadside and displaying the channel's rainbow logo painted on its door…I watched a cameraman standing near the van with his portable camera balanced up on his shoulder and obscuring half of his face, and cables trailing behind…a small crowd had gathered in close to him, though they mostly stayed at a respectful distance to his rear…everyone was gazing off at where the man was filming, but he kept the camera pointed well away from us, panning over the steadily smouldering paddocks. For a moment or two I enjoyed some more lungfuls of the clean, country air…up ahead along the roadside now, facing us, several voluminous tankers were halted in a row…I began to think that perhaps the authorities were only concerned about flammable goods which were coming the other way. Then the traffic around us started to increase speed… the string of vehicles along the road in front broke up and we moved with more ease in the new space…Stunt gave the windscreen a final squirt of water and a wipe. 'Ain't nature a bitch,' he announced. Beside me, his face was grey with a fine covering of ash…I touched my own cheeks, and grit came off on my fingers…I looked down and saw my clothes were filthy from head to foot.

'That was amazing,' I said.

'Yeah,' said Stunt.

'Really amazing,' I said.

Stunt didn't bother to respond to this...instead, he merely resumed his monologue and began philosophising about good old nature and how you could never count on her...sometimes I heard him break in on himself, as if interrupting a conversation...when he did, he described again the drive we'd just had through the fire...with each new account the whole experience appeared to be longer and more dangerous. I wanted to leap in and agree with Stunt...I also felt it had been hideous and exhilarating, and I wanted to add my comments, but he never seemed to give me a chance to contribute...rule number one with Stunt was to keep on listening. Early in the evening we reached Cathedral Square...I recognised it at once from photos I'd seen at some point...Stunt dropped me off by the rear of the stone church and he told me, unnecessarily, that this was the centre of town...I got out of the cab with my bag and Half-Arse and slammed shut the truck's door, thinking how nice it was to have arrived at last. I stood beside some skinny, mangled oak trees, stretching my tired back and limbs, and waved Stunt goodbye...he waved at me across the passenger seat in a hasty gesture, and I saw that he was already struggling to put the artic in gear again...I could easily imagine he was still carrying on our conversation at the same time...Stunt finally got the truck to pull away along the road, and next it merged with the traffic and was gone. I waited, feeling how the air around me was filled with the swish and sounds of passing cars...at length I roused myself a little, and walked along the side of the church until I paused in front of a large monument, a war memorial...the memorial seemed to consist of a bunch of bronze people gazing about and trying to ignore a half-naked angel who stood above them on a pedestal...the angel was straining her slim body and arms upwards to hold a sword aloft, and all of her, bare-breasted and slim, was streaked with green smears...I spent some minutes imagining where her nipples should be...this left me feeling strangely restored. Soon I started drifting around the paved square, searching tentatively for a phone box... despite the passing traffic, the entire place appeared deserted...there was only a lonesome-looking flock of seagulls, strutting and fidgeting on the steps before the church...after a while I reflected that Cathedral Square didn't have a real cathedral...furthermore, it wasn't really a square...it was just an odd space with a lot of tall, glass-fronted buildings arranged around it in a hodgepodge everywhere I turned and looked. Along the top of a building nearby I caught sight of an illuminated news-board with letters drifting in flickering orange lights across a screen...I'd never seen an illuminated news-board before, and it made me think that perhaps I'd come to a big, exciting city after all...with that I returned to my search for a phone box and found one at last by a plaster-walled kiosk in a corner...I squeezed inside the box and lifted the receiver...there was the whine of a dial tone, which helped me feel that my luck was in, and a chunky phone book hung from a chain by my shoulder...among the dry, curled pages near the front of the book I managed to look up the number for directory...I dialled, and spoke to the operator. I was able to get Struan's phone number by using his address, but there was no pen anywhere in the box for writing things down and I needed to rely on memory...for an embarrassing moment or two I begged the operator to repeat what she'd just said, and then finally I muttered Struan's number over and over until I'd finished dialling it...I pushed the long chrome button A when the ringing tone stopped, and waited. After some instants I could hear Struan's light, breezy voice...it was coming through on the line amid some clicks and crackles, as if from far off, but I knew immediately it was Struan from the careful way he always enunciated his words. 'Well, well, well,' he said, after I'd told him where I was. 'Didn't know you were rolling on into town like this out of the blue. Still, that's mostly your style, isn't it.' Then he added, 'Your sort of backward savoir-faire.' I wondered what exactly he meant, but Struan was chuckling to himself and didn't bother to explain... he was famous for his biting wit...I'd been hoping that Struan would be pleased to hear from me...the thought that he might not be too pleased had never really crossed my mind...but it crossed it now. 'And so, what do you want?' I heard Struan asking.

'Well, is there any chance I could crash for a while at your place?' I suggested.

I knew that I was letting the words tumble down the line...there was more anxiety in my voice than I'd intended. 'Yeah, of course. Stay as long as you like,' Struan said decisively. I felt a sudden welcome rush of relief...I almost missed what Struan was trying to say next...it was something about me getting my act together and hurrying, but Struan seemed to guess what was up and repeated himself in a severe tone. 'Look,' he said, 'I'm off to a big party this evening, so you really will have to shake a leg. Drag your shit over here fast. And I mean fast—because I expect

156

you've just invited yourself along for the ride, you lucky thing, you.' I started to say some garbled thanks, but Struan interrupted...he was telling me he lived not too far off and within a fairly good walking distance...I put in more coins so that he'd have time to explain the route...Struan said he was right next to the intersection with Victoria Street, and I got him to explain that too. After hanging up, I set off from the Square at a determined pace and didn't stop to pay much attention to the view around me...there was an old bridge across some sort of creek...there was a small pleasant park with a floral clock, but I kept my eye out mainly for signs up on the lampposts...they were indicating the streets Struan had told me to find...I kept my act well together and hurried, and on the way I reflected that in a big city a fairly good walking distance was always a long bloody stretch. At last I came up to the Victoria Street intersection... it had several roads all meeting and crisscrossing at once beside a fancy-looking ancient clock tower in one corner...I'd already started out across the complicated intersection when an exciting new thought occurred to me, that I should make a brief detour and keep on going straight up Victoria Street...at that instant, further up the long unbending stretch of the street, I could see only low commercial buildings and shops set hard against both sides of the road...the sun was so well down in the sky that it had one side of the road wrapped in shadow while the other side still gleamed with expiring yellow light...but somewhere up along Victoria Street had to be the offices for the Caxton Press. I was absolutely sure of it...the street's name was the same as the address in the *Landfall* I'd perused at Stokewood...I got myself over the intersection and past the nearest corner...I marched on up the road, hoping I wouldn't have to go too far. It was a bit of a job but quite soon I saw a sign for the place I wanted, across on the shadowed half of the street...the building was small and detached from the others on either side of it...immediately I headed over the road towards it, feeling thrilled by my own proven cleverness. But the Caxton Press office looked a lot less grand than I'd expected...it was just a tidy, two-storey converted cottage pushed up against the footpath, with a neat pitched roof and brick walls painted over in some sort of off-white colour and trimmed in black...there was a low veranda along the front, and beneath the veranda I could make out an ordinary grey-green door between a pair of large dark display windows. I reached the kerb and drew up in front of the building...the display windows nearby were strangely unlit and seemed bare, but I moved closer and spotted what appeared to be a swirling Caxton symbol facing out at me from one glass pane…I felt a renewed thrill at recognising what it had to mean… it meant that all this was a real publisher's. I stood still for a while on the footpath, resting by an iron lamppost…I was right in front of the office, just within an arm's length of the door…it was a temptation to reach out and knock and see what might happen…but I was too covered in gritty ash and my own sweat to think of going in…instead, I tried bending and peering into the interior of the premises through the display window next to me…but the display area had some sort of hardboard backing, and I could see nothing beyond the Caxton symbol and the dim, dusty cubbyhole behind it. So, I thought, straightening up again, this is a publishing house. I could easily imagine that, inside, people must be printing things…they were standing at massive raw-wooden tables amid a smell of sawdust and oil…they were inspecting factory-fresh copies of *Landfall* while the hot presses ran behind them…in my mind's eye I could see how their clothes were smutted with ink and grease from the typesetting, and how they smiled as at last they picked up and held the final products of their own long, monkish labour…they cradled the spines of the copies in their palms and they rubbed their thumbs over the sharp edges of the covers…just being there, before the building where it was all going on, made me want more than ever to write my novel. Next the indistinct shape of a figure appeared behind the glass panel in the Caxton-office door…the handle rattled as the door was pulled back and open…I saw a tall, slightly built man step out into the entranceway…he was wearing a brown jacket, a wide-collared plain grey shirt and a pair of rather close-fitting jeans, and he was coming out through the doorway while glancing back over his shoulder. The man had pushed both of his hands down into his jacket pockets…he seemed ready to get in a last word on the front step as he shuffled forth, but he turned, saw me and halted…he swayed a little as he paused, keeping the door open beside him with one of his jutting elbows…I could see now that the man had a lean, youthful face and that his dark hair was cut with a severe parting and a broad fringe that swept stylishly across his forehead…his hands stayed in his pockets… whoever was behind him had disappeared. 'Yes?' the man said quickly. I thought there was an odd look of amusement in his eyes. He asked, 'What do you want?' To me, it felt like a peculiar question…I was surprised he couldn't tell.

'I'm a writer,' I said, and shrugged.

'Good on you,' the man replied.

'I'm writing a novel,' I said.

The man pulled his narrow lips into a tight grin…it made a lot of lines come up on his face…I revised my idea of his youthful age and put him at somewhere perhaps in his forties. 'Well, isn't everybody?' he said. It was as though he was searching for something in my words to make fun of… but I dismissed that notion from my mind…I thought it might be best to get the conversation onto a proper, less peculiar footing, and I decided to press onwards, to be more articulate.

'You know, it's really not easy having a gift,' I said. 'I guess that artists must congregate at places like this quite a bit, at least until we're better recognised. So I could be wrong, sort of thing, but I suppose you're an artist too and I don't suppose you'd be all that famous yet either.'

The man visibly bristled…I imagined I'd been a tad too fast with my assumptions…I watched him hesitating. Finally he said to me, 'I'm the editor here, in fact.'

'Oh yeah?' I said. 'You mean like *Landfall?*'

The man was nodding his head, but I saw he was doing so with a hint of reluctance…I also noticed that not a hair in his delicate fringe was moving out of place…but the main thing was, if he was telling the truth, that I could scarcely believe my luck.

'Well, it's wonderful to meet you,' I said.

I held my hand out for the man to shake…I wanted to greet him as per etiquette, writer to editor, but he didn't reach for my grip…instead, for a moment we contemplated my hand in the small space between us… except for my smeared fingertips, the whole of my arm was powdered with thick black soot.

'I went through fire to get here,' I explained.

The editor let me lower my hand to my side once more…he hunched himself forward a mite from the doorway and looked past me down the street…he was bobbing lightly on his toes, as if he had things to do.

'I don't suppose you'd get out very much,' I said. 'I suppose, for you, reality must seem like quite a novelty.'

I smiled at the naive charm in my own witticism, because just like the editor I could act amused too…this could be the right moment, I felt, to make a lasting impression…but the editor didn't even bother giving me a reply…perhaps he hadn't really understood me, or perhaps my approach was just poor, and I realised that I might be missing a valuable opportunity by being too clever.

I asked straight out, 'Do you have any kind of advice for me?'

Even as I asked, I could imagine a highly polished brass plaque might one day be put up here in a special spot beside the door, engraved with something simple but profound...it would commemorate our meeting and what had passed between us...people would read the plaque as its etched inscription aged and darkened over the years to come...they'd marvel that *this* was where it had actually happened...they'd marvel that *these* were the actual words which had been uttered...then I realised that the editor had already started in on giving me an answer. 'Because I've just discovered a girl, a local student, lives in town,' he was saying quietly. He spoke in a pensive tone, as if half to himself. 'You know, someone with real talent,' he added. 'Quite a find, in fact. This girl, she can hit the ball out to the boundary line every time. You have to be able to do that, eh. Every time.'

'I see,' I said.

I was a little disappointed that I wasn't the find with real talent.

'Got anything else?' I asked.

'Illuminate the ordinary,' the editor announced. 'Try that.' He fixed me with a suspicious look, as if I couldn't illuminate my way out of a paper-bag...next he glanced up and down the street once more, and shrugged his shoulders. 'Listen, you just keep on writing,' he said.

'Oh, you too,' I said. 'You keep on writing too.'

I felt sure that what he'd just told me was a good tonic for all of us in the game...it was bound to be good advice...I also thought maybe the poor man needed cheering up.

'You know, you don't have to be an editor for always,' I said. 'Someday people will read *your* stuff. So what's your name again?'

But the editor had swung round in the open doorway...he lifted his hands out of his pockets, and I saw he had big gnarled wrists that were probably better kept hidden from view...he stepped briskly back inside, reached out and closed the door in my face with a gruff thud. I stood still for a while on the dim and empty footpath...a car went past, and then another, but I thought it wise to be patient and hang on for a jiffy...the editor was a busy man who'd most likely forgotten something crucial in his office...I thought he would soon come out once more and pick up where he'd left off...he'd be ready to hit the ball away to the boundary line himself...but slowly, finally, I understood that he wasn't coming out again until he was sure I'd gone. The load of this knowledge pressed down on my shoulders, and I turned away and crossed the stupid street...there was no traffic to worry about...there were no other people around anyplace that I could see...I began dragging my feet back where I'd just been along the deserted road. I was disheartened, though only for a minute or so...it occurred to me that the cruel grind of rejection had to be every writer's lot...sometimes editors could just hate to get their hands dirty... sometimes editors could even make mistakes about talented people as well...we were hard to spot. Before long I was on Salisbury Street, back around the corner...the street was a large multi-lane, one-way road, with a lot of cars that were hurrying past, and I soon reached the house with Struan's flat...it was exactly where it was supposed to be, crowded in beside a new commercial tower covered by slick white tiles...tucked in next door, the house was shabby, old and a bit slummy...it just looked like a two-storey wooden box. I stood for a moment on the asphalt footpath, eyeing Struan's place...it was narrow across the front, with two cramped pairs of double-hung windows spread along the top and a stubby bay window on the bottom floor, stuck into one corner nearby...the house's dull green paint seemed to cling forlornly to its brittle weatherboards and it was very close to the street, with only an unkempt red photinia hedgerow between the building and me...there wasn't a front door anywhere to be seen, but there was an uneven, patchy gravel driveway snaking alongside the house towards the rear. I started moving tentatively up the drive... no one appeared and stopped me so I felt a bit easier as I plodded forwards, though still I had to be careful of the deeply gouged potholes all around my feet...under the heavy shadows from the tower it was hard to make things out. But at the rear of the house I discovered a sizeable, grassy yard...it had a huge elm tree planted in its lawn at the far end, and the tree's branches were low and extended out towards me in full leaf... amidst the murky glow of the evening, the elm looked ready to explode with a kind of dark vitality...in fact, everything looked much more charming than I'd expected...further across the yard I could see the French doors of another low single-storey flat...the whole back area seemed like a small oasis hidden away from the street. I skirted the bottom of a badly-rusted iron fire-escape at the rear of Struan's building...next to it was an open passage with doors to the ground-floor flats and a stairwell lined with unpainted hardboard...I started climbing the stairs, keeping Half-Arse safe in one hand and my duffle-bag up on my shoulder...there was a

161

swollen pile of dried-out dog shit lying on the carpet runner near the top, and I stepped over it...solid wooden-panel doors were waiting on each side of the landing...I chose one at random and knocked. In a moment the door opened a few inches...Struan's face peered at me from the other side of the gap...his eyes rose and dipped, roaming as they took in what he could discern of my appearance. 'Oh my God,' he said. He pulled the door open wider...I could see immediately that Struan was rather different now from school...he'd cut his curly brown hair very short and on his upper lip he'd grown a dark, straggling pencil moustache...it all made him look particularly spivvy, like someone I didn't really know, but he drew the door back properly and motioned for me to come in. As I stepped inside, Struan moved to keep himself well away from my dirty clothes...his own outfit appeared brand new and from the high end of fashion...I saw his little, light physique was crammed into a small tan leather jacket, which he wore with a pastel-blue polyester knit shirt and some remarkably tight trousers...Struan was standing in platform shoes which gave him extra height, so that I was looking him in the eye as he shuffled back a bit to make room. He asked, 'What the hell happened to you?' I hesitated to reply, and paused just past the doorway.

'There was a fire,' I said finally, 'and it included me.'

Struan grinned, with his lips stretching crookedly up one side of his triangular face...it was what he always did when he was about to speak in a witty manner. 'Well that'll serve you right for smoking in bed,' he murmured. I didn't bother too much with showing any amusement, but instead I turned back briefly in the direction of the stairs...I pointed down the steps at the dog shit still lying on the threadbare carpet...I liked animals.

'Do you have a pet?' I asked.

'That fucking husky over next door,' Struan explained. He nodded, and stuck his chin out at the doorway opposite...then he gestured for me to hurry up and get further inside. 'Just be careful to, like, check the soles of your shoes, okay,' he said. But I was already shambling on into the narrow hall, eager to see what Struan had done with his flat...through another doorway on one side of the hall the living-room looked small and dark, and I entered and gazed discreetly about at it...the bare walls were covered with a rumpled brown scrim which hung slack in places but which extended round to some double-doors opposite...there was a crude brick hearth, stacked with unlit coal, a little to my left, and a flimsy-looking

162

record-player with a built-in speaker was on a box in one corner...hard up against another wall was a lumpy, discoloured beige sofa with no arms, and an empty wire coffee-table was arranged just in front of it...I supposed Struan was still developing the flat's potential. 'We're in a really big hurry, remember?' Struan announced. He took me impatiently by my free hand and started pulling me back from the living-room...my feet scuffed on the rough wooden floor...but I thought I rather liked the flat's uncluttered quality...I began to consider just what I might do with it myself to make it productive for a writer. Struan led me towards a half-open door on the other side of the hallway...he let go of my hand and pointed past the door at a tiny kitchen area...I could see yet another open doorway beyond the kitchen, leading into what appeared to be a narrow bathroom. 'In there. Better get out of your clothes and have a shower, eh. Quick as you can,' Struan said. 'I can lend you some clobber.' I bent down to put Half-Arse on the floor of the passage and slid my bag from my shoulder... then I walked into the uncomfortably poky kitchen with its ensuite bathroom...I spread my arms out and announced that the whole weird set-up, the whole crazy kit and caboodle, was wonderful...at the same time I saw a large clear bottle of vodka sitting on the bench by the sink...beside it was another bottle, a slim yellow one with a foreign label.

'You even have a bar,' I declared, and laughed.

'They're for cocktails, for Harvey Wallbangers,' Struan called from somewhere. Only at that instant did I realise he was no longer behind me...he'd already vanished off in the direction of the living-room again. 'Come on, hurry up,' I heard him shouting. He added, 'I'll mix you a drink, okay, and bring it to you in the shower.' He seemed insistent...I went into the bathroom and got undressed...I stepped into a long, claw-footed white tub and felt the cool of its enamel on the soles of my feet...the tub had a crinkly pink plastic curtain around it and a shower attachment hooked up on the wall at one end...the water was only tepid when I turned it on, but it felt awfully good to wash the grime off...the ash slid down over my legs in thin, wet layers and onto the bottom of the bath. After a few minutes I heard Struan come in...he handed me a Harvey Wallbanger around one edge of the curtain, waving it in the air for me to take...the cocktail was in a twelve-ounce beer glass with HANZ printed on it in yellow letters...I liked the whole concept of a drink in the shower...I took the cocktail and tried a taste, and thought it was just like orange juice...my stomach was more or less empty, so that almost immediately I could feel the alcohol rushing into my bloodstream. 'These are good,' I called. But Struan had disappeared again...it was all dash and go with him...after showering, I borrowed his razor and toothbrush...finally I wrapped a towel around my waist and ambled off for the living-room...I was swaying slightly from the effects of the drink and still holding my emptied glass, but I felt like a new man. In the living-room I discovered Struan bent over the record-player and gently manoeuvring its pickup arm onto an LP...with his free hand he was grasping a whole heavy beer-jug full of Harvey Wall-banger mix...I approached, and heard some tinkling music begin to issue from the record-player's speaker...over a piano that sounded far away a woman started singing in a throaty voice. 'That's Billie Holiday,' Struan said proudly. He straightened up...he gestured at my empty glass with the jug he was holding...I guessed it was an offer of a refill. 'I want you to call me Billie at the party tonight,' Struan added. 'That's my nickname down here.'

'No problem,' I said.

I let Struan pour me a fresh Harvey Wallbanger. 'And you can put your gear in the sunroom out at the back,' Struan was saying. He pointed off behind him with his other arm as he finished pouring, and my eyes followed his gesture to the sliding double-doors that I'd half noticed before... their glass panes were covered roughly by strips of brown paper, but I assumed the sunroom was beyond them. Struan said, 'You know, you're pretty much in luck. I haven't really got a flatmate for this place yet, eh.'

'So where do you sleep?' I asked.

Struan flustered a little. 'Didn't you see it?' he replied. 'It's the old master bedroom at the front. Off beyond the bathroom. There was another door.' I shrugged my shoulders...Struan continued to look embarrassed. 'Listen, I'll go get you those clothes,' he said. He bustled past me, and I watched him disappear off into the hallway...I waited and finished my Harvey Wallbanger...that didn't take long to manage, so then I pulled apart the sticky double-doors to get a peek at the sunroom. At once I stepped into what looked like a largish alcove...I could feel a wicked draught coming up between the planks in the bare floor and its chill made me notice how damp my towel was around my hips...there was a modest bed, a wooden desk with nothing on it but a small metal lamp, and a chair...across the entire far wall a row of dusty chintz floral curtains hung from the ceiling down almost to the skirting board...I briefly inspected the desk, and next I tried lifting one rough, furry edge of the curtains...they were covering a series of old sliding-windows in which the putty looked dangerously fragile, and several of the panes were badly cracked. But through the glass I could see there was a wide view down onto the yard below...it had grown even dimmer outside in the early twilight, though I could discern two figures out in front of the other single-storey flat...they were Maoris, both in white singlets, and they appeared younger than me...they were both of them bent forwards in a half crouch, circling each other and making short, rapid, feinting movements over the grass. I strained my eyes to watch...now the pair were slipping in and out of sight under the capacious branches of the elm, dodging nimbly after one another around the sides of the tree's broad trunk...through the smudges of light I saw one had impressively large shoulders and he had a knife grasped in his hand, and he darted and twisted and then poked with the knife at the other man...his counterpart came better into view...he was less solidly made, though I saw that he had a knife too. But they seemed to be simply practising...they were working alternately at lunges and parries, and they even laughed as they went on threatening each other...I lowered the curtain with my fingertips...a little gingerly I stepped back into the living-room.

Above the wailing of Billie Holiday I called, 'Hey man, there are two quite serious-looking guys training for a scrap down in your yard.'

Struan came in from the hallway...he was holding some clothes draped across his arm. 'Shh,' he said. 'Not so loud. I forgot to tell you about it, eh, but there's an actual gang living out in the rear flat. I know it's not the greatest, but—' He broke off and shrugged. Then he asked, 'You didn't open up the window back in there, did you?' I shook my head and Struan murmured, 'Good.' He added warily, 'Hey, listen, you'd better keep that whole thing locked tight while you're here. A few days ago one of those guys had a wee climb up the fire-escape. Probably going to rob this place, eh. My downstairs neighbour, he told me, and I don't want any kind of trouble with people like that.' I glanced back towards the sunroom...I wondered whether Half-Arse would be safe, being left there untended when we were gone...I didn't want any trouble with people like that either. But Struan was still approaching and he was holding the clothes on his arm out in my direction...I tried to focus my attention on them properly. 'These are some slacks I borrowed from my mother,' he was saying. 'I figure you should be able to get into them.' Struan lifted up a pair of pink spangled trousers and slowly let the legs fall...he leaned down and spread the trousers out with care across the coffee-table...next he held up a bright, red-and-gold tie-dyed shirt which had dramatically flared sleeves. 'And this is a sort of something I picked up in an op shop, eh,' he said happily, dangling the shirt from his fingers. 'It's a drag party,' he added. 'We're at the Ram.' I stared at the strange clothes and at their shiny, almost gossamer material...I started wondering what Struan was doing with his mother's slacks in his own flat...I wondered if perhaps a drag party might be like a Heads' Ball but in fancy dress. Struan said, 'You do know that I'm gay, don't you.'

'Oh,' I said.

Suddenly I wished I was wearing something more than just a towel... I wished I could recall how far exactly Struan had opened the shower curtain when he'd given me my Harvey Wallbanger...but it couldn't have been all that much, really, because I'd only seen the glass and the hand that was gripping it. I examined Struan for signs of anything especially gay...but I wasn't sure what to look for, and I couldn't even remember him singing 'The Teddy Bears' Picnic' at school...he appeared precisely the same as he'd been a moment before, except that he seemed nervous and was blushing intensely up to the tips of his ears.

'Well, that's okay,' I said.

Struan looked noticeably relieved...he took a long slow breath, as if he'd been unable to manage one for some time...his face began returning to a normal colour, and I was pleased he wasn't nervous anymore, because I suspected that I could be nervous enough for both of us. 'And so, you want to come to this party?' he was asking. 'I mean, it's a Gay Pride week thing. Absolutely everybody is going to be there.'

'Okay,' I replied.

I told myself again that a writer shouldn't pass up a chance for anything, especially if it was a chance to meet absolutely everybody. 'But you have to call me Billie,' I heard Struan insisting. 'That's the new me. I'm not Struan anymore, all right? I'm Billie.' He was waving vaguely in the direction of the record-player with the end of the red shirt, which was still clasped in his hand.

'Okay, Billie,' I said.

Struan beamed...his whole face lit up with delight...I was glad it took so little to make him happy...I reached for the clothes and went back into the sunroom to try putting them on. But after closing the doors, I couldn't stop myself from worrying a bit about being naked...several times I left off changing to double-check that I'd slid both doors properly shut…I even stopped to check that the curtains to the yard outside were pulled completely across the windows…but nothing weird happened, and I started to relax and concentrate on what I was doing. The slacks were so tight to squeeze into that they pinched hard around the crotch, and I wondered if it was something to do with the original owner not having a penis…the wide, loose arms of the shirt flopped about at my sides whenever I moved…I spent a lot of time considering how many shirt buttons to leave open on my chest…I didn't want to seem cheap…there was no mirror anywhere in the sunroom but that left me feeling almost grateful, because I guessed I appeared very gay in my new outfit. Finally I shuffled back into the living-room, and found that Struan had changed his clothes too and was already waiting…he was wearing a sleeveless blue polo-neck top that was stretched taut across his small chest…his legs were forced into some sort of jodhpurs for riding, with the bottoms tucked into calf-high black boots, and in one hand he was holding a colourful silk shawl to drape over his bare arms…but even more than this, I noticed that he'd rapidly put on a lot of heavy makeup…he was wearing false eyelashes, with a long earring dangling near one side of his face, and I thought now that Struan really did look like somebody new, like Billie…he was standing and swinging his arms a little self-consciously, staring at the floor, until he glanced up as if asking for my opinion.

'Outrageous,' I pronounced.

'Just some other stuff I borrowed from my mother,' Struan muttered. He was blushing again. 'Divinely decadent,' he said, and giggled. I'd never met Struan's mother, but I was beginning to feel I knew her…we drank the rest of the Harvey Wallbanger while listening to more Billie Holiday. 'The Ramada, the hotel where we're going, it's got an underground car park,' Struan told me. His tone was gently reassuring. He said, 'I mean, we don't have to be out on the city streets like this, eh. And I've got our ride all parked and ready out the front here, so don't worry. The thing is, we just have to make sure we don't meet any of the gang-boys in the back when we head off.'

I said, 'It sounds like being gay involves a lot of forward planning.'

Struan smiled his lopsided grin. 'Oh, you don't know the half of it,' he said.

We departed from the flat well after sunset…nobody saw us leave, and even out in front of the house the warm darkness felt velvety and comforting and hid us nicely...the streetlights around us, and off at regular intervals into the distance, were so dim that they illuminated nothing beyond their own high iron poles and small patches of the asphalt roadway. Struan's car was at the kerb nearby...it was a low-slung red MG sports car with the top off...I thought it looked sensational until we approached more closely, and then through the poor light I began to notice the rough spots, the dents and the scratches on the bodywork. My door on the passenger side squealed when I opened it, as if I'd just done it harm...the car was terribly old, but I felt sure that an MG still had to be cool...I struggled to find space for my legs while I slid in over the badly worn upholstery...Struan wouldn't let me try to adjust the seat. 'That's a bit broken,' he explained. He had to coax the starter motor several times and the engine growled harshly when at last it turned over, so that I supposed the muffler was in no better condition than anything else...we pulled out onto the wide, one-way road and wriggled immediately into the centre area...the engine was grunty as well as loud when Struan opened it up...he drove with an extravagant intensity that felt almost equal to the roar from under the bonnet...he gripped the car's small steering wheel with his arms out at full stretch, using several lanes along the middle of the road as though they were his own territory, and driving faster and faster. I was pressed back into the seat and my hair was blown violently away from my scalp behind my ears and neck...I glanced about us, and saw the footpaths were empty on both sides of the street and that there were no other vehicles anywhere...all in all, I decided that not meeting any other traffic had to be a good thing.

'How can you afford a set of wheels like this?' I asked.

Struan didn't seem to catch my question...I had to shout it again above the car's raspy mechanical sound, even though I was right beside him.

I added, 'Everyone always reckons students don't have any money.'

'I'm not a student,' Struan yelled back. 'I quit.' We were now negotiating a corner at a fine speed...my side of the car was straining to lift under me, as if ready to become detached from the road...one block later we pulled up with a lurch at a red light. 'I'm a trainee chef,' Struan told me suddenly. We were idling and it was easier to speak...Struan was keeping his eyes fixed on the dark, deserted road across the intersection. He announced, 'I can get a loan for anything I want.' The lights changed, and we lurched off once more...rather than replying, I tried instead to protect

168

my hair by pressing it against my head with one hand…for a strange brief moment I was acutely aware of myself, seated in somebody's sporty car and worrying in vain about my evening to come…I supposed this nervy, helpless sensation must be how girls felt on a first date. After a few minutes we turned off the street with a squeal from the tyres and swept into a low, echoing concrete garage under a hotel…we'd arrived…a short way past the entrance Struan halted the car and pointed with one hand over to an open doorway below an exit sign…then with a deft swing of the wheel he backed us into an empty parking space…he switched off the ignition, but the engine went on grumbling and shuddering for several seconds before it died. Struan ignored the engine's convulsive noises and got out of the car, slamming the door…he hastened ahead of me towards the exit sign and I clambered out and tried to follow, watching him march in his outlandish clothes and boots…he was hurrying with a quick, buoyant step, and I thought he seemed very keyed up…he seemed like someone anticipating the performance he was going to give in public. Past the exit we tramped down a short, tiled corridor…there was a solid metal door at the far end that was heavily scuffed at the base, as if someone had given it a good kicking…Struan pushed open the door with an effort…it led us directly into the sounds and smoke of a hotel bar. The bar before us, the Ramada, was a large, spacious rectangular room, with a lot of nooks and alcoves off it making what looked like hidey-holes, and I saw it was all decorated in a self-consciously modern style…there were tracks of multicoloured lights on the ceiling that winked and sparkled and rather irritated my eyes…there was exposed grey-concrete along the walls and the thick dusty carpet at my feet had patterns of wide, gruesome purple-and-orange swirls…Struan plucked at me agitatedly by my elbow…I'd halted just past the doorway, and we shuffled further inside together. Red crepe-paper streamers had been Sellotaped up here and there on the ceiling, and they were sagging loose and downwards about us…I had to brush one end of a twisted strand away from my face…I saw that a broad hardwood dance floor with a flashing mirror ball overhead occupied much of the centre of the venue and that most of the guests were mingling on the far side of the area, standing or leaning at a row of tall tables…they were dressed up in clothes like ours, in colourful varieties of drag, and were listening to some soft instrumental jazz on the sound system, and they all had an expectant, rather frightened air…the place was not anywhere near as crowded as I'd imagined it would be…in fact, it was disconcertingly empty. The dance floor was still unused...somebody in front of us flitted across its bare space, waving anxiously to a friend on the other side... one or two people away at the tables were staring at us, and I thought that perhaps our arrival was news. Struan led me round past the edge of the deserted dance floor...I saw that nearby was the bar for drinks, set into a recess along one wall...there was a small group of guests that had gathered close to the counter, standing with glasses in their hands, and together Struan and I joined the group...behind the counter, the bar staff in their badly-fitting white shirts looked as if they were already working hard and were happy to have something to do...one was trying to insert a big tray of chopped-up lemons into a fridge and I heard the slosh of a bag of ice being tipped into a bucket. All at once a tall, raw-boned man wearing a shiny blue party-dress, a low-cut tubular thing that finished near his knees, came up and bumped against Struan from behind...Struan paid him no attention and appeared to be gazing off at somewhere else in particular, but I couldn't help glancing at the man's face...he looked maybe forty years old and he had shoulder-length strawberry blonde hair which was falling in great waves and curls around the sides of his head, and which was cut in a shaggy style about his cheeks...I thought the piled-up hair might even be real...he had a long jaw, small red eyes with mascara on the lashes and a pronounced aquiline nose...his generous nose made his features seem especially beaky, and I could see where swipes of thick pale foundation makeup were covering his rough facial stubble. 'Well, after a lot of fiddle faddle this place is at last starting to fill up,' the man said in a deep, flat tone. He nodded back towards the door that we'd just used, though I saw he was ignoring me and talking directly to Struan...in response Struan offered only the most distant of smiles, still without bothering to meet the man's eyes. But I turned away and stared in the direction the man had indicated...I saw that quite a few more people, whole groups of them in fact, were now entering from the car park...the sound of their new noisy talk was beginning to lift and swell through the room in a genial fashion...when I turned back, I found the man had moved close up alongside me...I could smell his deodorant...he had a large gold lamé purse ostentatiously dangling from the crook of one arm and it was swinging about between us. Still not really acknowledging me, the man reached with his unencumbered arm over to the bar and picked up a cocktail glass decorated with a pink-striped paper umbrella...I watched him pin the glass between two long bony fingers and then take a casual sip. 'Hi,' he finally said to me in his deep voice, over the edge of the drink. 'I'm Frannie.'

'Nice to meet you. My name's Andy Ingle,' I said.

'I haven't seen you around here before,' Frannie said. He lowered the cocktail glass and gave me a wide grin.

'I'm visiting from Palmerston North,' I replied. 'I'm a friend of Billie's.'

'Do you like my boobs?' Frannie asked. He nodded down towards the low neckline of his dress...I could make out some very distinct cleavage...the white tops of the breasts were bulging upwards, swelling as he breathed. 'They're new,' he announced. 'Frannie's a transsexual, eh,' Struan declared, cutting in quickly at my other side and surprising me. Clearly he knew Frannie after all. He said, 'You know, she's had the big operation and everything, had it for ages.' Struan pinched the back of my arm while he spoke...he seemed both happy and afraid that I'd actually started mixing, and I supposed he was concerned at how I'd cope...but Frannie was still standing there, swinging slightly back and forth...she moved further in front of me, twitching her shoulders about like Roger Gascoigne on TV...she was still waiting for an answer on the new boobs.

'They're perky,' I said.

'Would you like to dance?' Frannie asked.

'All right,' I said.

The Harvey Wallbangers and the atmosphere had made me feel daring...I'd never danced with a man before, and it had never occurred to me to try...but in this room I thought maybe I'd keep that information to myself. We walked the short distance over to the hardwood floor area... Frannie still had her drink clasped firmly in one large hand and drained it as we went...I was a little worried that I might get caught in a slow dance, but the soft music had changed into something louder and jazzy...a rich, raucous saxophone was playing the lead...already some other people had come forwards onto the floor and were hopping about. We began to dance around too, Frannie and I...Frannie kept her knees tight together in the narrow dress and wriggled...she swung her elbows out into a shimmy...I thought she did it well, since she also had to hold the purse and the empty cocktail glass up close to her hips...it was all energetic work and hot... soon my skin was starting to prickle with sweat in my own constricting clothes. From our position on the dance floor I could see that still more people were coming into the hotel room, bringing with them some of the cooler, fresher air from outside...they were in old-fashioned clothes with lacy Edwardian ruffles, in pimps' costumes with wide hats, and they were wearing glitter on their cheeks...everybody seemed to be keen to make the party bubblier, and the dance area was becoming more and more crowded...not far away I saw two plump, moustachioed men under the mirror ball who were openly cuddling. 'That Jean-Pierre,' Frannie called. She'd noticed me looking and, still prancing about with her boogie moves, she bent forward and hissed into my ear, 'Two drinks and he's anybody's.' After the song ended Frannie shook her neck and shoulders, as if relieving the tension in her tall, rangy frame, and insisted that we get some cocktails...we trotted off the dance floor and threaded through a rapidly growing crush around the bar...Frannie had no trouble parting the crowd...I looked about for Struan amidst all these people, but I couldn't see him anywhere. Frannie put her glass up on the counter and drew the attention of the barman by reaching over and grabbing at his white shirtsleeve...next she began telling me something about her job...she ran a local tropical-fish supply store out Papanui way...for several minutes Frannie explained a lot of stuff concerning grooming and cycling fluid and thermometers. A very short, very chubby woman came up close beside us while Frannie talked...the woman's fat figure was crammed into a long-waisted, frilly pink-and-white dress, and I could smell where it had been dabbed with perfume...she had bobbed, massively curly blonde hair and heavily-made up cheeks...the woman stood gazing at us through a pair of badly attached, droopy eyelashes and it was clear that she was waiting to be introduced, but Frannie seemed reluctant to break off in mid-conversation with me... even so, the woman kept smiling and nodding in obvious enthusiasm while she listened...she kept acting as though she was already engaged in talking to us both. 'Yeah right. This is Trudy, eh,' Frannie huffed and said to me at last. Frannie scrunched up her nose in annoyance...she was visibly fuming...she gestured at the woman beside us with one of her long arms, and her purse flapped about. She said, '*He's* an old friend of mine, Trudy is, eh. But even if he ran for mayor, you know, he wouldn't get any kind of votes at all.' Trudy reacted to this by shrieking in a high, scrappy voice... she reached up and pummelled one of Frannie's shoulders with both of her podgy hands...at length she turned to me with the look of somebody waiting for her share of applause, but I offered nothing back except a little grin. Then she said to me a lot more quietly, almost confidentially, 'Don't let Frannie be a bitch.' Perhaps she was remembering some unhappy past experience, and I hoped I might lighten things.

'Why, is Frannie a bitch very often?' I asked.

But Trudy didn't reply...instead she merely gazed up at me and jiggled about a lot, giggling and wheezing as if thrilled at my existence...I supposed it meant I was beginning to be a social hit...it felt best to press on with my advantage and I asked Trudy what she did for a living. 'Oh, I'm a mail sorter at the post office,' she told me quickly. Trudy giggled again...she gave Frannie a long, sly glance. 'You know, like, the whole time putting all those letters into pigeonholes,' she said. 'For people who'd never want somebody like me, eh, touching their things.' 'Oh, let's face it, darling,' Frannie cut in. 'You love it.' She rolled her eyes for dramatic flair and drawled, 'You've always been a perfect one for stuffing things that nobody wants into holes.' Around us the other partygoers who were also waiting to get their drinks all burst into high-pitched, girlish laughter... plainly everyone was overhearing our conversation.

'I see,' I said.

Trudy caught my eye, and this time she said quite seriously to me, 'No, I do night shifts usually, most of the week.'

'So what's that like?' I asked, trying to sound serious too.

'It's a hell of a racket,' she said. 'I mean, the noise, eh. There's mailbags moving about over your head in all directions and there's all the franking machines going full blast.' Trudy added, 'I can do just a bit under a thousand letters in half an hour.' 'What's that happening there on that other side, hmm?' Frannie suddenly asked over this. She'd manufactured a bored edge to her voice...I saw she was pointing off across the room at a woman who looked like a transsexual or similar, standing at a table...the woman was wearing a denim skirt and a lacy Mexican-style blouse with a pillow tucked inside...the pillow's bottom edge was hanging out below the blouse but she was holding the padded bulge gently to her stomach, rocking it up and down. 'Oh, it's that Tim, you know,' said Trudy, adopting a new and scornful tone. She'd raised her voice loud enough for the people around us to hear, and I realised with a rush of insight that she was behaving exactly like an actor with an audience. 'Always calls himself Gloria, him,' Trudy said. 'From Radio Avon.' 'That mud-kicker,' Frannie growled. 'He's come along pregnant tonight, eh,' Trudy added, and arched her short, heavy neck. 'I mean,' she said, 'if some people thought it'd give them a chance to be the life and soul of this party, eh, they'd crawl in over barbed bloody wire.' Frannie heaved a large sigh. 'Tragic,' she said. The barman interrupted us by putting our cocktails up on the counter, ready at last...Frannie insisted on paying for us both and pulled some money from her purse...she gave me my glass but spoke next to Trudy, indicating somewhere off in the distance once more. 'What about that Robert crouched over there in the corner, hmm?' Frannie said. 'Now, he's a real little sex symbol.' I marvelled at all this, at how Frannie's manner could be so intimate and yet so public. 'Oh, that dearie definitely likes to put his mouth where the money is,' Trudy replied in just the same sort of voice as Frannie's. 'Oh, you watch, eh,' she added. 'He'll be down on his knees in Press Lane later this evening.' Around the bar, the crowd that was spread behind us had grown deeper and people were beginning to jostle, impatient for their drinks...I decided to try and leave...I made tentative noises while I started drifting off through the crush, holding my cocktail glass...a little to my surprise Frannie and Trudy didn't bother to stop me. I headed aimlessly through the now very busy room...the clammy heat was making me thirsty, and I kept sipping from my drink until it was almost empty...everywhere was congested with rambunctious people and I had to twist and change direction to make progress, until I wondered why I'd bothered to come to a drag party at all...I considered the wisdom of finding and using the toilets...I wished I'd thought to go for a pee before leaving the flat. When I got to the far side of the room, I spied a short, grossly overweight man who appeared rather out of place...he was wearing a white pinstripe shirt and a pair of navy-blue trousers, a businessman's clothes, with a crinkled black necktie hanging down across his corpulent tummy, and he was standing with his rounded back pressed up against the concrete wall behind him...he was squirming a little, showing restless energy, while he'd half settled a plump forearm on a high table beside him in obvious discomfort and impatience...I saw the man was middle-aged and almost completely bald, so bald that just a small thin edge of ragged brown hair extended back around his head... his buttony eyes were gazing everywhere about him through his horn-rimmed glasses as I approached, as if maybe he was expecting something major to break out at any second...his jacket, a different, lighter shade of blue from his pants, was rolled up into a dishevelled ball under the table by his feet, and he'd been perspiring for some time into large, wet patches below each of the armpits of his shirt. 'Hot. Dreadfully hot,' the man muttered when I drew near. His voice sounded so quiet that I couldn't be sure whether he was really talking to me...he hadn't even been looking particularly in my direction as he said it, but then the man smiled and raised his chubby hand from the table, gesturing for me to join him…I saw that he was holding an odd, long brown cigarette between two of his thick fingers, more or less as though he'd forgotten it…in fact the man seemed to notice the cigarette at almost the same instant I did, and he began to smoke from it eagerly. 'Crazy party,' he announced between puffs. 'Crazy, crazy. Crazy party.' I went round to the other side of the man's table and leaned up against the wall…the concrete felt pleasantly cool on my shoulder blades…the song in the sound system over by the dance floor appeared to have changed…it was an emotive melody, a jangly thing, with a woman singing in French, and I could even hear someone at another table crooning along to the singer's reedy, foreign tones. 'Edith Piaf, you know?' the fat man said beside me. '"Milord." Hell of a famous tune. There, up there, Piaf.' The man's accent was slurred and American…he was leaning towards me and waving his strange cigarette vaguely before his face, pointing with it towards a cloth-covered speaker near the ceiling…from up close I could see the man had the faintest stringy goatee growing, poised, on his ample chin…the goatee wobbled a little beneath his lower lip as he went on talking. He was saying, 'Shitty, shitty life—sacrificed it all. Great songstress.'

'Well, I guess that's how it works with a vocalist who's the real deal,' I said, mostly for something to say. I put my emptied cocktail glass down next to me and then I asked, 'You're not dressed up?'

'I'm not even gay,' the man said in his quiet voice. He was very hard to hear…he glanced at me across the table, and through his chunky spectacles his hazel, weary eyes appeared magnified and a bit alarming as they kept roaming around…his cheeks were jowly, pink and shining with perspiration, and they seemed to be sliding on his face as he spoke. 'I just kind of come here because it's so tough to find a decent party in this one-horse town,' the man said. 'I'm a professor out at Canterbury. You know? In English, the lit business. Criticism that is, literary criticism.'

'Well, I'm not gay either,' I confessed.

It was almost a relief to say so…amidst so much outrageous flapdoodle I was glad of an opportunity to tell the plain truth at last.

I added, 'I'm a writer, eh. And I've never met a literary critic before.'

I introduced myself and held out my hand. 'Prof Bradley Bingham,' the man said. He took my hand in his large, damp palm and then shook it a little suspiciously…perhaps he felt it was a strange thing to be doing in a gay bar. He asked, 'So, what type of stuff do you write?'

'Oh, novels,' I said. 'But I haven't finished any yet, sort of thing. That's because I'm having a bit of trouble getting started.'

'Everybody has trouble getting started in this goddamn town,' Prof Bingham said. He took another steady pull on his long cigarette. He exhaled a small grey cloud of smoke which swirled about before his mouth, and added, 'You know, this is the kind of provincial set-up that makes you think Armageddon might not be so bad.'

'Oh, I know it's important to stay creative if you want to get right into it, I mean, deep into the juices of the muse,' I replied. 'But I really am having trouble sitting down to start.'

'Just park your arse and write it,' Prof Bingham muttered. He stared off, gazing away at the crowd again. 'Absolute, cacophonous fucking chaos, that's your point of departure,' he said much more clearly. 'No wonder you people can't snaffle yourselves up a sense of identity in this country. And stay away from all that frou-frou Katherine Mansfield crap. I'm warning you, right, New Zealand critics can't see a thing in her beyond the life, and they never see anything in her queer and nasty life but themselves. What you do, yeah, you try what good old Jack Kerouac did. Just sit down and write whatever trifle comes into your head.' I thought all this sounded like the most brilliant advice...I determined that, when I got back to the flat, I'd do exactly what Prof Bingham said...I'd sit down to write with Half-Arse and stay away from Katherine Mansfield. But Prof Bingham was still talking, and I could tell he was saying something more about literature...he was dropping pearls about Hemingway and Faulkner and Joyce in Paris, so I was pretty glad I recognised some of these top-notch names...in Paris Faulkner was too shy and weeny to go into a cafe and shake Joyce's hand...it seemed that Paris had an incredible, vibrant cafe scene, not like Christchurch. Prof Bingham told me solemnly that Stendhal wrote in Paris...in Paris, Stendhal wrote the whole of *The Charterhouse of Parma* in just seven weeks...Stendhal would never have written shit in Christchurch in seven weeks...I made myself a quick mental note...Paris was the place, the definite place, to write a fast novel...but Prof Bingham had already moved on without a break. He seemed scarcely aware of me, and continued peering eagerly around him and smoking as he talked...he began saying that Indian literature was well developed, despite the country's poverty...compare that to Christchurch, he declared, where everyone had plenty of stuff and there was simply no culture...it was all happening in Indian writing, but there was no Indian

176

writing in goddamn Christchurch...after several more minutes of this, Prof Bingham finally appeared to notice that I was listening, and he suggested I come out to the university sometime and sit my arse in on one of his lectures.

'Sounds good,' I said.

But I needed to get the words out quickly because Prof Bingham had gone right on talking once more, as if intoxicated by his own speech. 'That whole goddamn college is chock full of pussy,' he was muttering half to himself, 'all of it in long leather boots and big floppy sweaters, and jeans so tight those girls should be just dying to get them off. But most of that pussy, see, is way too stupid to know how to put out. You should come over there sometime, though, and meet my cute little third-year squeeze. I'm educating her through her cunt.' As I listened, I couldn't help thinking that a college sounded like an impressive place...I thought how happy I'd be to meet pussy there, even pussy that was too stupid to know how to put out...I thought it would be fascinating to meet people who wanted to talk about literature while they took their jeans off...I let Prof Bingham continue pronouncing gravely on this topic for a little while longer...his insights were probably important, but I couldn't pay very much attention...I was over-stimulated by Hemingway and Faulkner and Joyce and Stendhal, and it felt as if I'd already heard more than enough to occupy my mind. In the end I made an excuse to go use the loo...by now I was fairly busting to pee...even so, I couldn't seem to focus on anything, not even on some business as basic as emptying my bladder... I took a few steps through the mob of guests in a direction that might just lead to the toilet, but then I went off in search of Struan instead. I found him over in a far corner of the room...Struan was standing at a table with one of his arms up around a man's shoulders...the man was small, dark haired and olive-skinned, and he appeared to be in his early thirties...as I approached through the crowd I could see that Struan, with his arm still draped possessively round the man's shoulders, was moving to bend away into the corner and twist himself into a half crouch... it was obvious that he was trying to conceal himself while he drew back hard on a wrinkled, hand-rolled smoke. The man standing beside Struan regarded me with a serious look as I came up to the table before them... the man had his hair permed into tight curls and cut very short, and he wasn't in a costume but instead wore a stylish, close-fitting brown jacket and slacks...it was exactly like the sort of jacket I'd seen on Struan when

I'd first entered his flat, and something made me guess that this person must be the model for Struan's new image. Struan had paused from all his clandestine puffing...he held the smoke cupped under his palm, gripped between his thumb and index finger, as he straightened up once more... his other arm stayed still firmly clasped around the man beside him... Struan's eyes were lit by a look of triumph, and I was fairly certain I was dealing with marijuana again. 'Ah,' Struan said to me with a hoarse grunt, 'this here's Mike.' Mike grinned at me and nodded some kind of greeting, but his eyes kept their serious, level gaze...I supposed he was puzzling over how I might know Struan. 'Hey, you like some of this joint?' Struan asked me in a raw voice. His fingers were trembling as he held out the smoke, and he glanced inquiringly at Mike...I saw Mike shrug, so I figured it was okay...I took the joint and had a puff...the familiar sour grassy smell from the car back over near Masterton spread around me and I held my breath for as long as I could, but nothing happened.

'Amazing shit,' I said, as I let the smoke go from my lungs.

Mike grinned again, an almost fulsome smirk this time...he seemed very satisfied with my verdict...he reached out and, with a polite hint of hesitation, took the joint from me. 'Mike and I, like, we're going to his new place together tonight,' Struan announced quickly. 'So look, the thing is, I'll have to drop you back at the flat with the key, eh. And don't you go losing it, or I'll kill you and bury you in a shallow grave where the coyotes can find you.' He smiled lopsidedly...he was pausing for me to admire his witticism.

'Okay, Billie,' I said.

I didn't bother with any more of the dope...the drinks had already made me sufficiently cheerful and groggy...I thought it might be better to let some of the booze gradually wear off, though I managed to go on drinking anyway. Struan gave no sign of leaving the party soon...I checked around for Prof Bingham, but he looked to be good and gone... I spent some time chatting to Frannie and Trudy again, and at this point they felt like old friends from happy earlier days...I even danced with them, shaking to a little more boogie-woogie out on the floor, to help burn some of the hooch from my system...Frannie kept pestering me about escorting her to the drag ball on New Year's Eve, and I had to find excuses...I didn't enjoy lying to her, but I also supposed it was my own fault that I needed to, being here under false pretences. Finally Struan drove me back to the flat...he seemed to regard this as doing me a rather troublesome favour, and he dropped me at the kerb in front of the house without saying more than a simple word or two...he left me alone and I watched him pull off again into Salisbury Street, revving the engine and straying across the empty lanes...he was in no better condition to drive than I was, and I was glad to fathom this only now after having been given a lift, and not before. I stumbled along the drive towards the rear entrance of the house...I was trying stay steady as I trod on the uneven patches of gravel, but it was hard work and I had to put my arms out in front of me so as not to fall...from halfway up the drive I found there was some sort of hooley happening among the gang members, far off across the back yard and inside their own flat...they were making a tremendous lot of noise and I could tell the lights were on behind the curtains over their windows...fortunately they all seemed to be gathered indoors, out of my way...it wouldn't be a smart idea for me to interrupt such big doings while dressed in a weirdly flared shirt and a woman's pink slacks. Upstairs at last in the sunroom, I wasted no time changing into the spare clothes from my duffle-bag...my hands were even trembling as I pulled the folded garments out and shook them loose to wear, and it felt terribly pleasant to be putting on normal things once more...I could scarcely contain my sense of being released from some kind of imminent danger, either from downstairs or off on the street, and this made me think for a moment of how precarious Struan's life had become. After I'd finished changing, I saw with relief that Half-Arse was untouched on the desk, just where I'd left it...I stood in front of the typewriter and removed the scratched plastic cover...remembering Prof Bingham, I then took out my packet of foolscap, tore it open and rolled a coarse sheet into the trundling carriage...I was tired and perhaps a little overwrought...all I could properly understand was that my head felt heavy and my ears were ringing, but I was also determined from this very instant to write something, anything, whatever came into my mind. I sat down gingerly at the desk and took a second to enjoy the comforting feel of the back of the chair on my spine... but it was time to get stuck in, right now, and I tried to focus on my own thoughts...the problem seemed to be choosing just which thought to begin with...also I didn't know how to touch-type, and that was going to be a whole other problem...I wasn't sure quite how I'd manage, once I started my typing up...could I go at it fast enough, tapping away, to keep pace with each specific new idea? I sat for a while longer, pondering all this...I stared, poised and ready, at the keys...they were faced upwards, waiting, almost taunting me beneath my hovering fingertips...I stared harder and harder and harder, but after several minutes I was only looking into my own empty hands...whatever else I might be, I was no Stendhal. Just then I was disturbed by a sudden huge burst of stereo-noise...it swelled up around the back of my ears, but next the piercing music just as abruptly stopped...in the near-silence that followed some frenzied yelling was soon audible, and it didn't take a lot of nous to guess where the racket was coming from...I switched off the desk-lamp and stood up, and very gently moved to the window...even though I was inside and far away from the other flat, it felt best to proceed in secret...with the most unobtrusive gesture I could manage, keeping myself as distant from the glass as possible, I lifted one edge of the curtain. The French doors to the gang's flat, down across the far end of the yard, had been flung wide open...from within a sharp light came streaming out, spilling into the yard...its dramatic orange glow was spread all over the elm tree's trunk and made one part look fiercely bright while the other was left still lost in darkness. Some gang members were treading carefully down over the brick steps at the flat's entrance and heading outside, and I realised that many more were already moving around on the grass...they were well obscured below me by the half-lit abundance of branches and leaves on the tree, but I could catch glimpses of them lumbering in and out of the shadows, rocking their hips and their broad, sloping shoulders...they were all gathering themselves into a large, scraggy circle in the night... the whole yard was rapidly filling up with people. Nobody, none of them, looked anything like the kids I'd watched practicing earlier in the day... among the shuffling crowd taking up their positions it was grown men I was seeing, mostly slouching and muscle-bound...several were in sleeveless, ragged denim jackets with circular gang patches on their backs, but soon I saw there were some women with them too...the women were wandering about on the far edges of the circle and calling to each other. I started to stoop down, softly as I could...I told myself that no one would notice any brief flutter of the curtain...then I squatted and stayed watching, avoiding the slightest motion, confining myself to a tiny corner of the window. After a moment my eyes lit on a particularly heavy-limbed Maori man in a sleeveless denim gang jacket, a man with shaggy black hair that dropped down across the shoulders of his massive upper frame...he was shambling about in bare feet...he was in the midst of the circle, but standing too close to the tree for me tell what was happening...the big man kept reaching out somewhere in front of him with one hand, making some kind of gesture...finally I saw that, lazily and easily, he was pushing away from him a much smaller man. The big man was herding the smaller man, getting the smaller man round into the centre of the gathering...I could see where the big man's bare biceps were poking from the arm-holes of his loose and ungainly jacket...his arms shone with sweat along the knots of his muscles each time he reached forward with slow, simple movements and shoved. Three more women were coming outside in a bunch from the flat, the last people perhaps, since they had the appear-ance of having just woken up...one had a blanket draped around her shoulders...they were talking in high, sleepy voices, and their faces glowed with the orange light as they attached themselves to the group... inside the circle, the small man was still staggering back from being pushed, over and over...he was dressed only in a T-shirt and shorts, and kept his head down...he looked skinny in his flimsy clothes, and I saw his chest was heaving with each breath...his arms made shadows as they went up and out for balance. The big man kept saying something to the small man each time he advanced...it was spoken too low for me to under-stand, but it had a delicate, almost caressing tone...both of the men were shifting in and out from view beneath the tree...I saw the small man was trying to step sideways, hoping to escape, but the circle was closing in on him. A woman at the back with a long, heavy jaw started calling, 'Go on! Go on!' Other people were laughing...a mood of anticipation was swelling across the entire yard, and it seemed to rise up and crawl into the room beside me. I heard someone shout clearly, 'Plant the bastard!' But the big man stayed very calm...the little man kept right on backing off, and by now everything in his body expressed fright...he raised his hands with his palms up, as if he didn't want to use them...another man reached out and shoved him from behind, and the little man stumbled. From where I was crouching I began to sense something heavy and brutal, thumping hard, until I realised it was the loud pounding of my own heart...it was so unaccountably noisy that I worried it might give me away...but at almost the same time, the big man made an agile movement with his hand...I could hear the dull, dead wallop of a blow...I saw the small man falling backwards with his arms going wide, sprawling onto the rough grass, and he started trying to scramble up again in a desperate hurry, half away from my view under the tree. But the big man stepped forward after him...I heard the big man grunting as he laid into the little man, who still seemed to be only up on his knees...the big man was punching down with long, heavy swipes into the darkness beneath the branches...he bent lower, and went on and on...he appeared to be gathering further strength from his own rage. At last an older, portly woman forced a path for herself into the circle...she was wailing theatrically...her eyes were wide in her round, fleshy face...she stepped away from my sight under the branches and then suddenly back into view, dragging the little man along on the ground by his limp arms...I watched her stop and squat beside him, and continue with her slow wailing. Another man came forward and he kicked the little man in the stomach...it was so hard that the little man's knees jerked...but the big man slouched up again and hissed, as if to drive everybody else off...next he turned on one heel and stamped on the little man's head...the little man lay doubled up on the ground very still, and it occurred to me that he could be dead...it made me wonder about ringing for an ambulance, or maybe the police, but I was far too scared to stir. Some of the other women in the group were wailing now as well, but it sounded quieter and indifferent, and already people were turning away, moving off...I could see they were beginning to shuffle back into the flat and even hurrying to get inside...the stereo noise started up again...soon only two women were left in the yard, hauling at the little man's slack body, until at last they dragged it up over the low brick steps and into the house...someone closed the doors, and within a moment the whole empty yard was in darkness. For a long while I stayed motionless, still hunkered down and listening to my own shallow breathing...I didn't dare change position till it felt completely safe...finally I let the edge of the curtain drop and got up. I crept over and stretched out softly on the bed, lying on top of the thin sheets in a nervous state...I wondered if there was anything more to drink in the flat...it was likely that we hadn't used up the last of the vodka and the other stuff...I was convinced that it would be impossible to close my eyes...quickly, though, I began to feel overwhelmed with tiredness, and in the end I fell asleep.

I woke up late and hearing the repeated screeching sound of birds... there were a lot of them, and they seemed to be enjoying themselves at my expense...I was still lying fully dressed on the top of the bedclothes, but I was on my stomach and my nose was crammed down into the pillow...my mouth felt scraped very dry and my head was aching. After a bit I rose sluggishly and peeped out through the curtains...some raucous, fat sparrows were singing in the tree outside, but the flat across the back yard was quiet, and its doors were closed…I watched, waiting for some time… nothing in the flat appeared to stir. Finally I gave up and shambled into the kitchen, listening to the sound of my own sloppy footsteps…I guzzled some cold water from a tap over the sink and felt slightly better…then I took my dirty clothes and Struan's gear and left the house, heading off to find a laundrette…I'd remembered seeing one in Victoria Street the day before, near the Caxton Press office. I located the laundrette again without difficulty and managed to bundle all the clothes with me into a handy machine near the door…there was a dispenser in one corner where you could buy washing powder…it was soothing at first, just sitting on an upholstered bench for some minutes and hearing the wet clothes churn around in the washing machine, but after I changed everything to a dryer I started to become restless…more and more I began noticing the traffic going by on the street outside, and I felt strangely energetic, tired and irritable all at the same time. Back at the flat later, I fixed myself a slow brunch of toast and coffee, having it while standing up at the bench in the kitchen, but soon there was a sharp, rhythmic knock on the door that interrupted things…when I opened it, I found Struan waiting alone before me on the landing…he was wearing what seemed to be badly fitting, borrowed clothes, and he had his party gear draped lazily over one arm… his eyes looked red and a little puffy, and I supposed he hadn't got much sleep…I thought he appeared very pleased with himself. 'Hi,' Struan said. I didn't bother making a reply and simply let him in…Struan followed me to the kitchen, passed into the bathroom and dumped the party clothes on the floor…then he came back and tried to make a show of looking embarrassed in front of me…but I purposefully didn't ask him any questions about Mike or anything else and got on with eating my toast. 'Well, you had a good night, eh?' Struan inquired after a while. He just couldn't hide the cheerful tone in his voice…he'd already begun spooning some instant coffee into a cup for himself…he shook the electric jug to check that it still had some hot water.

'Yes, fine thanks,' I answered.

'So what are you up to today?' he asked, pouring water from the jug into his cup.

'Don't know,' I said.

I didn't feel much interested in writing…I studied my own coffee cup and continued to be out of sorts…what I'd seen in the yard the night before had left me depressed over writing anything, any kind of tittle-tattle scribbled on paper...instead my thoughts swirled round and round but stayed curiously empty...I was beginning to wonder what on earth I was doing here...perhaps Chloe had been correct, and it was pointless and silly and wrong to chase a distant, febrile dream. 'But that's all, whatever happens,' I heard Struan pronouncing firmly after a moment, 'because I've got a couple of members' tickets for the races at Riccarton this arvo. That's if you want to go.' I realised I'd been too lost in my own gloom to notice that Struan was inviting me to something...now he paused. Then he repeated a little shyly, 'You want to go, eh? To see the gee-gees?' I glanced across at Struan, who was blowing in a nonchalant manner onto the wisp of steam rising from his freshly made coffee, and suddenly I felt a tremendous sense of gratitude springing from within me and directed both to Struan and out to the world in general...it occurred to me that I'd begun to learn how there was an awful, awful lot in the world which was new...I was also beginning to understand that I was a real drongo for temptation.

'You know, I've never been to the races before,' I said.

I had nothing fancy to wear either, not to get all dressed up in for someplace like Riccarton...Struan told me that the whole business was going to be a super-classy affair...but he assured me that once more I could use a selection of his clothes, and he seemed to have a plan in mind...I followed Struan into his bedroom and he showed me where his gear was kept...most of it was in an old black wardrobe and a chest of drawers that were both pushed up against one wall, facing the bottom of the bed, though other clothes and wrapping papers and even makeup items were scattered about everywhere...I tried to imagine how it was going to be to look classy, but I couldn't manage it from the sight of the room. Struan pulled a smart pale-grey three-piece suit out of the wardrobe for himself...he told me there was an older one lying around somewhere, kept as a spare...after some rummaging he found it folded away in a drawer, and he handed it to over me along with a spare shirt...the suit was light blue but similar in cut and style to Struan's, and though the waistcoat was ferociously tight about my ribs when I tried it on, it had paisley colours that looked pretty sharp...I was able to squeeze into the trousers and jacket with a little effort. I examined myself in a mirror set up behind the door...the jacket had lapels almost as wide as Struan's did, which felt cool, and anyway I'd need to keep it on because the arms of my shirt were much too short...unfortunately there was no real alternative to wearing my dirty sandshoes with the trousers, but the trouser cuffs were very low and kept most of my feet out of sight...I decided that this effect gave me an offbeat, maverick air. When all our preparations and fuss were finally complete, we drove out towards the racecourse in the MG... in the meantime the sky had grown overcast with a thin dappled-grey layer of herringbone cloud, but still we wore sunglasses to make sure that we'd look the real deal...despite our late start, Struan insisted that we stop at a pub for warm-up drinks on the way...we sat in the lounge bar, staring from its picture window at a broad intersection and the parkland beyond as if we were well accustomed to this whole kind of thing. Afterwards, Struan drove us off for the track again...we passed down a long straight suburban road and turned at last into the grounds...Struan showed our tickets at the gate and got us a parking slip...the road beyond the gate immediately grew rougher, and the parking area, when we reached it, was just a wide scraggy paddock where Struan had to manoeuvre the MG across bumpy grass between rows of parked cars...after a few minutes he got us backed into an empty space near a line of spreading birch trees...through the trees I could see the tantalising white fence of the racecourse in the distance, and I heard the echoes of announcements on the tannoy. A garishly dressed woman came waddling by past the front of our car, moving with difficulty in her high heels on the clumpy, muddy turf...after her padded a pair of heavyset men wearing suits and florid ties, who both looked excited and drunk...I watched one of the men lean on our bonnet for a moment and wipe his forehead before stumbling off, but Struan ignored them all until they were completely gone and only then climbed out of the MG...once he'd closed the door, he paused and carefully pulled down the cuff of each shirtsleeve inside his jacket...it was such a nice flourish that I got out and tried doing the same with my own cuffs, tugging hopelessly at their edges...both Struan and I began heading in the direction of the track and within a minute or so there were a lot more punters all around us, but I thought we must easily be the smartest, coolest visitors in the whole place. We crossed a narrow gravel path and moved towards the enclosure...a light breeze, chilled and crisp, patted at my cheek...now I could hear clearly the scratchy noise of racing talk being broadcasted from the loudspeakers...I could see a striped marquee and people carrying chilly bins, and I smelled barbecuing sausages...but when I started pointing out the elderly stewards in white coats who were loitering amongst the growing crowd, Struan only made a show of looking dismissive...maybe he thought they were just obvious to everyone.

He turned to me and declared that we ought to try a little flutter...Struan said he knew something about the betting game because Mike owned a racehorse...he gestured at a big red arrow above a sign for the racing-club hall, and he began to hurry me along with him in the direction it indicated...soon we were approaching a large wooden building attached to the back of one of the stands...there was a set of braced double-doors at its entrance which were painted a drab olive green and which made the hall look a lot like an oversized farm shed...Struan led us to a gap between the doors, and half pushed me through. 'You'll want to put basically a few bucks down, eh,' he announced. Inside, the hall was long, crowded and busy, and as we advanced I could smell smoke and sweat in the confused, draughty air...the room's beige walls had heavy brown curtains to hide the outside view, and the light from the ceiling lamps high above was thin...the bettors all around us held copies of tattered race books, and fidgeted and lit cigarettes while they stood about...I thought they looked unusually anxious and expectant...their talk and nervous laughter appeared to amplify in the vaulted spaces overhead and left a peculiar, almost hushed echo...my shoes started scuffing on something slithery until I glanced down and saw a litter of old betting slips beneath my feet, strewn across the badly worn, diamond-patterned carpet. Many of the horsemen and racing aficionados were queuing at the counters of the betting windows which ran down one side of the hall...a man clutching a newspaper bumped past me and rolled his eyes as if I was in his way on purpose...I realised that we were actually crossing and interfering with lines of impatient people. So, I thought, this is a gambling house. Struan was studying a chalk-smeared signboard not far from us for information about the field and scarcely took his eyes from it as we joined the back of one of the queues...when we finally got up to our counter, the punters in other lines nearby were jostling us, threatening to push in and complaining that the windows were going to close at any moment...but the man working at the barred window before us seemed happy enough when we both slid a few hasty dollars at him under the white-painted grille...he was wearing a spivvy tan suit that looked rather like ours, so I thought perhaps he recognised quality customers when he saw them...the man kept his head bent warily over the drawers of cash beside him and cocked one ear towards us as we talked...he didn't appear the least perturbed when we struggled with the terms for explaining what we wanted in the next race, so that in the end we managed to put a couple of dollars each way on a mare Struan liked. Afterwards, I had to hang around while Struan went off to the toilet…the race was already starting when we made our way through the back of the hall to a stairwell for the members' stand, and we could hear the excited drone of the race-caller coming from some speakers as we trotted up the narrow, lino-covered steps…the commentator sounded as if he had a little money on the outcome himself…somewhere in the near distance above us I could sense a sudden tension among all the people gathered in the stands around the racecourse…it seemed to build, thrillingly, and it was spilling down into the stairwell towards us as we reached the lower landing…together we stopped and listened in a more wholehearted fashion to the commentary…the race-caller kept repeating our horse's name, saying it with stronger and stronger emphasis, and we started scurrying onwards again up the stairs, but it was too late and a noise erupted up above of cheering and the stamping of feet. Struan halted once more, turned, and clapped me on the back…I heard the race-caller's voice beginning to wind down in an exhausted tone…but our horse had won…we hadn't even seen the track yet, and already we had to return downstairs to fetch our winnings…I decided that I liked gambling. Some minutes later, with the windfall cash in our pockets, we found a bar in another room off one end of the racing-club hall… we celebrated by forking out for a bottle of Marque Vue and we would have bought drinks for everyone else in the bar as well, except that the place was empty…as soon as the bottle was handed to him by the barman Struan unwound the wire and popped off the cork, and he poured some of the bubbly into a pair of plastic cups on the counter…then while the barman was distracted, I lifted a whole pile of more cups and slipped them under my jacket…I thought they might come in handy as extras. We polished off a drink each on the way to the door…we'd had a couple more by the time we finally got ourselves upstairs and into the members' stand… Struan and I commenced searching for our seats amongst the rows, and as we stumbled around we made a lot of noise…we didn't care about the racket, though neither of us was really drunk…we just felt excited enough to pretend that we were. We leaned on the hardboard-covered dividers between sections and called out our seat numbers over people's heads… perhaps we hoped that somebody in the crowd was going to welcome us…I had my sunglasses propped up on my forehead as I lurched about, checking for bum spaces, and Struan was anxious that I'd get sticky champagne all over the suit he'd lent me…several people looked irritated when

187

I told him not to be such a clucky old woman. At last we located our seats, well up in the stand and right in the centre of a row...we shuffled to get to them, hurrying and clumsy...Struan threw a cup at me, but we had cups to spare...anyway he missed and hit somebody else. When we found our places and sat, I thought the members' seats were hard and surprisingly plain...they were nothing but wooden benches, white-painted and warped, running in continuous lines along each of the rows...there was a single plank for our members' bottoms and no support for our backs...several middle-aged ladies wearing fussy floral dresses and elegant hats were seated in front of us and I saw that most of the women had their handbags up on the benches beside them, safe from the grit and rubbish on the floor.

'You know what? These are the bloody plebs seats,' I complained out loud to Struan beside me.

Struan didn't say anything...he just raised another cup to throw...I had to remove it from his hand.

'Dork,' I said.

On my other side a pretty girl was sitting next to me, and now I took a moment to concentrate on her...she sat with her long legs stretched out before her and crossed at the ankles, and she was wearing a smart navy-blue trouser-suit that had pairs of large gold buttons along the front...her clothes looked businesslike, but I thought the girl was maybe our age... she had a thin fair freckled face and a lot of wiry red hair in loose curls that tumbled down almost onto her shoulders...the girl was trying to ignore me while I scrutinised her, and with one hand she carefully wiped back her fringe from her eyes and stared ahead towards the course, exhibiting a stern sort of attention. I followed the girl's gaze to a complex of white fences surrounding some lush green turf near the track...there on the grass I could make out only one horse...it was proud, shivering and skittish, and being led around in circles by a trainer...past some more fences and a trim row of hedges were the empty starting gates, where the staff were bending to get ready the machinery...the layout, the equipment, all of it seemed to involve nothing that I could really understand, but I could tell that the girl beside me seemed to be alone...I let out a cheerful sigh, because I was so delighted to be with her.

'Would you like a bit of champagne?' I asked her, and turned in my seat.

I could hear a slur in my voice...I was holding out one of our cups for the girl, though for a moment she didn't move...maybe she was tired of how the upper classes insisted on behaving at the races, but I saw her lips pull back into a small smile, as if she was conscious of her own attractiveness to me...then she reached out in a slow, deliberate manner and accepted the cup. I had to work at keeping my arm steady while I poured the hooch for her, and it was tricky...it appeared I'd been misjudging just how much champers I could handle. 'My name's Catherine,' the girl said quietly. She held the dripping cup away from her with the tips of her long fingers...evidently she was hoping not to let anything land on her clothes...Struan leaned over to join us, and the three of us tried clinking our cups together...I felt disappointed when the plastic refused to make any noise. 'Do you two have some kind of interest in a racehorse?' my long tall Cathy asked.

'We do,' I lied. 'We have several interests.'

I took a generous sip from my cup...but as I raised my arm, I was mostly aware of the over-padded shoulders in my jacket lifting awkwardly towards my ears.

'I'm Andy, and this here's Billie,' I said to cover any embarrassment.

I was making a brave effort to enunciate properly, because it was high time to disguise the fulsome effects of the bubbly.

I added, 'We're men. We're young men about town. And what do you do, eh?'

By now, sitting here at the races in a suit next to a pretty girl with whom I was sharing champagne, I was feeling oddly detached from myself...it even seemed strange to me that I hadn't bothered to tell the girl about my being a writer...but in fact I didn't feel in the least like a writer at that moment. 'I work as a secretary in town, for a real-estate firm,' Catherine was saying.

'Well, we're company directors,' I cut in.

Secretly I was impressed that someone my age might be doing real work for a living...I saw a name that was spread across a large hoarding, far across the track, and had a small flash of ingenuity.

'We're at Skellerup,' I continued in a rush. 'You know, gumboots, wet-weather gear, tennis shoes. All that razzmatazz.'

I pointed down at my own filthy sandshoes, acting as if they were an eccentricity in which I liked to indulge...Catherine smiled faintly once more. She said, 'You look a bit young to be company directors.'

'Well, not when your name is Skellerup,' I insisted. 'My dad and my uncle run the good old firm.'

I turned and gestured at Struan...he'd been sitting quietly at my side, watching me go through my patter.

'Billie here's my cuz,' I said.

'That's right,' Struan said. There wasn't much persuasion in his voice, but I saw that he was nodding his head.

'We're the Skellerup boys,' I declared, and laughed.

I took another sip and found I'd finished my drink...my head was buzzing with the wine...after a few minutes we all three decided to go back downstairs and place some bets...as we got up, I kept checking that Catherine would actually join us and I gave her my arm to walk on...I was determined to behave as though plenty used to dealing with secretaries. At the rear of the stands we picked our way with care down the narrow steps to the betting hall...Catherine kept her long arm willingly in mine... she leaned into me and I could feel the stiff wire of her brassiere rubbing against my elbow...Struan was well in front, and at the entrance to the betting hall he halted and watched us descending...I thought his eyes were bright with mischief as we approached. 'Just don't spill any plonk on my suit,' he whispered when we drew level. But the next two races were a bust...it didn't matter that we went back to our seats and stood up at the exciting bits amongst all the other shouting punters, cheering for our horses...it didn't matter how much we yelled our hearts out and stamped and threw our hands into the air with frustration...the bloody nags came nowhere...each time we sat down again afterwards feeling deflated and deprived of energy, and I was conscious of just how hard all three of us were trying to look as if we still knew what we were doing. At last Struan and I decided to pool our resources...putting a decent bet together on another race was going to eat up the remains of our cash, but suddenly I was sure it was going to work, whatever horse we picked...I could imagine us winning and me making all my moves with Catherine...I felt thrilled...I could feel the devil sitting close on my shoulder and almost tickling my ear, because I was entering a state of mind where everything began to seem possible, even easy. Once again I helped Catherine downstairs and enjoyed each second of it...there were lengthy queues already in place in front of the betting windows and we had to join a line far at the rear...Struan tried studying the horses' form in a borrowed race book, but I just let the names of the animals play over my charmed mind...I kept my arm tight around Catherine's small, slippery waist as we waited. The three of us moved forwards in a steady shuffle up to the counter... when we reached it, I pulled Catherine even closer and put my other arm over Struan's shoulders…he looked delighted, and I stared each of them in the eye in turn…that way, they couldn't notice how my uncomfortable jacket's sleeves were riding up.

'Pick a horse,' I said loudly to them both.

Back in the stands, we stood and began cheering from the very start of the race and went at it until our throats felt raw…a late sun had come out at last amid the scraps of cloud overhead…it was glinting richly on the colours of the grass and on the jockeys' silks above the galloping horses as the leaders approached the far side of the course…we watched the riders, all crouched in their saddles, flitting by against the fence-line…their outstretched arms seemed to shunt back and forth in time to our rhythmic yelling as they bobbed onwards. Some of the horses broke away and went wide as they left the back straight…just past the final turn the jockeys started whipping at the animals' shoulders…the crowd rose around us and we strained ourselves forwards…the race-caller was screaming above the ever-growing roar…our lovely mount came romping in first. At the flashes of photos on the finish line, I turned and kissed Catherine hard…her hair was bouncing on my cheeks…I felt her shiver…I pressed myself in against her, and she slid her tongue deep into my mouth… when we were done kissing, it was a job to concentrate on what was happening around us. But the next race was going to be the last of the day…I was desperate to get a bet on…I was convinced my bet was going to win, more so than I'd ever been of anything else, and the idea ran back and forth through my overheated mind that company directors were always winners. The three of us went downstairs to put our money again on just one horse…I was insisting that we had to stake all of it, every penny… I cajoled and pushed…in front of the betting window I took the time to kiss my Cathy again…we picked a nag without giving even the least proper care to the odds…I just had us slide our fingers quickly down the race book's list and select a runner almost at random. We were cheering upstairs from the moment when the horses plunged out of the starting gates…I kept grabbing at Cathy and whooping…the sun had gone back into cloud, obscuring the view, but at the far turn we could see our horse led the group pounding along beside the low white fence-line and I became very aware of how much I looked right, every inch of me, working my role…the trackside punters were leaving their places and pressing up against the rail before the course…the crowd around us tensed and moved in a shrill, gasping body…at the final turn the horses seemed to spread out wider across the track, kicking up bits of muddy turf, and someone behind me started complaining that the ground was really far too soft. Our horse stayed on the fence coming into the home stretch...it was pulling several lengths out in front...it was finishing in style when it reached the post...Catherine jumped and hugged me so hard that I thought I'd get her clothes off right there on the spot. Once the race was done, the three of us each caught our breath and watched the jockeys beginning to stand upright in their saddles, raising their heads under their caps as they let the horses run on...then Catherine gathered the tickets from me and went off downstairs to collect our winnings...Struan and I considered going with her, but we wanted to linger and see our winning animal come round into the birdcage. For some minutes we were preoccupied with imagining how we'd spend all the money...I felt that the members' stand had been lucky for us...I noticed some wiry red roses were growing on bushes trained along a rail opposite the front of our stand, and I thought they must have been planted there for people like me...it was good to be a member. 'You know, I'm going to have to take off for work at the restaurant soon, eh,' I heard Struan saying after a bit. He sounded tired but happy. 'Why don't you squire Catherine to the varsity Stein?' he suggested. 'There'd be a party on out there tonight for sure.' I wondered what kind of party exactly a Stein was, but I pretended that I didn't need anything explained.

'How would we get there?' I asked.

'Just hop in a taxi, man,' said Struan. 'You can afford it.' At that I realised I could, too...with my winnings I could get a hotel room...tonight I could bang my little secretary silly...I gazed fondly in the direction of the stairs...some of the overdressed racegoers were shuffling past us along the row of seats in order to leave.

'She's taking her time,' I said. After a while I added, 'Maybe she had to go the toilet, eh. Girls do that when they get excited.'

Struan said nothing...still Catherine did not appear...I stared off at the birdcage, where our horse stood held at the bridle by a trainer...the horse was shifting from one leg to the other and pawed occasionally at the ground...it was under a blanket now, but its bare, exposed flanks rippled with the power in its lean muscles. The minutes ticked by...the head of the Jockey Club began making a speech...he stood stiff and straight at a microphone set up out in front of the grandstand, and a small group of dignitaries were gathered behind him...he kept nodding his bald head obsequiously at an elderly woman standing nearby, who was wearing a huge, tawdry hat. Many of the punters at the trackside had gone, and most of those still around us were leaving…for a bit longer we hung on, but it was growing clearer with every drawn-out moment that Catherine was not coming back…Struan shrugged…when I didn't react, he shrugged again. 'Well,' he said philosophically at last, 'that's that fucked.' I busied myself with looking down at my feet, hoping to match his stoic mood.

'At least the champagne was sort of free,' I said.

We stayed waiting in our places a little more, and then gave up… Struan had to go to his restaurant…I decided that I'd go to the varsity Stein in any case…it meant walking the whole way, but I'd never been to a Stein before. In the car park outside the grounds, Struan gave me directions and assured me that it wouldn't be too far…I waved him a curt goodbye, still embarrassed at how I'd lost our money, as he drove off in the MG…for a few minutes I gazed at the back of the stands and reflected on life, though nothing but disconnected thoughts rose into my head…then I left the grounds and began trudging along what Struan had told me was Yaldhurst Road…the light was going, and heavy blue shadows stretched out from the fences and power poles across the footpaths and the asphalt on the street…Yaldhurst Road seemed bleak. My troubles weighed down on my shoulders and I tramped along in a slump, trying not to think… soon the sun was gone and my feet were sore, but at last I could see half-lit, grassy landscaped areas running far back from the road I'd just turned into, and the dark slabs of official buildings…I'd arrived at what appeared to be the edge of the university campus. I decided to accost some students for information…a handy pair were waiting a little further up the footpath at a bus stop, bent over together in the shadows under a street-light…they looked like a couple, whispering to each other in a comfortable way…I interrupted them and asked exactly where on earth the bloody Stein was. The guy out of the pair straightened his back and stared at me, but after a moment he inquired in a respectful tone whether I meant the Stud Ass party…as I nodded, I realised I was still dressed in my three-piece suit, and supposed I looked like a businessman…the guy told me to try the first floor of the Student Union…fortunately, he raised one skinny arm and pointed the way with a nervous gesture…I saw he meant a long, two-storey building in the near distance, set well back from the street on a broad lawn that was planted with withered cabbage trees… I marched off without bothering to thank him, because I figured that was how businessmen behaved. The Student Union was made of raw concrete cast in a complex jumble and looked very modern…a number of yellow lights illuminated the stark exterior in places and, as I approached, I could discern small ornamental balconies tucked away here and there in the concrete, each covered with a rough wooden cladding…I located the entrance, and inside found a grand, cement-walled concourse and some wide metal stairs leading to a mezzanine…I headed for the stairs as quickly as I could, feeling low in spirits…there were students everywhere with shoulder-length hair and dirty jeans, moving about and talking, and lots of them up on the mezzanine…I could hear competing, busy echoes from them all around me as I started trudging on the stairs, trying to forget the tenderness in my feet. A sleepy-faced, bearded student wearing wire-rimmed glasses leaned down from one of the black railings above and waved, and I almost waved back until I saw his cobber come past me with a hand raised in reply…I felt sure that I could only look out of place in my stupid suit, and even surer that people were staring at me or purposefully ignoring me as I hustled along…but at the top of the steps I could see where the Stein must be. It had to be at the opposite end of the balcony on the mezzanine, where several large groups of students stood gathered outside a doorway in a corner…people kept arriving, and the students waiting to get in through the door were all greeting each other in the cramped area as if they knew everyone else…everybody was pretending that they were not the least bit in a rush, but something was quite evidently holding them up…I heard crowd noise and the soft boom of music coming out from inside over their heads as I drew nearer and joined them. Most of the students milling around me were male and dressed in loose woollen jerseys, checked shirts and jandals…I thought they appeared very casual, standing together in their scruffy, careless clothes, and I fretted again over my embarrassing outfit…a few of the guys were talking amongst themselves about forestry papers, though the music made the gist of their words hard to catch…then I realised that it was paying an entrance fee which was slowing everybody down…a girl was sitting by the door with a blue metal cashbox balanced on her lap, only taking people's money one by one…she was stamping the backs of people's hands from an ink pad, but I had nothing to get myself in with, despite my suit, not so much as a penny in my pocket. I began jostling deeper into the midst of a group of students, shoulder against shoulder… there were several moments of collective confusion while I tried acting as

194

if I was in amongst a congregation of some good old pals...I kept chattering about forestry with the people next to me, about trees and soil and planting things, and tried to be lively...the students responded by moving away as though they couldn't wait to get rid of me...but suddenly, just as I'd hoped, everyone went through the entrance into the party at once in an anonymous body, and the girl didn't attempt to stop us. Past the door, I let my gang of new friends go off ahead on their own and lingered for a while before wandering through a narrow, concrete-walled room...it was a poorly-lit sort of foyer with a low ceiling, almost empty except for some badly upholstered green couches scattered about here and there... already a slow dribble of students from back at the entrance was overtaking me and filing by...but I turned a corner and finally discovered what I'd been traipsing halfway across town for...I was at the far end of a longer, bigger version of the previous room, low-ceilinged and dim like the other, but packed now with people, amplified noise and smoke. I saw the students in front of me were all standing and gazing off in the same direction towards the room's other side, watching a band...most of them were rocking back and forth where they stood...everyone was displaying an almost competitive look of absorption...as I pressed in closer, I could feel the heavy fug of the stale air and catch the smell of deodorants working hard on the limbs of the partygoers around me. So, I thought, this is a Stein. Far across the room the band was crammed onto a small, spot-lit stage and only the musicians' heads were clear in sight above the throng of people...one or two of the band members were even bent down a little to avoid the constriction of the ceiling-beams...it was a large group with three guitarists and a drummer, but including as well a trumpet player, some kind of special percussionist and several backing singers...right now they were all running through a song that was restrained and soulful, but it felt as if they might break into something jumpier at any moment... through the crowd I could see that the dance floor just in front of the stage appeared close to full with people shifting and swaying to the laid-back rhythms. But I was still out of sorts, and I pushed my way in hard where the crowd was loosest, sidling past some people and behind others until I joined a group of partygoers clustered at one edge of the room... they were holding drinks and some were leaning with their shoulders on the rough, unpainted cement walls...a few of them turned to inspect me as I drew closer, but then they moved and put their backs to me, keeping their distance...I decided to thread my way further forward into the gathering, but I couldn't shake the impression that everyone here had their own friends with them and around them, everyone except for me... people kept shifting to get out of my path or inviting me to go on by, though I didn't really want to go on by...I just couldn't manage to find a group to attach myself to. While stumbling along I remembered there were some cigarettes in a crushed packet in the rear pocket of my trousers...they were the fags I'd bought on the ferry when coming over here to the South Island...I stopped to take them out and lit a smoke, but didn't enjoy it all that much...next I offered the battered packet to a tall, gaunt fellow standing near me...he took it from my hand and at once disappeared into the crowd. With that I began to think maybe I should leave and just slope off to the Salisbury Street flat...I still had Struan's key and could let myself in...maybe I could pick up my novel where it had got left off, though I'd never felt less like writing...I'd never felt less literary since my moment of inspiration on that day at the family dinner-table in Palmerston North...I just wasn't sure, not anymore, that writing could even be done...you needed to be one of those genius guys to write, but I was never going to fit the bill. With a little more judicious pushing I drew near the edge of the parquet floor that marked the dance area...I wondered if I could maybe steal myself a drink...there were three half-full stubbies abandoned in a row where the red and yellow hardwood in the parquet floor started...nicking one would be the highlight of my evening. Then, close-by through the knots of people, I saw a girl dancing about in a languid manner, half circling at a little distance from her partner...the girl was wearing a dark-toned, purple satin evening dress...the dress was held up at one of her shoulders with a bright gold clasp and it draped in flattering contours down over her slim waist and thighs all the way to her ankles...it seemed every bit as over-elaborate as my suit. The girl's bare swaying arms revealed themselves clearly against the dress's glossy material...her arms looked thin and pale as she shifted back and forth in the rhythms of the dance...despite her hints of makeup I could see she had a fresh complexion and a small, oval, fine-boned face with large winsome eyes and delicate features...her long brown hair was tied up into a pony-tail that displayed her slender neck...from where I stood watching, I thought her eyes were green. The girl swung completely around, still dancing in her preoccupied way...her dress was low and open at the back, and it revealed the sensuous, milky skin across her shoulder blades...I felt a sudden cramp in my heart. Now the girl's elbows swung up once

196

more against her willowy figure...once more she turned, gazing off past me as she moved with a new energy...my throat closed, and I felt sure that she was the most beautiful person I'd ever seen...I'd no idea until this moment that such beautiful people could even exist and breathe and carry on through life. The overheated crowd around me was distracting, dull and boorish...I wanted to get away from them all and yet I wanted to stay right here...now more than anything else I just wanted to absorb each aspect of the beautiful girl as she turned once again...but watching her there from the edge of the dance floor only made me feel wretched and even more depressed than I'd been earlier. Then the music's slow beat stopped, and everything was collapsing...the girl started crossing the inlaid floor away from me with the dark hem of her dress flicking at her heels...but I couldn't bear for her to leave...I hated her for it...I wanted to weep...it was torture, this speed with which I could be overcome by my own ravenous passions. In front of all these people I longed to shout, to howl out her name, her unknown name...I groaned...I guessed what was troubling me...this was love...this was *love*!... the awful feeling seemed to force itself out from the centre of my being. But the girl didn't even bother to look back...I was completely broken up inside...I was struggling to find a proper breath...I gazed in the direction of where she'd gone with my mouth hanging open like a bag. For a long while I stood quiet, frozen in place, alternately hopeful that the girl would return and forlorn when she didn't...but there was no reason left to remain because she had definitely vanished...the truth of this demoralised me all over again. Sometime later I made the inevitable trek off into town in the dark, heading for the flat...it was a long way on confusing, night-time streets and my feet were still rubbing in my shoes...the people I approached for directions, those who were out at that hour and prepared to answer me, said why not just take the bus, but I couldn't see a bus stop anywhere. After a while I began to slog across a very broad, level park, treading on a thin asphalt pathway through the spread of the grass...the path kept meandering further and further from the road into open fields and wooded areas until I could no longer see clearly to the edges of it all...the far-off streetlamps tossed down their light only in hazy, desolate patches...the bare misty spaces around me were unlit, and more and more I felt alone in a deep, surrounding darkness...I heard an occasional car's drone fading into the distance...a hidden bird screeched something weird when I passed under some trees. I supposed I should take care to check behind me...I should think about avoiding the worst of the dark places...but there was only the plodding noise of my own footsteps for company and I could care about nothing except my nagging, miserable memory of the girl. Finally the main road came up again through the damp and creepy night, and I crossed an old bridge...the bridge had white filigreed railings that seemed to stand out against the clinging gloom, but I was free of the park and walking on a well-lit street...next, after a block or so, I left the street and started to cut across another grassy space, this time only a small public square consisting mostly of grey lawn...the square was flat and featureless, and had trees and clumsy-looking benches arranged along its borders around me, and its high streetlights imposed faint shadows at angles over the turf...an out-of-place-looking lamp was shining in the square's otherwise empty centre...I drew closer and saw the lamp was set on a cast-iron post that was anchored into a bulky concrete base...at length I came to a stop alongside. The lamp was stained with rust and soot and its tall post was curiously fluted...the dim light at its top shone from an ornate glass cage...up beyond the whole quaint contraption, I could see where the pale edges of the clouds had begun to bulge and part...a half-moon was showing itself in the broad black sky. I thought of how both lights, the lamp and the moon, seemed to rival each other...I couldn't make out which was the stronger, so I kept on gazing upwards until my balance faltered...the ground was threatening to slip away beneath me and the sky swirled a little, but I went on staring up into the heavens with my eyes wide. I felt my heart swelling up again...it swelled up so bloated and shivery that it almost consumed me...I pondered all those great and destructive questions about the universe...I decided that, if there was a God, part of Him must be what we aspire to and die trying to achieve...next I swore a momentous and binding oath. I swore that I was going to be a writer...I was going to do grand things and win glory...I was going to write books more marvellous than the fat moon and the stars in the sky...then I would be famous, so deeply famous that the girl on the dance floor was going to know all about me...she'd recognise me, even though I'd no idea of her name...she'd remember me, even though we'd never really met. Hot, bitter tears sprang down over my cheeks...I could scarcely believe the idiocy of my own heart...but it was *my* heart that I was lost in...I stared up into the lights and swore anyway.

Much later that night I woke up with a shock...I felt too dazed to think properly and my blood was pumping hard...all I understood was the vague, visceral sensation of my own fear…I was lying on the sunroom bed in the flat in my T-shirt and underwear, and I wasn't sure how long I'd been asleep. But the doors to the room were half open…they'd been pulled gently back and someone else seemed to be there, near me, in the darkness…I could hear little noises from furtive, stealthy movement… they seemed to confirm there really was someone in the room…finally I realised that it was Struan.

'What are you doing?' I asked.

I was surprised by the sound of my own words, spoken out loud… my eyes were coming rapidly into focus…Struan was dressed in his work clothes and bent over, slipping off his shoes…he straightened up and got himself tentatively onto the edge of the bed…he looked as if he was going to lie down on the sheets. 'I am so tired,' Struan whispered. His voice was very close. He added, 'Let me just, like, stretch out here for a bit, okay.' I dithered, wondering what to do…the charitable thought came to me that he must be drunk, or perhaps he'd simply gone into the wrong bedroom.

I said, 'Look, I don't think it's—'

'Just for a wee while,' Struan murmured in a firm tone. By now he was half reclining on the bed…I wasn't sure what else I could say…maybe I should tell him that I was tired too…after all, that was why I'd been sleeping.

'Listen, Struan,' I began.

'I'm Billie, remember?' Struan whispered. There didn't seem to be the slightest hesitation in his voice…he was extending his legs out along the bed and I felt him put his head up beside my pillow. 'Just go off to sleep again,' he said. But I couldn't just go off to sleep…I lay on my back, fretting, with my eyes wide open…I stayed staring in something like fright up at the marks on the cobwebby ceiling and tried to concentrate on making myself breathe normally. It was unpleasant and silent in the dark, and the distant sounds of traffic that I dimly remembered falling asleep to were all gone…I wondered if perhaps Struan really was tired and only wanted forty winks…perhaps I was overreacting to something pretty harmless… at any rate it was his flat to sleep in, the whole place, wherever the mood took him. I reminded myself too that Struan was smaller and probably not as strong as me…I felt a sudden sense of comfort in thinking so…but next I felt uncomfortably queasy once more at realising that I did need to think this way…after that, while I was reminding myself all over again that I was still the stronger of us, a pair of soft arms slid up around my neck.

'Struan,' I said.

I took one arm and pulled it off...I felt a flush of terrible embarrassment...I couldn't imagine which was worse, that Struan would put his arms around my neck, or that he'd think I'd enjoy it. 'Just, let's just sleep,' Struan mumbled.

'This isn't going to work,' I said. 'I'm not sleepy, and I don't feel like—'

But there was movement up near my face and a smell from warm wisps of breath...somebody was kissing my cheek...it had to be Struan... there was no one else in the room...the kissing was damp and distressing, and I tried raising a hand to brush Struan off...then I sat up quickly in the bed and pulled my knees up almost to my chin.

'I don't think this is such a good idea!' I wailed.

I heard Struan asking, 'Really, are you sure?'

'I'm sure!' I said.

'Well, you know, I thought you might like to try it,' Struan said. He spoke in a high, artificially playful voice, but already I was getting myself out of the bed...my feet touched the wooden floor and the boards seemed cool and safe under my bare soles...I stood in the middle of the sunroom and tried to think of what had happened...my face and cheeks felt hot in the dark...I was beginning to feel shaky with rapidly accumulating anger.

'I don't want to try it!' I shouted.

I hoped that sounded resolute...Struan shifted and sat upright amongst the sheets...I wasn't confident about what he'd do next and by instinct I backed further away from the bedside...suddenly I thought this must be how a woman would feel, how frantic for escape, whenever a man made unwelcome advances...all at once I felt an immense sorrow for the whole of womankind, and their lives struck me as precarious and infinitely valuable. Struan had swung his legs down onto the floor...it was a relief to see that, at least, he was still fully dressed...he got up and sashayed past me to the doorway, but then he halted at the threshold...he leaned with one thin forearm propped up along the doorframe...I wanted more than anything for him to go, and I wondered how on earth women endured this sort of thing. 'You won't tell people, will you?' Struan asked. It hadn't occurred to me...who did he imagine I'd want to blab all of this to?...but even while I seemed to think about it, Struan repeated the question more urgently.

I did my best to sound calm as I promised, 'No, I won't tell anyone.'

In the dim grey light Struan appeared to be smiling. 'Billie's going to

get some beauty rest now,' he muttered. He dropped his arm to his side…
with a flouncing movement he started walking off into the living-room…
finally it came to me that I should ask just how he'd himself got into the
flat in the first place, but already he was gone. I pulled the doors closed in
front of me…I tried not to make my actions seem too hasty…there was no
latch or lock anywhere I could find, but I went on looking for one anyway,
and at last with a sense of reluctance I lowered my haunches back down
onto the bed…I stayed sitting motionless for a long time, facing the door
and staring at Struan's shoes, which were still lying on the bare floorboards exactly where he'd left them. I told myself that the hush of the
night was reassuring…I also pondered what kind of plan I should have in
case Struan came back…but he didn't appear again.

FIVE

When I awoke, it was already late in the morning…through a crack in
the curtains the hot summer light was tumbling down from high up in the
sky and shimmering in an intense yellow glaze along the edges of the curtain's fabric…the light warmed the room and appeared to be striving to
announce the new day. Gradually I began to recall what had happened…
as an extra hint Struan's shoes were still lying abandoned on the floor near
the bed…his suit and the shirt that I'd borrowed the afternoon before
were still draped across the chair…I supposed that I'd slumped over and
fallen asleep while trying to keep a watch for him coming back. I got up,
dressed in my jeans and went on tiptoe into the living-room…there was no
other sound anywhere in the flat…the morning sunlight was illuminating
broad sections of coarse scrim on one wall…on the sofa I saw a large cardboard cut-out of a whisky bottle, propped up against an armrest and looking like some kind of advertising paraphernalia…perhaps it was something that Struan had brought back with him the night before and forgotten
amidst all the weirdness and confusion. There was no suggestion of any
movement from the direction of Struan's bedroom at the other end of the
flat…I stood still for a moment listening, but could hear nothing…it was
difficult to imagine that Struan could be off in there, peacefully asleep…
but I felt fairly sure that he was and I went on listening even harder, with

deep concentration, as if this might prove something. Then I returned to the sunroom and gathered up my gear to leave…as I went through each guilty action of packing it seemed more and more important not to make any noise whatsoever…at last, when it was done, I picked up my old duffle-bag and Half-Arse with the very ends of my fingertips…I slunk out into the living-room again and winced in alarm at every creak of the floorboards…I left the flat and entered the stairwell, closing the door behind me with the very faintest of clicks. The dog pooh was still there on the landing…it looked dried-up now, pale and shrivelled…as I stepped past it I bade the whole mess a silent goodbye…I felt bad to be running off like this, but I wasn't going to write anything in the flat…I needed to find somewhere else to start on my novel, someplace where I could write the first things that came into my head. Once outside and onto the street I waited for a moment, standing on the footpath with my bags in my hands…it was Sunday, and a mild, warm wind was blowing down the road onto my back…I was feeling fine and free, and wondered where to go…it seemed sensible to begin by walking into town…I took a deep breath, and then another… then I set off at a brisk new pace. I retraced my steps from the other day back in the direction of Cathedral Square…despite being close to the heart of the city, the streets around me were broad, empty and unnervingly quiet, and had a spooky Sunday feeling…after a few blocks I entered a small park…I reached a stream which I dimly remembered and saw the wide lawns on both sides down to the riverbanks were cut so close that the grass appeared almost manicured, with the edge of the water lined by willows and toetoe. Suddenly I guessed that this stream must be the Avon, the river of Shakespeare, and that I was starting to cross this Avon on an old-world, weathered iron bridge…the bridge seemed charming and quaint, though the river itself below me was choked in places with reeds and Christmas lilies and looked disappointingly shallow…all the same I thought maybe I'd try seeing where the Avon headed…maybe a river, even a little one, would lead me to some answers. Beyond the bridge was a small meandering road that was following the stream's course and I made for it, waving off a few sandflies…as I plodded along the road's uneven cement footpath on the edge of the riverbank I could see a lot of ducks quacking and bobbing nearby on the placid water, the only creatures of any kind around…the ducks didn't seem to be harbouring any major problems of their own on a warm summer's day…but then, they were ducks…ducks didn't want to be writers…they didn't suffer the exceptional burden of art. I began to think of what I might write if I could use those fine first thoughts coming into my mind…I considered what it would be like to roam about in my own ideas…finally it occurred to me that, after all, I might not be such a blank canvas…my feet were padding over the cracks in the footpath, and a faint and pleasant coolness came off the river's marshy, narrow waters, but I was soon lost in remembering something that had happened to me…it was so long ago that it felt almost as if it had happened to someone else…it was back during primer two, far away at Winchester School in Palmerston North. I could recall how mighty glad I'd been to get out of primer one, because primer one was taught by Mrs Watson…she was an intense little elderly woman who had greasy white hair, a small angry mouth and a glass eye, rigid on the left side of her face…she wore tweed clothes that smelled of camphor, and she was constantly hobbling with a stooped and jerky gait around the tables at which we sat in her classroom…oh how we dreaded her pausing at our backs in her habitual irritation with her freakish face hidden just out of sight…oh how we dreaded it when she bent down, pushing that wrinkled, twitchy head next to our cheeks, to warn or scold us. In Mrs Watson's room there was a large plywood doll's house set up for the girls to play with…there was a long strip of blackboard painted across the back wall for us to write on in chalk…but Mrs Watson was mostly famous for the way she dealt out discipline…she was every bit as pitiless as she looked. In my second week at school I watched her strap two big kids from the standards…they were brought into the class by another teacher one morning and made to wait before us…they stood in bare feet on the edge of the mat while we surveyed them from our seats around our tables…they were fidgeting in front of us and wiping their fingers against their pants, and they tried not to shiver from anticipation when Mrs Watson ordered both of them to stretch out their hands, palms upward…the big kids didn't hesitate when they raised their arms, but they still couldn't help flinching as Mrs Watson produced her long leather strap from a cupboard…next she started whipping them on their hands and the inner parts of their forearms, one kid and the other, over and over, and she raised red wheals up to their elbows. The kids were rough and dressed in ugly, cast-off clothes…they had military haircuts which gave them square-shaped heads and made them look like the types who wouldn't mind a bit of pain, but both of them began crying and whining as the hitting went on…at last they went out of the room, whimpering with hurt, and as the door closed on them I decided right then and there to be good or, even better, not to get caught...I could see the vital importance of not getting caught by Mrs Watson. I didn't feel safe, though, until I entered Miss Hughes's class in primer two...Miss Hughes was young and pretty, and she had ringlets of curly blonde hair that hung about her cheeks...her class was busy and fun, but her class also had several big boys who always sat in the back row...the word was they'd been kept behind for a year...mostly they stayed slouched with their stubby arms folded at desks that seemed too little for them, looking bored or sometimes helpless. But the big boys in our class were old enough to go up to the rugby field at playtime, past the incinerator and far off across the school...the real primer-two kids, the rest of us, were only allowed to be out at the front of the school playing simple games like hopscotch, tag or patter-cake...among the big boys in our class was a rugged, stocky kid named Wayne and partly for fun, and partly for protection, I became his friend...he asked me one morning if I'd like to come along at playtime over to the rugby field, since he and his mates always had a bit of a game going there...that set me thinking, because I'd never been all the way up to the footy field before. At half-past ten, Wayne began leading me across the school...we passed through a long slim gap between the caretaker's shed and one side of a classroom, and at the rear of the shed I spied the rusting and sinister hulk of the 44-gallon drum incinerator...I'd never been any deeper into the school than this...next we skirted a high, corrugated-iron fence that was peeling its flaky paint and there, suddenly before us, was the footy field. It was not so distant and not so large as I'd first imagined... it wasn't even a real football field with goalposts and marked lines and things...it was just a wide sweep of uneven and muddy turf, bounded on one side by a welded-steel jungle-gym...the other side fetched up against the stuccoed back end of a classroom block...but there were noisy big kids, lots of them, playing and jumping not so far from us. Wayne led me forwards onto the field and my jandals kicked into the gooey clumps of grass cover...I watched a group of very large boys moving nearby...they were mostly in dirty grey flannel shirts and shorts, and they were sliding on the mud and grass in their bare feet...then I could see some of them were running and passing an oval leather ball along a row, and they kicked the ball and changed direction...one boy threw himself at another's knees to make a tackle and grunted from the impact of collision. I stood still, small, waiting on the field...but mainly I was paralysed by my own sense of enchantment...there was no namby-pamby hopscotch or patter-cake here…it was all just so busy with people playing, really playing, everywhere around me…it was so much more confusing than anything I'd expected, but then I'd already forgotten what I expected anyway. Some of the boys had started a little run in my direction…one of them zigzagged with the oversized ball gripped in his hands…they were all coming up at me fast…I observed them with pleasure, their big pumping knees and elbows, the powerful sounds of their feet…I didn't make the least, not the tiniest movement…a massive boy ran straight over me as though I wasn't even there. My back was spread out flat on the wetness of the ground…I was gazing up at nothing but mountains of cloud in the huge blue sky… warm blood was dribbling from my nose…a few moments later I understood what had happened and started to cry hard. Wayne had vanished from view, but several girls who were older than me, from classes I didn't know, began to appear and stare down at my face…I was crying and bleeding, and the girls made a fuss…they pulled me up from the ground with eager hands…they made me stand very erect with my head tilted far, far back…I stood there in my vertical posture, crying and bleeding, while the girls commented with appreciation on all the blood. After a minute or so some of the girls decided they'd better walk me over to the office…that sounded serious, and I started crying harder…finally the girls marched me from the field, with my head still kept well back as if my life might depend on it…they were fretting together and getting more and more excited…they led me slowly in a convoy round past the incinerator, past classrooms and gawping kids, and in the direction of the office…I'd never been to the office before. My neck was sore, and I was aware now of a slick of mud caked along my bottom and thighs…I couldn't see well for tears and blood and the strange way my nose was pointed at heaven…but I could tell that still more girls kept on gathering around me, with a trail of them following behind…I began to cry even harder because they all seemed to be enjoying themselves so much. At last we reached the red wooden door of the school office, went in through it and started along a corridor…the girls pushed me before them down the passage in an experimental fashion…I shuffled meekly on the clean and polished lino amidst their noisy talk, but another door further up in the corridor opened and Mrs Watson stepped out…she stood there half bent over, lopsided and quivering…she was clasping a wooden ruler in her hand and demanding to know what on earth all this racket was. My escorts vanished…one last girl, the bravest, remained beside me for a moment, hesitated and then ran...I thought of running too, but I was slow and injured, and Mrs Watson came up and held my arm...she examined me sideways out of her single good eye...she growled something down into my ear...I felt abandoned, bereft in front of this crazy old woman.

'Been up at the football field,' I managed to snivel.

I was too miserable to think of a lie...I even said the whole word 'football' in order to speak properly...but I knew in my heart that it wasn't going to make any difference...Mrs Watson hit me with the sharp edge of the ruler around my legs. She told me I wasn't allowed up onto the football field...she told me and told me, and while she told me, she went on hitting me...but it made no difference because I'd already been there... all I could do was keep on crying, and my sorrow extended outward until I felt it encompass the entire sad, dishonoured world...who were all these people, these raging intruders and deserters, who seemed to populate every fucking inch of my childhood? It occurred to me now that Mrs Watson was just like Evan Blake, yet another adult with no off-button...I was still tramping along the footpath next to the Avon, half under the shade of some venerable-looking poplars that were heavy with leaf and sloping away from me towards the river...I glanced past the trees across the water and saw a fancy band-rotunda which was set on the opposite bank amid a shiny clipped lawn, guarded with a long stone border...the day was starting to get uncomfortably hot, but part of me was still remembering Mrs Watson, who was out there somewhere...how I would've liked to lay my hands on a time machine, because with one of those I could go back into the past and teach the old bag a lesson...I amused myself for a few moments as I trod along, thinking of all the harm I might do to her. Gradually the road and pavement me led me away from the river...I crossed a wide intersection and entered a much smaller street beyond it...parked at the kerb on the far side from me, in front of a row of imposing two-storey villas with high red roofs, was what appeared to be a lone, derelict car...I thought the car was a newish Corolla that had been somehow spectacularly neglected, with its patchy white paint scraped bare to the metal in places and spattered by bird shit...the grille even seemed stuffed with a material like bits of weeds...as I drew nearer, I saw that all the bodywork on the roof, the bonnet and the sides of the car was covered in a thick layer of grey dust. I couldn't help heading over the road to examine the whole thing more clearly...then I noticed the vehicle wasn't empty and that a man was actually in there...some of his chubby face was in view, pushed up hard against a side-window...the man was very fat, and I guessed he was sprawled in some ungainly way across the front seats...probably he was asleep. I got up close to the car at the driver's side and leaned down, gazing in, and sure enough the man was slumbering spread out on his back and his plump belly was on display, rising and falling...he had a small, flabby-looking arm flung over the top of one seat and the rest of him was twisted into a corkscrew posture, with his legs poked down into the footwell and his face up at the window-glass just in front of me...the man's spectacles were askew on his temples and sticking up loose along his bald head, and his pink mouth was wide open... he was definitely snoring...the sunlight was flooding in onto him and it occurred to me that, in spots at least, he was going to get badly burned... but next I realised that it was Prof Bingham there in the car before me. I reached up and tapped on the car's roof...it took several tries at tapping to get Prof Bingham to waken, but he raised his head at last and his glasses fell off...I watched him half sit up and make a dive down to the floor to retrieve them...he was wearing a pale-blue sweatshirt, and his wide back seemed to wobble beneath it as he fumbled about...when his face came up to the window again with his glasses on, he looked flushed and muddled. Prof Bingham was unshaven...his little goatee stood out amongst the black stubble across his jaw...he started rolling down the window until he had it almost completely open, and I saw his sweatshirt was badly stretched around the folds of his short, bulky neck. Without meeting my gaze, he asked quietly, 'What the fuck?'

'Professor Bingham, it's me,' I said. 'We met at the party. You know, it was two nights ago at the Ramada. Don't you remember?'

Prof Bingham made a noncommittal grunt...he manoeuvred his considerable torso so as to sit up straighter, sliding a little on the vinyl of the seat...finally he leaned an elbow out on the sharp rim of the lowered window-glass and craned his neck, straining upwards to survey me. 'Oh, yes,' he mumbled. 'The young writer with the confused sexual orientation.'

'No, I'm not at all confused about sex,' I objected. 'At least, not so far. But, Professor Bingham, I really am confused about writing.'

I stepped back and put down Half-Arse and my bag on the warm, smooth asphalt...I was standing almost in the middle of the narrow street and felt a bit exposed to the traffic, though it wasn't likely that there'd be any other cars popping along such a tiny road soon...I figured it was time to have a go at pleading my case.

'I've been trying to follow your advice, eh, and write whatever comes into my head,' I said, 'but that's not as easy-peasy as it's cracked up to be. It turns out that a writer's head is a pretty phenomenal place. Anyway, the thing is, I found out that basically I need to get myself somewhere good to do it all. And I can't find anywhere, eh. I left the flat I was in and I don't know where to go, and now the whole show seems to be sort of slipping backwards. The world is a very unaccommodating scene for artists—'

'The world is just fucking unaccommodating,' Prof Bingham interrupted in agreement. He waved with one fat hand and nodded at his own words, as if he'd just finished refining a great truth...then he gestured vaguely behind him into the grimy interior of the car. 'I mean, look at me,' he grumbled. 'I'm homeless. My bitch of a wife just slung me out. Said I'm too degenerate to live with. That dumb, vain, greedy shrew. That woman's been living on my paycheck for years and never done squat, just moan, moan, moan. And she thinks *I'm* immoral.' Prof Bingham sounded a little as though he was speaking to convince himself, but he went on describing his wife's worst features in considerable detail, warming to his theme...he talked and talked without pause in a continuous garbled harangue, speaking even while he was taking a breath, as if that might save time...Prof Bingham was bitter, because he'd been married for so very many years...he thought he'd seen it all, until now...but now it turned out he hadn't really seen it all, not by a long motherfucking chalk. I wondered what might actually have happened with his wife, but that didn't take very much effort for me to guess...Mrs Bingham had most likely objected to his educational methods. 'If she goes to the V.C., I could get the can,' Prof Bingham was groaning. 'I'm praying she won't, because then she'll want alimony, or maintenance, or whatever the fuck you people call it in this country. Oh, look at me, for Christ's sake. I've got my whole life in this car here.' Prof Bingham paused for my reaction at last...possibly his own exhaustion with marriage had caught up with him...I stared down through the dusty rear windows into the back seat of the vehicle...there were a few old record albums lying on the seat, with the pressed marks from the disks inside showing through the covers, and there was a small, garish, higgledy-piggledy mess of clothes. That seemed to be all...it didn't look like a very full life, but I thought that probably literary critics were a bit like writers...probably they weren't all that tuned into material things.

I asked, 'So what do you reckon you'll do?'

'Well, it's hard to say,' Prof Bingham muttered. 'I guess it's either camp out in the office at college—that means sleeping on the goddamn floor—or take off to the West Coast. I don't know.' He grunted…he shifted about restlessly on his seat again inside the car. Next he added, 'I bet I could find a commune of some sort over there on the Coast, you know, to hang out in.' Prof Bingham twisted himself further towards me…he crossed both podgy arms and laid them along the top edge of the open window…he was peering up at me once more from his seat, as though this time more genuinely intent on my response.

'The Coast sounds great,' I offered.

'Yeah,' he said, 'I guess. I've done the office thing on way too many occasions. The bitch'd figure out where to come find me, and like, we all know what happens then.' But I didn't know what happened then…in fact, I was quite keen to hear exactly what might happen when the bitch found him at the office, but Prof Bingham had halted…he was still turned in my direction, though he was gazing blankly off along his shoulder towards the front windscreen.

'You could probably get a whole lot of literary criticism done over on the Coast,' I suggested.

'Literary criticism is dead,' Prof Bingham whispered. He sounded distracted now as he spoke. 'Dead and gone. Little papers on the hillside,' he said. 'It was too good to last.' Finally he appeared to rouse himself and come back to the present…while he went on murmuring something under his breath he waved for me to walk around to the passenger side and get in…it seemed like a good idea, so I grabbed my gear from the road and trotted round past the bonnet of the car…when I opened the passenger door and clambered onto the empty seat beside him he was still talking, though sitting up straight with his hands on the steering wheel… I shut the door and occupied myself in arranging Half-Arse and my bag somewhere convenient down by my feet. Prof Bingham was saying softly, 'All washed up and gone to hell. Shit yeah. Nobody cares about literature anymore, nobody feels it. Nobody feels it down in their gut.' He started rubbing at his own generous gut under his sweatshirt…the shirt rode up his belly and showed a scoop of navel amid a mass of tangled body-hair. 'Life is where it's at,' Prof Bingham pronounced. He scratched himself philosophically and continued. 'Life. There's no time to put it on paper. I mean, it's too varied. It's too interesting. We should each have ourselves a pair of lives, one to do everything in, and then another one to think about it all in afterwards. Now, I know, I know what you're going to say,' Prof Bingham protested. He was staring out over the soiled bonnet of the car and I felt unsure whether he was really addressing me or not. 'Everybody goes on and on about the "university of life",' he said, 'but hell, in my extensive experience of the education racket you can't force people to get off their arses and study shit, not even in a metaphorical context. So we don't need a university of life, hell no. I mean, what do people like to do? Shop. That's the answer, shop. No one ever had a problem with a Spiritus Mundi based on shopping. So what we need is a "supermarket" of life. A supermarket of life, with bargains and discounts and the whole shebang. Tons of stuff all over the shelves, and trolleys that don't goddamn wobble. Pretty girls at the checkout. Cash or credit. Yeah, everybody should be encouraged to shop around a little in the supermarket of life.'

'I agree,' I cut in. Thinking that I needed to stay focused for both of us, I added, 'And I'd really like to go with you over to the Coast too, and find a commune. But that's because, for me, I want to write my novel there. I really think an isolated place might be best to get away from all these hassles.'

'A lot of loose pussy on a good commune,' Prof Bingham mused. He smiled, looking lost in his own thoughts again…it was as if he could see the loose pussy in his mind…then he seemed to snap out of it and turned to me. He asked clearly, 'Why don't you just accompany me and be my Boswell?'

'Okay,' I said.

I had no inkling of what he meant…I wondered if being someone's Boswell might be a new type of degeneracy…but by now I knew how much I was prepared to go along with, more or less, if it would at least get me somewhere to write…also I didn't think I'd have too much in the way of trouble with rule number one from Prof Bingham…rules weren't really Prof Bingham's thing. 'Fuck it,' he was announcing. 'Let's make it an adventure.' He reached out for the car's key in the ignition and turned it… the starter motor whined in a kind of agony, but nothing else happened… Prof Bingham pressed the key harder, jiggling his backside up and down on the seat, and finally the engine caught. Above the new growling sound from the motor Prof Bingham asked me, 'You got anything else you need to do in a hurry before we head for the hills?'

'Not me,' I replied. 'A writer needs to seize the day.'

'Good fucking attitude!' Prof Bingham barked in delight, and laughed out loud until his whole roly-poly body shook. After that he stamped his foot on the accelerator and gunned the engine hard...the entire car appeared to strain on the spot...at last it pulled away from the kerb with an ugly roar, though a lot more slowly than I'd expected, drifting towards the centre of the road...something out front under the bonnet was beginning to rattle dramatically. 'It's the camshaft belt,' Prof Bingham explained without waiting for me to ask. He grimaced. 'At least, that's what the skanky guy at the gas station told me. What does a camshaft need a belt for anyway? It hasn't got any pants.' He giggled like a silly-billy at his own joke and added, 'Don't sweat the thing. They tell me it's nothing to worry about.' Prof Bingham turned us into a large, one-way street and gradually he managed to convince the car to gather up some more speed...we started merging with other traffic...by now we were moving at a new and decent pace, with the rattling still happening under the bonnet, and we turned several times and seemed to flow into roads with an ever-greater number of vehicles...it wasn't very long before I saw that we were driving out past the airport. After that we soon left the city behind and the traffic thinned...we began heading through the flattest and most civilised-looking farm country I'd ever seen...we drove alongside beautifully maintained boundary-fences into a smooth pastel-brown landscape, with the paddocks spread in a sweeping, level vista out around both sides of the car...the view was broken only by the grazing stock and a few dark, elegantly arranged shelterbelts of pines and macrocarpas...but before us the highway pointed itself straight at a mass of mountains far in the distance...they arched up in a line, blue-black across the horizon, as if to bar our path. Prof Bingham switched on the radio, perhaps to drown out the ominous sounds emanating from the engine, but he couldn't seem to get anything to work on the dial...with the tuner knob he strummed back and forth across the wavebands and found only static, until at last he gave up and muttered a few words about hunting for a cassette...he felt around the sides of his seat with one hand, definitely hunting for something, and I watched him drop his chin onto the top of the steering wheel to help drive the car...not for a second did he consider pulling over or even slowing...instead he let go of the wheel entirely, scrabbling with both hands everywhere down along the floor...gradually his head slipped off the steering wheel into his lap and he was grumbling impatiently from someplace down near his knees...the car was mostly steering itself. I promised Prof Bingham that I'd do some hunting for the tapes...I tried to coax him back to sitting up and looking through the windscreen at the road...I insisted that we'd be better off if he was actually driving the car while it was moving...Prof Bingham gave a grunt, as though he didn't mind either way, but eventually his face came up and he took hold of the wheel with his hands again. I turned and leaned far over across my seat into the back of the car...for some time, bent like this, I searched around hard amidst the scanty clutter in the rear, checking the clothes and the folds of the seat-cushion and its edges, while my own seat's top banged against my stomach with each movement of the vehicle...after a lot of trying I could dig out only one cassette...I held the thing up and examined it just below the ceiling as the car continued bumping along...the cassette was old, a copy, and labelled *Tex Morton's 20 Golden Greats* in black felt-tip. I wriggled and sat myself down in the front again, and as I reached out with the cassette Prof Bingham seized it from my hand...without glancing at it, he tried jamming it into the car's stereo-player...he had to dab at the thing hastily with his fingers to push it home, but after a minute or so some yodelling country music droned across the car's interior...the recording didn't sound too good...it sounded as if maybe the tape had stretched...I thought Tex Morton's yodelling came over as remarkably flexible. 'That's it? Oh hell, that's all we've got?' Prof Bingham asked. His shoulders slumped and he looked dejected. He started to moan, 'And you think that crap is music? Eewww. Because there's no goddamn way that's the real McCoy. Imitative bungle if ever I heard the stuff. I mean, what a typical bunch of Kiwi idiots.' But then all of a sudden Prof Bingham straightened up again...he began squirming about on the spot and once more couldn't be bothered with watching the road...instead he bounced his buttocks up and down on his seat-cushion and turned to me. 'I've got it,' he hissed. His heavy jowls were trembling with excitement. 'Hell's bells, I've got it! That's my wife's tape. That's it. That's it. That explains it!' He looked me triumphantly in the eye. He shouted, 'I'll bet the bitch of a woman broke my fucking radio on purpose. Just so I'd have to hear this crap. On purpose!' Prof Bingham returned his gaze to the road, but he kept repeating the words 'on purpose' to himself with obvious satisfaction...finally I started agreeing with him, hoping it was the best course... time passed, and the mountains grew nearer and nearer, and Prof Bingham settled back into delivering his usual mumbled monologue in a manner even Stunt would have admired...he was accompanied by the engine rattle and endless elastic yodelling, since Prof Bingham didn't appear to understand that the tape might keep on repeating…it continued playing side after side on an unceasing loop, and occasionally Prof Bingham surfaced from his thoughts and complained about the music, although I didn't bother to help him make the crooning stop…he was muttering yet again through Tex's slurred version of 'Click Go the Shears' when we reached the foothills. Once in the mountains the terrain around us quickly grew rougher and scrubbier, and the highway became a lot more crooked…through the dust on the windows I saw the cold bleached-blue colours of clumpy tussock grass on both sides of the road…the outlines of the mountain slopes were now sharp and clear, and the car began labouring at each bend as we climbed and Prof Bingham talked…Prof Bingham had long since launched into other topics than his extreme hatred for his wife and Tex Morton…he was giving what sounded like a lecture on new Commonwealth literatures, a particular interest of his…at length he left off to reminisce about a recent visit an actual living author had made to the university, and I started straining harder to listen. 'That was because he's not white,' Prof Bingham was murmuring. 'Though, you know, he's Oxford-educated. I mean, a hell of a lot better educated than anyone in the English department. But he's never fitted into that whole European-tradition thing that kicks off with Shakespeare and Cervantes and God knows whatnot. And he wrote all those books about permanently ruined Third-World countries. Little places full of vicious claptrap that never get any better.' Prof Bingham was shaking his head from side to side…he had a look of something profound, like sympathy, on his face…but I wasn't sure whether it was sympathy for the writer or the entire Third World.

'So, pardon me, just who is this fellow and where was he from?' I asked.

I had to put my question over a snatch of warbled song…Tex was singing about someone beating up a man called Sergeant Small…I worried that perhaps the noise from the music and the engine would make me miss hearing Prof Bingham's reply and this gun writer's name. But in any case Prof Bingham ignored me and said, 'Out here on a British Council grant.' He was keeping his eyes fixed now on the upward-winding switchback road…the tarseal cover before us was uneven and showing long, snaking cracks. 'Oh, he's an Indian,' Prof Bingham added, as if my query had registered at last. 'Don't you know about him? Must be familiar with his work, surely. Major, major stuff. The department people put him up in some crummy hotel, for Christ's sake. Maybe they reckoned they had to

213

save the Council its money. I mean, really, what were they thinking? The guy was already very touchy. He felt he'd taken a lot of discriminatory-type questions at Victoria, after his lecture there. But I mean, they didn't even give him a goddamn chance to lecture at all to our crowd down here. And the department only sprang for dinner at the staff club, the tightwads—but you know, even that might have worked out. The guy brought along a bottle of wine he'd found, which it turns out he really wanted to try. But man, those morons from the department, they didn't want anything else with the meal but beer. And they served up a roast. He's a Hindu, for God's sake! What the fuck, they thought he'd like a home-cooked meal? No one ever noticed that he's a vegetarian. No one goddamn noticed! Typical bunch of Kiwi idiots! And then you!' Prof Bingham broke into his own story...he stared across at me with new vehemence. He shouted, 'You want to be a writer, yeah? In *this* country? With nothing—with nothing but its woolly-brained, sick-hearted and sad-arsed animals, and I'm not talking about the fucking sheep!' He'd taken his hands off the steering wheel again and he kept waving them, lunging around in my direction. He yelled, 'Do you have even the slightest idea how they treat real writers here? In this country? Well, *yeah*? Do you?' The car was steadily veering leftwards off the road...it was heading us at an angle into the crumbling rock-face alongside us, but Prof Bingham was still waving his hands around while he involved himself in answering his own question...as the rock-face came near I gasped for breath...involuntarily I pulled my knees up towards my chest, and I thought in fright of reaching for the handbrake...the car smashed across a white marker-post...Prof Bingham grabbed at last for the steering wheel...we swerved violently back into the road, crossed completely over to the other side and at once started scraping with a thick shriek of metal along the safety rail opposite. 'Shit! Shit!' Prof Bingham cried. But by now he'd regained some control of the car... we were moving back towards the road's centre and following the white line...Prof Bingham went on driving, but a little more carefully...we didn't bother stopping to check for damage. For several minutes afterwards Prof Bingham lamented his luck...he complained that I hadn't said anything to him as a warning and tried to make it all my fault...but I was too upset to reply...the adrenaline was still throbbing fast in my neck and shoulders...gradually Prof Bingham seemed to sense that I might be annoyed and he began to adopt a more chastened tone, even while making a lot of critical remarks about the local road conditions. 'Well hell,' he finished up.

He wiped his cheeks with one hand, and I saw that he'd been sweating. Then he continued, 'I suppose I was a bit too preoccupied thinking about that bitch woman I married, and her sitting there that day at the staff-club dinner. Visiting writer, you know, and she's only there with us all in a printed sundress, very low cut kind of thing, like she's just come off the beach. I mean, she was right opposite the H.O.D. Flashing herself, really showing off the goods, acting like butter wouldn't melt in her arse. Waste of effort in the end. The H.O.D. wouldn't know what to do with a bit of cleavage. Shorts and sandals, the entire lot of them round that table, like a bunch of schoolboys. You know that the cook out back had to make up a quick salad? Nearly couldn't manage it. And then all through the meal, the Media Studies people, those rednecks, they had no conversation.' Prof Bingham chuckled to himself...he glanced across at me and clicked his tongue with happiness, but I was still taking deep, even breaths to calm my nerves after almost getting killed...I was only half listening, and so Prof Bingham actually spoke louder. 'The Humanities people, huh,' he began saying. 'They're all just talking to each other about water-blasting somebody's swimming pool—it's like the guest's not even there. And so all through the meal the poor guy sits as if he's not really paying attention to a thing, you know, but now and again I thought he did come out with a few words. Showed he was aware of what's what. Anyway, I got the job of driving him back to the hotel. Jesus Christ, it was some dump, I'm telling you, not exactly the Chateau. So, well, I dropped him off and headed away for home, okay, and there's a call from him as soon as I get to the house. Already. Second I walk in the door. And the guy's crying down the phone. Crying. Saying this country's defeated him. He can't take it anymore.' Prof Bingham fell silent for a while and I took a moment to try and visualise an Indian writer...I could imagine him, the writer, sitting terribly alone and sobbing...I filled in some dreary details of the hotel with my mind's eye... it didn't look like such great shakes being an author, but at the same time I rather envied this man...the writer knew exactly where it was in life he wanted to be, even if he wasn't in it at that instant. Inside the car the air all around our legs was becoming unpleasantly cool, and I checked that the car's heater was on...it was, but it didn't work any better than the radio... before us the pale tussock cover on the mountains had thinned and was starting to disappear, so that the slopes we were heading into seemed to show nothing but bare banks of rock and scree. 'Goddamn country,' Prof Bingham began muttering. He said it over and over under his breath.

'So what did you do about the writer?' I inquired at last.

'Oh, the guy told me the wine had made him sick,' Prof Bingham replied. 'Made him "ill." "Ill" was the word he used. He said he couldn't sleep on the bed in his room. He had a whole long list of complaints. Go figure.' Prof Bingham shrugged. 'So in the end I just rang off and called the QE2 Council liaison man. But then I felt kind of responsible, you know, so I drove over to the hotel and saw the liaison fellow had come by. He was heading up the front steps into the place. Tall, blond, heavily-built guy, yeah. One of your rugby-types—thick neck in a cheap suit and eyes way too close together. Looked like his parents hauled in some favours and found him a job, you know? Probably a whole lot of favours. Oh boy, I just remember waiting, and this brontosaurus of a guy plodded back out with a little Indian man weeping on his arm. Quite a sight. The QE2 guy took him away and God knows what happened.' Prof Bingham gave a brisk, cynical laugh…he reached forward with one hand into the glove-compartment and I watched him pull forth a bright red packet of cigarettes, juggling it in his palm…slowly, by pressing the packet up between his hands on the wheel, he eased himself out a cigarette and got it into his mouth…he kept steering with whatever fingers remained available…I noticed the cigarette was of the same long brown sort that he'd been smoking when I first met him. Prof Bingham glanced at me…perhaps he'd seen how closely I was observing things. 'You want one of these?' he asked, speaking with the end of his exotic cigarette jammed in between his teeth. He tossed the packet towards me and it fell onto the seat by my lap.

'Okay,' I said.

Prof Bingham hunched forward once more to rummage in the glove-compartment…he produced a lighter, flicked it and, while the car jolted along, manoeuvred the flame up towards the end of his cigarette but away from his face…I got myself a smoke, took the lighter from Prof Bingham's clammy grip and used it too…I thought smoking might help me forget that, as of this moment, I was definitely cold…also I was starting to feel hunger cramps in the bottom of my stomach and it occurred to me that a hot home-cooked roast dinner would be pretty good about now. We were well up in the mountains and yet we continued to climb…we hadn't met another car in a long, long while…a wide gorge had opened up sometime to our right, and there was a narrow, meandering river far below us in the murky haze…to our left, the way was so winding and steep that in places there seemed scarcely room for the road…the country around us looked empty, harsh and a little threatening, and the sun had just gone down behind the far tops of the mountain peaks, so that the remaining light was grainy and shadows reached across the car...I saw dull white, dirty patches of snow were appearing here and there at the roadside. Prof Bingham switched on our headlights...he'd gone back to muttering about new Commonwealth literatures...I wondered if maybe these remarks were his stage-two lectures. After some time we started up an especially steep incline...the car slowed, and soon it was slipping a little on some fragments of fallen stone scattered along the tarseal...we were struggling, working more and more with each scrabbling motion of the wheels, until at last we were merely inching up towards the top of the rise...Prof Bingham pressed the accelerator to the floor but the car's power continued to drop away...he lifted his foot and shoved it down on the accelerator again, though if anything the engine grew quieter. Then the road flattened and we crested the top of the slope...we dipped downwards...the car began to coast and I thought we'd be all right, but at that moment the engine suddenly ceased altogether and the glow from the headlamps vanished... within an instant the rattling noise died away...the whole car was kaput and we were rolling downhill into the gloom through a new, eerie silence. There was no more country music...there were no lights shining at us in the dashboard...even Prof Bingham had stopped talking...I watched him turn the key in the ignition a couple of times, but nothing happened... instead we trundled on, gently, soundlessly downwards, and I began to miss the engine's crazy rattling. Finally we drifted to a complete stop at the end of the slope...we'd halted on one side of a low, rocky bend in the road...the car's nose was pointed off the shoulder of the highway at a patch of badly stunted grey scrub in front of us...we were gazing out of the windows at angular branches bunched all around among heavy shadows. I strained to stare upwards above the scrub and mountaintops, and saw there were black clouds in long bulky folds coming towards us across the dimming sky...the clouds were moving in fast...they seemed to lean in close and press down against the sides of the slopes...at the same time there was even more cold gathering in the interior of the car. 'Well,' Prof Bingham said, 'it's not the camshaft belt.' He turned a little and asked me, 'Know anything about engines?'

'Nothing,' I said, 'I'm a writer.'

'That's your answer to everything, isn't it,' he growled. Then he sighed deeply and added, 'Well, I do know this, we're fucked.' But Prof Bingham didn't look the least bit fucked...I noticed that he didn't even look very cold...he sat leaning with his fat forearms on the wheel, smoking the last of his cigarette, and I envied him the insulation he carried in his extra weight. My breath was misting in weak flurries before my face...the increasing darkness around us was now galloping in and I focused on the red glow from the tip of my own cigarette beyond my fingers...it appeared attractively warm...I took a lengthy draw on the cigarette, kept the smoke down and reflected for a minute...I felt that two such articulate, literary people as ourselves shouldn't be stuck for ideas at a time like this, but we were two articulate, literary people without a clue and in urgent need of real help. Next there was a small smack as something touched the front windscreen...I looked up and heard another tap on the windscreen, and another...there were wet flakes of snow landing on the glass, more and more of them...most of them immediately began to melt, but a few stayed on, clinging to the glass as spatters of ice...at last a lot of snow started to float down in tiny flecks and streaks, and these twinkled and danced about with a shiny life of their own in front of the car. So, I thought, this is a snow-fall. It was the first time I'd ever been snowed on...all of it looked so nice, so appealing, and it was going to freeze me to death...Prof Bingham was absolutely right...we were fucked. I stubbed out my cigarette in the dash-board ashtray...then I bent down to open my duffle-bag at my feet...rapidly I began to pull out all the clothes from the bag and to try putting them on, fumbling around...I had my spare jeans, some socks and a couple of extra T-shirts to use, but it was hard and awkward work in the tight space. Prof Bingham took the hint...he turned and reached for his own clothes in the back seat...one by one he dragged them all over into his lap, and I could see that they were mostly light summer wear...Prof Bingham puffed and snorted as he wriggled to get everything on...soon he was dressed in three bright green-red-and-gold Hawaiian shirts...there was one left untouched beside him that he'd given up trying to get into, so I took it and put it on as well, over the other gear I was wearing...by now we couldn't see anywhere out of the windows for snow, but we looked snappily dressed and ready for the beach. 'What is it with the goddamn climate in this country?' Prof Bingham groaned. The dark had set in almost completely, work-ing in weird contrast to the remaining bluish gleams off the snow...we were both shivering as we sat and the cold was still getting worse...I could hear Prof Bingham's teeth clacking, though it was difficult to discern the features on his face beside me...I supposed we really wouldn't last the

218

night if no one found us, but we didn't even have any headlights to indicate our presence…I kept my arms wrapped about myself, and started rocking back and forth…it didn't seem to help much, but it felt like something to do. After a while, I thought I'd better get us both up some sort of signal for assistance…I pushed open the creaking door on my side of the car and stepped out…the sharp raw air stung my nose…I could hear no reaction coming from Prof Bingham inside the vehicle, so I pushed the door shut behind me and took a few steps, and my shoes crunched in ice crystals on the solid asphalt…it was brighter out in the open than I'd expected, amidst all the snow flapping around…I paused and attempted to brush the steadily gathering damp flakes off my shoulders, but the stuff was coming down in a big way and my layers of clothes kept on getting wet anyhow. I took a lot more trembling steps further up along the rise of the road…already this was beginning to feel like a mistake, but it was important to battle onwards…I glanced back for the car to check how far I'd got, but the car had shrivelled somewhere into the snow and was hard to see…I tried forcing myself to walk on for perhaps a little bit more, and finally put my arm out against a rocky scarp beside me for support…my feet were getting awfully numb and strangely heavy. It was going to be better to double back…I turned, but felt myself slipping…my shoes were sliding on the loose scree and some treacherous patches of snow grass…plodding back to the car would mean a ton of effort…besides, I couldn't see anything…I sat down hard on the edge of the highway and thought that this had to be helpful, because I really needed a break. I wasn't going to rescue myself or Prof Bingham…instead, nature seemed determined to crush the life out of us…since I was sitting down anyhow, there was a bit more comfort in leaning up against the jagged rocks of the slope just behind me…a few of the stones were poking into my back, but I could scarcely feel them…it occurred to me that I might die, and I didn't want to die with my novel not even properly underway…I wondered just what on this freezing, forlorn earth I was going to leave behind me if I died, because no one would ever know about the first things that had entered into my head. For a moment there came a tremendous flush of panic rising within me…then I took a deep, calming breath and told myself it didn't matter…I hadn't learned much up till now in Prof Bingham's marvellous supermarket of life, but I was plenty old enough to know the score…nothing lasted, and nothing would confuse everything into itself in the end. I sat on, pondering vaguely about getting Half-Arse…it would be good to type up some sort of final note, but I couldn't move a muscle…I was wet through, and I had a sensation of sleepiness that was like being nagged at beyond any mercy…the soft snow was caked all over my shoulders and legs, and formed remarkably pretty piles all about me…perhaps Prof Bingham was in the same shape that I was, somewhere off there in the car…I thought perhaps he was sitting calmly and smoking and enjoying the complete lack of country music. I'd already closed my eyes for a little time when, under the eyelids, I could sense a strong glowing light…I told myself a light could only mean one thing and that it was necessary, vital even, to make a last big effort…if something was coming, what happened next was going to be crucial…to my surprise, I succeeded by instinct at getting to my feet…finally I struggled to step forward into the road, forcing myself to raise my arms. I tried looking into the almost vanished distance for a vehicle…I was fairly sure now that one was out there…it had to be coming towards me from someplace…besides, if it ran me over, it'd be doing me a favour. Soon there were some blazing lamps, a pair of them, shining up into my face…I thought I could hear a door being opened. 'Jesus Christ!' a voice said distinctly. Now was the right moment for me to speak, but my mouth refused to cooperate…someone gripped my arm…I was being pulled forward, and my legs were even offering encouragement, but then without the least warning I was being pushed backwards…I fell back, still without uttering a word, down across something spongy, the cushioned rear bench seat of a car…I was staring up at a low curving roof quite close to my face, and casually I considered whether this car might be a Volkswagen…but before there was any opportunity to ask, the door by my feet was slammed shut. Next I could hear Prof Bingham speaking some palaver in a mumble…the door was pulled open once more and admitted a fresh gush of cold air…I was jostled, and my trousers were being dragged off my legs, first one pair and then the other, with rough, repeated efforts…I was hauled into a sitting position, and both my arms were raised and forced into constricting sleeves…at last a baggy, itchy layer of cloth was shoved down all over me hard and, when my head became free again, I began to see better and found myself gazing into a face of extraordinary beauty…it was the beautiful face of the girl I'd seen at the Stein the night before, but it was only a glimpse, and just as quickly she disappeared. I was aware merely that the car was bumping along…I wanted to find the lovely girl once more but it felt too warm to move…it was nice to be warm, and it would be even nicer to fall sound asleep.

I woke up slumped half over onto my side with my face down and one cheek pressed flat into the seat of a car, the back seat because my eyes were focused on the slope of some seats in front...the cushion's springs beneath me were jolting a little against my jaw from the vehicle's motion, so we were definitely going somewhere...I glanced at my shoulder and saw it was covered by something thick, red and black, a swanndri...I could feel my T-shirt under the swanndri on my upper body, but the swannie's wiry wool was scratching at my bare skin down around my knees... with one hand I felt along the edge of my leg, and found I had no pants or underwear on...except for the mysterious swanndri I had nothing on at all over my lower half, but my hand dropped and brushed past Half-Arse and my duffle-bag, deposited near me down between the seats. I started twisting and wriggling about onto my back...the roof-light above came into view and shone starkly into my eyes, but despite the glare I could tell that I was gazing up quite close at somebody's features...I was looking at the beautiful girl again, who was peering down at me with what looked like intense curiosity...immediately the same sensations came over me, the agitation and the pleasure, that I'd felt upon seeing her at the university...she was here, she was still actually here, sitting beside me... then she glanced off away from me in an excited manner. 'It's all right. He's all right,' I heard her announce towards the front seats. Above me I could easily make out the girl's small chin as she spoke, her small mouth and the delicate mounds of her high, wide cheekbones...it was hard to believe that she was real, she was here with me...it was as if some fluttering presence in the universe had truly wanted us to be together...I could remember everything from the Stein about the girl, and every detail that I recalled appeared so simple and yet now so full of meaning...she lowered her head and looked down at me again with her lively gaze...her eyes were a breathtaking bottle green. 'We were worried about you, eh,' she said. 'No we weren't,' said somebody else. It was Prof Bingham's voice coming from the front of the car...I sat up in an awkward hurry and the back of Prof Bingham's big unmistakeable head slid into my view above the top of the front passenger seat, poking up round and pink...there were tufts of his rough, loose hair hanging about the rear of his bald pate...I saw another woman was in the seat next to him and that she was doing the driving...even with her back to me, I could tell that this new woman was stocky, maybe powerfully built, and sitting with her broad shoulders hunched forwards and her arms well up to grip the wheel...

221

she had long shoulder-length hair, unkempt and sandy-coloured, and cut in a fluffy, feathered style that hid much of her face from me, and she wore a large shapeless black jersey that I felt looked unpleasantly mannish. Prof Bingham turned half towards me across the seats, and I saw his eyes were scrutinising me up and down…I thought how an awful lot of stuff could go and happen while you were unconscious…he reached back high above me and switched off the roof-light. 'Snap out of it,' he muttered, and arranged himself on his seat again. In the fresh gloom of the interior he added, 'We've been picked up and rescued, buddy boy. And you, you almost got yourself made into an ice candy.' 'Well, I thought you were very brave,' the beautiful girl whispered alongside me, and I flinched at the sound. She was so close in the semi-darkness…I wanted to look directly at her but couldn't muster the strength to try. 'Well, *I* thought you were an idiot,' Prof Bingham declared. The woman in the driver's seat laughed heartily at this…she tossed her head a little and glanced back towards me, and I saw her large, heavy-featured face amid the broad curls of hair slapping against her cheeks. 'Welcome back to the living world and things,' the woman growled in a deep, throaty voice. 'You were pretty well out of it for a while there.' The woman turned away from me and refocused her gaze on a narrow patch of pale-blueish space in front of the car…it appeared to be all of the road that was illuminated by the headlights. 'I'm Dulcie,' she added, without looking at me again. As Dulcie drove on, she soon told me that this was her car we were riding in…it was her lucky spare swannie I was wearing…also it was her cousin Gizi, sitting next to me, who'd persuaded her against any vestige of common sense to stop.

'Pleased to meet you both,' I plucked up courage and said at last.

Prof Bingham mumbled something more from the passenger seat… Dulcie heard it and started chuckling…I was annoyed that I couldn't catch his comment. But I saw with satisfaction that we were perched in an old Volkswagen which was shuddering along…we were descending quickly on a steep, winding incline through the dark and at each turn the headlights kept sliding over the edges of sharp, rocky bends…most importantly, there was no sign anywhere outside of snow. 'You know, I've never seen anything other than a fraction of the South Island before,' I heard Gizi saying beside me. I guessed she was trying to make polite conversation, but I still felt nervous about her sitting so close and couldn't concentrate on replying…it wasn't every day that I almost got run over by someone I was in love with…my eyes were growing more accustomed to the subdued light and at last I tried stealing a furtive look at her. Gizi was wearing a loose blue jersey that was a size too large for her, much like Dulcie's but prettier, and its long sleeves nearly covered her dainty hands…I saw how petite she was, and that her dark brown hair was drawn back into a severe pony-tail, just as at the Stein…I would never have dreamed she and Dulcie were related…Gizi had picked a woollen fuzz-ball from her jersey which she was tearing to pieces with tiny movements in her fingers while she returned my gaze. 'We're on our way to Franz Josef,' she said to me. Now I definitely needed to make some kind of polite response…I clenched my teeth, trying to think of conversation… the small car was creaking a little as it rounded each narrow bend…its swinging motion seemed to keep nudging Gizi and me closer together. 'I'm from Wellington,' she added.

'My name's Andy,' I managed to begin.

But I had no idea what else to say…I felt far too happy to risk ruining this moment with Gizi by saying anything more…instead, I contented myself with gazing at her further…below the loose hem of her jersey she was wearing jeans and oversized ugg boots…Gizi was raising one arm a little between us and I thought perhaps she was conscious of being so carefully watched, but she was only moving to straighten some stray wisps of hair by her ear.

'I saw you in Christchurch, at the varsity Stein,' I said, as she lowered her arm. 'You were on the dance floor while the band was playing and I could see you fairly easily. You were dancing round and round.' I was embarrassed now at speaking in such a rush, but it was almost a relief to talk. I added, 'I think it was, oh, a couple of days ago.'

'You were there?' Gizi asked. I nodded.

I said, 'I noticed you. I couldn't help it. You were wearing a rather sensational purple dress.'

Gizi smiled…her smile gave her a delightful, impish quality, as though she knew just how enchanting she'd been out there on the dance floor…but she made no reply, and I was left asking myself if maybe I'd said the wrong thing…the car's heater was blowing hard so that it was getting hotter with each minute, and the whole interior of the vehicle was smelling of pungent drying wool…for the second time I became aware that I was sitting next to the most stunningly beautiful woman in the world and I had no pants on…what was worse, I couldn't find two words

223

to put together that might charm her. We stayed sitting there in silence…
the silence swelled and seemed to fill the entire car…I wondered if I was
the only person amongst the four of us that it bothered. Gradually amid
the shifting shapes in the darkness the road brought us down into some
sort of valley…the widening slopes and escarpments around us appeared
more overgrown with thick tangles of scrub, and far off a building
loomed…it was such a long time since we'd spotted something human
outside amidst the night…the building was substantial, an old-style hotel,
with bright lamps shining on a lot of broad, curtained windows and over a
curved, filigreed iron balcony along the front…then at the edge of the
road the car's headlights lit up a small yellow sign for a township…a minute later we were on a street of sorts, and other sparse lights of houses
began to emerge here and there nearby, scattered around unevenly in the
dark. After a few minutes we arrived at a skimpy line of poorly lit shops
that were huddled together along one side of the street…Dulcie slowed
us to a halt, idling before a shop that resembled a narrow, makeshift
shed…we stared at it through the car's windows…it had rough corrugated-iron walls and there was a hand-painted sign on a board in front
which advertised fish and chips…a gleam of fluorescent light was spilling
from the place's frosted-glass door, but that was the only hint of anything
going on within. 'I'm starving, eh,' Dulcie declared, and her raspy voice
filled up the Volkswagen. She asked, 'So any of yous fellows want some
greasies?' I thought all of us seemed to hesitate, but Dulcie had already
switched off the engine and the headlights…she pushed open the door
beside her, grunting at the effort, and got out…she wasn't waiting for an
answer…we watched her marching with rapid, stiff-legged paces round
the car to the shop. Gizi and Prof Bingham began to follow but I stayed
put in the vehicle, pretending to be lagging behind…as soon as they were
all gone I commenced hunting, quick as possible, among the damp
clothes down in my duffle-bag…I didn't want to go outside with my arse
quite so exposed…then it occurred to me that back up there on the mountain someone must have taken off my trousers, and even my underwear…
I blushed with shame. The clothes in my bag were a jumble of spare gear
and wet things from when I'd been covered with snow…the wettest stuff
had damaged the foolscap…after a minute or two of sorting through the
mess I eased my bottom off the springy seat and pulled on some grundies, some half-dry jeans, and socks and shoes…the jeans felt unpleasantly cold but I was determined to wear them, and when my changing was

224

all done I got out of the car at last...Dulcie pulled open the door of the fish-and-chip shop from inside as I reached for it. 'Hurry up,' she barked into my face. 'You could've just put your strides on in here, eh.' I nodded to try and please her...she led me in...under the shop's harsh lights I could see a distinct line of hair was growing across Dulcie's upper lip and, thinking about it, I blushed again even harder than before...I was hoping like mad that it wasn't Dulcie who'd taken my strides off up on the mountain. Inside, the shop was even narrower than it had seemed from the car...it had pale-brown walls that smelled of lard and brine, and a high counter along one side separated us from the hissing fryers...there were no other customers, but behind the counter stood a thickset, swarthy man wearing a striped butcher's apron and a white T-shirt...he was stooped and busy talking quietly to Prof Bingham, who was resting his portly frame up against the counter's edge...Gizi was waiting a little apart in the far corner. I shuffled further in and stood closer beside Dulcie, watching the pronounced hump that stuck up along the back of the man behind the counter...the man had penetrating eyes and coarse black hair, and he'd started to scratch furiously at his head with one hand...despite his disfigured posture he began swaying back and forth, still talking, between the fryers and the counter, and he went on picking at his scalp in an unhappy manner...Prof Bingham kept his elbows propped out wide along the countertop and he was nodding his head and even tapping his fingers to some rhythm in the man's conversation...but suddenly the man dropped both hands down onto his hips and all at once he began shouting. I worried about Gizi...it surprised me that I'd forgotten her, since up till now I'd been acutely aware of her at every second she was near me...I thought that all of us, not only me, ought to be looking at her...but she'd remained standing in the far corner, scuffing the rounded toe of one of her boots against the dirty lino on the floor. 'The other day I get a ring and they tell me, hey, you come down Hokitika way,' the man was booming at Prof Bingham in a foreign voice. 'Hey, you know, go get some fucking fish.' The man turned away in a huff and slid some sticky, battered fish down into the sputtering fryers...the hiss from the oil flared up louder and just as quickly died away into near-silence...next the man spun around again and lunged with his whole head across the counter, staring straight into Prof Bingham's face...he was yelling once more. 'And you know, you got to start shit quick, eh, because these deliveries is not regular and no fresh quality, eh. Yeah, and it is always the other

225

bloody people take things, so I go fast. I mean fucking fast, you know?' I
saw Prof Bingham was still simply nodding, in spite of the man being so
close to him...Prof Bingham bumped his belly patiently against the side
of the counter...the man wiped some flour off his fingers on his apron and
then put out a large hand covered with black hair...he took hold of Prof
Bingham's arm and sniffed heavily. 'And this cop, this fucking traffic cop,'
the man rumbled, 'is near the river. This cop, he stop me and he say, "You
speeding, eh." And I am thinking, I say, "Yeah, I speeding," because I
serve him in the shop five years, eh. He say, "I give you ticket," and me,
hey, I am thinking that's okay, because what the hell, you know. And he
open up the book and say, "What's your name?" You know, it is just,
"What's your name?" I say, "What? What is it the *fuck* you talking about,
eh?"' The man was straining his badly hunched body further and further
forwards across the counter...he held Prof Bingham's arm tighter. He
shouted, 'Yeah, I mean, already you know my name. That is what I am
thinking. I serve you in the shop five years, eh.' Prof Bingham merely
clicked his tongue, and finally he gave the man a wink...the man paused,
and out of one corner of his mouth he spat onto the floor...I felt a crazy
need to go protect Gizi...although I actually did nothing, it made me rel-
ish my own sense of bravery in her presence. 'Bloody, bloody cop,' the
man had straightened up and was yelling again. 'He say me, "What's your
address, eh?" Ah, hey fuck, you know? You seen that flash new station, it
is that station they got in Grey? Bloody nice, eh. I go there the other day,
it is for paying the fucking fine, and me, you know, hey me, I am buying
that building!' The man let go of Prof Bingham's arm...he turned away
from the counter and stood with his arched back towards us, rattling each
of the handles on the bubbling baskets in the vats and lifting them out to
drain...he pulled four white sheets of paper from a pile and spread them
on some newsprint on the counter...for a moment he arranged each sheet
delicately with his stubby fingers, and finally he emptied the dripping baskets onto the papers one by one...I watched as the man upended a large
jar of salt over everything...he held the jar clasped in the middle of his
hairy fist and the contents fell everywhere steadily across the gleaming
yellow edges of the freshly cooked chips. 'Salt?' the man asked after a
while. The man wrapped up the newspaper parcels of our takeaways, but
when the time came to pay I realised to my embarrassment that I didn't
have any money...I whispered to Prof Bingham that back in Christchurch
I'd lost every penny at gambling...I hoped perhaps he'd be impressed,

but he paid for me only with bad grace. We went outside to the front of the shop and tore off the corners from the chip packets as we shuffled a little along the street...a metal lamppost was nearby and the four of us halted within its meagre circle of light...in a hurry we pulled out steaming chips and pieces of fish with our hands from the partly-torn packets, and I watched Gizi juggling a hot morsel around in her fingers...to me, it was almost inconceivable to see her doing something so down-to-earth...even the hesitant way she peeled the gooey batter off a bit of grey fish had me captivated. After some time Prof Bingham and Dulcie began edging away, talking between themselves quietly off beyond the thin glow of the light... I smiled at Gizi, and inclined my head towards the pair of them to suggest that I knew what they were on about...Gizi smiled back at me a little shyly in return...I held out a chip for her and she took it and smiled some more, and I hoped her happiness was connected with me...Prof Bingham and Dulcie came back, and when we'd finished eating we dropped the chip papers into a nearby bin and got ourselves settled once more in the confines of the car...Dulcie was leaning on the steering wheel and watching Prof Bingham as he slid onto his seat beside her. Then with an abrupt movement she straightened up and announced, 'Yeah, I reckon we're all set. We're all right, yeah?' Dulcie twisted herself round towards the back seat, and said to Gizi and me in a decisive tone, 'We're going to head off for the Coast to Greymouth, okay? Yous got any objections?' Gizi answered with a tiny cheer, and the sound of it went on echoing in my mind like something magic...up front Prof Bingham was bobbing about gleefully on his seat...Dulcie hunched forward again to start the engine and the motor leapt into life...I thought the car itself just couldn't wait to go... Dulcie fiddled the gear lever into position and the Volkswagen shoved off with a jump...Prof Bingham was already jabbering away to no one in particular about the merits of Caribbean literature. The highway before us continued flat at first as we drove, but soon it began to descend rapidly once again...there were big clumps of damp-looking fern everywhere along the roadside, visible in the headlights, and even some stringy, wind-bent trees poking through the darkness whenever we swung round a bend...Prof Bingham kept on and on with his flow of whispered patter... he kept waving his hands up and down good-humouredly...he leaned over a lot in the narrow space between himself and Dulcie, and I got the impression that this was his way of flirting hard. Alongside me Gizi was also talking, but I wanted so much to absorb everything she said that I wound up focusing on nothing...I struggled to concentrate on how her father was working in some sort of international line...Gizi was speaking about Spain and about living there, and she was telling me that she'd spent some time staying in Madrid, not actually so long ago. 'We were in an apartment which was pretty small but really nice, and it had this balcony with an old iron railing. It was in the Barrio Salamanca, just on the edge of it. That's quite near Calle Serrano, eh,' she said. I was enchanted at Gizi speaking those Spanish words right next to me...I thought she even seemed a little Spanish as she said them...she slurred her r's marvellously in her high voice...I tried to look as if I understood quite a bit about Calle Serrano.

'And so how was that like?' I asked.

I thought of all Prof Bingham had said concerning Hemingway and Joyce...I thought of Stendhal knocking off his novel in Paris in seven weeks...I couldn't even imagine that this real person beside me had been there in that sort of fantastic European capital. 'It was just so awfully hot and crowded,' Gizi was saying. 'And I didn't know anyone.' I supposed that made sense...I guessed that, of course, any big city must be crowded and maybe hot too...there would be people walking everywhere on the narrow footpaths alongside the busy, traffic-crammed streets...the passers-by would skirt rows of grimy wrought-iron railings which barely separated them from other groups of people sitting at cafe tables, that kind of deal, people on chairs gesticulating and chatting...all these locals and tourists out on the street, overdressed and overheated in the muggy summer air, they had places to go, important places, and they had conversations to frame, conversations of significance...how easily they'd disregard an old stone apartment building nearby, its facade stained by city soot and mould, with a discreet shaded recess at its entrance, and they'd miss Gizi, standing and waiting in that cool tranquil corner by the door, waiting for someone she knew. How I wished I could have shown Gizi all around...I wished I could've had Gizi at my side in Madrid...then, surely, I'd have been living in a state of permanent inspiration.

I asked at last, 'Well, what did they say about New Zealand over there?'

But Gizi simply continued with her own talk...she had nothing to say about New Zealand...instead, she was telling me something of going to see paintings in the Prado...the museum building had long galleries inside to walk, several floors of them, and they had vaulted ceilings, marble columns and ropes in front of the popular pictures, with intimidating

228

guards alongside…she spoke as if it was really possible to stroll about through the collections for the whole day, and I assumed that most of what she was saying must even be true since, after all, she had no particular reason to lie to me. 'It's because there's just *so* much art in there,' she said. 'Rooms, the spare rooms, they're full of the stuff.' I remembered all the books I'd paged through back at Wynyards…now it appeared that I'd loved them with more than passing interest…now it seemed like fate. 'The whole place was incredible,' Gizi finished up with a happy sigh. She was lying back against the gently bumping seat of the car…she turned her head towards me for my reaction…but under the pressure of her gaze I couldn't think of anything special to say…all I could manage was to admit that her story really got to me and fascinated me so much because I was a writer. 'Oh, I've always admired writers,' Gizi said. I watched her blink at me under her long lashes…she was scrutinising my face, and I wondered what she was seeing…perhaps she was staring at a famous author in the centre of a desperately adoring crowd, or perhaps not. In a soft voice Gizi added, 'I can just remember that little single piece of poetry from school, eh. "Let us roll up all the universe into one ball."' Oh, Gizi knew poetry!… my heart went into a riot…I felt sure it was perfect poetry that she must know…for a moment it was the only thing I could think about.

'Well,' I swallowed and said, 'I imagine that Madrid is full of writers. I suppose the streets are probably paved with writers.'

'Not real ones,' Gizi said, and I could hear kindness in her voice. 'But the Prado is different,' she went on. 'It's got real pictures.' My mouth felt dry and a bit salty from pure excitement…Gizi was starting to talk about the Prado some more…she was peering ahead towards the front seats with her eyes shining…I guessed that this must be what inspiration looked like from the outside. 'I'm probably going to take art history at varsity next term,' Gizi was saying. But I'd lost the ability to concentrate on her speech because up front I could see Prof Bingham and Dulcie were holding hands…their palms were clasped tight together over the rounded top of the gear lever…I reached out and took Gizi's slim fingers in mine…she fell quiet, but she didn't stop me. The car continued drumming along in the dark…it ran with an easy motion, although I didn't care anymore where it was going…Gizi and I were resting our backs into the cool, quilted padding of the seat in a wonderful, tense silence, still holding hands…this life was so perfect, I felt, that if I died now it would no longer be a problem, and in fact the mere thought of Gizi missing me, gone prematurely from the earth, made my eyes brim with grateful tears...suddenly I wanted to commit suicide right then and there and felt a powerful urge to jump for her out of the car...only the slender recollection that I had a novel to write stopped me from getting myself under the wheels. At that very instant I glanced forwards...in the front seats Prof Bingham was sitting with a hand stuffed up inside Dulcie's bulky jersey...beneath the jersey's woolly cover he was methodically massaging one of her heavy breasts...I couldn't tell if Dulcie was enjoying it or not...she kept an arm out on the steering wheel and sat still, driving us onwards into the dark. Later, somewhere close to the edge of Greymouth, we saw a blue flashing motel-vacancies sign up ahead on a pole and pulled off the highway into the motel's wide gravel drive and parking area...a block of single-storey, attached units with fibrolite cladding on the walls stood in a row beside us, facing the road...I could see the owner was hurrying out from his office nearby and slapping its screen-door shut behind him...he was a big, clumsily built man, with a beer can gripped tight in one hand like a valuable possession. The owner marched across to where we were halted and Dulcie rolled down her window...he bent beside it and began staring into the car at us with bloodshot, searching eyes, looking as though he'd much prefer us just to clear on out...but Prof Bingham leaned across Dulcie and asked if by any chance there were two units available...in response the motel owner fished up some triangular key-tags from his pocket and gestured with a nod of his head towards the office behind him...Prof Bingham got out of the car and went into the office with the owner to sign the book...Gizi and I stayed with Dulcie while she picked a spot and parked before the row of units. We were climbing out of the Volkswagen as Prof Bingham returned, and there was a moment or two when we all stood around and stretched, taking in the good fresh night air...but soon, not saying a word, Prof Bingham grasped Dulcie's elbow and I watched them both begin to walk away across the gravel with their footsteps making loud, brassy crunches...they were striding together up to the dimly lit entrance of one of the units. The pair of them paused under the square yellow porch lamp over the unit's doorway, looking every inch a couple...Prof Bingham hunched down a little and tried turning one of the keys in the lock...the key briefly resisted, until I could hear Dulcie call it a cow of a thing...finally the lock opened with a snapping sound and Prof Bingham and Dulcie bundled themselves inside, closing the door, though a few seconds later Prof Bingham pulled open the door of the unit again, and with a harried look on his face he tossed me the key to the other unit...the key-chain flopped onto the gravel near my feet, and as I bent to retrieve it I heard Prof Bingham slam the door shut hard once more...Gizi and I were alone. I straightened up and stared along the row of units at the nondescript arrangement of porches and their lamps facing the highway...there was no other car but ours parked in front, and the whole place appeared to empty except for us...I weighed the key in my palm and shrugged...it was a gesture that I didn't really intend for Gizi to see, but I noticed that in any case she'd begun to head on her own towards the next-door unit. I hesitated, and then went and poked about in the unlocked car for Half-Arse...it meant I had to scramble to catch up with Gizi on our unit's doorstep but she stood waiting patiently for me by the entrance, looking a little tired...I couldn't have explained what I was doing exactly by bringing a portable typewriter with me, though fortunately Gizi didn't ask...she didn't even suggest that I fetch any other bags from the car. I got the door open, reached round and clicked on the light-switch inside the unit...the low-watt bulb in the ceiling lit up a lot of peeling wallpaper that had sometime been painted over orange and red...we shuffled tentatively into the uninviting room and both of us came to a halt before a wide, sagging double-bed, still unmade, with a pair of chrome lamps sticking out of the wall above its badly scratched headboard...I saw that to my left there was a wooden table surrounded by tubular-steel chairs, and up on the rear part of the table sat an antiquated TV set with rabbit ears...I put Half-Arse down on one of the chairs...at the far end of the room was a simple kitchen, and I could see an open doorway that appeared to lead to a bathroom and toilet, but neither Gizi nor I made any move to explore. Instead I took Gizi's hand in mine again and stepped with her round to the side of the bed...after a few moments we sat on one edge of the mattress, kicked off our shoes and lay down together across the bedclothes...our weight made the springs sink and the headboard slope awkwardly in towards us...the headboard was almost touching and covering my right side but all I could feel conscious of was the warmth near me in Gizi's living, breathing body...she made me think of sad, sentimental things like butterflies and angels...I put my left arm up around her shoulder, felt her nestle into me against my chest and fought off an urge to weep. 'I've never had a real boyfriend before,' Gizi murmured. She shifted slightly for comfort inside my encircling arm. She added, 'I remember at intermediate school we just used to have these absurd sort of crushes on girls in the other classes, eh. Don't ask me why. It was kind of like the thing to do. Lots of squealing and heavy panting, you know, when the right girl came into the room. But, you know, that's all.'

I asked, 'Well, what about Spain?'

I was surprised by the hoarse catch in my own voice as I spoke. But Gizi was already whispering, 'Oh, in Madrid no one ever paid me any mind.' I considered for a moment how an entire city that didn't notice Gizi must be a town full of idiots, but what I wanted most was just to lean down and kiss her...I was yearning to kiss her, but I felt too overwhelmed to risk it...I raised my eyes to the ceiling and implored God if He was listening... obviously it would be better to let my overwrought emotions out a pinch before they exploded, though the difficulty was there were so very many, an abundance, an immensity of emotions all threatening to come forth together...I reckoned that bedroom operators really couldn't afford to carry a swag of these things around...I was beginning to wonder how they managed. My mouth was half open but once again I had nothing to say... we were cuddling now...that was all...Gizi seemed quite content to think I was a gentleman...I felt so peaceful next to her that it distressed me to consider how I wasn't. Then the headboard alongside me started to shudder...soon it was making a small, regular series of creaks...from somewhere I could hear a rhythmical, guttural groaning...the groaning sound was coming through the wall from the adjacent unit, louder and louder and more urgent...I understood at last that it was Prof Bingham and Dulcie fucking...they were fucking like rabbits. The sense of desire within me began rapidly to retreat, but Gizi didn't appear to be disturbed...I couldn't see her beautiful face pressed up against my ribs, and I thought perhaps she was asleep...for some time I lay without moving, feeling embarrassed and disappointed...the luxurious groaning from the pair next door went on and on for ages...for a man who talked in a mutter, during sex Prof Bingham liked to make a lot of noise.

In the morning I awoke with Gizi sleeping next to me...neither of us had moved much from lying sideways, stretched out, across the bed all night...Gizi's head was perched on my shoulder...her hair was tied up in yesterday's pony-tail and I saw where some loose strands had come free...I couldn't resist admiring them and, keeping very still, gazed at them and at where they blended into a small fuzz of baby hair trailing along the delicious curve of her neck. After a while I admitted to myself that my arm was numb...I reached out for a pillow and gently I eased Gizi's head onto it...

232

she stirred, but didn't seem to wake and went on breathing through her nose in a fashion that was steady and deep...I slid a little away from Gizi and thought how utterly perfect she looked, though since I was so much in love with her, how she could possibly look otherwise?...I pondered the simple mystery of this for a bit because it gave me an excuse to go on gawking at her...but eventually I got myself up from the bed. There was a scungy travel alarm clock over on top of the old TV, and I could hear its droning tick-tock noise...the plastic hands on the clock's dial were showing close to lunchtime, even later in the day than I'd expected...I crept about quietly, put on my sandshoes and opened the door of the unit. Outside, the air felt moist on my skin and almost unnaturally calm...I was staring across the car park and the tarsealed highway and into the remains of a dewy morning mist...the mist was gathered low along the densely forested slopes of some hills beyond the road, and creamy patches of the fog lay settled all about...I sniffed and caught a scent of pine sap hanging with an odd heaviness in the wet air...I glanced down and saw a copy of the local newspaper on the porch at my feet, folded and wrinkled up with moisture...I reached for it, tucked it under my arm and strolled with it along to the next unit. The door of the unit was open and there was a low light on inside...Prof Bingham and Dulcie were up...Prof Bingham came wandering towards me at the entrance while holding a Pyrex mug of coffee...he looked vastly satisfied. 'Robert Lowell,' he announced, as if letting me in on a secret. Prof Bingham stopped in front of me by the doorway...I could see Dulcie padding around in the unit behind him. 'Lowell,' he repeated softly. 'Crazy old cocksman went and kicked the bucket a couple of months back. On his way to meet his wife in New York—his real wife, that is, not the other one—and he dies of a heart job in the rear of a yellow cab. Well, who wouldn't? Probably more than the old guy could handle, facing up to the dragon again.' Prof Bingham paused to sip at his coffee and finally he launched into an ugly, chesty cough...he had to hold the coffee mug away with his arm extended to prevent anything from spilling onto him...at length he ceased hacking...he gulped to swallow the phlegm. 'Ah, that slut really gets my rocks moved,' he gasped. He grunted and nodded over his shoulder in Dulcie's direction, so that I wondered whether she might have heard him...Prof Bingham was looking remarkably red in the face and I thought it possible that he'd been getting his rocks moved this morning as well...for an instant I even wondered whether he might question me about my own night and any rumpy-pumpy I'd had with Gizi, but instead he

233

reached out and took the newspaper from under my arm...Prof Bingham tossed it behind him with a flourish. 'Many thanks, junior,' he declared. I didn't bother to inquire whether Prof Bingham had a paper of his own...he turned, and I watched him go back into the unit. Afterwards it seemed to take a long time for us all to get ready for leaving...I had to fetch suitcases for Gizi and Dulcie, and Gizi showered and changed her clothes...Dulcie appeared to be in and out of our unit every few minutes...she and Gizi both blow-dried their hair in our bathroom, standing hunched forwards over the dryer, one after the other, with the blast from the nozzle pushing up into their faces...they both complained that they'd have to use the same woollen jerseys from the day before...I was able, at last, to give Dulcie back her lucky swanndri. Sometime later I had a chance to get into the shower and wash...after that I put on my sole remaining cleanish pair of underwear and wriggled into my other dirty clothes once more...it was the best I could do, but when next I saw Prof Bingham again I thought that he hadn't even bothered to rub himself down over a sink...I was amused that Dulcie could put up with it. Finally we climbed into the car and headed for the town...the mist had lifted and left the bleakness of the rolling hill country exposed, and we passed damp, scrubby portions of farmland and some derelict saleyards...a large cemetery came up on our left showing a disordered jumble of graves and then we were among houses, with hints of the nearby sea flashing between them as we went past...the road broadened and we seemed to be entering Greymouth, but I saw only low buildings and warehouses, and a few cars parked before empty stores here and there...I went on wondering where the town really was, where the main shopping street might be or even the eency-weenciest bit of city stuff, but Dulcie didn't stop...the road had split in two around a long green median strip, and Dulcie just kept us sailing onwards in a hurry while saying over and over that she was starving. Across an intersection I finally saw some shops and the familiar sign for a Wales bank, located up on the very next corner...I made a fuss until Dulcie pulled the car over for me right in front of the bank's doors...I got out, flustered, and headed across the footpath with my passbook gripped in one hand...on entering the bank I half wondered if I'd bump into Penny inside, but the place was deserted except for a middle-aged, grey-faced teller standing at his counter, having a cup of tea...then I had a moment of worry, a sudden panic that the others in the car might not wait...hurriedly I withdrew all the rest of the money in my passbook, the whole lot, and scampered helter-skelter outside for the street once more, feeling relieved to see the car was still there and grinning as though I'd just staged a robbery. Gizi opened my door and I jumped in…we took off again, with Dulcie changing quickly up through the gears, and I felt more settled…I was pleased that now I'd able to pay back Prof Bingham for the fish and chips and also the motel room…as we rattled along I counted out the money, using the showiest gestures, and passed it to him. Soon we went by a tiled public square with a nondescript white-painted fountain and then bumped over a railway line that was sunk down deep into the asphalt road, until all at once Dulcie slowed just past the tracks and stopped…the wind was much sharper here and buffeted the car…we were halted on an empty corner close to a row of decrepit commercial buildings, and I saw the end one, the nearest and the biggest, was a two-storey hotel with a broad, mustard-coloured plaster front and a badly bent iron veranda sheltering its ground floor…a collection of grimy, double-hung windows on the top floor were shaded by pink awnings, and miscellaneous drainpipes and black electric cables were crisscrossed over the outside walls, giving the whole place an air of improvised renovation… Dulcie shoved open her door and tumbled out of the car, heading for the cover of the veranda…the rest of us got out and hurried to follow. 'Boy, oh boy,' Prof Bingham bubbled. He clapped his hands…he sounded as if his day just kept on getting better. We approached the hotel…by the nearest corner was a buckled metal door, which I supposed must be the entrance to the public bar…it was tucked back a little from the footpath, nestled in a broken wooden frame and covered by chipped layers of yellow paint… Dulcie pushed the door open and led us all inside. 'Boy, oh boy,' Prof Bingham said again. He went in just behind Dulcie while Gizi and I brought up the rear…the pub inside was large and painted in shabby browns and tans, with a smell of stale hops and a radio playing somewhere…a pool table was in use in a near corner with a couple of tough-looking characters bending over the cushions, and I could make out the solid wooden counter of a bar way across on the room's other side…but in the middle of the room, together on high stools among three rows of tall, Formica-topped tables, a lot of scruffy hoon-types were sitting hunched over on their elbows amid a mess of glasses, beer-jugs and ashtrays…they were in bush clothes, some wearing damp tartan swannies and torn grey shorts and some in black oilskin parkas with leggings, and each and every one of them wore gumboots…though none of them was watching us, they seemed somehow very aware of our arrival. But Dulcie kept striding towards the hoons without looking around, acting as if she had somebody to meet urgently on the other side of the room...we followed Dulcie in our little file...Prof Bingham was waddling along happily behind her, with Gizi walking a few paces behind him, and finally there was me...I wondered if perhaps I was the only one among us who appeared nervous...none of the hoons so much as glanced at us while we passed, but I felt that they were growing tenser and drawing even closer together...I felt they continued sitting in their group on the narrow stools in a way that was even more hunkered over, if anything, with their legs splayed even further apart. But next Prof Bingham stopped and lit one of his fancy cigarettes...stuck halted behind him with Gizi, I was full of the heebie-jeebies as we waited near the hoons and listened to the smack of pool balls from the corner table...after a difficult moment we could move forwards again and we reached the bar...we drew ourselves up in a little row before it and I watched Prof Bingham drop his smouldering cigarette into an ashtray...he leaned sideways over the counter past the taps, straining at an angle towards the solitary barman. 'Oh boy, oh boy,' he announced. Prof Bingham put a pink hand under his chin...he inclined his bald head upwards with a confidential sort of air, and with his other hand he started stroking his goatee almost flirtatiously...I thought he looked even more American and different than usual...the barman didn't say a word. 'So, what do you all got that's good?' Prof Bingham purred. The barman was an elderly, long-waisted man in a discoloured red cardigan, with his shirt unbuttoned low at the neck...I could clearly see some grey fuzz of chest hair sticking out by the wrinkled collar...he went right on not saying a word, but he picked up a hefty glass jug from a wire rack...then he held it, tilted, to the nearest tap, and his hands appeared to tremble a little as he began filling it with beer...he stared silently out into space beyond us as if our presence had thrown him deep into a mood of self-pity. Prof Bingham retrieved his cigarette, muttering, and put a bunch of money on the counter...by now the big jug was filled to the brim...the barman set it down and stepped back, scooping up the money in a hurry...Prof Bingham took hold of the jug in both fat hands and Dulcie grabbed some glasses off the counter, and together with Gizi they walked away towards the closest table...Prof Bingham was moving stiffly to avoid spilling a drop of the brew...I was left at the bar all alone. I pointed at another jug and the barman picked it up...as he proceeded to fill it, I held his gaze and after a moment nodded over in Prof Bingham's direction...I rolled my eyes...I thought the barman smiled faintly as he poured

236

out the beer. By the time I got to the table where the others were sitting, Prof Bingham was talking a lot more loudly and in great excitement...I gathered it was something concerning the seminal influence of Gertrude Stein on Hemingway and the early Moderns...Gizi was wriggling about in an effort to rest her ugg-booted feet on the base of her stool...she held her glass up in both tiny hands and looked pleased with herself...I dragged up a free stool and sat close alongside her. Prof Bingham went on and on talking in fine, noisy form...occasionally he leaned across and nuzzled at Dulcie's neck without even slowing down in his monologue...Dulcie kept chuckling and grunting 'yeah, yeah,' as if agreeing with everything he said...Prof Bingham only broke off from his speechifying once or twice in order to pull hard on his cigarette...he smacked his lips in exuberance with each puff. But I noticed an enormous hoon had detached himself from the group in the middle of the room and he was beginning to shuffle up towards us, moving at a snail's pace on massive, unsteady legs...gradually though he was getting nearer to our table...I could see where the hoon's pink belly was poking out under his clothes...he was wearing a woollen hat over hair that appeared thin, dark and greasy, and his pale face was half-hidden by a long, shaggy beard which seemed to nestle on his chest...in one hand, in the grip of tattooed fingers, the hoon was holding up a beer-jug which was full to the top. I thought there was an expectant look in the hoon's narrow eyes and I started keeping my head down, but still I couldn't help seeing him approach...he came around the back of us to stand right at Prof Bingham's shoulder, holding his jug high up as though almost tired of it, waiting for some attention...but I supposed the waiting might take a little while...Prof Bingham was quite the early Hemingway fan. 'Hey!' the hoon barked. We all looked up in time to see him raise the jug to his lips...the hoon was patting down his unruly beard with his free hand, as if to give himself more space...next we watched him arch his head back and begin to tip the jug's contents into his open mouth without ever seeming to swallow. 'Marvellous, marvellous,' Prof Bingham commenced mumbling. He leaned away on his stool to see better, but not before glancing about to make sure we were all gawping along with him... the level of the beer in the jug was sinking quickly. 'Marvellous oesophageal dexterity,' Prof Bingham muttered. 'Think Beowulf. Think of mead. Think the Anglo-Saxon horn.' But by now the hoon had already finished... he put the empty jug onto our table with a thump and the thin remains of the beer froth ran down the glass...he burped, and patted his substantial gut with satisfaction. 'You're not from round here, eh,' the hoon declared in a gruff voice. I saw Prof Bingham nod and say, 'Hey, not even from close to round here.' Prof Bingham flicked the ash from his cigarette onto the floor. Then he asked, 'If I get you another one of those doohickeys, could you show me that again?' The hoon appeared surprised and had to give this some serious thought...I could hear a lot of sniggering from behind him, back where the other hoons were sitting at their tables and evidently paying us careful attention. 'Yeah, I reckon,' the hoon said at last. He added, 'Just go over there and ask Lionel.' He gestured off towards the barman and grinned, though suddenly something like malice came into his eyes. Next the hoon said, 'But I reckon you ought to show me first what you can do, eh mate.' 'All right, hang on,' Dulcie interrupted. She reached round in front of Prof Bingham for one of our jugs...it was only half full and slopped in her grip as she hoisted it up to her mouth, but she started at once on guzzling the liquid...her thick throat bulged from the effort. 'Fuck,' the hoon said beside us in appreciation. Some of the other hoons over in their group were making a big thing of laughing, but I noticed they were most of them sitting up straight as they watched. 'She's a keeper,' Prof Bingham agreed. He puffed on the remainder of his cigarette...when Dulcie finished, he blew out a long, triumphant mouthful of smoke.

'I'll go get some jugs,' I offered. 'Lionel and I are on the same wavelength.'

But all at once it seemed everybody from the other tables wanted to join us...the hoons were coming over in a rush...they instantly merged with us into a single delighted gathering...they even shifted over some extra stools to sit on...they started sharing their drinks with us, despite our protests...somebody poured Prof Bingham a glassful to knock back and then everybody wanted to offer him one, and he quaffed them all. We were busy swapping names and forgetting them, and exchanging cigarettes...everybody around us, everyone at the same time, had decided on becoming extremely jolly...before long I went across to Lionel and bought some more jugs anyway, and there were also pies to get, and bags of chippies that were torn up and opened...we watched the hoons show off at drinking games in front of the tables...the party went on and on through the muddled afternoon. Prof Bingham got drunk and soon he became wildly agitated...he kept jumping up and down on his seat and waving his arms while shouting about Structuralism...he threw an ashtray across the room and screamed that it was not a symbol...the hoons thought he was hilarious...Dulcie watched his performance with a proud grimace set across her features...even Gizi was animated and fearless around him in her delicate way, and I felt everybody in the place was charmed by her sense of gaiety. One of the hoons buttonholed me and wanted to talk about his brand-new tow-truck service...it was a scheme that he ran on spec from a local garage...I didn't have much choice except to listen and nod while he rambled on, but at last I really was fascinated by tow trucks and how they worked...I thought of Prof Bingham's car, which we'd left way the hell up on the mountain waiting for rescue...I considered mentioning this handy line of business to Prof Bingham but I could see he was beyond the slightest interest in anything other than his own craziness...he'd started banging his glass against a tabletop and bawling for someone, for anyone, to do the savage dance, though the hoons just kept acting as if amused by him. But their tolerance only appeared to arouse Prof Bingham further...after a moment he leapt up from his stool with his arms above his head, kicking and pumping his legs as though doing some kind of dance himself...then we all watched him slip backwards with a crash onto his own table...he fell and lay prone on the lino amidst a wreckage of broken glass and spilled beer...the whole mob of us in unison let out a roar of approval. At length the hoons entertained us with what they called super-coordinated chunders...we cheered on a hoon who swigged from one jug and vomited everything up into another...by now we were too confused with drink to understand much... it seemed the coordinated part was when the hoons did it over again in pairs. Much later, we all of us staggered out from the pub in a loose, boozy and merry body...behind me people were yelling at each other to get some half-g's from the bottle store...I gazed around in wonderment that it was still the same day outside as when we'd arrived...the heavy cloud was forcing the remaining light from the sky, and I could feel the dampness of the morning's mist had returned to the air. Some of the hoons were already reappearing from the bottle store and they were marching here and there in front of us on the footpath, looking happy... they had bulbous, sloshing flagons of beer clutched against their chests... they hadn't wasted any time and I could guess that, unlike us, the hoons knew exactly what they were doing...I heard them calling out to each other, shouting over each other's voices about heading off for a ride... there was a woozy clamour to find some cars. We soon got to our Volkswagen, parked where we'd left it...only at the sight of it did Prof

Bingham appear to understand what was happening, and he began prancing up and down on his little legs again in the middle of the road...he was still shit-faced drunk. 'I'm going to handle this, yeah! Me! I'm going to drive!' he was announcing. He flailed with his arms around in front of us. He was very aggressive, and he screamed at everyone in a high voice, 'Look, two hands! The two-handed motherfucking engine!' Prof Bingham opened the Volkswagen's door and climbed clumsily into the driver's seat...Dulcie got beside him up front, and Gizi and I slipped into the back...I saw the hoons were pushing each other in a tremendous rush into some cars nearby, and I hoped the cars were really theirs to take... they were slamming the doors and there was a lot of bellowing and screeching...one car had its bonnet raised and a long-legged, skinny hoon was leaning in beneath, fiddling frantically with the engine. Prof Bingham had trouble getting the Volkswagen running because he was far too drunk to manage the key in the ignition...then the engine caught, and we listened to the starter motor shriek while Prof Bingham kept right on trying to turn the key...up ahead of me in the passenger seat I could hear Dulcie beginning to complain...most of the other cars had pulled out now and were departing...I listened to the hoons honking their horns and saw their vehicles were weaving off in a hurry away from us and along the road in the gathering dusk...I noticed that even the hoon working under the bonnet had finished, and he slammed the bonnet down and dashed to hop into his ride just as its wheels were rolling forward. 'Yeah, I reckon I'll knit me new arsehole,' Dulcie growled, 'because we are well and truly buggered, eh.' She offered up a helpless giggle, and beside me I also heard Gizi giggling along with her...but Prof Bingham had finally given up on trying to start the car...he put it in gear instead, and immediately we lurched into the street with a mighty thump, surging forwards and bouncing over the railway lines in the direction the hoons had gone...I felt a pleasant sensation of increasing speed, making me loll on the swaying back seat...I had the impression that this was all an incredible performance, a drama that I was witnessing from someplace comfortable and distant...our tyres squealed like the soundtrack from a film as we rounded the corner of the next intersection. Then suddenly I realised that I couldn't see Prof Bingham anymore, even though he was the driver...there was nothing of him on show except his podgy knuckles clinging to the steering wheel...the rest of him, his whole head, seemed to have slipped down under the dashboard instead of looking out at the street, and I reflected

that he made rather a habit of this stuff…through the windscreen in front
of us there was only the bare, careening road in sight, coming up before
our eyes…within a few moments I could hear Prof Bingham's voice rumbling from low in the footwell…he appeared to be asking where the fuck
the rear-view mirror had got to. We were sweeping still faster along the
wide, veering road…Gizi reached for my arm. 'Boot it!' Dulcie started
screaming in the front seat. 'Boot it! Boot it!' The metal base of a lamppost
swerved into view as the car rushed towards it…I saw Dulcie lunge over
to pull at the wheel…we all swayed violently and I held my breath, but the
lamppost had disappeared…the hoons remained somewhere out before
us…Prof Bingham's head came up above the steering wheel again, but as
he drove I could see that he kept glancing around strangely over his
shoulder and out of the side-windows…he was talking to himself beneath
the increasing whine from the motor, and I couldn't tell whether he was
expounding on new theories of literature or not. Soon we caught up with
the tail end of the hoons' cars near a long corner…Prof Bingham cut off
one of the cars in a deft move and got in front of it…the hoons now driving
behind us flashed their lights and put up an indignant frenzy of honking…but without warning Prof Bingham slammed his foot onto the
brakes…the sheer suddenness of our halt made me turn and gaze to
check through the rear window…I saw the car behind brake too, with its
bonnet dipping and the wheels stopped hard as it still kept on approaching us…I'd never seen a vehicle do that before. The hoons' car skidded
into the back of us with a crunch and shoved the whole Volkswagen forward…my neck muscles felt wrenched by the impact…Gizi gripped my
arm even more deliciously tight with both of her hands…at once Prof
Bingham started driving the Volkswagen off again, but for an instant our
wheels spun on the spot…next there was a brutal squeal of metal as we
parted from the car behind us…the Volkswagen swung itself forwards
down the road with tremendous momentum, and again we were heading
away in the direction of the others as if nothing had happened. We drove
for some while, until even the idea of going someplace had become mean-
ingless…at last we were only conscious of racing at speed down a stretch
which was long and very straight and unchanging, and so we all four of us
opened the windows…we stuck our heads outside and yelled into the
night, with the cold air whipping our faces and grabbing at our hair…we
went on and on like this, faster and faster, until it was impossible to hear
anything else around us but the sound of the engine and our own loony

shouting...every other feature of the view had vanished into the surrounding darkness that hurtled by...finally Prof Bingham, or perhaps it was Dulcie, thought to put on the headlights. It was much, much later, but I had not the remotest idea when, that we slowed and turned off onto a bumpy, poorly metalled side-road...the cars soon fell in together and became a convoy, and each driver among our group worked at keeping close to the vehicle in front...the track before us was rising and dipping in our collective lights as the cars all jounced wildly along. Finally the wind-damaged trees and scrub on both sides of us fell away in the dark, and after a few more minutes we came down to a beach...I could see the other vehicles halting one by one where the road met the edge of the dunes...Prof Bingham drew us to a stop near the end of the group and let the engine idle...the cars' headlights were all sloping onwards past a tumble of flax bushes, dune grass and narrow mounds of sand, and the beams spread down across the long gravelled seashore...I saw where they were shining on shells amid rocks and on wet, weird shapes of driftwood... there were some twisted strings of kelp out in the distance, and beyond them the black water in the sea shifted about and churned. Then all at once Prof Bingham proceeded to leap out of the Volkswagen, slamming the door behind him as he went...he was wailing and whooping on the sand and waving his arms...he reached down for the bottom of his sweatshirt and began to drag it up and off his torso in the lights in front of us...I thought his energy was remarkable, and we watched his pasty, flabby chest emerge...he hopped about as he started hauling off his pants, and at the same time I noticed that some of the hoons were also getting out of their own cars...Prof Bingham stepped out of his underwear to a cheer from the gang of hoons gathering near him, and one of them picked up his discarded sweatshirt and began flourishing it overhead. In an instant Prof Bingham was skipping around stark naked amongst the clumps of flax bushes...only his glasses still bounced about on his nose as he hooted and pranced...his limp cock was flopping up and down below the fat folds of his heaving belly. 'Why's he doing that?' Gizi whispered next to me. But I was too busy straining to see for myself to reply...I scarcely registered that Dulcie had started climbing out of the car...then Gizi tried her own door and found it wouldn't open properly, and I had to help her clamber out with me from my side...we stepped down onto the sparse sand at the road's edge with the wind blowing the grit up everywhere against our legs...I saw Prof Bingham suddenly turn and run, galloping off past the dunes and heading towards the water...I had no idea why he was doing it, and thought perhaps he had none himself. Prof Bingham jumped and swung his arms out as he picked his way across the jutting stones on the beach...at each step his large pink bottom seemed to wobble behind him with a life of its own...far off beyond him we could hear the ceaseless sounds of the surf in the dark pounding in over and over along the shore, while the raging wind coming in at us smelled sharply of brine. 'What a sorry-arse bum!' someone was shouting. A vague sense of envy was spreading amongst us all. An almost sorrowful voice nearby yelled, 'What a brown-eye!' Prof Bingham's saggy white figure had reached the shallows...I watched the surf hit his body, and he leapt up away from the cold...he was raising his flabby arms high in shock...Prof Bingham started to splash into the water up to his calves and for a minute he managed some hopping in the low, foamy undertow as he avoided the breakers, but soon we saw him turn and make his way back for the beach...I supposed that he'd already had more than enough of the icy waves...he began trotting unsteadily up towards us. But immediately one of the hoons grabbed for Prof Bingham's abandoned clothes...next everyone seemed to make the same decision at the same instant and I knew what was going to happen...everyone clamoured to get back into the cars. 'Hurry, hurry!' Dulcie shouted unnecessarily at Gizi and me. I heard the frantic slamming of doors around us as we piled ourselves in...Dulcie was already up behind the wheel...she started us into reverse and the tyres squelched on the sand...Prof Bingham was still somewhere off in the distance, tottering over the stony beach...I could imagine him trying to holler and go on tiptoe as fast as he could...all the cars were turning in confusion to get themselves facing along the rutted road. We were going to be the final car away, and on the edge of our swinging headlights we saw Prof Bingham coming up near to the dunes...he tried waving and gesturing with his arms at us in desperation, but Dulcie got us driving off at the back of the row of other vehicles as quickly as she could manage...only Gizi seemed to feel any pity for him...she picked up the morning's newspaper from where it had been left on the seat and I watched her fling it with one hand out of her open window...I supposed it was to aid Prof Bingham's modesty, since he was naked and alone. We accelerated hard into the dark and for a few minutes we bounced uncomfortably on the uneven track...I guessed we were somewhere near the main road when, all at once, Dulcie braked because the cars in front of us had drifted to a stop...one of the hoons in a car up ahead got out, and we watched him leave his door open and sidle up the road towards us in our lights...Dulcie wound down her window...as the hoon drew close, he began self-consciously brushing the short fringe of his hair away from his forehead and we could hear him calling something. 'We better turn back, eh. Bloody better go back,' he announced. He came up to the driver's side of our car and leaned down at Dulcie's window. Then he said more quietly, 'What do you reckon? I mean, we really ought to, yeah. Obviously we can't leave the poor bastard this bloody far from town in the middle of the night.' But Dulcie was all for leaving Prof Bingham this far from town in the night... she kept raising one hand from the wheel as if to push the hoon away...I thought that now it might be Prof Bingham's turn to die on the roadside from exposure...but then Gizi started in on pleading for him...I was surprised at how much she appeared to care and it made me think of her as wonderfully tender-hearted. 'He's good value,' the hoon agreed when Gizi had finished. Dulcie still looked reluctant, but the hoon began moving away and retracing his steps to his own car, and one of the cars up ahead was already turning itself around...some of the other vehicles started to follow, shunting laboriously with their engines straining...it was difficult work in the narrow space amongst the trees. At last we were all turned round and we began to drive back, but after only a few bends we met Prof Bingham coming towards us...he was stooped down and hobbling over the rough hollows on the road...he was shivering, while below the bare curve of his belly he was clasping tight the pages of the newspaper Gizi had thrown...even so, his skin had a ghastly pallid look from the cold... Dulcie stopped our car just in front of Prof Bingham and got out...in the headlights we watched her go up to him and hug him around the top of his bald head. 'Oh boy, oh boy,' he was saying. He said it again and again above the noise from his own chattering teeth...other people had climbed from their cars and were milling about, and everybody had started laughing off the whole thing with a faintly embarrassed air...one of the hoons brought over Prof Bingham's clothes...Prof Bingham got dressed on the road, and then joined us in the Volkswagen and sat quietly in the front seat with the heater going...occasionally he stirred to try and shake the sand from his sweatshirt and pants. We followed the hoons in a trail of cars back to Greymouth...at length in town we all pulled up and halted around the edge of a wide intersection next to a small park...most of the hoons climbed out of their cars with a great deal of slamming of doors and entered the park, calling to each other and wandering through the dim light under some stunted, sparse-looking tea trees…Dulcie, Gizi and I got out of the Volkswagen and watched from the footpath, though Prof Bingham stayed put…a couple of hoons were fetching the half-g's from the cars and I could hear someone doing his best to rustle up a few glasses. There was a neat section of asphalt occupying the middle of the park amongst the grass, with an imposing, square-shouldered, granite cenotaph at its very centre…several of the hoons made for the cenotaph, and in the dim wash of the nearby streetlamps we could see them sit down and arrange themselves on the low chunky steps around it…they leaned back and propped themselves on their elbows as if they'd done this sort of thing many times before…one or two of them waved for Dulcie, Gizi and me to come on over, and we shambled towards them…from their attitude they appeared very likely to spend the rest of the night here…I supposed that this must be the hoons' happening place, but I felt a bit reluctant to join in any more of their games out here when it was so late. At last I took up a position almost automatically beside Gizi, sitting with her close to the top of the cenotaph's steps and with hoons sprawled everywhere about us…I'd lost sight of Dulcie, and Prof Bingham was still back warming his bones in the Volkswagen…I half envied him, because the steps were nice and broad but produced a killing cold beneath our bottoms and on the undersides of our legs…we all of us commenced work at polishing off the half-g's, though only with fitful interest, and the hoons' voices around us became subdued, despite the intermittent slamming of car doors that went on and on…I thought that we must be the only people making a noise in the whole of the night until I noticed a faint, lonely chirping of crickets someplace off in the near distance. Behind me, up by my shoulder, I could just make out some bronze plaques set into the cenotaph's pitted stone…they were below a list of the places that the Anzacs had gone to and saved…the word 'France' was there in the centre, and I thought of how much I really needed to get to Paris to write…but Paris was way off beyond the sea, so far off that it couldn't even be nighttime there yet…I nudged Gizi and pointed up at the word on the plaque… I meant France, the word, as the country next to Spain…but Gizi glanced at it and simply sighed. Then I saw Prof Bingham had revived and was out of the car…he came shuffling across the grass towards us, rubbing his hands…he sat on the edge of one of the cenotaph's bottom steps and lit up a cigarette…somebody gave him a flagon to drink from and he propped it between his knees and began muttering over it, offering up an exposition on Milton to a hoon who was lying stretched out prone on the asphalt beside his feet...Prof Bingham looked so at home with the hoons that I had the impression he was one of them, and it occurred to me that he probably wanted to have this sort of booze-filled hooley almost every night. 'So hey, yous jokers got a place to crash?' someone was asking in a loud voice. I glanced about in the darkness...the man who'd asked the question was a big, round-shouldered hoon sitting near the bottom of the cenotaph...he was bent forward with his arms shyly clasped around his knees, and I could see where his denim jacket was too small and riding up high along his back...then Dulcie appeared from somewhere out of the night...she drew closer to the hoon and stood above him, inclining her head. 'Well, yous can all come over to my mate's place in Cobden,' I heard the hoon say clearly to her. 'There's yards of room, eh. Probably should see you right.' I saw Dulcie nodding...that seemed to arrange everything...after a while I got wearily with the other three into the Volkswagen again...we followed a single carload of hoons who guided us, their red taillights swaying near and far before us in the dark, out towards Cobden...it was somewhere across town but I could get no sense of direction from the deserted, hopelessly suburban streets...I'd long ago given up trying to guess what hour of the morning it might be. Finally we halted at the top of a steeply sloping road and Dulcie pulled the car over hard against the kerb...alongside us the broad, ragged jumble of what appeared to be a boxthorn hedge crowded out across the footpath...it was leaning and bulging forwards at us in the night with a look of barely contained menace...the streetlamps had come to a lonely end further off down the road below, though someplace past the hedge's swollen contours I could make out the shining of distant lights up on another far-away hill. The hoon who had the place to stay approached our car, and I saw him bend over beside the driver's window and summon us with a casual wave...we got out of the Volkswagen and then roused ourselves to gather our gear, opening the car's boot and fishing about for the stuff we needed...when we were ready, the hoon walked off and we began trailing behind him...I was carrying Gizi's suitcase for her, together with my duffle-bag and Half-Arse...Dulcie brought her own suitcase, and Prof Bingham didn't bother carrying a thing. The hoon led us to a narrow gap at the far end of the hedge...he pushed his way through with an effort and we followed, although the prickly twigs and stiff leaves of the bush caught at us as we

246

passed…beyond, I peered into the gloom and saw there was an asphalt path heading down into a shallow gully, with the pale shape of a weatherboard house nestled near the bottom…the hoon went slouching in front of us along the path…in the limited light as we descended from the street I could see the whole pitched iron roof of the building and, when we moved a little closer, I noticed its eaves were sagging…on the section around it there was a lot of summer growth that had long since got away and was choking the remains of the lawn and garden. The trail soon narrowed so that we trudged further below in single file…everywhere beside our legs the path was tangled with thick weeds…a few biddy-bids stuck to my jeans…we were down now, almost level with the house, and I saw that in places the scrub actually rose to its windows and vines were clinging to the blue-grey timber on the building's walls…there were even skinny saplings poking up amongst the shrubs, the bindweed and brier around us, and there was a smell of rubbish somewhere, going off. The hoon led us up onto the porch and fiddled to put a key in the front door's lock…next he pushed the door open, and we went in behind him as best we could…but the lights inside didn't work…we heard the hoon clicking the switch several times in a series of pointless efforts, until at last he gave up and moved on into the dark…we all followed him, stumbling and bumping against the damp wallpaper in the blackness of the corridor… my eyes grew accustomed to the gloom but I kept on smacking Gizi's suitcase by accident into my knees. The hoon took us through to the living-room, where a dull glow from outside slanted in from the uncurtained windows…the large room was completely empty down to the skirting boards round the walls, and the nails in the bare floor creaked under our clumsy, heavy steps…Prof Bingham asked if this house was maybe recently abandoned…in reply the hoon only shrugged in his short jacket. 'It's okay to use the place,' he said finally. He appeared embarrassed by our disappointment. He added, 'Stacks of space, eh.' We accompanied him as he went on into the kitchen…past the entrance we had to watch where we put our feet because the lino across the kitchen floor was badly buckled…I saw there were some roughly made cupboards around the walls, an old stove and a bench and sink, and that was about it…there was a shiny-topped wooden table that seemed to be propped up precariously in a corner…otherwise the kitchen was as empty as the living-room. The hoon set the key gently on the table…Dulcie put her bag down onto the floor and I did the same with the gear I was carrying…it felt good to be free of the load…then all at once the hoon turned with the sound of a tight squeak from his boots on the lino and tramped away into the living-room again, not bothering to say a word…I thought he was going to come back, but after a minute we heard the front door being pulled shut. Somewhere the wind was rubbing a branch against one of the windows…for a while none of us seemed to know what to do…at last Dulcie walked over to the sink and turned the handle on one of the taps…the metal in its mechanism scraped but no water came out, and the prolonged squealing struck me as sharp with melancholy…Dulcie contemplated the dry tap, sighed and looked up. 'Well,' she said. Then quickly she went over to Prof Bingham, reached out and took his hand. 'Come on with me, Fido,' she announced. She started to lead Prof Bingham in the direction of a passageway…I assumed they were heading off to find a bedroom…Prof Bingham appeared to think so too, because he followed willingly and stopped only to pick up Dulcie's suitcase as he went by…he began hauling it behind him with his free hand and they slipped off down the corridor, though I could hear Prof Bingham banging the case carelessly along the bottom of the passage wall. For a stupid second I wondered why it was always like that, why the pair of them were always going someplace together to find a room on their own…then the obvious reason popped into my mind, and at the same moment I heard the thud of a door closing and everything was immediately quiet…even the branch outside had ceased hitting the house. I told Gizi to hang on for a bit, and hoped by putting firmness into my voice to hide my own inner turmoil…my hands and fingers were jittery…next, walking as softly as possible, I did a quick reconnoitre down the same passage that Prof Bingham and Dulcie had headed into…there was one closed door in the corridor which I presumed they'd just shut and I found two more doors that were open…both of them seemed to be for small, empty bedrooms. The bedroom furthest from Prof Bingham and Dulcie looked to be the better choice…through the doorway I saw the room had some shredded greyish curtains covering most of the windows, which could be helpful…in the centre of the room there was a single-sized iron bedstead with a thin, quilted mattress and no blankets or pillows…my heart sank at the bleak simplicity of the bed, but I stepped up to it and examined the spongy kapok mattress, and told myself that the whole thing was basically all right…when I turned to go back, I saw a dark-coloured wardrobe in the corner behind the door with a rusty wool-bale hook lying in front of it…I stretched out with my shoe to push the sinister hook away, but changed my mind and left it...if need be, something like that might just come in handy as a weapon. I returned to the kitchen and found Gizi waiting...I took her by the hand in the dim light and led her forwards and we shambled along the passage again with the bags, but when we entered the bedroom everything around us seemed unforgivably ugly and grim, and my courage deserted me...I started apologising and couldn't stop...as an answer Gizi put her forefinger up to my lips, and for an instant I could feel the thrilling warmth in her fingertip against my skin...then she put her suitcase up on the bed, opened it and started lifting out her clothes, her neatly folded tops, a spare pair of jeans, her underwear and even a brassiere, the entire contents...I watched her lay it all across the bed as blanket cover, and with her colourful things spread up and down along the lumpy mattress the room seemed brighter. After a few minutes I went away to find the toilet...in the corridor, as I passed Prof Bingham and Dulcie's door, I could hear the rhythmical noises of bedsprings grinding...I guessed Prof Bingham was already getting his rocks moved again...I tried to ignore the sounds and crept by towards the end of the passage, but the pair of them had started to groan, over and over, as usual...beyond any control I felt my mutinous cock beginning to swell. I pressed on and found the bathroom pretty much where I supposed it would be, at the back of the house...it was lined with cracked grey tiles that were laid everywhere across the floor and which extended halfway up the walls...it was also perishing with cold...but there was a mould-stained toilet inside next to the bathtub, and I thought the bog looked functional...by now I was having trouble with the hard-on poking upwards in my pants. I had to wait a bit before being flaccid enough to pee...the wind had risen once again, and I distracted myself by listening to the gusts whistling around the corner of the house...when the flow of my urine came, it steamed slightly on the side of the bowl...after finishing, I remembered the kitchen tap and doubted that the cistern would work, but I yanked at the chain several times anyway...the result was just a forlorn clunking noise and no gush of water, and I left the bog with the idea that it might have been more hygienic to pee out of a window. Back in the bedroom I found Gizi was lying curled up on her side in the middle of the mattress...she was nestled, fully dressed, among a thin covering of her spare clothes...she even had her ugg boots still on her feet...I bent down quietly and stretched myself out behind her along the bed...Gizi turned with a little grunt and put her arms up and around me, hugging my chest…together we cuddled for warmth. My heart was pounding like mad…Gizi was clasping my hand and holding it to her…she put it here and there, as if trying to find the right place for it…I was beginning to get very excited again…next we were kissing, breathing hard as our mouths made contact…we started to slip our chilly hands under each other's clothes, and beneath Gizi's jersey and T-shirt I put my palms round and over her small firm breasts. We were both shivering and gasping with the cold and with nerves…Gizi had her fingers running along my back and she pushed the tips of them into my underwear…I plied my hands downwards and slid them past her slim, smooth waist towards her jeans…the jeans were pressed tight against her warm skin so I unbuttoned the top, and I could scarcely contain my joy when Gizi didn't try to prevent me…we paused, hugging each other once more with our faces up close together…the loose bedsprings squeaked satisfyingly as we moved about. 'Dulcie told me I had to go on the pill,' Gizi whispered breathlessly. I was lying half on top of her…she was gazing up at me with her lips very near my cheek. She asked, 'Do you think it's made me gain any weight?' I leaned away, and looked down at her pale, exposed breasts…they were on show where our efforts had got her T-shirt and jersey ridden up almost to her neck.

'I think you're perfect,' I said truthfully.

'I'm a virgin,' Gizi confessed in a whisper.

'So am I,' I confessed back.

I hadn't meant to say it straight out loud like that…I hadn't meant to say a thing, except from an urge to match her honesty…but I also thought how we wouldn't need to go on admitting it for much longer. I began to pull down Gizi's jeans and panties, and she let me…at the same time she began pulling off her jersey and T-shirt and even commenced kicking off her boots, which complicated matters…but I tried not to let that or anything else slow me up…her body, appearing before me, was even more beautiful than in any form I could have imagined it…Gizi's skin was flawlessly white and smooth and shapely…I saw the patch of pubic hair in her crotch had a soft, exquisite curl. I began peeling off my own clothes so fast that they seemed to keep clinging to my knees and elbows as I hauled at them…I shook the things away and felt the cold cutting suddenly into my bare shoulders…my quivering erection was red and almost bursting, but I didn't make even the slightest attempt to hide it…Gizi looked startled at the sight…I supposed this was the first time she'd ever had one in a bed with her...my hard-on appeared to stand up there on its own between us. But I didn't think I had very long left to last before coming...if we were going to get rid of our virginities, we'd better hurry...I manoeuvred Gizi's legs apart, lay between them on top of her and pushed. Nothing happened...my cock met an unyielding wall of muscle...I thought for a moment that maybe my cock wasn't in the proper place...I reached down with one hand and checked about carefully for what I wanted to find...but that was definitely a vagina all right. I pushed myself again, and Gizi gritted her teeth...again nothing happened...I was starting to become desperately confused...if ever I needed *The Little Red Schoolbook*, that time was now. 'Shouldn't it be further in?' Gizi asked, sounding muffled beneath me. It wasn't in at all...I had to remind myself to stay calm and focused...this was turning out to be hard work.

'Leave everything to me,' I whispered.

But I could see Gizi clenching her fists amongst the clothes on the mattress...I shoved, and then strained with effort at the job...I grunted and squeezed my whole body forward...I was still on the outside...below me, I heard Gizi beginning to cry. 'It's my fault,' she wailed. 'I'm too tense,' she added.

'No, it's my fault,' I said, trying my best at being chivalrous.

But I didn't really think it was anyone's fault...we were just starting out at this, and perhaps it was bad fate...I thought that perhaps, in the great plan for the endless world, we were not meant to be doing this together after all...Gizi was still crying...she was whimpering into my chest with bewildered sobs...I looked down and saw her eyes were swollen, and the tears were streaking across her unwashed face.

'Don't worry,' I said.

I rolled over and lay beside her...I put my arms up around her limp shoulders.

'Don't worry,' I said. 'Don't worry.'

For a few moments I held Gizi closer, pressed to me, and then I cried too...I really didn't want to, but the tears burst out of me...they rushed down my cheeks while we lay there, miserable together. Oh how I loved her!...how so very much I loved her!...this was not at all what I'd imagined my first time at sex would be like...I wasn't even sure if it really counted as a sexual experience.

251

I woke to silence in the watery, early light...it was morning, and immediately I thought about the night before...every detail of what had happened came rushing back...Gizi was still sleeping peacefully beside me...we were both lying, clothed again, on the ugly mattress. I realised my legs were painfully cold...they were almost numb...I got up quietly and in a hurry...next I stood at the bottom of the bed and saw that Gizi hadn't stirred...I watched her sleeping amongst her clothes and not making even a hint of movement...she was using a wadded-up blouse for a pillow under her head and had one petite arm up beside her, as if to protect her cheek. I felt now that I knew every facet of her life...I felt I even knew the things about her that she hadn't told me yet...there was nothing, nothing in the least, that I didn't know...Gizi wanted someone who would bring her bouquets of cut flowers wrapped in newspaper...she wanted zany mid-winter picnics and shared laughter at private jokes...she wanted someone to pause, halting in the average day, while thinking of her and what she might be doing...she wanted her own small hand held warm and tight whenever she was lonely. But I'd long since leapt those stages, and every other stage too...I had us drawn together forever in space and time...I had us immortal in love and literature and wild devotion...I had us binding the infinite reaches of God's universe into a single solid atom...the sheer, unalloyed power of my own emotions tore at me...that was no basis for a relationship. In any case, I felt that Gizi was somehow superior to all these thoughts...I found I'd put my arms out while standing there watching, as if to touch her anyway...I had to check the impulse, and I lowered my arms to my sides again. At last I started to move off...I managed to collect my duffle-bag and Half-Arse, holding them slack in my hands...the floor betrayed me by creaking a little as I slunk across it...the house seemed to be objecting to me making any kind of departure...but if the universe didn't mean for Gizi and me to be together, I couldn't face telling her goodbye. I was running away from her...it felt like a cowardly, awful thing, to be running away from Gizi... but a declaration of eternal, worshipful, limitless love was all I could think of to offer her...it wouldn't help. I trod as carefully as possible along the crooked wooden floor of the passageway...the house looked different in the daylight but everything remained quiet as I nudged open the front door...outside, on the path up to the hedge, I heard the sound of a number of chirpy finches mocking me from the treetops nearby…a loose, fresh breeze was coming in from somewhere and creeping up the slope of the hill…it was a cloudy, chilly, cold-hearted sort of day. Dulcie's Volkswagen was parked by the kerb, just as we'd left it…the little car looked terribly dinged up in the places where the rear had been hit…I tried a door, and it opened with a sorrowful, scraping sound…the newspaper from the previous day was still lying bedraggled on the floor, and I reached in and picked it up…the thought occurred to me that, for a newspaper, it had seen a lot of action…I also thought it might just possibly have information to help me get out of town, so I squeezed the damp pages into a roll and stuffed it all deep into my duffle-bag. Then I simply walked away on the uneven asphalt footpath…my legs kept picking up a faster and faster pace as I trod down the steep, curving slope of the road…within a few minutes my dirty clothes felt less chafing with the open air wafting against my skin. I continued heading downhill for some time until I came to a dairy…I could see it from a good distance away on the corner of an intersection, built into one end of a house and hard up against the footpath…the dairy's blue-and-orange-painted walls and even some of the wide windows were covered with ads and posters for fresh bread and Tip Top ice-cream, and a small red veranda attached by cables was shading the storefront… several wire newspaper billboards showing headlines and magazine posters were propped up along the area beside the entrance…I halted for a moment at the door…none of the lights were on inside, but I pushed the door back a little and stepped into the dim, cramped interior of the shop. The familiar goods and cartons arranged neatly on the shelves looked reassuring…a thin, round-faced Chinese man appeared through a curtain of green plastic strips behind a service counter at the back of the store and stood waiting…he smiled briefly at me in the semi-darkness and so I smiled in return, and waved with a small gesture meant to show that I wasn't ready yet…the Chinese man retreated behind the curtain, but I could see him standing quietly on the other side of the loose strips, keeping me in sight as I moved about. I ended up buying a pint of milk and a cream doughnut…outside on the footpath once more, I perched myself on the dairy's bike-rail at the edge of the road and gave the milk bottle a vigorous shake…gulping the cold milk down soon settled my stomach and helped chase away the headache left by the previous night's beer…with satisfaction I munched the oily doughnut, and when I'd finished I threw the empty bottle and the bag into a rubbish bin and pulled yesterday's newspaper once again from my duffle-bag...the damp pages were hard to unfold, and it would have been better just to go back into the shop and buy another paper, but I didn't want to bother... instead I ripped out the part I needed for bus times or trains and hunted around. After a moment my eye was caught by one of the classified ads at the top of the ragged page...it was a few simple lines asking if anyone wanted to share a ride to Picton...it mentioned only a phone number and that the ride was for today, but Picton sounded perfect...Picton sounded like just the sort of place that I'd like to get a ride to, because Picton was completely in the other direction from Gizi's trip to Franz Josef. Not far off at the corner of the next intersection I could see a tall red phone box...I approached it, pushed its heavy door inwards and lifted the receiver, grateful to hear a dial tone coming from the earpiece...in the tight space the door seemed impossible to close and so I braced myself against it with one bent knee and my shoulder, and worked on dialling the number from the scrap of newspaper...I let the phone ring...after some while it was answered by a woman who sounded elderly and spoke in a strong, refined Scottish brogue...she told me immediately that her name was Mrs Macalister. I started to ask about whether the ride to Picton was still on, but Mrs Macalister interrupted...she explained sternly that it was her husband who'd done it...he'd gone ahead and positively insisted that she put the notice in the paper, and she wasn't exactly sure if it was such a good idea, but really that was the kind of man he was, and you couldn't expect to change a person after so many years now, could you...Mrs Macalister kept on like this, yet there was something timid under the severity in her voice and I thought it best not to stop her...obviously she didn't enjoy talking to strangers, and her manner suggested she might hang up...but despite my care and self-restraint, I couldn't resist asking about the ride again as soon as a chance came. 'Oh dear, oh dear, yes,' Mrs Macalister said softly. 'Oh dear, I don't know.' But when she began speaking some more, I jumped in and talked over her...I introduced myself very politely to prevent her from ringing off...I rushed out some mumbo-jumbo about touring the South Island and an urgent need to get up north for a vital appointment tomorrow morning at nine on the dot... meanwhile Mrs Macalister had commenced hemming and hawing in a tone that implied she didn't believe a word of what I was saying, but I found her scepticism annoying and pressed harder. When at last I'd finished, she announced down the line, 'Well, I'm afraid you've rather gone and cut it all a little too much on the fine side, young man. I was only now preparing to be off and away.'

'Yes,' I said, 'but, you know, if you could just see yourself clear—'

Mrs Macalister ignored me. She said, 'So that's how it is. I'll be departing directly.'

'Well look,' I said, 'I'm actually one-hundred-percent ready to go myself, right this instant.'

I hoped this would be a clincher, but I had a terrible feeling this old biddy was going to desert me in my hour of need.

I started to say, 'Even if you could just take me part of the distance—'

'Mind you, my husband did rather suggest it would be better,' Mrs Macalister interrupted, 'safer, really, that's his point, to have some type of travelling companion.' Mrs Macalister sighed, as if sharing this information was a burden. Next she said, 'Strictly speaking, well, no one else has actually answered the notice. I mean, apart from the one foreign-sounding man, that was, whom I really just had to put off.' Mrs Macalister paused, and asked me shrewdly, 'You're not at all foreign, are you?'

'No, not even a little bit,' I said. 'I'm from Palmerston—'

'Well, Silky and I are going to be in need of the company,' Mrs Macalister cut in.

'That's good,' I said, 'that's extra-curly.' With a glow of gratitude I asked, 'Is Silky your husband?'

'Why, no,' Mrs Macalister sounded severe all over again. But then I thought maybe she liked sounding severe and returned to it out of habit. 'Whatever gave you that remarkable idea?' she demanded. 'Silky's my cat, of course.'

'Yes I see,' I said.

I wondered about being cooped up in a car with a fucking cat…I wondered about being cooped up with Mrs Macalister too, but I felt there was no choice…the phone box's bulky door, still propped up hard against my shoulder, was becoming uncomfortable…I asked Mrs Macalister if she could find me on the road out of town, because I was already on my way…this was true, or perhaps more of a half-truth, because I couldn't know if I was on my way since I'd no solid idea of where I was.

'I'll be the one carrying a duffle-bag and a portable typewriter,' I added.

Mrs Macalister seemed to regard this as all very eccentric…she began cautioning me that it didn't sound to her how real New Zealanders behaved, but after a moment she softened again…she agreed to do her best to keep an eye out for me, and I started in on thanking her profusely. 'Well, you know, I certainly can't make any definite promises,' she declared and rang off. I left the phone box and headed lickety-split on a route that I hoped would lead me to a main street...after a while I did get out onto a larger sort of road and almost at once discovered a signboard pointing me north...with this I proceeded a lot more confidently, though still as quickly as I could...but it seemed reasonable to think that I was going to get ahead of Mrs Macalister, wherever the old hen was coming from with her direct departure. Before too much time had passed, I was walking out of town on the edge of the state highway...it was only a nondescript road I was on, a thin asphalt strip tracing a line between a bushy green escarpment and the shoals of a broad, shallow river, but I was managing my exit from Greymouth...as I trudged onwards, a cutting wind funnelled by me along the riverbanks and across my back, and the cold made me hope that my ride was going to turn up soon...then at last I heard a vehicle approach and slow down somewhere behind me...I turned and saw a two-door light blue car not far off, pulling over onto the gravel shoulder of the road...the car looked tidy and well kept, with a sloping rear that made me think it might be a Datsun, and I started walking back up the side of the road towards it. 'Mr Ingle. Mr Ingle, would you be?' a voice was calling in a distinctly nervous tone. I could see that the passenger window of the idling car had already been rolled down...the driver was bent well over across the vinyl seats and was twisting to get a glimpse of me out of the open window...I saw a large woman with an anxious, heavy-featured face, and I thought she seemed exactly like my mental picture of Mrs Macalister. I came up and stood squarely before the car, bending across the flimsy bonnet to take a good look in through the front windscreen... Mrs Macalister was a chunky, muscular old woman wearing a floral, yellow-and-pink cotton housedress that was pinned up at the neck with a prim turquoise broach...she had grey hair tied back into a bun and wore gold teardrop glasses, and I noticed traces of talcum powder on her broad cheeks...she was still trying to ask through the window with a queasy inflection if I was not perhaps the young man who had phoned. But I wasn't going to give her any chance to get away...I scooted around the edge of the vehicle without a word...I opened the passenger door and watched Mrs Macalister manoeuvre her matronly carcass back onto the driver's side, shrinking from me a little...then I got in and slammed my door shut hard.

'It's good to meet you,' I said.

I arranged Half-Arse and my duffle-bag at my feet...next I turned round and saw an obese tortoiseshell cat behind me, lying on a tartan rug spread across the rear seat of the car...the vinyl cover of my own seat crackled under my bottom as I shifted a bit further to size the cat up...I didn't want any unpleasant surprises from a bloody animal...but it stayed half asleep on the rug, curled on top of its own legs, paying me no attention.

'Good to meet Silky too,' I added, and turned again to the front.

Mrs Macalister had taken up a position ready to drive once more, sitting slouched at the steering wheel with her head forwards over her strong shoulders...both of her hands were gripping the wheel tight and I could see where the backs of them were lined with lumpy purple veins... but her face was bent a little towards me, and suddenly I understood that she was really in the midst of appraising my filthy clothes and hairy chin.

'Been doing a lot of bumming around,' I said. 'I'm seeing something of life, eh.'

After a long moment she asked, 'And are you eating properly?'

'Very well, thank you,' I replied. 'I had milk for breakfast.'

'Oh dear,' Mrs Macalister said.

'Let's just go, shall we,' I said. 'I'm in a hell of a hurry to get out of this town.'

That appeared to do the trick...Mrs Macalister put the car into drive and nudged us back onto the road...we set off, and went at a sensible pace for some time through a long, boring valley and round the sides of hills... we travelled past tiny townships without any names that I could discern, scattered amongst the bush and pasture here and there. Mrs Macalister didn't waste her energy on idle chitchat...in fact my presence seemed to have stunned her into a kind of silent resignation...while driving she continued to watch the road anxiously with her head craned forwards, peering at the windscreen for whatever was in front of us...she kept her hands up on the steering wheel, positioned at quarter to three, and at all times observed the safety speeds marked on the yellow AA signs at each bend...when eventually the highway came out of the hills near the coast, the road narrowed and she took special care...it was slow work, but steady. On one side of the switchback road that we were following the choppy grey Tasman Sea was spread out below us, stretching away, with more of it coming into view past each bend...on the other side of the car was a seemingly endless, bush-clad slope…it was crammed with an unchanging cover of black mud and thick fern and dripping ponga trees…we went winding this way and that above the coastline for over an hour…I was starting to feel almost hypnotised by the scenery. Finally Mrs Macalister broke in on the long silence and announced, 'Well, I do believe it's past the time to give Silky her breakfast.' She didn't take her eyes off the windscreen as she added, 'The poor wee dear, after all this while she'll be feeling just that much more peckish for waiting. Poor wee thing.' I glanced at Mrs Macalister without making a reply, startled by this new dip of hers into garrulity. 'And yes, she'll also need to be getting her injection,' Mrs Macalister went on. She was now staring across from the wheel at me, and her thin lips had formed a determined, pinched compression at the edges of her mouth.

'I see,' I said.

Mrs Macalister drew the car gradually over to the side of the road… she slowed us to a lengthy, cautious stop and at last we sat parked on a straight portion of the highway that was grim and even eerie in its lonesomeness…I saw the sea was breaking hard across a narrow strip of beach far off below us, and the water looked forbidding and cold…down in the surf dark, tortured stands of rock were sticking up, bashed by the spray, and heavy, crumpled clouds were spread across the sky above us… it was difficult to believe that anywhere as sunny as Australia might be out there on the other side of the horizon. Silky stood up on her rug behind us and yawned…the cat seemed to know what was going on…meanwhile Mrs Macalister bent far down into the footwell and began groping about under the driver's seat…presently she pulled up a rustling white New World shopping bag and took out a tin of cat food, a can-opener and a bowl…she put each item down one by one in the space between us. 'Now, I'll require you to give me some assistance, young man,' Mrs Macalister declared. She was breathing heavily from her efforts at reaching under the seat. She asked, 'Could you get all this arranged somewhere on a nice clean spot out by the roadside, well away from the traffic of course, while I gather up Silky and bring her? I think the poor wee dear needs to be settled first.' I glanced again at the cat…it didn't look poor or even particularly wee, and it looked a lot more settled than I was.

'No problem,' I said.

I scooped up the food things and eased open the car's door on my side…the crashing sounds of the surf hit me and a stiff, salty wind blew hard into my hair...I took a few steps from the car, put down the bowl and started using the opener to work the lid off the tin of cat food...when I bent down and shook the contents of the tin into the bowl at my feet, the sight of the sticky jellied meat made me think that I was hungry too. Mrs Macalister came up with Silky draped over her arm...she placed the cat down on the roadside, and it roused itself in its flabby way and shuffled over the tarseal towards the dish...we both stood and watched, leaning slightly into the wind, as the cat began dutifully to eat...but after a moment or so Mrs Macalister went back to the car and returned with a small plastic syringe and a clear Tupperware case in one hand...she prised the case's lid open and began to remove a short needle and some sort of glass vial...Mrs Macalister concentrated, working with her large fingers, until she got the needle and syringe fitted together. 'It's terribly sad,' she said in a voice raised against the gusty wind. She added, 'Silky's a diabetic, and I'm afraid she has been for some considerable period. But then in this life we all have to make adjustments, don't we.' Mrs Macalister focused her attention on expertly filling the syringe from the top of the vial...I saw a hint of impatience passing over her wide, papery-skinned face. She said, 'You'll have to give her the shot while she's still eating.'

'Me?' I asked.

Mrs Macalister removed the syringe from the vial and held it up... she squeezed a drop out of the needle and then looked squarely into my eyes. She said, 'Well, Silky has to have her insulin.' I peered down at the moggie on the road.

'I'm not jabbing a cat,' I said.

'Just take her by the scruff of the neck and push this down into the skin,' Mrs Macalister explained. 'After that you depress the plunger. That's all there is to the whole process. Hurry now, she'll be finished eating soon.' I stared at the cat some more...it had its saggy back to me and was bobbing its head, still bent over the bowl...it was calmly tossing a chunk of meat about in its mouth...all around us I could hear the rumbling of the sea continuing to thrash at the shore.

'Why can't you do it?' I asked after a while.

'My husband always manages this,' Mrs Macalister said. She sounded brisk and matter-of-fact. As I went on gazing at the cat she added, 'I just get everything ready. Tish tosh, you hurry along now.' I tried to think of some new sort of objection to raise, but there didn't seem much room left for discussion...I thought that Mrs Macalister really knew how to negotiate...after a few more moments I took the syringe from her, stepped over and leaned downwards, almost to the road. The cat was concentrating on chewing the last piece of meat...I grabbed at its neck in a hesitant way...the cat went right on ignoring me, and I held my breath and stuck in the needle, feeling it sink under the flesh...but there was no reaction at all from the animal...maybe it regarded this as simply normal...I eased the plunger down and was glad to get the needle out just as Silky was swallowing her final mouthful...I straightened up and gave Mrs Macalister the empty syringe.

'Have you been married long?' I asked with a flush of triumph.

'Long enough to take care of a cat,' Mrs Macalister replied. But she looked satisfied. She added more confidentially, 'You know, my husband usually manages things like the driving, too.'

'Oh, would you want me to have a go?' I volunteered, hoping I sounded bright and competent.

I'd never driven a car before, though until a minute ago I'd never given a cat an injection either...besides, I was fairly sure that Mrs Macalister's car was an automatic...I'd had plenty of time to observe what she was doing, and I thought I remembered most of it...I thought I could manage driving every bit as well as she did. 'Oh, I don't know,' Mrs Macalister was saying. But I could already imagine myself at the wheel...I headed eagerly past her for the vehicle. 'Have you ever had an accident?' she called to me.

'Not even once,' I called back.

I opened the driver's door in a hurry and almost tumbled in...Mrs Macalister was still out on the road, still tidying up her cat stuff...the key was in the ignition and I started the engine, which made the whole car shudder pleasantly...next I reached across to the passenger's side, picked up Half-Arse and the duffle-bag and threw them over the top of the seats into the rear, so that they landed on Silky's tartan rug with a thump. Mrs Macalister appeared and climbed into the front seat next to me, clutching her cat and her paraphernalia...she attempted to lecture me on being careful, but I made plenty of noisy revs with the accelerator and drowned out most of her little speech...I figured I knew how to negotiate too, and at last Mrs Macalister seemed to give up...she let her assorted things fall down beside her feet and kept Silky hoisted on her lap...the animal curled around itself once more and didn't look as if it wanted any trouble. I put us into drive...the car set off with a violent jolt...Mrs Macalister's whole body lurched and her glasses nearly flew from her nose, and she clutched even harder at Silky. 'Oh dear,' she said distinctly. She said nothing else at all for a long time...Mrs Macalister appeared too tense to speak...occasionally I noticed her twitch a little in her seat, though mostly I saw she was just holding Silky with one hand and gripping the armrest with the other...but I could spare her only a glance now and then, due to the sort of speeds I was heading us up to...I saved my attention for the highway like a real driver. We followed the signs for Picton... at length we turned inland and left the sea behind...the road began to hug an interminable series of heavily forested bends...next it climbed and dipped and wiggled around the edge of a long gorge...I thought we still seemed to be taking forever to get anywhere, and my solution was to go even faster...everyone knew the AA signs were only a guideline, and Mrs Macalister already looked so frightened that it made no difference to her. I discovered that you could corner a lot more quickly if you used both sides of the road...it made the tyres squeal in odd spots, but that meant everything sounded more exciting, and I decided the main problem was resisting any urge to touch the brake...we drove on for a few hours like this and nothing changed, except that sometimes I used the wipers to scrape bugs off the front windscreen...I was tired and starting to feel a little shaky with hunger, but driving fast was relaxing and I understood now why people put up with sitting in cars over such huge distances... it was awfully easy just to let your mind drift. I supposed that I was Mrs Macalister's idea of an adventure, so after a while I began telling her what it was like to be a serious writer...I thought it would help when she gossiped about me to her friends later...my explanation of writing took quite a lot of time, but no matter how carefully I phrased it all Mrs Macalister seemed to lack any consistent interest...it occurred to me that perhaps she wasn't so enthusiastic because she didn't read very much... but then, neither did I.

'It's my job to transform the things I know into art,' I said to her.

On impulse I pushed the button that rolled down the driver's window...as the window descended next to me, the air from outside started rushing past my right ear...it meant I'd have to shout to set forth any more opinions, but it felt exciting to imagine my opinions flying off into the open world.

'Writers like me,' I yelled, 'we're in a specialised line of trade. You see, we get in touch with the first ideas in our minds, and then we use that to dig down and reproduce from the balls of the universe. We get ourselves in really deep.'

I listened to the sound of this, and tried to consider what it was that I might be learning from all these experiences...but it was a complicated business, driving, expounding, theorising and evaluating all at the same time, particularly when I was in such a wicked hurry...I turned to look across at Mrs Macalister while we accelerated onwards...she was still sitting rigidly with Silky held tight in her lap...she had the back of her neck pressed up hard against the top of her seat, her eyes wide, and the corners of her lips were pulled apart as she made small, sharp, sucking noises...travel didn't appear to agree with her.

'We also illuminate the ordinary,' I bellowed above the wind. 'One way or another, it's heady stuff. You know I've got a novel in the works? But I can't say anything more about it right at the moment, eh, because that might have a detrimental effect.'

Mrs Macalister said nothing in response at all, and I wondered why on earth she kept staring at the road so much if it bothered her that we might crash...for some time we'd been passing along a river flat, skirting the ragged, rocky banks by the water, but next our route began heading away on an uneven though fairly straight piece of road...it was a good opportunity to see what maximum speed I could crank the car up to... it turned out that I could still crank it up a whole lot...a little later we came to a town and I saw from the signs that it was Blenheim...soon I got some useful practice at stopping which I hadn't quite expected, but I was confident by now that I could drive any type of vehicle pretty much anywhere. After Blenheim the sky cleared and the highway before us started winding through shallower, greener valleys and occasional built-up areas, bright under the sunshine...my eyes were sore and my back was aching from having had to sit still for such a long time...I wasn't really seeing the road anymore so much as feeling my way...we circled some kind of flat grassy square that appeared to signal the beginnings of a town...soon we were among other cars, in traffic that insisted on only crawling forwards...I followed the other vehicles through the slow, increasingly suburban streets beside tranquil-looking houses with berms, and I thought that this evidently was Picton. Within just a few more minutes I could see railway lines nearby, running along the foot of some low glistening hills...next there were warehouses around us, lots of them in a busy jumble...we reached several rows of signposts indicating parking and I found that I was driving in a lane, and I'd never done that before…finally I saw the ferry terminal through the traffic, just up ahead. I didn't think to ask if the wharf was where Mrs Macalister actually wanted to go…instead it occurred to me that I could catch the ferry back to Wellington from here, and I remembered that Wellington, off across the water, was Gizi's hometown…going there would mean I'd leave an entire stretch of blue sea between Gizi and me. All at once the thought of Gizi crowded out everything else as her lively, exciting face rose up in my mind with an astounding clarity…it was dramatic…I could make out her green eyes and the dimpled edges of her smile. Why on earth was I running away from her?…suddenly all I wanted to do was hold onto that vision of Gizi forever in my head…the mere idea of not managing to hold onto it caused me pain, but I was reassured to hear the familiar pattern of her voice somewhere in my ears…almost unconsciously I'd eased my foot from the accelerator…I let the car drift more and more slowly, because it seemed too much of a bother to be driving any longer…I was too preoccupied with maintaining the vision of Gizi's perfect face, up close before my eyes. We were swinging a little leftwards…I swung us back harder to the right…it meant we started into a turn, so I thought we might as well go on heading that way anyhow…I thought there were lots of small, interesting-looking cross streets coming up, and we'd probably get into one or other of them…it might even be a good idea to pull over someplace. There was a bad, dull thud around us which reverberated throughout the car…everything jumped and skidded, and I heard a mysterious, long squeal…then I realised that the squeal was coming from me, because my hands and shoulders were being showered with glass…something had slammed into the edge of my side of the car, up near the engine, and we'd been shoved hard over towards the left half of the road…the car had stopped moving, which was just as well since I wasn't driving it anymore…I wasn't doing much of anything, except for thinking how my head felt rattled and a bit twitchy on my neck. The truck that appeared to have hit us was coming to a halt just a little further up the street…I noticed its wing-mirror was half torn off, and the left side along the cab looked pretty well smashed…I could scarcely believe the whole event was all over, and I seemed to have missed a lot of it. So, I thought, this is a traffic accident. I glanced across at Mrs Macalister…she was still there, sitting almost motionless, with Silky still clasped in her lap… she had her face craned forward and was staring at the intricate cracks in what remained of the front windscreen...her features had settled into a peculiar, frightened smile that suggested nothing was wrong. With an effort I pushed open the damaged door next to me...I stepped out into the street, and thought the whole car looked as if a giant had tried using it to make a milkshake...underfoot there were bright, slippery globules of safety glass spread out on the tarseal in a beautiful twinkling sheet...I could see that the truck driver was already hurrying towards me around the side of his cab...he was a big, rough-faced man dressed in loose, grease-smudged olive-green overalls, and he was stamping on the road with each step in heavy steel-capped boots. 'What the bloody hell were you doing?' the truckie yelled at me as he approached. He was trembling from anger and perhaps from shock...I raised both hands with my palms up and out to show that I didn't want any fuss...I opened my mouth to apologise. The truckie moved closer and caught me on the jaw with his fist...the blow was solid...it flung me back against the bonnet of Mrs Macalister's car...I sank downwards to the road and spent a moment taking in what had happened. The urgent panting of the truckie's breathing was just above my head...I glanced up and saw he was standing almost right over me, glaring down, and so I started getting to my feet...I had to use the car's tyre as support... my sandshoes slid amongst the safety glass...without waiting for me to be properly upright in front of him, the truckie swung at me again...his blow brushed past the edge of my cheek. 'I'll fucking kill you!' he yelled. He seemed sincere...after all, my face hurt, and he'd already had one good try at running me over...but while I was considering this, the truckie collected me with a solid punch once more...my entire body jerked from the impact. 'You bloody little, fucking, bloody bastard!' the truckie was yelling. At least, he was probably shouting something like that, because by now I'd straightened up and was too hell-bent on escaping to pay careful attention...I concentrated on circling round the rear of the car to keep some space between myself and another attack, but the truckie was coming after me fast...I skirted along the passenger's side in an effort to put still more of the car between us...within the vehicle's interior Mrs Macalister's head and shoulders suddenly came into view nearby through the windows...I saw she'd reached up with one arm to clutch in desperation at the top of her seatbelt strap, next to her cheek...her lips were moving as if she was repeating some sort of phrase and I thought it might be 'oh dear,' since that was the gist of the message on her face.

'I'm sorry, Mrs Macalister,' I called to her.

The truckie was still coming for me gamely...he was still shouting, but I was glad to see his heavy boots were slowing him down...I kept scrabbling and circling round the corners of the car to try and hold him at a distance, and within a moment or two I got to the open, shattered door on the driver's side again...quickly I dived in and reached past the front seat for the rear of the vehicle...I lunged for my bag and Half-Arse...Mrs Macalister shrank away, and from her lap Silky astonished me by hissing at me in fury.

'I really am sorry, Mrs Macalister,' I yelped.

I wriggled myself out of the car and found the truckie had managed to get close again...this time I swung hard at him with Half-Arse and backed him off...it felt like a small victory for literature...then I started to run pell-mell up the road with my duffle-bag and the typewriter...the truckie responded by chasing me some more...evidently he hadn't finished trying to kill me and believed there was hope. The thought popped into my mind that it was morally wrong to turn tail...it was possibly illegal, but I was an artist and I felt an obligation to future readers to keep myself safe...even so, I'd never heard of a major author who'd fled for safety from a long-distance truck driver before...for a few instants I thought he was actually going to catch me...but I ran as if my life depended on it, which it probably did...gradually he seemed to tire, and I just kept right on going. I reached the ferry terminal at a determined jog-trot...my lungs were burning and the sensation went all the way up into my windpipe, and it took me some considerable while to recover my breath...I still felt bad about leaving Mrs Macalister, but the feeling didn't last for long...she struck me as the sort of over-cautious person who had miles of insurance...now she was going to be glad of it. Inside the terminal building I found the ferry was due to sail within only a few minutes...this was helpful, because I could hear a police siren wailing somewhere in the distance...as I went up to buy a ticket, there was a final announcement over the terminal's loudspeakers...they were already calling visitors off the ship. The plump, middle-aged woman who served me at the ticket counter had a soggy red face and she started preparing my boarding pass in a manner that suggested we had all the time in the world...I abandoned any pride...I leaned across the counter at her and begged...I said that I really had to please get on that boat, the one just outside, right this instant...it flustered her, and after a further minute or two she handed over my ticket, but in her haste the woman gave me most of my money back by mistake as change...I felt that my luck had returned, and scurried out to the boarding ramp clutching my duffle-bag and Half-Arse in one hand and waving the brand-new pass from the other at anybody who might be in my way. Once up on the boat, I tried heading off into the vehicle deck to hide...an officious crew member in a neat, freshly-ironed white uniform barred the door down to the empty cars...I poked my ticket at the plastic buttons along the front of his jacket and explained myself with a series of lies...he stayed resolute...after that, I hung about in the corridors until we cast off...I was still worried at being somehow recognised as on the lam. At last the boat lumbered into the harbour and then drifted lazily through the Sounds...I went up top and watched the wake spreading away behind us...it washed out towards the steep capes and inlets, dense with growth down to the shore, that lined both sides of our passage along the water...I pondered gloomily on the vow I'd formed to get myself literary glory...getting myself a free trip across Cook Strait instead wasn't really any kind of progress...I was going to have to raise my game. It took quite a while before we left the shelter of the Sounds, but eventually the ferry began rolling and pitching in long, predictable movements on the open sea...I went below to search for the cafeteria, thinking that the ship could lift and drop me as much as it damn well liked...I was going to take Mrs Macalister's advice...I was going to start eating properly.

A few hours later I was in Wellington again...some heavy rain seemed to find us coming through the Heads and to follow the ferry in the direction of the harbour...the wet weather turned the messy bush cover on the hills nearby into a greasy, murky shade of green, and the wind came up in gusty bursts as the boat crawled in against the wharf...I disembarked and walked from the terminal into town, hunched forwards while the sweeping wind made the raindrops feel as though they were shooting past my face and shoulders...the drops dug into my clothes and blew skidding along the footpath at my feet...I used every scrap of cover that I could find to keep me dry and it was a relief to get away from the exposed area around the new Beehive and duck in under the verandas of some stores. I wondered where on earth I could manage to head for now...it was more imperative than ever to find a place to get started on my novel...if I didn't get writing in a hurry any impetus I had would drift off somewhere beyond my grasp, and so I pushed on at top speed further into town, hoping that something might turn up. Soon I began to march along Willis Street again past a wide, fenced-off building site up close to the road...I walked on the footpath beside the rough panels of a hoarding that screened the front of the site, with most of the pathway running under the protruding shelter of some bulky steel scaffolding...I used the dry places where the scaffolding's platforms covered the pavement, and I crouched a little and watched where I put my feet...then there was a slapping noise which interrupted me, coming from something high overhead...I looked up and saw a long wooden plank falling and banging against the scaffolding several storeys above but dropping down at me fast. I knew at once I should move out of the way, and felt what a pity it was that I didn't have even the slightest chance...the plank hit the footpath end on just in front of me...the wallop of its impact was so swift and hard that it bounced up again to my shoulder height...the first time I'd been too slow to react to it coming down, so this time I dodged deftly away...the plank landed once more and flopped onto its side. I gazed up through some of the gaps in the scaffolding, trying to see what had happened...from many storeys far above, almost up in the sky, a chippie's face was staring down at me as if I was a big deal...I noticed he was wearing a bright yellow safety helmet. 'Struth!' he shouted. Something in the chippie's tone made me start shaking with fright...a second or two later a low wooden door at ground level in the hoarding creaked open a bit ahead of me...another man, a new one, now put his head out through the door's confined space...he was half stooped and ruddy-faced, and I watched him twist his neck and check cautiously upwards...the man was also wearing a safety helmet. I waited as the man opened the door wider...he emitted a loud grunt from the back of his throat and began manoeuvring his large, heavyset frame out onto the footpath...he struggled, and while he did so I could see he was dressed in an old brown suit with his shirt and tie partly hidden under an orange safety-vest...his long red face showed a lot of lines from blood vessels trailing beneath the skin of his nose and cheeks...the man straightened up in front of me at last and looked me over...he kneaded his back with his hand for a moment and mumbled that he was the Project Manager here. 'You're all right, eh,' the Manager said to me quietly.

'Well, no thanks to you,' I replied.

By now I was feeling so scared that my shoulders were twitching about...I felt my stomach contract, and fought off a sudden urge to vomit by standing very erect and still. At the same time I could hear the Manager growling, 'Yeah, but I mean you're basically all in one piece, eh.

I mean really, mate, you could have—' He halted in mid-sentence, and I saw he was eyeing me in an amused way...his lips even parted in a brief smile, as if he was contemplating what might have occurred and didn't think it would be all that bad.

'I'm not your mate,' I hissed.

But the Manager only ignored this...instead he leaned closer towards me and spoke louder. 'Oh, I reckon nobody's ever got the least flaming idea about the whole problem of putting up a fifteen-storey building,' he said. His tone was firm...it appeared he was trying to explain himself to me...it was as though I, of all people, should be expected to sympathise. The Manager said, 'Everything, and I do mean every bloody thing, has to be humped way the hell up to the top floor, you know what I'm talking about? Especially the bloody gib board, eh, when it's too big for that half-pie lift. I mean, Jesus.' The Manager halted once more...he seemed only now to have noticed my poorly restrained shivering. He added, 'Look, you've got to watch your step, mate. It's just common sense. I mean, a few things are bound to drop off a building site once in a while.'

'Well, I don't give a fuck,' I said.

The Manager reacted by poking one finger angrily at my chest... perhaps he felt his own common sense had been called into question... but he swallowed and hesitated, and for a moment nothing came out of his mouth. 'Well, it's the law of bloody gravity,' he declared at last. 'I mean, sooner or later people are bloody going to get hurt.'

'I *still* don't give a fuck,' I announced.

'Oh, wait on, mate,' the Manager started. The loose skin tightened along the base of his large jaw...he spread his hands and, involuntarily, I took a step back...I felt sure he was going to give me some sort of push, or maybe worse.

'You nearly fucking killed me just now!' I screamed.

I'd had enough...I'd had a gutsful...screaming out loud felt a lot better than just letting my bones shake through my shoulders and legs...it was my second accident on the same day, and I was tired of being assaulted afterwards.

'I should fucking get the fucking law onto you!' I yelled.

I'd already noticed that the Manager was bigger than me, so I kept well back while I went off crook...I started calling him a fucking hooer and all the rest of the names I could possibly think of...it seemed like a good way to drive home my point, although the Manager didn't agree...

we stood in the centre of the footpath and shouted at each other with every ounce of breath we could muster. Some people who were attempting to pass by halted and gathered around us...they collected wherever it was conveniently dry under the scaffolding's platforms and waited, watching the fun...the Manager kept up a lot of stupid bellowing that regulations and supervision couldn't always stop accidents...I went on swearing and swearing at the Manager, and I swore at his family, at his friends and at their families and their families' friends...I read the company's name from a sign on the hoarding and started swearing at that too...finally I gave up on any chance of bringing off some sort of elegant variation and simply waved my arms and screamed 'Oh, for fuck's sake!' at everything the Manager said. In the midst of all the ruckus a big black executive car with a long bonnet and a wide chrome grille pulled up at the kerb next to us, though I was too busy to notice much more...I paid the car no real attention until the passenger window began to roll gently down... then I turned sideways and saw how the car's dark gleaming bodywork was shedding raindrops off its slick wax coat and how its chrome wheels stood out against its tyres...it was a Jag perhaps, or a Daimler, or some other kind of businessman's gee-whiz make. But I could see a middle-aged lady was peering up at me through the car's open window...she was leaning over a little awkwardly from where she sat in the driver's seat, and definitely she was watching me...she had a large, round and puffy face with almost bloated cheeks, and a shaggy mass of blonde hair fell about her head and bare shoulders as she strained to keep me in view. 'Get in,' she called. I'd run out of insults, so the timing seemed pretty good...also the lady was already pushing open the car door on my side, and the door was large enough to swing well across the footpath between the Manager and me...quickly I picked up my duffle-bag and Half-Arse, climbed in onto the passenger seat and hauled the heavy door closed...it shut with an authoritative thump...I took a moment to think of a solid exit line to end my argument with the Manager, but I needed to hurry because the automatic window beside me was rolling up.

'Fuckface!' I called, before the window sealed.

I saw that we were sitting in a comfortable, real-leather interior...the wide dashboard just in front of me had a polished wooden finish, and everything around me in the car appeared to smell of the lady's soapy perfume...we were moving, pulling out into the road, and the Manager was already gone from sight...I noticed the lady was holding the steering

269

wheel gently by its lower half and she shuffled it nimbly about in her fingers while she stared at the windscreen before her...she was wearing a shiny, close-fitting navy-blue dress, a sexy thing held up by spaghetti straps, and I could see it looked tight all the way down to her ankles...she was driving in bare feet with a pair of high heels on the floor beside her, and was busy watching the road as we turned and she nosed us across the traffic. The lady made other vehicles coming from both directions draw to a stop, and I supposed maybe she thought the outrageous size of the car would keep us safe...after a few seconds her gaze flicked towards me and her chin jutted out as she broke into a broad smile...we finished turning and started cruising at a steady pace up the other side of Willis Street. 'Do you like tea, or do you prefer coffee?' the lady asked, glancing across at me again. For an instant or two I floundered...I was distracted by the deep wrinkles that I could see under her makeup near her eyes... she was wearing a lot of makeup, an awful lot, and there were more wrinkles by her mouth, tucked in along the edges of her glossy lipstick...I was about to ask which of tea or coffee she preferred when the lady interrupted my thoughts. 'Don't worry,' she said. Then she smiled even more broadly, shaking her head a little...I saw her hair was kept stiff with hairspray and looked peroxided. 'They have both, eh,' she added. The lady shuffled the wheel to make a left turn...as she leaned towards me to manage it, the front of her interesting dress sagged lower and I could see through the gap in her cleavage...I was staring downwards into her wired bra at a pair of long white breasts...I tried to avert my gaze, but the lady didn't seem in the least to care...soon we drove into a narrow lane, headed round a small bend and pulled to a stop...we were halted up beside a broad concrete abutment next to a parking-building, though it didn't appear that we were going to bother with parking inside the building itself. 'I really thought you looked damn good, standing out there on the footpath,' the lady said. She switched off the ignition and appraised me, up and down, through drooping eyelashes...after a moment or two she opened her door of the vehicle and motioned for me to get out from mine, but at the last instant she stopped and leaned back into the car towards me...the lady ran the fingertips of one hand along my forearm. 'I hope you're not annoyed by me saying so, eh,' she said.

'No, no, I don't mind,' I said.

I clambered out with my things, and the lady locked the car...she'd slipped into her high heels and they clacked against the asphalt as she led me away, walking in front...we stepped down a covered alley nearby and then came out onto a bustling central street, which we had to duck across together quickly to avoid the rain...this sudden scamper seemed to relax us both and we began grinning shyly and happily at each other...on the far side of the road we continued marching at a brisk pace under the veranda of a large department store, shoulder to shoulder now, with the wind nipping at the backs of our legs...we approached the store's main entrance, which was a pair of automatic doors positioned right at the building's corner, and as the doors slid open I followed the lady inside. The lobby within had a brightly polished grey stone floor and marble walls of a pinkish colour, and was lit by a collection of gilded lamps set high overhead...there were one or two women jostling past us who held bunches of large, glossy white shopping bags dangling from their fingers, and I could hear music and distant chatter from further inside the store...suddenly here the lady's expensive dress didn't look so especially out of place...in fact, it felt silly to be carrying a grimy duffle-bag over my shoulder, and even sillier to be holding Half-Arse. I padded after the lady into the stuffy interior of the building, until she put an arm up and stopped us before a row of lifts... the ancient metal door for one of the lifts opened by lumbering back in folding sections, and the two of us got into the elevator car alone...the lady reached over in front of me and pushed the button for the top floor...the lift closed and we swung upwards slowly...I wondered if something was likely to happen between us as we ascended, whether we'd fling ourselves onto each other, but the lady didn't move and neither of us even said a word...after the door had rolled back, we stepped out into a large open area under a high, barrel-vaulted ceiling. It was an old-fashioned tearoom that stretched before us, a huge barn of a place with dark, lacquered timber-panelling around its walls...a row of massive and very pink marble pillars divided the room at its centre, and jumbles of potted palms and bunches of blue-green peacock feathers were arranged on stands by the pillars and in corners...there were rows of tables running along each side of the room, all of them covered with elegant white linen...I could see a lot of customers were sitting at the tables, and at once I felt that I'd made a mistake in coming up here...but the lady took me by one hand and led me forwards...we trod over a heavily-patterned green carpet that had me worrying whether the soles of my shoes were clean, and I needed to concentrate hard so as not to sneeze in the dry air. As we passed by the pillars and among the tables I noticed that all of the patrons appeared to be

271

middle-aged women, and I thought how overdressed and fat they looked in their hoity-toity, middle-aged clothes...they had chunky handbags stowed down on the floor close beside their chairs, and they drank from floral teacups which they held with difficulty in their big fingers...around us the women's sombre talk made a peculiar echo and there was even a clicking noise coming from them spooning up cakes off their thin china plates...I could tell that everywhere about me these women were glancing at us and then meeting each other with their eyes...by now the lady was gripping my hand tightly in hers and she reached out and pointed a little artificially ahead of us at the service counter across the room... it was still uncomfortably far off. 'We'll just let these bitches have a good long gecko at us,' the lady whispered in my ear. The lady swung my hand back and forth a bit while we strolled onwards...over beside the service counter, waiting for us, I could see a frightened-looking Maori girl who was evidently an assistant...she had a plump, round face and was standing rigidly to attention in a plain brown dress which she wore under a frilly smock...the girl kept both hands clasped tight in front of her waist in a manner that made me feel sorry for her, because in this fussy place I knew how she felt...when we drew near, the girl avoided my gaze and mumbled something at me that sounded rehearsed, and it took me a moment to comprehend that she was asking whether I wanted tea or coffee...I decided to ask for tea. 'We'll both have coffee,' the lady snapped and let go of my hand. The girl reached out nervously in my direction and gave me a pair of faded green cinema tickets...I took them and could feel how greasy they were from use...beside me the lady was starting to gesture at a two-tiered, glass display-case up on the counter next to the cash register...it was filled with cream cakes and buns. 'Would you like a sticky thing, eh?' she asked me mysteriously. She giggled in an odd, high-pitched voice... the giggle seemed especially ridiculous in someone her age.

'No, thanks,' I replied. 'I ate on the boat.'

I could be mysterious too...but the lady turned on one heel and marched us towards a nearby wooden table which was crowded to its edges with two large stainless-steel urns and a collection of silver trays, cups and saucers...now I noticed for the first time that all this was guarded by another assistant, a dumpy, elderly woman standing on the table's far side...the old woman had a face which had long ago collapsed into furrows, although she was wearing the same type of dainty smock as the girl and with a small serving hat perched up on her coarse grey hair

272

for good measure…I thought she was eyeing us with an attitude of sullen authority…she thrust out an arm that looked thick and brawny along the wrist. 'Tickets, please,' she growled. I presented her with our tickets… she took them and put them into her pocket. 'Would that be tea or coffee?' she inquired.

'Coffee,' I said.

I was getting the hang of this…the disgusting old woman poured out some coffee into two cups, placed the cups on saucers and set them on a tray which she held up before me…next she signalled by nods of her head and by raising her eyebrows that she wanted me to remove the whole thing from her hands…I took the tray and gripped it with some difficulty while also juggling Half-Arse from the typewriter case's strap…then I began to stare about me, ready to follow the lady I was with, but she was no longer anywhere nearby and I saw her gliding away past a group of matrons towards a vacant table…for a moment I could appreciate how shapely her legs seemed, muscular and fluid, through the slinky material of her dress. I went after the lady and caught up with her as she was sitting…I put the tray down on our table, pulled out a chair and sat opposite her…high in the ceiling above us there was a revolving fan at work with its blades chopping round and round, and I thought for a second of how I'd never seen a revolving fan before…I was only aware of them in movies, where they suggested that a place was seedy, uncomfortable and hot. 'My husband owns half of this whole pile, eh,' the lady announced. She spoke as if what she was telling me was a dreadful bore…I tried to meet her gaze while reaching for my cup and saucer… she ignored her own coffee and left it sitting on the tray. 'At least,' she was saying, 'whenever he can bother himself with being around and about— that's when he thinks and acts as though he's the owner. But really, he's the most unscrupulous man you'll ever come across.'

'How does he do it?' I asked. 'Maybe I could learn to be unscrupulous.'

The lady leaned back and laughed hard…her eyes wrinkled up and she showed her yellowed teeth. 'I thought I'd like you,' she said. Next she raised her chin and began to glance with a haughty demeanour around the room at the customers…she appeared to be daring the other women to react, but their conversations remained subdued. 'You see, my husband, if that's what you can call him, he used to be an accountant with a big hardware store—not here,' the lady said to me in a loud voice, still glancing about her. She declared, 'Back in the 1950s, that was, when he was only

273

getting started, eh. Well, he just slowly made sure that all of the hardware store's import licences were put into his name, sort of thing. That was perfectly legal in those days, you know, thanks to the idiot government. And afterwards, see, he left the store and took all the import licences with him, so they were his now, and that's how he could go half shares on opening up this little place here. All perfectly legal. But what it really meant was, he had a virtual monopoly on every one of the items he had a licence for, eh. So was that enough for him? No, no, not for my Ted.' The lady shifted about awkwardly in her chair to get herself comfortable...at the same time she began to eye me once more with a careful, searching gaze...then she leaned forward across the table, adjusting one thin shoulder strap of her dress...it gave me another fascinating view down into the ample hollow of her cleavage...the lady started talking again, though much more quietly. She half whispered at me, 'What he used to do was, he'd import a certain amount of something, and he'd get into messing with the invoice. And what that meant was, he'd diddle the paperwork so that the number of items he'd list was down, but the price per item was up. So anyhow the total sum was the same, you see, on paper. You get the idea, eh? He'd take the first batch of the goods, the first half, and he'd sell them off at these big prices to the all people who were supposed to be having them, all his government cronies, and sometimes with maybe a special discount for his rich pals. But the thing is, now he's got about half of the imported goods which no one knows about, eh, and he'd sell that stuff right here. In the shop.' The lady pointed down at the floor below our feet. 'He'd go and sell it all at the official bloody mark-up set by the government,' she said. 'Oh, it was impressive.' For a moment the lady seemed lost in admiration...she thrust out her jaw and smiled. Next she lifted her bottom a little from her seat to lean even further across the table, and whispered almost into my ear, 'They'd have two cash registers, right, and he'd ring up the declared goods on one and the undeclared on the other, see. This went on for, oh, for years. I mean, it built this business.' Her voice had tailed off nearly into silence...she was waiting for my reaction.

'Ah,' I said.

The lady sat back down on her chair again so hard that it squeaked. 'And what exactly do you do?' she asked loudly, in an ironic tone. She leaned away from me and began pushing herself a bit out from the table. She said, 'That's if you can surprise me, yes, and happen to do anything at all.'

'Well, it's kind of complicated,' I said. 'I'm a writer. But I'm having a lot of trouble with my novel at the moment.'

'Oh, don't call yourself a writer, dear,' the lady said and sighed. She propped one elbow up over the back of her chair and waved a finger at me in an exaggerated manner. 'Call yourself a man of letters,' she insisted. 'That's what all the other layabouts do.' In the silence which followed, the lady continued watching me with her attitude suggesting I was merely somebody who tilted at windmills...but I decided not to descend to her level.

'You know, every artist's problems are unique,' I said. 'Mine is just that I can't find a place to sit down and write for ten minutes.'

'You *are* sitting down,' the lady growled.

'No, I'm leaving,' I said. 'Thank you for the coffee.'

I slid back in my chair and started getting to my feet...I reached down to pick up my bag and Half-Arse, but the lady bent quickly round the side of the table and seized my arm. 'Wait,' she said. 'Hang on. I'm sorry. Look, I'm sorry if I cast aspersions.' I paused, still feeling that it would be the smartest thing to go...I was already three-quarters out of my seat, but I'd rather liked the flutter of panic I'd seen in the lady's face.

'Well, you can be as sorry as you want,' I said, 'but the truth is, I've had more than enough aspersions cast all over the whole flaming show for one day.'

'Just wait a minute,' the lady was saying in a soft voice. She'd kept hold of my arm and her eyes were darting about...from the look of her it seemed she was going to tell me yet another thing she didn't want anyone else to hear. The lady said, 'Listen, okay. I sort of need someone to partner me to the International Ball at the Wellington Club tonight. That's all. Really, I couldn't bear to go to it on my own, eh. And I just thought it was an experience you might enjoy.' She tried hard to grin at me through her layers of makeup. Then she added, 'I'm sure we could find a place for you to write later. Even the Wellington Club might be persuaded, eh.' I sat myself down again, and let go of my bag and Half-Arse...I'd heard about how writers had clubs, and how they usually went off to their club to compose essays and drink whisky in elaborately fusty rooms...it was where they encountered other artists and the town's movers and shakers, and chatted on the issues of the day over fat cigars...I'd never been to a club before.

'Well, I've got nothing proper to wear,' I said.

The lady's grip left my arm and she straightened up in her chair...but then she reached out for my knee under the tablecloth, almost as though I'd been leaving it available. 'What's a store for?' she said teasingly. She gave my knee a definite squeeze and immediately I started feeling a warm rush around the groin...for a strange second it occurred to me that we hadn't paid a penny for our coffees...but the lady had commenced leaning forwards and whispering to me again. 'You know,' she said, 'if you're intent on being a published author, sort of thing, well right there, you'll need to let me train your imagination. So I want you just to close your eyes.' Her hand was sliding firmly around the underside of my knee...I closed my eyes. 'Now,' the lady murmured, 'I want you to imagine me spread out on some silk sheets. Spread out naked.' She asked, 'Can you imagine that? Can you? Eh?' I sensed she was reaching further upwards, her fingers drifting higher along my leg and pinching the inner muscle of my thigh...my heart jumped...at the same embarrassing moment my cock was developing in my pants. The lady began muttering, 'Just imagine me getting myself screwed by some animal, eh. Just imagine it. Me among those sheets, all naked and blissful, and being screwed by, let's say, an especially well-hung donkey.' Her fingers started brushing up towards the edge of my crotch. 'How are you doing with that?' she purred.

I swallowed hard and confessed, 'I'm having a little trouble visualising the donkey.'

My leg was released, and I heard a noise...I opened my eyes, blinked, and saw that the lady was laughing in a manner every bit as artificial as she'd acted when we first walked into the room together...next she began bustling to get up from her seat, and she motioned for me to do the same, but I didn't really want to move so soon...I was going to need a good few minutes for my pants to calm down before I attempted anything like leaving...I went on sitting, spoiling her theatrical exit, aware of how my face was tingly and hot, with my skin feeling scarlet all the way to the back of my ears.

At last, the lady got me downstairs into the clothing area of the store...a bony-faced salesman with a tape-measure slung round the nape of his neck approached us when we halted at the glass-topped sales counter in the middle of the menswear section...on the lady's instructions he proceeded to run his tape-measure across my shoulders, doing so with the air of a person behaving against his own better judgement...after some time he and the lady chose me a dark pinstripe suit from a rack in one corner...together they brought the suit over, and the salesman draped it with a flourish along the counter beside the three of us...he ran the tips of his fingers down the whole outfit and informed me that the material was pure wool.

'Well,' I said, and shrugged, 'if that's all you can really manage.'

The salesman drew the lady some distance aside and they both deliberated with each other in hushed, heated tones...I amused myself during their powwow by admiring a smart black-leather bomber jacket which was on display...it was being modelled on an improbably handsome, rock-jawed mannequin a little further over across the aisle... after a minute or so the lady came back sporting a triumphant look... she saw me fingering the leather jacket and immediately pulled it off the dummy...without a word she tossed it onto the counter next to the suit. Things happened quickly now, with the lady very much in charge... another salesman was summoned and despatched to get me some shoes...I had to go to the men's toiletries area to find myself a shaving kit and a small bottle of cologne, and the lady took great pains over picking me out a nice shirt and tie...finally I took everything along to the gents to change and spruce myself up a bit, and the lady escorted me there with the leather jacket slung over her arm and then stood in wait outside...I stumbled into the toilets and found no one was using the urinal or the narrow empty stalls, so I pulled all my clothes off in front of the basin and washed a little...but I thought it best to get the whole clothes-off business done in a big hurry, because it bothered me that the lady might use any tardiness as an excuse to come in herself and grab me. I shaved, and dressed quickly in the shirt and brand-new wool suit, though for a few seconds I paused before putting on the tie...I told myself that this shindig was a lot like a trip to the races, only more up-market, so that wearing a necktie couldn't be the least bit childish or even schoolboyish...I put the tie on...it cost me some trouble but at last I had the thing done with a decent knot and the edges tucked under my collar, and I approved of the result...I shoved my old clothes and sandshoes into my duffle-bag and walked out of the toilets looking an entirely different fellow. 'Well there, now you're presentable,' the lady drawled at the sight of me. But I was an elegantly dressed young man still clutching an old duffle-bag and a portable typewriter...the lady at once wanted me to give them both up, but I steadfastly refused...I wouldn't even let her hold them for me...I was pretty sure she'd try to throw my stuff away in secret. A taxi was rung for by somebody on the staff, and when the lady and I came out through the front doors of the department store the cab had already arrived and was waiting for us...I saw that, in the interval while we'd been guzzling coffee and shopping for clothes, the weather had worsened and it was now raining like a bastard...the taxi was up at the kerb with the driver peering anxiously in our direction from inside...the lady and I hesitated for a moment in front of the shop windows and then we dashed forwards together from under the veranda, trying to dodge all the water as we covered the gap to the car...immediately the base of my neck, my hair and one shoulder started feeling damp...we piled into the rear of the cab from the same side and slammed the door. The driver accelerated away, so that we were pressed back into the cushions of the seat...we began checking ourselves in satisfaction to make sure we weren't too wet... big transparent beads of rain splattered noisily off the taxi's windows, washing all the colours of the city beyond the glass into blurred streaks of grey and soupy green...we turned a corner and joined the rear of a lengthy queue of cars, some with their lights switched on against the wild downpour...the driver worked us steadily along in the traffic and up a narrow slope...after some time the taxi pulled to a halt, and I guessed from how the lady leaned forwards with a new look of anticipation that we'd arrived at the Wellington Club. We were parked beside a massive pohutukawa tree growing up from a space cleared in the footpath... through the window I could see the tree's thick trunk was divided in half and rose terribly high, with its dark branches out of sight above the roof of the cab...I tried cracking open the taxi's door a little and saw how the pohutukawa appeared to offer us some protection from the foul weather, but a curious shrieking noise was coming from somewhere up over me... it was enraged birds, sheltering in the tangled branches of the tree's canopy. 'Don't let any of those things crap on you,' the lady announced beside me. She shoved me out of the taxi with both hands, so that I had no choice but to run for the entrance of the nearest building...almost at once I heard the lady coming behind me in her clumsy high heels and she pushed me inside through the building's doorway...in the lobby we paused to collect ourselves, panting and laughing as if yet again we'd just had an extraordinary adventure, and I saw there were other people gathered over by the lift...they were adjusting their clothes, brushing off raindrops and making a show of being very relaxed...I could tell that they had to be fellow guests because they were all of them dressed like us. We crowded into the lift and rode to the fourth floor…when we got out there were even more guests standing before us in what looked like a large foyer, an open area dimly lit by some track lighting far up on the ceiling… the guests were milling about in loose groups, collected mostly around the edges of the room against the foyer's pale beige-coloured walls… they were all putting on a fuss of appearing absolutely thrilled to see each other, and I watched them scrape their damp shoes across the deep red carpet as they went about shaking hands…the lady led me across to the cloakroom half hidden in a recess nearby, where I handed my new leather jacket over the counter to the uniformed attendant and then followed it with my bag and Half-Arse…the attendant seemed to touch my gear with an affectation of great distaste and his expression made me worry that I might never get any of it back. But before I could say a word to him the lady was leading me away through the chattering crowd and towards a curving staircase over at the far end of the foyer…there were paintings in heavy gilt frames everywhere on the walls around us, hung in well-judged positions that caught most of the angled ceiling lights nicely across their canvases…I paused, leaning on the brass banister at the bottom of the stairs to admire them…but the lady took me by the elbow and hauled me up the steps, pinching my skin hard.

'You know, in the Governor-General's residence you get time to browse,' I complained.

At the top of the stairs I could hear a hum of music, some sort of band playing a twangy and old-fashioned guitar tune…it was coming at us from the broad, open doorway of a room further off along a corridor…the lady put an arm through mine so that suddenly we seemed like a couple, but still I had to work a little at getting into the part…I patted the lady's wrist as if we were dear old friends, and we strolled with a mutual, pretended idleness down the passage…when we drew level with the doorway, I saw we were approaching a wide and brightly lit ballroom. A busy noise of music and conversation rose up at us as we entered…the party appeared to have been going on for some while and there were large numbers of well-dressed people in front of us, standing in tight bunches with drinks in their hands, bent forwards a little and struggling to hear each other above the music and the sounds of shouts, bustle and energetic laughter…I saw the room had a vaulted, sloping ceiling, covered in some spongy material that looked like red upholstery, and above the heads of the guests I could discern the ruffled tops of a series of red curtains drawn across banks of windows on the far wall...one or two curtains had gaps that still let in a bit of late-evening sunlight...we shuffled further into the party and far off through the crowd I could see where a four-piece band were performing on some sort of low wooden platform...they'd just finished a song and were starting into a rather restrained version of 'Rock Around the Clock,' and the lead guitarist was stamping his heel to encourage his fellow musicians. Close to us, by one of the ballroom doors which had been folded back inside against the wall, was a narrow makeshift bar...a particularly cheerful press of people was gathered around it and behind the bar the staff in their white shirts were handing out glasses of wine as quickly as they could...it struck me that the barmen were the only other people I could spot in the place who were really my own age...a man showing large sweat-stains under the armpits of his jacket was hustling about nearby, holding a camera...he kept aiming the camera at random and the flash went off every time he took a picture...suddenly I felt the lady withdraw her arm from mine, and I guessed she didn't much fancy being photographed with me clasped tight in her grip. But then, abruptly, the lady left me...she marched in a flurry up to a couple standing nearby...she kissed both of them on the cheek in an animated, self-conscious fashion and said something familiar to them...after an instant she disappeared past the pair and off into the room...I was left waiting all alone, still in the rough vicinity of the doorway. Far across where the band was, I could just make out a few guests jiving with some rockabilly moves on a small dance floor, and so I started wandering over in their direction...I wondered why, for an International Ball, I couldn't pick out any interesting foreigners... everyone around me looked more or less Kiwi, but perhaps the types of people from other countries who got invited here were not really foreign enough to be noticed. 'Jolly good do,' a deep voice called to me. I turned, and saw that a frail, elderly man dressed in an expensive black suit was hobbling towards me with an unsteady gait...he was keeping his thin arms up for balance as he inched his way to my side...the man was tall and emaciated, and the discoloured bluish skin on his sunken face and along his drooping jaw was heavily wrinkled.

'Jolly good do,' I mumbled back.

I nodded for good measure...with difficulty the man moved a little further round in front of me...he smelled repulsively of embrocation and I could see how the loose flesh on his neck was lying in folds above the tight collar of his shirt. 'You're not Stanley's boy by any chance?' the man asked in his gravelly voice. In spite of his terrible age, his small eyes were fixing me with a firm gaze.

'Certainly not,' I replied.

'Well, good chap,' the man said with approval. For a moment I wasn't sure if he really meant me or Stanley. Then he added, 'Just can't have it, you know—shall not pass and all that. Best to stay away from Stanley.'

'Consider it done,' I said.

'So, what sort of thing do you get up to, eh?' the man asked. But already he'd ceased staring at me and seemed to have spied someone he recognised off at a distance.

'I'm a man of letters,' I replied.

'Jolly good,' the man said.

Even as he spoke he was slowly turning his back on me...the man's feet were scuffling almost in place at the bottom of his thin legs, but soon he started shambling away as though I no longer existed...I watched him go and then drifted for a while myself amongst the crowd, still unsure of what I was doing here...I wondered if Gizi had ever felt this way in Spain...I hoped to find a group somewhere that would be talking about literature, but instead I found some men discussing Bastion Point with an air of amused competitiveness, as if each was trying to show the others that he was the most detached from his own opinion. Near them I overheard a woman saying, 'Of course, he was the one who briefed poor Norman Kirk on the economy when Labour got in. Knew his *Bible* chapter and verse.' A waiter, easily visible in his cheap white shirt, was walking about offering drinks off a wide pewter tray...he carried the tray in front of him with two hands and indicated by a smile that people should take whatever they wanted...as the waiter came past, I picked up a heavy cut-glass tumbler of what appeared to be whisky. 'Get me one of those as well, would you?' a man said from behind me. The man sounded bored, though still remarkably insistent... the waiter had already moved too far away from me, so I turned and handed my own glass over...the man took it without a word of thanks...I saw that he was wearing a dark pinstripe suit similar to mine, but he was middle-aged, small and misshapen...he was standing awkwardly with his little chest out and his narrow shoulders pushed well back into his jacket...he wore black horn-rimmed spectacles on his beaky face and his thin sandy hair was receding far up from his forehead. The man had curled his long fingers all the way round the front of my whisky glass...he held it for an instant, and then raised it and drank most of the contents in a single gulp.

'No point in staying sober at one of these god-awful things,' he said, gazing at the glass with satisfaction. After a moment he glanced across at me and grinned. 'Who squired you here?' he asked.

'I don't know,' I said.

The lady had never given me her name…it occurred to me that this, too, was probably done on purpose.

'Ted's wife,' I managed at last.

But the man seemed to have forgotten his question…he was staring away from me into the room with a distracted air. At the same time I heard him say, 'Spent the whole damn day at the Reserve Bank, reading bloody reports. All of them on how hard it is for students to get summer jobs, that sort of thing.' The man heaved a sigh through his pigeon chest…I watched him swirl the skimpy remains of the drink about in his glass. 'Can't imagine why it's hard,' he said, and glanced at me again. 'You know, I never had any kind of trouble getting a summer job when I was at varsity.'

'Why do we even bother to care?' I asked.

'Indeed,' the man replied, and chuckled. 'It can't go on,' he added. He raised his glass once more and tossed off the rest of the whisky.

'You're not one of Stanley's boys, are you?' I asked suddenly.

'No, no, not at all,' the man said. For a minute he pretended to take an intense interest in something further off, but finally he twisted round to meet my gaze again. 'Just who do you mean?' he asked.

'Indeed,' I said.

I nodded gravely and turned on one heel…I began walking away in a stiff manner that I hoped made me look as though I was parting from riff-raff…for a moment or so I concentrated on getting as much distance between the man and myself as possible. But a little further across the room I saw a woman in her forties, short and a bit plump, who was standing alone…she was wearing a long yellow wrap dress that didn't really suit her and she had a round face, large features and bushy dark hair that swept back from her forehead and fell almost to her shoulders…she was clutching a brown leather bag with both hands and, as I drew nearer, I noticed she kept raising herself onto her toes, bobbing up and down while staring off at the doorway…I coughed politely to get her attention… she turned towards me and I realised I needed something to say.

'Hullo,' I said.

'Oh,' the woman replied. She seemed taken by surprise that anyone would approach her...she got up on tiptoe once more and began craning her neck to gaze even harder at the door, and I marvelled how no one at this party would ever look me in the eye because they always had something better to do. But the woman settled herself again, and in a rapid, husky foreign accent she announced, 'My husband is just around in the room. Is just gladding a few hands, you know?'

'I see,' I said.

It seemed best to introduce myself...I said that I was from Palmerston North and didn't really know anyone here...I asked if it was all right to talk to her...at this the woman looked at me in a shy fashion and said her name was Marcela...I asked Marcela what country it was that she came from...she told me, and I thought it sounded pretty much like some place in South America. 'My husband is embassy people, and—you know?' she said. I didn't know, though I was interested in how she appeared to growl out certain English words...it was nice at last to hobnob with one of the international guests...Marcela lifted a hand to play with a long gold pendant which hung from a thin chain near the base of her neck. She added, 'For these events he is just liking me to come sometimes with him, you know? And well, for tonight that means nobody can go in my salon.'

'Oh, what salon is this?' I inquired.

I'd heard of people having salons...they had clever discussions and things there, witty encounters that embodied the spirit of the age...I told myself that this might be a useful artistic connection. 'My hairdressing salon,' Marcela said in a happier tone. 'Is just really a miracle, a miracle that I do not get the hair all over me now.' She dropped her hand once more and made energetic sweeping motions across the material of her dress. She said, 'That hair stuff, it sticks in everything.' I couldn't help feeling disappointed, but I decided Marcela's sort of salon could be interesting too.

I asked, 'What do you do with all the cut hair?'

'Oh, is just throw out in the rubbish,' Marcela replied. 'But hey, it sticks in everything, you know. Every six month I must ring our plumber for checking the washbasins. And some people's hair, it just smells, you know.' Marcela tilted her head back and began to laugh...I thought her frankness seemed very appealing in this otherwise snooty room. She said, 'Don't get me started on that.' But I could see how Marcela wanted me very much to get her started on that...I could see she was relieved, as I was, at finally having someone to chat with...I thought of her husband working in the international side of things and pondered the wisdom of asking if he might know Gizi's father...then suddenly I wished Gizi herself was here...what could she be doing now?...I forced myself to concentrate instead on what Marcela was telling me. I heard her saying, 'And well, the old people, you know, it is they just don't washing their hair so much. But some peoples, their hair just always smells a lot after you wash it, you know. There was this day, one of my hairdressers, she was put the rods in this old lady's hair, this thing was right after we washed it, and my hairdresser, she was just sitting that whole time beside a bowl of disinfectant. A big, big bowl of disinfectant. Was just for making her nose close into the bowl. Pheeew.' Marcela vigorously waved off a smell. She added, 'That bowl, you know, was for to get away from the pong.' We both laughed, savouring the moment...but that same instant somebody gripped my elbow with the power of a vice...I turned, surprised, and saw the lady I'd come with was beside me...I could see how much the makeup on her cheeks had smeared in the growing heat of the ballroom, so that the wrinkles across her skin were easy to notice...she looked older, and her eyebrows were narrowed into a serious expression...she pulled me by my elbow in closer towards her damp, dishevelled face. 'Well, you've been a naughty boy,' the lady whispered into my ear. She spoke as if this was something we were both very aware of, and it made me wonder what I'd done...but the lady was already leading me away in a manner that pre-empted any objection...I'd no chance even to say goodbye to Marcela. 'You naughty boy,' the lady repeated. 'Why'd you run off and desert me like that?' I wanted to protest, but the lady was preoccupied with steering me across the room...we shuffled along in an ungainly hurry, bumping past other people...up ahead of us was the dancing area, and I saw the band members on the little platform were checking their instruments after some sort of break...when we reached the dance floor, the lady let me go from her grip...I tried to move away but at once she spread her arms up around either side of me and stubbornly corralled me into the dance floor's centre...she didn't seem drunk, though I still wondered if perhaps she might have had a few. Almost immediately the band started up again, and they were playing a slow dance...there were just the two of us out on the floor and there was plenty of space, but the lady took my arms and shoved them around her waist in a rough bear hug...she insisted on us dancing in this lovey-dovey style...she wriggled her podgy shoulders in as close as possible to me, hugging me tighter and tighter...I was relieved when some other couples began to join us on the floor and sway about. The music droned on through the first chorus and the lady started rubbing herself against me...I could smell her harsh perfume coming up from the warmth in her breasts...with my fingers clasped behind her I could feel the edge of her panties shifting on her buttocks, and it didn't take long for my cock to respond and swell...my erection began to bloom out and upwards, and I felt angry at getting a hard-on in the middle of a dance floor...I wondered why my cock always had to have such a powerful will its own, but the lady merely acted as though delighted...she was pushing herself even closer, more obviously, up against my groin, and then sliding her belly along the hard edge of me. 'Oh, you,' she said into my ear. Her fake blonde hair was all over my face...I was too embarrassed to look anywhere but down into the curve of her shoulder...the dance appeared to be taking forever...under the back of my jacket the lady's hands were now massaging my arse...it felt unbelievably good, and I wished she'd stop teasing me. Suddenly the thought of Gizi rekindled itself, and the idea of how much I wanted her to be the one I was dancing with...I shuddered, and couldn't bear that it hurt me so badly to remember her...I loved her, and loved her even more by thinking of her...why had I left her?...in my unhappy mind I pictured Gizi's beautiful face again, sad and delicate. But the lady seemed to know that I was off the job...she'd worked one of her hands round my hip and along to the front of my trousers...she leaned her head back and grinned at me with her puffy cheeks spread wide on her face, and with a deft movement, still keeping herself in close to me, she unzipped my fly...I felt her fingers struggling and reaching inside my trousers...they slipped down past the elastic waistband of my underwear, and finally the lady had my erection cupped rampant in her hand. I shivered with shock...my knees began to buckle...the pleasure was unmanageable, though I supposed it might be bad form just to ejaculate right away...but then, I also supposed it would be bad form to ejaculate at any time in the middle of the dance floor of the Wellington Club. I was too scared to step back and risk having people see what we were doing...Gizi's image had almost faded from behind my eyes...I fought hard not to let that image vanish... the lady twisted her hips in against me and thrust her face into my neck. 'Tonight, oh, I am going to screw your brains out,' she murmured vehemently with her chin nuzzling my shoulder. But all of a sudden the lady let go of my cock, wrenched her hand upwards and withdrew it from my pants...she took a long step back and started to gaze around her... next she joined everyone in making polite applause, patting her palms together...it appeared the band had finished playing...other couples were striding off and leaving the dance floor, though a few people near us remained standing about...but I was aware more than anything else of the atrocious crimson heat in my own face, and also I was desperate to hide the extraordinarily inflexible penis that I felt pretty sure was poking up in my underwear from my open fly...it meant I had to busy myself with dipping forward in an odd crouch and work at buttoning my jacket into some type of screen. I was breaking out with sweat, and troubled, and my fingers were slippery...I glanced up at the lady as I continued straining to fasten the jacket around my equipment...she was staring at me from a few paces away, pretending to be still slowly applauding the band...an expression like scorn had come into her eyes. 'Go rustle us up a couple of drinks,' she ordered. I got myself covered and began to slink off, feeling awkward and hoping that, to the other guests, I might look pitifully sloshed...at the same time I kept trying with one hand beneath the jacket to hitch my member back inside my trousers, but there seemed an awful lot of penis to force back into such a small space...across the ballroom groups of people made way for me and I staggered past, though that only led me further in amongst even more people, who were gathered and watching...I sensed tears of bafflement rising in my eyes...someone tried to ask me if I was finding it all a good show...I went on scuffling by without being able to answer. At last I left the ballroom altogether...I searched for a gents toilet and found one along a corridor...I went in, stumbled to the urinal and started readjusting myself properly...by a piece of luck the entire toilet was empty, because I discovered that it was all terribly sticky down there amongst my cotton underpants...without actually coming, I seemed to be leaking into the fabric of my grundies. For a while I stood on the slick tiled step of the urinal and stared into the drain...it was hard work to try and focus on calming down...whatever sort of creature the lady waiting for me back near the dance floor was, I was fairly sure she included a vagina, and my virginity appeared set to take a fatal beating... tonight, finally, I could get my brains screwed out, and already my brains were feeling well and truly knocked around in any case...I didn't think I'd have many problems with managing to stick my thing into this woman... she was all muscle control. But where, I asked myself in an instant of self-pity, was Gizi, and it hurt again to realise that she was nowhere and immediately I began to pine for her...I'd succeeded at zipping myself back in and was standing more comfortably, but more than ever it was Gizi I just wanted to be with, and the idea of her continued to ravage my heart...I stared up close into the well-polished mirror above the urinal, gazing at my own face while it gazed back at me like a stranger...I thought I looked wretched...I tried leaning even closer but there was just more of me on show before my eyes, looking even worse, and it was still Gizi I loved...thinking of her made me groan aloud and squirm in front of the mirror-glass. I felt miserable at my own weakness out on the dance floor... but I felt weakness must be exactly what this whole deal was...I was tired of being led about constantly by my own penis...in my thoughts I attempted to send Gizi a tender message, but what I really wanted was a reply, and that wasn't going to happen...in fact I decided with a new resolve that none of this, none of it, nothing would happen. I left the toilet at a march, putting a determined look on my face just in case I might change my mind...outside of the loo, I headed briskly along the corridor to the staircase and padded downstairs into the foyer...the entrance area was deserted and I could hear trivial piped music coming from somewhere near the ceiling...there was only the attendant to be seen, waiting in his cloakroom, standing behind the counter with his arms stiff at his sides... he had a blank, bored expression on his face until he was disturbed by my appearance in front of him...then he gave me a condescending smile. I asked for my things...the attendant half turned and reached behind him, rummaging about...after a minute or so he handed over my leather jacket, the duffle-bag and Half-Arse...while he pushed them across the counter towards me his oily smirk stayed set upon his thin lips, as if I had a guilty secret that he had guessed.

I asked, 'Is it still raining outside?'

'I'm afraid I have no idea, sir,' the attendant replied.

'Well, try bloody keeping it that way,' I said. 'Because smart doesn't suit you.'

I rather hoped the attendant would come out of the cloakroom and start something, since I was good and up for some argy-bargy...I was ready to fight him or anyone else who might be available, but the little bastard didn't react...he simply resumed his former blank expression... at last I stopped facing him down and turned to go...I got into the lift with the heavy jacket slung over one arm, thinking that at least it might serve as a souvenir of this experience...I'd already learned that there was nothing in the world I couldn't run away from, but this was the first time I'd ever run away from a certain fuck. Outside the building the sun had just gone down, though the streetlights hadn't come on yet...the air remained blue in the semi-darkness and the rain had eased to a feeble drizzle that wasn't too bad to handle...I dodged the shadowy pohutukawa and its branches and started to run with all my gear, heading from the safety of one veranda to the next...after a few minutes I scurried across the road and down a steep flight of steps...the concrete on each step was smooth and damp, and I had to take care as I pattered along, but my descent soon took me out into the midst of a downtown quay once more... in the near distance I could see one high shoulder of the railway station terminal with all the lights inside each storey turned on, and I decided to make for it. When eventually I reached the square in front of the station building, I saw how the golden blaze coming from the building's banks of windows flooded gorgeously out onto the ground across the grass and flowerbeds, but I made myself head without any further shilly-shallying for the grimy steps up into the terminal...a large group of street kids was sitting on the steps, waiting by some wire newspaper billboards propped against the weathered grey base of a pillar...I had to skirt round the kids to get to the station's broad row of entrance-doors...one of them called to me as I attempted to go past...I could hear him demanding fifty cents. I halted and wondered why me, why it was he'd picked on me to try, when there were several other people who were passing up and down through the entrance beside us looking nonchalant and clearly happy not to be hassled...then I remembered that I was still dressed in my poncy pinstripe suit...I thought maybe these street kids were the same as the ones from the Cuba Mall the other day, but if so they wouldn't recognise me now like this...I reached into my pocket and scooped up my loose change...I handed it down towards the kid who'd asked me for money... he took it, and I waited for him to say 'thanks' or call me 'mister,' but he stared at me sullenly as though he resented what I'd just gone and done. I moved on past and went inside the chilly entrance hall, my footsteps knocking and echoing against the slick stone floor...I tried to remember being here a while ago with Penny, after the unit had arrived from Upper Hutt, but instead the height and grandeur of the hall reminded me more than anything of the Wellington Club...even so, the broad concourse when I marched into it instantly seemed dirty and bare...the floor surface changed to bitumen underfoot, and the long clay-coloured walls on each side of me, which were lined halfway up by dingy brown tiles and had rows of broken wooden benches scattered before them, looked shabby in the sombre lighting from overhead…a lot of pigeons were waddling on the ground and as I approached they jumped, screeching, to avoid my legs…they began flapping up onto the benches to escape me, and even more of them were getting onto ledges in the low, sloping roof above. I didn't remember any of this at all, and for a moment I halted again and glanced around…to my right I saw a solitary ticket window was still operating over in one far corner, with a refreshments kiosk opposite that was shut for the night and barred…just behind the kiosk the dark, draughty exit to the platforms yawned open…the whole concourse appeared empty except for several passengers milling together in a sort of huddle close to the ticket window…they stood hunched, gripping the handles of their bulky suitcases and talking in subdued tones, as if they were too despondent to go outside to the trains. I made my way past the passengers and across to the ticket window, and I set down my things in front of it…I straightened up again and spoke to an overweight, doughy-faced woman who was standing in the booth before me…she was leaning heavily on her counter behind a thick, protective sheet of glass…I could see she wore a poorly fitting navy-blue railways blazer over a white shirt, with an official-looking cap drooping at an angle on her head…the glass between us made her appear strangely far away.

'What's leaving soon?' I asked into the glass.

The woman gazed at me with a sleepy-eyed, impassive manner and didn't utter a word…perhaps she hadn't heard me, or perhaps her shoes were hurting from having spent the entire day on her feet dispensing tickets…for an instant it occurred to me that getting on a train meant putting myself at an even greater distance from Gizi…but that was all I could really do, and it needed doing in a hurry…it was the only solution I had to my longing for her.

'Please,' I tried asking louder. 'What's the quickest train out of Wellington?'

The woman behind the counter shrugged her large shoulders as though she didn't care…I supposed that by the end of a typical day she'd met a lot of people who were in even more of a hurry than I was…I thought fucked-up and forlorn people probably came mumbling to her window all the time…then I realised the woman was actually giving me an answer. 'Fifteen minutes till the Northerner departs,' she was saying.

'Where's that go?' I asked.

'North,' the woman said. Still she stared out at me with a show of complete indifference. 'Auckland,' she added.

'How do you keep so much information in your head all at once?' I asked.

The woman merely blinked at me. She said, 'Are you leaving or not?' I took out some money and thrust it into the gap under the window-glass…I asked if it'd be enough to get me the whole way to Auckland… the woman only replied with an air of satisfaction that there might not be any seats left, but I watched her scoop up the notes with her plump hand… she pushed them away into a drawer without giving me any change…for a man in a brand-new business suit, I was going to be broke pretty soon.

'Look, can you—can you at least tell me which platform the train leaves from?' I asked.

'No,' the woman said. She became preoccupied in writing something with a ballpoint pen on a slip of paper, and I saw that it was most likely my ticket she was preparing…after a few moments the woman put her pen down and seemed to weigh her options…next she poked the ticket reluctantly under the window-glass…I didn't miss my chance to grab for it. I marched off with the ticket towards the platforms, but then I spotted the entrance to the station toilets and made a detour for the gents instead… once inside, I felt the toilet's white tiled walls and exposed copper plumbing looked damp and forbidding and smelled of piss, and I was grateful that the whole place was empty…I headed over to the wooden stalls and discovered none of them had doors, and also that it was hard to find a cubicle which was anywhere near clean…finally I entered a stall almost at random, peeled off my suit and shirt, and hastened to put on some of the clothes from my duffle-bag…I kept shivering and hoping that nobody would come into this bloody awful bog while I was changing, and for a few minutes I stumbled and banged frantically against the side of the cubicle as I tried to climb into my jeans in the cramped space…with only a T-shirt to wear on top, the leather jacket was going to be handy in the cold. When it was all done at last and I came away from the toilets, clutching my bits and pieces of stuff in both hands, I felt much better…in the concourse again, just before the exit to the platforms, I saw a thin and dishevelled old man sleeping on one of the benches…he lay stretched out on his back with his arms up over his chest…he was wrapped in a greasy-looking black raincoat and there was a loose pile of newspapers propped beneath his neck for a pillow…as a bed the bench didn't look too comfortable. On impulse I went up and stood by the man...I could see that his unkempt, long grey hair was spread out in a fan around his head and he was unshaven, and as he slumbered on he breathed in and out regularly with a kind of desperate peace...I put down my bag and Half-Arse, and then laid the suit and shirt across the man as extra cover...for a moment he stirred from his dreams and looked at me with foggy, puzzled eyes, but he didn't try to get up...after a second or two I reached out with the shaving kit and put it by his face...next I placed my new pair of leather shoes under the bench.

'Don't forget to wear a tie,' I said.

I straightened up and draped the necktie across him too...finally I collected my duffle-bag and Half-Arse once more and turned to scan the rail yards and the long narrow platforms...there was only one train out there and I made for it...a few other passengers were also on the platform, hugging friends and saying their goodbyes...the rain rattled fitfully on the corrugated-iron of the canopy above us...gusts of wind blew cold air onto my feet and pushed bits of paper and plastic litter along the tracks in circles. I found my carriage, stepped carefully over the gap and got up into the entranceway...I opened the door to the interior and went in...the carriage itself was cramped and stuffy, and its aisle was very narrow, so that I struggled to move between the high backs of the seats on either side of me...I had to grab at the seats' padded tops as I tried to thread my way along...in front of me some of the other passengers stood easing their bags up into the wire luggage-racks overhead...a young couple were bending to tap against their window and wave out to the platform. Eventually I located my seat...it was going to be on the aisle...the other seat next to mine was already occupied by an elderly man...I nodded to him in what I hoped was an amiable fashion and sat down, stowing my gear at my feet. A few minutes later there was a sharp blast from a whistle...it was followed by the muddled sounds of doors slamming...at length the train jolted forwards, but every bit as suddenly it stopped...the eccentric movements shoved everyone up and back in their seats...then after an instant the train started again, this time more gently, and began to pull away from the station.

SEVEN

Despite what the ticket woman had told me about there being few seats left, the train wasn't nearly as crowded as I'd imagined, so I supposed we were probably going to collect more people along the route...the carriages shook and groaned when the wheels changed tracks heading out of the station, but soon we were rattling onwards at an increasing speed and making our way around the edge of the harbour...then all at once the dim, steadily receding view of the city vanished as we entered a tunnel...with a flicker some yellow ceiling lights in the carriage came on...but the lights were weak and scattered, and they seemed only to emphasise the dark still nestling in amongst us. Even the old man sitting just beside me was half hidden by deep shadows...he appeared to be having trouble arranging his legs in the small space around him next to the window, so with one foot I pushed my bag and Half-Arse under my seat to give him more room...the man was round-headed, bald and had large ears, and he wore a thin green woollen jersey and grey slacks over his heavyset, blocky build...he was not especially tall but he certainly was restless, because he kept on shifting his knees up and over to the right or the left...he rolled his eyes and began muttering, as if trying to convince himself of which way was less uncomfortable. The train came out of the tunnel and I saw that now we were wandering through pitch-black cuttings and past dark, sporadic streets...the overhead lights in the carriage remained on...I drew the leather jacket closer around my chest and at last the man beside me seemed to settle, if only from sheer tiredness...there was a disappointing lack of clickety-clack sounds as we trundled onwards, though the carriage rocked a lot on the track's narrow gauge...next to me, the man began shifting all over again...he craned his neck to look through the window and pushed his knees up together and muttered. But there was nothing worth seeing outside...there were only the dim outlines of nearby weatherboard houses and pale, glowing patches from behind their curtains...in the distance further dots of light from yet more houses were all there was in view across the dark and solid shapes of the hills...after a while I asked the man if he'd like the aisle seat so he could stretch his legs. 'No thanks, I'm good,' he replied. But he didn't seem good...I saw some people further along the carriage were standing up and getting out into the aisle to haul open their bags... they were unpacking and repacking everything and talking to each other in lowered tones...the man just sat and fretted...after some minutes he turned half towards me, and for an instant I could see his sharp, pitted nose in some passing road-lights...his small eyes looked hesitant and strangely bright, but he turned away from me again for the window, murmuring to himself.

'Is something out there?' I asked.

The man continued staring away from me. He said in a slow, distinct voice, 'Last time I was on this train line heading along here, it was over thirty years ago.'

'You don't say?' I said to encourage him.

'Yeah, coming back from the war,' the man said. The man was speaking in a steady baritone, but its timbre sounded hoarse and thinned by age. He added, 'That was after the troop ship got in to Wellington. Jesus, I thought we'd never arrive here. I always remember telling people how good the gorse looked up on the hills. They thought I was mad.' He gave a short, precise laugh.

'World War Two, eh?' I said.

The man didn't answer...he was still gazing out of the window into the darkness...I took a moment to ponder solemnly what the war must have been like...after all, it was the war that saved western civilisation.

Finally I offered, 'You were probably away a long time.'

'Seemed like eternity,' the man agreed and nodded his head. 'But I got sick as a dog at the end of it all,' he continued, 'and that's why they sent me home.' The man turned to me once more, looking in my direction a little shyly...his eyes were darkened again by the carriage's shadows, though I could tell he was staring at me hard in the half-light...his lips quivered as if he was going to say something, but at first no sound came out. Then suddenly he rasped, 'Smallpox.'

'What, isn't that fatal?' I asked.

'Only if you die,' the man said.

'Oh,' I replied.

For a few seconds I thought about how it was really quite amazing, what you could learn on a train trip...but the man was still talking and I wanted to pay attention. 'Everyone got vaccinated by the medicos, see, before we embarked. But mine didn't take,' the man was explaining. 'It's a long story.'

'Well, I've got time,' I said.

The other people further up the carriage had mostly settled again...

the whole train appeared to have lulled itself into a sleepy, contented mood and we were gliding more smoothly on the tracks...except for the faint, far-off chug of the engine, it was quiet everywhere around us.

'I'm going all the way up to Auckland to see something of life,' I said.

But the man was ignoring me...he'd just discovered the lever that made his seat recline and he was reaching round behind him, below his armrest, and tugging at it...he kept pushing himself further and further back with one hand while clutching at his round belly with the other, though the seat didn't seem to go far enough to make him really comfortable. After giving up on his efforts, the man grunted and said, 'Well, I'm just off home to Levin.' He flexed his shoulders on the half-reclined seatback and did his best to relax. He added, 'Been seeing my daughter down in Wellington today, she's going to have a baby soon. That's not easy at her age, eh. It's hard to know what you can do to help.'

'What about the smallpox?' I asked.

'Get her some sort of pressie, eh, take her mind off things,' the man finished up. He was muttering to himself again...but then he registered my question and lifted his head. 'Oh, that's a very long story,' he said apologetically.

'Well, I'm interested,' I said.

There was a lengthy silence...the train was jiggling along at some speed now...I stared up at the gently rocking luggage-rack and the lights overhead, and thought maybe I should work at getting some sleep while I could...but after a moment the man started speaking once more. 'That was in April '44, when I was in Palestine,' he said. He spoke in a flat tone and softly, as if he didn't want other people to hear. 'I felt sick, mind, and the nearest place was a Scottish hospital somewhere between Jerusalem and Jaffa. That's where they sent me. I remember the doctor was checking the soles of my feet. I asked the orderly, I said, "What's wrong with me?" and he said, "Didn't they tell you? You've got smallpox." Well, I was already feverish, and just after that I was pretty much delirious for about five weeks. The only real thing I can remember about it is, I thought the poms were trying to prevent me from going home, eh.' The man paused to chuckle...his large head was lolling against the top of his vinyl-covered seat...I felt he was already lost in his own tale. 'Because,' he was saying, 'you know, New Zealand troops were being sent home in rotation from Cairo by then. Yeah, so one day I even got out of bed and started looking round for my clothes. I didn't know they'd been burned. Anyway, all hell broke loose because this dying man was up and announcing that he'd had enough of their pommy war and he was going to head home, I mean *now*. My nurse, she was this tough Scottish woman named Sister Mary, and she stopped me and said, "Show me your arms and I'll see if you're fit to go home." So I did, and she stuck a hypodermic in. I just managed to say, "That's a dirty trick" before I passed out.' The man stopped talking...the train had begun swinging a little, moving through more open country... the lights from houses seemed further away and were spread much more sparingly across the hills...I thought that, beyond the windows of the train, those lights all trembled delicately like stars off in the distance...it was difficult to think of each of them as somebody's home.

'How did you get better?' I asked after a while.

'Oh,' the man said, 'when I was first admitted, the medico told the nurses, "Don't worry about him, he'll die in forty-eight hours." But Sister Mary, she was a stubborn woman, eh, and she was going to prove something to those lardy-dardy doctors. Anyway, it's the dehydration that kills you apparently, so to stop me drying out she tried to give me some water. But I just complained that I wanted a beer. So in the end she actually went down to the mess and got me one. What happened was, she tried to give this thing to me in my fever, you know, through a feeding cup, but I kept complaining that New Zealanders drank beer from a glass. So the poor woman, she went and got a glass, and every day she fed me beer out of it. That's all I had for five weeks.'

'So your life was saved by beer,' I said.

I couldn't help grinning...I liked the notion of letting the Scottish nurse know what New Zealanders drank from...but the man looked troubled, as if I'd said the wrong thing, and he was wrestling around in his seat again...I realised I'd simply blurted out whatever had come into my head and it was stupid. 'Yeah, I reckon,' the man said at last. But I could tell he didn't agree with me and I regretted my comment...I wondered if the man understood I'd spoken that way to disguise the sorrow at his story that I was really feeling. By this point all the lights outside the windows were gone, and with them all trace of anything existing beyond the carriage...I saw some people in other seats had covered themselves with long woollen blankets...they were holding the tops to their necks and letting the bottoms drape down across their knees...a couple nearby up the aisle were trying to play cards...I sat, still feeling my embarrassment, until suddenly the man turned and started to speak once more. 'Those weeks, mind, I didn't really know what was going on,' he said. 'But I did have a special beer ration.' I nodded my head and the man continued. 'Well, after all that time Sister finally needed to have a go at feeding me, and she said how do you like your eggs and I said, "Scrambled." So she got me some scrambled eggs and I ate three of them. By then she knew I'd make it. Anyway, I had this huge, puss-filled infection all over my face, and I used to try and scratch this thing while I was out with the fever. So they tied gloves on my hands, you know, and one day while I was completely out of it, I patiently worked these bloody gloves off and I put my hands up on my face and broke the scab in half. God, it felt great. Scarred for life, I should have been. Hell to pay.' I gazed at the man as carefully as I could in the carriage lights...he had no obvious scars on his large face...there were only some rather ordinary indentations on his nose...the man seemed to comprehend what I was doing, but he didn't stop me or turn away. 'Perhaps because the scab just broke in half,' he said. Then he added, 'My face was bright scarlet when I was able to get up, eh. But otherwise I felt fine. I remember when I got out of bed, it was D-Day. Anyway, after that they put me in quarantine for ten more days to be sure. I spent it all alone in this thirty-man hut surrounded by barbed wire. No newspapers, no books. They just brought my food to the gate, and I wasn't allowed to approach till after the joker with the tray was gone. God, I nearly went out of my mind.'

'What did you do?' I asked.

'Nothing. I told you, I nearly went out of my mind. Doing nothing'll make that happen fairly quick.' The man sighed. 'Mealtimes were the big event. The rest, I just tried to go for walks around the hut, because I was still feeling pretty weak. Then they sent me to Cairo and I spent two weeks in a New Zealand hospital, and after that, home on a hospital ship. That was another five weeks. Scary too, because they had all the ship's lights on at night to show up the red crosses. No blackout. But there wasn't any trouble, eh. When we got in to Wellington, I had another medical check and the doctor said, would I like to go back into the army?' The man gave a bitter laugh. 'I just managed to say, "I'm not all that fussed," and I was discharged. After I finally got off the train at Levin from so long away, my own mother didn't even recognise me. I mean, she just walked past on the platform and my sister had to point me out—because I'd lost so much weight, eh, and I had no hair at all, not even eyebrows. And also my skin was still bright red. They took me home and put me to bed and I slept for thirteen hours. It was ages before the horrible colour faded and my hair grew back. But everything came right. Till I went bald.' The man sat quietly...it seemed to be the end of his tale...he'd moved a little away from me, suddenly self-conscious, and had turned to focus on the window beside him once more. I didn't know what to say in response this time, but I thought that now I could imagine his condition long ago...the man was lying in a wooden bunk on a hospital ship with the other casualties...I could see him, sprawled out on his back amongst some sweat-stained sheets...he was staring upwards at the roof of the cabin, praying silently so that the others wouldn't notice...he was praying that he wouldn't be torpedoed before he got home at last.

'Well, that's a remarkable story,' I said. Then without thinking I added, 'Maybe in the end you were lucky. I guess maybe that's all anybody can be.'

'I reckon,' the man agreed. But he went on looking at the window and said, 'You know, things were supposed to be completely over for me, the whole deal. Can't really believe I've lived so much longer.' He shrugged. 'You get your moment—if you're lucky anyway, and then that's it.'

'Not for me, that's not it,' I said. 'I'm a writer. We leap over death.'

But the man didn't hear me, or if he did hear me, he didn't bother to answer...I was grateful for this, because I'd just shot my mouth off again as usual and I didn't know how to explain what being a writer meant anymore when people asked...after several further minutes of us not talking, I checked on the man and could see he was dropping off to sleep...I only hoped that telling me his tale had made him feel a little better...soon he was beginning to snore gently, in and out through his nose, and I kept very still on my seat so as not to wake him. A short time later through the windows on the other side of the train I caught a brief glimpse of the sea's pale spray in the dark...the waves were smashing onto some rocks hidden from sight, up along the edge of the coastline, and the spray jumped and writhed as though with a life of its own...but next we turned and appeared to be moving inland once more...at length the train pulled into a station that had to be Levin and we drew slowly to a halt, level with a poorly lit asphalt platform...outside someone blew a whistle and next to me the man suddenly stirred...I heard a few doors slamming further up and down the carriages in a series of peculiar metal squeals and thuds, and there was a muffled announcement from a loudspeaker inside the station building that I couldn't make head nor tail of. The man stood up in a hurry with his eyes bleary from sleep...he manoeuvred past me between the seats, not waiting for me to shift out of his way, bumping against my legs...in the aisle he turned and nodded goodbye in an embarrassed fashion...then he stumbled off from me towards the front of the carriage and was gone.

Once the train started again, I was left sitting completely on my own... that gave me plenty of room to spread myself over the pair of seats...I tried leaning down sideways across the cushions, putting my head on the armrest by the aisle, and ignored any discomfort to my neck...this let me stare dreamily at my reflection in the window-glass and at the bits of murky view that I could make out while the train went on trekking northwards. After a while I dropped into a kind of doze with my eyes half open...I wasn't sure how long I lay like that, but eventually the track curved and we approached a pattern of lights that somehow caught my attention...we were entering a township, and gradually I recognised the streets as Longburn. Longburn, the little town, seemed marvellous in all its familiarity...I knew, I actually knew those simple, regular rows of houses we were bumbling past, the timber fences, the tubular-steel letterboxes at the gates, the flat areas of the front lawns and patchy gardens...not far off I spied a broad suburban intersection coming up alongside us, lit by streetlamps and with triangular Give Way signs arranged neatly on posts at each of the deserted corners...the train spat out a blast on its air horn as we went over a level crossing...we passed some tennis courts where somebody had forgotten to switch off the floodlights, and the courts were laid out with fresh white markings in the brilliant, spooky glow. We plunged into farmland and darkness once more, but soon a number of new random lights made the landscape visible again and suddenly we seemed to glide between some damaged-looking concrete pillars, part of an old road-bridge going by overhead...we slowed further, and at length slid up alongside a substantial stretch of asphalt covered by a sloping roof, and it took me a second to understand that I was staring at the platform of a railway station...at almost the same instant the train pulled to a dead halt with a thump and a lurch...the impact clattered the couplings, and despite the shaking and swaying of the carriage some people in front of me began rising abruptly out of their seats...I sensed others were moving around behind me, and felt my seatback shift and shiver in someone's grip... doors were being wrenched open and slammed all along the carriages. There were bent, shadowed figures outside who were hurrying across

298

the platform under the hazy lights from the station awnings...I watched them hunkering and vanishing off into the night...with a small shock I realised that I was back in Palmerston North. I was just a short walk away from Rangitikei Street and the Square...in the Square's centre the old illuminated clock tower would be showing the time at the top of its flat, four-sided face...under the Japanese bridge on the little ornamental lake the ducks would be slumbering with their heads curled behind them...of course, the shops and everything else were probably shut up tight now, but the streets would be exactly the same as always...I was back. For some reason this idea made me think of a time long past when I was nine years old and I'd first ridden the bus alone into town...the winding route finished up by taking me to a draughty, green-painted, corrugated-iron bus shelter located in the very middle of the Square, and I remembered jumping down over the great gap from the bus's steps as I alighted onto the footpath and arrived, in town by myself...all afternoon I wandered about, and at last I bought a copy of Gerry Anderson's *Thunderbirds* annual and carried it home with me like a reward...I got it at Wynyards, I remembered, so I'd actually been in there a few times in my pre-literary days...there was a sleek red-tipped rocket on the cover of the annual...the rocket was landing amidst a blast of grey engine smoke with all systems go. It struck me suddenly that, if I got out of the train now, I could easily pop off home if I wanted to...at this hour my father, my mother and brother would all be in bed sound asleep...I could just go to bed at home and pretend to wake up in the morning as if nothing had happened. My ticket was for Auckland, but here might be the best place for me to stay and write in spite of everything...in fact, I could picture myself with no difficulty as an old man living in Palmerston North...I'd become white-haired and looked a little slipshod in my charmingly out-of-date clothes, and I walked everywhere bent over with a cane wobbling in my unsteady grasp...each day I'd shuffle on a morning constitutional out of the house, planning to totter down to a place I'd once nicknamed 'the ghastly trees,' an area of scrub which blocked the end of our street where it met the river...my family were calling, asking me if I'd be long because lunch was ready, but I waved them away, lost in contemplation...I was deeply knowledgeable about local things, and I was also a bit of a character. The simplicity and comfort in this appealed to me, and the appeal had a sense almost of nostalgia...I could imagine my future self thinking of a time far off in the past, meaning now, when I'd had adventures...

I hesitated...it was midnight according to the station clock perched up on a pole beside one of the platform lights...the train would be stopped for only another few minutes. I took my duffle-bag and Half-Arse and stood up...after some more moments of dithering, I shambled with my gear out of the carriage...I stepped down onto the dim platform, planted my feet amongst the painted lines spread over the cracked asphalt and gazed at the ugly modern station building nearby...the open entrance to a small set of concrete-block toilets was not far off up against one edge of the building, and having a leak first seemed like a good idea... swinging Half-Arse and my bag in each hand with vigorous movements, I walked across the platform and made my way over to the side for the gents...I had to duck my head under a low cement arch and then stepped through into darkness. In the confusing space around me there was only a single pinch of light...it was coming from a jagged slit high up which illuminated the pitted blocks at the top of one wall...I paused for an instant to let my eyes adjust...next I put my things down, got up onto the stainless-steel tray of the urinal and unzipped myself...I started peeing, and had almost finished when I heard footsteps padding into the bog...somebody, a man, was standing somewhere behind me. After a moment I heard him say, 'Nice jacket that, eh.' I guessed he must be talking about the leather bomber-jacket I was wearing...but it also occurred to me that, in fact, he shouldn't know anything much about my clothes in all this darkness.

'Thank you,' I said, and tried unsuccessfully to glance back over my shoulder while zipping my pants up. I added, 'I like it too.'

I turned round towards the entranceway, and now I could see things a little better...there were two men standing just inside past the opening, blocking my path out...their figures were large and indistinct...I stepped off the urinal, bent down and slowly picked up my bag and Half-Arse, hoping to put casualness into my every movement. 'You don't really look like you're from round here,' the second man announced in a slightly higher voice than his friend. He spoke as if stating a simple truth. But I still wondered how on earth they know anything about me here in the gloom of a cramped public toilet. The same man continued, 'So where'd you spring from?'

'Oh, I'm from Palmerston North,' I said.

'Go on,' the first man said. 'You don't sound like you're from round here, eh.'

'Well, I am,' I said.

I tried taking a very tentative step forward...the two men didn't start to move aside...I halted.

I added, 'I was born and raised just up the road.'

'Yeah? So what is that, eh? That means you're calling me a liar?' the second man said. He spoke delicately in his high voice, in almost a patient tone...at the same time, though, I could feel the blood throbbing through my heart and how my fingers were beginning to tremble...I was shuddering from fear, and was aware of the danger in letting them sense it...I wished I could discern something useful about the two of them as they went on standing there in front of me, but their faces were deep in shadow, leaving only the vague shapes and hollows of their features amongst the darkness...I could smell piss, unflushed, in the urinal, and I guessed it was my own...I couldn't work out for sure whether the pair were happy to continue playing with me, or whether they'd already justified to themselves what they were going to do next...the train was certain to depart at any moment.

'Tell you what,' I said. 'Why don't I give you this jacket? As a present.'

I started to shrug the jacket off from my shoulders, acting as calmly as I could...I got a sleeve down along my right arm before realising that I was stuck because I was still holding all my gear in my hands...then one of the men stepped forward and hit me in the side of the head... he connected with terrific force...I could hear Half-Arse and my bag clatter chaotically onto the ground around me even while I was falling... an instant later I was down too, with my face scraping along the damp concrete floor. Fast as I could manage I began scrambling, getting myself back up to my feet, worried that either of the men might kick me...but even as I stood I was walloped in the stomach, and the air left my lungs and I strained for breath, feeling my legs buckling and my body double over...before I could collapse, I was punched a second time in the ribs...both of the men were laughing, excited, encouraging each other...I sank to my knees and the jacket was pulled off me hard, tugged over my bent head while the sleeves were dragged down my arms...then I was hit from above on the back of the neck. I dropped to the concrete once more and tried curling into a ball...suddenly one of my eyes felt a dramatic burst of pain, as though somebody had stamped on my face...I retched, searching for air...I couldn't move my legs properly...I groped around for anything to hold onto...but no one stopped me or hit me anymore, and after a moment I could sit myself up against the cold metal edge of the urinal. Outside, a fussy voice was making some sort of announcement over a loudspeaker...a whistle blew, twice...I got to my feet with my knees feeling shaky and my whole body shivering...my things were all gone...I was alone. I staggered out from the toilet and across the platform...with each stride I felt the asphalt and its markings were pitching around crazily beneath me, but I could see the nearest carriage-door in the train was still open...in a frantic hurry I climbed in and up the carriage steps, but there seemed too many for me to deal with and I fell, sprawled just inside the entranceway...looking back over my shoulder, I saw a man approaching on the platform...I flinched, until I realised he was a guard dressed in a dark uniform with glinting gold buttons on his jacket. 'So how many jars have you had, eh mate?' the guard called out at the sight of me on the floor. He giggled while I struggled to get my legs a bit further into the entranceway...the guard had come close enough to the carriage for me to hear the keys jangling from a bunch on his belt...then he reached out and slammed the door shut right in front of me. I made a huge effort and actually stood up...for a moment I could watch the guard's big callous face under his railways cap just outside, staring at me through the glass in the door...but the train began to shudder, and next it was hauling itself off from the station...he drifted out of view. I leaned for several minutes on the door to the interior of the carriage... I could feel how each of the separate parts of me hurt...my stomach and neck muscles were cramped with pain and there was blood on my face from some scratches...I thought my left eye was already turning black...even one of my knees ached from when I'd landed awkwardly upon collapsing in the carriage's entranceway...somehow this struck me as especially unfair. The jacket and my duffle-bag were gone...all my money and the empty bankbook had been in the bag, and I was on the way to Auckland with nothing except a train ticket in my pocket...and Half-Arse was lost...I didn't have anything left to write with...Half-Arse was gone, I was bereft!...I didn't know what I was going to do from now on. My lower lip kept twitching, ready for me to break out into tears, but I slid open the interior door and started tottering back through the carriages to find my seat...it was hard work to stop myself from crying in front of the other passengers...I half wanted some kind of sympathy from anyone around me who might notice, though no one did...in my

302

seat, at last, I sat with my fists clenched tight and pressed into my sides to control my own sorrow and pain. For a long time afterwards the train laboured, heading at varying speeds ever upwards across the central plateau...most of the carriage lights were off, and there was only a thick darkness all around us...it squeezed in at us from outside amid the monotonous jostling of the carriage's motion...I became listless in my seat, and thought we seemed to be moving over an interminable version of nowhere...through the windows everything looked the same, minute after minute, in the soupy blackness...I could merely see some vague sandy soil down near the tracks...it was lit by our headlights and was shifting past in a tedious series, on and on. Inside the carriage, amongst the shadows at the far end, I noticed two people who appeared to be Maoris get up and pull a guitar from the luggage-rack...they sat down again with the instrument and one of them began to strum the strings as if feeling for the sounds, trying just a few bars of 'Wooden Heart' and 'You Are My Sunshine'...next he settled into a tune and the pair both sang to themselves quietly, somewhat apologetically, in the dark...but soon there were voices from other people in the carriage, humming and singing along...I joined in and tried a little too...it was something to do, and I didn't think anybody else could hear me. It had started to turn very cold, and the chill tightened my sore neck and I felt hungry...I wriggled about across the creaking seats, hoping in vain to get comfortable...I leaned the right side of my head, the side that wasn't so bad, up against the icy, damp-smeared window...through the hard bump and rattle of the glass I gazed up at the sliver on show of the poor old moon...it had come out now faintly, past the satiny edges of some cloud cover it was shining on...I wiped away some of the condensate to see better, but the moon still looked far off in the large grim sky. All around me the airy, limitless darkness kept coming in and pushing on my shoulders...I started shivering a little along the back of my neck and under my legs...I wished I had the jacket...I wished I had Half-Arse for company. But then all at once, staring up into the dark flood of space above me, I felt my own mind seeming to soar...I felt myself expanding...the impulse began to lift me further and further until I was almost out of the train somehow, with my thoughts gone...for a moment it felt as though I too, I also, might just be without limits...I was only a very tiny part of everything, but I could sense that same everything was joining with me...I was in the pale moon, the rumpled clouds and even the long, dark, enveloping expanse of nothingness…these things, too, had a fleeting, infinitesimal part of them in me. The Maoris were still singing nearby and the seats of the train rocked us all steadily…I could hear soft, mingled whispers around me and could smell the close, communal sweat of people under their woollen blankets…but my pulse was roaring…but my breath, oh, how dry it was, how tight it caught in my throat!…in my mouth I could taste the tingling of salt and I felt touched by a tremendous inrush of exhilaration…I wanted so much to cling onto this, but as soon as I tried the sensation already appeared to be finished, and left me with a strong impression of enormous lightness and the icy window-glass banging against my cheek. I sighed, and closed my eyes…I realised I was exhausted…then I shifted about, a little disgruntled, till I fell half asleep.

EIGHT

Early in the morning the train reached the outskirts of Auckland and we dawdled through a flat, suburban spread of houses that went on and on…Auckland was a big place…I remember, for those few who may read this, that the sun was already shining broadly and leaving long, sharp shadows down one side of the railway carriage…I was stiff after my night spent lying, clumsily bent, across the seats…my left eye was sore, but I could still see from it without too much trouble…once in a while I had to remind myself not to touch it. At last the train got into the station and I stepped out from the carriage onto a covered asphalt platform… everywhere around me, the yards, the canopies, even a wide clock on a wall with big numbers on its face, looked so exactly like a station, so terribly familiar, that it felt as if in the end I'd not really left Wellington… for a short time the platform was crowded with groups of other passengers alighting…they were mostly paunchy businessmen, but a scruffy few like myself were genuine travellers…I watched them all bustling by me, carrying their assorted bags, overnighters and backpacks a bit reluctantly now that they'd arrived. At length I followed behind this loose gaggle of people down a long, high-walled passageway…the sunshine coming from the corridor's upper row of windows was divided into shafts of intense light which lit up the dust motes in the air and smothered my face until I felt dizzy, faltered, and had to pause for a moment or two...when I got through the terminal building and came out to stand before the entrance under a low veranda, almost everyone else appeared to have already gone. A few of the last passengers were piling themselves into cars and taxis along the kerbside, and slamming the doors...the cars each drove off quickly down a steep, curving approach road and bumped over the gutter before disappearing into the traffic beyond on a busy street...within a few minutes I was alone, waiting aimlessly in the warm air...I kept staring down towards the vehicles heading by on the big main street in front of the station, all of them with somewhere to go other than here, somewhere important. After a while I simply began to walk off...I wandered along beside the approach road, which skirted the edge of a broad sunken garden...the whole garden was laid out with lawn and flowerbeds and a variety of trees, including even a few shaggy palms, and it was ringed by an elegant cement border that had steps down onto the grass...I thought of going in there and sitting, and just staying put...the grey trunks and sagging green fronds of the palm trees looked bright and welcoming in the morning glare, and I could see where wrinkled brown leaf mulch had been spread around the bottom of each tree and where a pile of grass clippings lay in one corner for removal...I halted and breathed in the sweet, sticky aroma of the clippings...I listened half entranced to the lulling hum of the passing traffic, rising and falling, while I gazed all about. A solitary man off behind me was walking down the same road in my direction, coming from way back at the station's entrance...the man was in his late twenties and wearing jeans and a T-shirt like me, and he looked every bit as rough and raddled as I was...I watched him moving across the smoky-red brick frontage of the building, striding along in jandals with a lazy, rangy gait...he had lank blond hair falling almost to his broad shoulders, but the hair was thin over his crown and it was clear that he was balding prematurely...the skin on his large face was wrinkled, fair and pinkish, and I supposed he was getting burned quite a lot from the harsh light...as he drew nearer, I saw the man was squinting straight at me with an oddly quizzical gaze, and he was definitely heading towards me. Presently the man seemed to pause, looking as if he was thinking to turn and retreat away from me up the road again...then he changed his mind and continued approaching...the man started nodding at me in a friendly but embarrassed manner...I nodded back as well. When the man was near enough, he said, 'You look like a fresh young rooster who's just got into town, eh.' He spoke tensely and loudly, as though a little unsure of himself...but perhaps there was just more traffic rumbling by beyond the garden than I'd first thought.

'That's me,' I said.

I shrugged and didn't know quite what else to add, but the man moved closer to stand right in front of me...he had a small blue backpack on his shoulder and he dropped it to let it dangle from his forearm... the backpack looked new, and its straps hung and dug into his pale-pink wrist. 'How'd you like to make ten bucks?' the man asked. He leaned in closer...he slid the backpack down the side of his leg and with an almost exaggerated care he deposited it at his feet...I stared at him in suspicion.

'I'd love to,' I said.

'That's all I need to know,' the man said. He grinned...he reached up and wiped his mouth with the edge of one hand. He said, 'What I'd bloody want you to do is, yeah, you'd have to take this bag across to Parnell. You reckon you can do that, eh?' The man didn't bother with waiting for my answer...instead, he pointed somewhere off towards the street...he was starting to give me detailed directions and a house number. 'It's just an old blue villa,' the man finished up. By now he seemed very eager. 'And when you get there, eh,' he added quickly, 'knock on the door and bloody hand this thing over, you know, and you tell them the delivery fee is ten bucks.'

'That's it?' I asked.

'It's easy money,' the man agreed. He paused again and squinted at me some more...I could see he needed a shave as much as I did, and I wondered if maybe like me he'd spent the whole night on a train. 'Now, I'm trusting you with this bag, eh,' the man said. He picked up the little pack once more and held it out, but at the last instant he hesitated...he went on keeping his grip closed tight around the straps.

'You don't have to worry,' I said. 'I could really use the ten dollars.'

'I reckon,' the man said. He glanced about, not saying another word, and thrust the pack across at me, and as soon as I took it he began walking rapidly away...I watched him go, swinging his arms and looking everywhere around him...he headed down past the end of the approach road and trudged into the garden...then the man turned and gave me a quick, nervous wave...I wasn't sure if his wave meant goodbye or to hurry things along, but in any case he marched beyond some of the trees and

306

disappeared. I hoisted the pack up over one shoulder…it wasn't heavy…I tramped out onto the main street and made for the direction the man had told me, enjoying my newfound sense of purpose…I felt good having a bag on my shoulder again and I liked the gentle way it banged rhythmically against the top of my hip…I didn't even care too much that it wasn't really mine. The street that I was walking on was wide, with several lanes, but in places it had no footpath and sometimes trucks came by me almost at my elbow…the old warehouses and industrial buildings I began to see around me were low and far apart and had their windows boarded up… after a while I approached an ancient, iron railway bridge that was mostly hidden from view by torn and sun-bleached hoardings…I passed beneath it as per instructions, and the underside of the bridge was so severely rusted and damp that I wondered if the thing might no longer be in use… according to the man's information I was getting into Parnell. The road before me curved upwards at the edge of a small park and grew steeper and steeper…I kept doggedly padding along…there were several shops and a slim block of flats on the other side of the street, and I thought each building looked as if it was inserted into the ground at a crazy angle behind the sloping footpath…the number of the place I wanted seemed to be well off, close to the top…soon there were a lot more stores lining both sides of the street around me, and the number of cars increased and their traffic began clogging the roadway…most of the vehicles coming uphill by me were labouring as much as I was, and even the cars parked in close along the kerb had their bonnets up and their handbrakes straining. At last I passed a church and was fairly sure I could see my goal off in the distance…I was heading towards a uniform row of pale, two-storey weatherboard villas on my side of the road…the old Victorian houses must have been fancy once in far-gone days, but now they all had a gently ruined appearance, and as I approached I could observe how they sat grouped together in semidetached pairs along the rising slope… they had tall brick chimneys sticking up from the edges of their sagging iron roofs, and at the buildings' sides hung complicated arrangements of bulky iron fire-escapes with bolted-on balconies and ladders…each house had a cosy-looking covered porch and front door, and large bay windows upstairs and down, but the bottom windows of the houses jutted out only into cramped, overgrown gardens and tiny front yards. Coming closer, I saw that one villa near the middle had to be mine…all of the curtains in its windows were drawn tightly shut, as though the place was empty or abandoned...I also saw a huge black scorch mark on one corner of the house that ran off in a sweep towards the rear, suggesting some sort of nasty blaze which had only just been caught in time...the fire had left a lot of the blue paint blistered on the weatherboards and even cracked parts of the wood...I stopped at the open gate by the mailbox and gazed at the broken paving on the short pathway up to the porch...I was feeling a bit overheated, a bit flustered and odd after my trek in the brilliant sunshine. Next something made me turn and look behind me, and I saw a white police Holden was parked on the opposite side of the road...there were two policemen sitting in the car, watching me intently as I stared at them...I was near enough to see that the driver wore a drooping ginger moustache in the middle of his chinless face...he was all dressed up in his uniform, with a white shirt and necktie, but he didn't seem to have a hat...I went on scrutinising him and his funny friend until finally the cops started to glare at me, and I turned my back on them again. I straightened the bag on my shoulder and trotted up the path to the porch of the house...there was a lot of old white fretwork around the top of the porch, hanging low, so that I ducked automatically as I stepped up under it...a rusty bell was set in the middle of the front door and I started twisting its mechanism...it didn't make much sound beyond a tinny rattle...I tried a little discreet knocking on the frosted glass in the door's upper half...some smears of dirt came off onto my fingers. But eventually I saw a heavy grey curtain being pulled back a bit from one side panel in a bay window by the door...then a hand let the curtain go and the lower sash of the window panel was shoved up with a squeak...a pretty girl put her head out and leaned her elbows across the worn paint on the narrow sill...the pretty girl looked only a few years older than I was, and she had a round, smooth-skinned face and butter-coloured hair left in a big shaggy mass of curls...she had flirtatiously large blue eyes, and full lips that she was pursing into a mild grin at the sight of me... the girl shifted a little on the sill to make herself comfortable, though she didn't say a word. I gestured at the door shut tight before me, but at the same time I kept looking at the girl...she was wearing a man's large, loose white shirt, with its sleeves rolled back to show off her plump and tanned forearms...I was close enough to see down through the window to where the ends of the shirt hung free outside a pair of jeans...the rough denim in the jeans was rubbed smooth in places and revealed the nicely rounded outlines of her thighs. 'You know, that door doesn't really work,' the girl declared at last. Her eyes seemed to shine from the mischief of what she'd just said, and I watched her deliberately looking me up and down. Then she added, 'You can get yourself inside through the window here if you want, eh.' The girl moved away into the room, and I didn't hesitate...quickly I put one leg up over the sill and lowered my head... it was tricky getting myself in through the tight space, even with my head down and my back bent, and I struggled...meanwhile the girl was explaining that some nitwit had gone and lost the key, but like no one was exactly sure who...I tried to listen, nod, scrunch lower and keep the bag on my shoulder all at the same time as I slid my bottom across the window frame. Finally I stepped down onto the bare planks of an uneven wooden floor and shuffled forwards...I was alone with the girl at one end of a wide living-room which had the untidy feel of a place inhabited by lots of people...waxy brown wrapping-paper had been used to cover the walls, and there was an old sofa nearby upholstered in grimy floral chintz, along with some chunky armchairs...all of the furniture had been pushed back to the sides of the room to leave the centre-space empty...in one corner ahead of me there were the stacked-up components of a large stereo, with the turntable cover still open...a beautifully-inlaid brown mantelpiece was off at the far end of the room and below it was an old-fashioned, tiled fireplace full of ash and twists of newspaper. The girl moved behind me and drew the curtain closed...a faint musty smell was lingering in the air, as if the place needed ventilation...I noticed that in the high ceiling above us all the lights were on...the girl reached up and down the edges of the curtain, checking that it was pulled properly across the window, without any gaps...I thought she was tall, almost my own height, and despite her loose shirt her vigorous build looked buxom and enticing...I saw how her heavy golden hair seemed to bounce against her face and shoulders. After a moment or so she turned to me and asked, 'What the hell happened to your eye?'

'Nothing,' I said. 'Some bloke hit me.'

I felt pleased at how interesting this had to make me sound and was going to say more, but the girl interrupted...she told me her name was Sammy, which was short for Samantha, and she asked whether I was a friend of anyone in the flat...her amused tone suggested she didn't think I was...I shook my head and slipped the pack off my shoulder, holding it out to her...I hadn't removed it when clambering in through the window because I'd reasoned that I would look cooler keeping it on.

'My name's Andy,' I said. 'A guy told me to bring this here, eh, to your flat, and say the delivery fee is ten dollars.'

Sammy didn't attempt to touch the bag...instead she turned quickly away from me and marched off across the room, heading for an open door into the hall...Sammy passed through the doorway and called, 'Georgie!'...then she stepped out into the corridor and I could see her standing with her broad back to me, leaning one arm on the worn wooden banister of a staircase. 'Georgie! It's here!' she shouted up the stairs. 'What?' a muffled voice called from somewhere far off. 'It's here,' Sammy repeated. 'Moondog. It's here.' There was a sudden thump and bumping noise from up above...Sammy swivelled round towards me. 'He'll be right down,' she said to me through the doorway. But already I could see a man who I guessed must be Georgie bounding into view down the steps of the creaking staircase...he had a lot of short curly chestnut-coloured hair and a bedraggled moustache, and he wore a baggy brown jersey that hung loose in the belly, with a small leather coin purse swaying from a strap across one of his shoulders...I thought he looked only a little older than I was, but he was puffing from all of his hurry...near the bottom of the stairs Georgie spied the pack I was clutching and he halted with one foot in the air above a step. 'Oh,' he said. He gazed at me hard. 'Oh,' he repeated. After another instant he continued on down the staircase... he passed by Sammy and bustled through the doorway towards me. 'Amazing,' Georgie started muttering to himself, 'that's really amazing.' He came up to me, nodded and took the pack from my grip...clumsily he unzipped the top, and with greater care he moved back the flaps and began staring inside. 'Amazing,' Georgie said again. He straightened up, glanced off at Sammy in the hall corridor and turned to me once more. 'It's really amazing!' he announced. At that moment I noticed another man had appeared in the hall...he was holding a white china teacup in one hand, and I thought perhaps he'd been interrupted at something and had come to check on us...the man looked just the same age as the others only he was more slightly built, with his slender frame nearly lost in an old red T-shirt and jeans...there was a lot of lank sandy hair falling about his long lean face...the man stood together with Sammy at the doorway and I saw him watching me cautiously, twisting his head on his narrow shoulders...an extensive streak of pink acne was in plain view on his neck. 'I think it's—you were, oh,' Georgie was saying in front of me. He paused, as if trying to put his ideas in order. Finally he asked, 'Well, like did Moondog send you?'

'I don't know. Suppose so,' I said, and shrugged.

Georgie seemed delighted, and I felt glad it was the right thing to tell him...he was grinning at me so broadly that his lips appeared to stretch up almost to his ears...I judged it best to smile back.

'Also there's ten bucks delivery,' I added.

'Oh—oh, that Moondog,' Georgie said. He raised his head and laughed loud and hard...he even swung in the direction of the doorway as though to share his laughter with the others...I saw Sammy and the other man were already chuckling together anyhow...Georgie turned back to me, and with his free hand he commenced searching deep in the pocket of his corduroy trousers...a look of mild concern came over his face. 'I just can't find my—oh—yeah, not that one,' he muttered. He put down the pack...using both hands and with hasty movements of his fingers he pulled open the leather coin purse slung across his shoulder...I could see there was nothing in the purse but a single crisp new banknote, neatly folded in half...Georgie lifted it out. He asked, 'You got change for twenty bucks?'

'No,' I said. 'Sorry.'

'Lonno,' Georgie asked, 'have you—' He glanced towards the doorway...the man with the teacup shook his head. 'Oh, okay. Well, better make it twenty,' Georgie said. He thrust the still-folded note out towards me...for an instant I was reluctant to take it, but Georgie began jiggling the note and telling me not to worry...even so, I couldn't help looking over at Sammy to check...she was nodding her lovely head, so I reached for the money and put it away in my back pocket. 'Hey, you want a smoke?' the man named Lonno asked me from where he stood beside Sammy. 'Smoke, yeah?' he repeated. He bunched his fingers up at his lips and mimed taking a long drag.

'Sure,' I said. Then I thought to ask, 'You mean dope, right?'

'Oh! Really amazing!' Georgie said.

Everybody was chuckling once more, as if I'd managed to come out with something terribly witty...Georgie picked up the pack...with a pat on my shoulder he led me over to the hallway and I followed everyone deeper into the strange house. At the far end of the passage was a white-painted panelled door, and as we drew near it was pushed quickly open...a lanky-limbed, very skinny man came through it in a hurry towards us...I saw he had a small, oblong face with a soft jaw and a beaky nose, and also a short mop of hair that was curly, brown and somehow girlish... he was wearing a grey argyle jersey that seemed much too tight for him and which made his bony elbows and shoulders stick out as he moved... just before bumping into us the man halted, straightened up and glanced at us all in surprise. 'Guess what Moondog did, eh,' Georgie announced to him, and waved the bag. The new man grinned shyly...in an awkward fashion he started backing away from us into the room behind him, and we followed. 'Got no kind of trouble from the pigs outside?' the man asked and giggled. He spoke with a high, effeminate voice...he was squirming, and he rubbed one hand on his hip...I wasn't certain exactly who the man was talking to, though he kept giving Sammy a particular sort of look. We were entering a narrow dining-room lined halfway up its walls with bare brown-timber wainscoting...it was another room with the curtains drawn across the windows and the ceiling lights on...a wooden dining-table, very cluttered, and a collection of straight-backed chairs took up most of the space, and at the table a heavyset man sat over a mug of tea and puffed at a cigarette in his hand...he had bristly black hair, shorn down nearly to a military cut, and sideburns that tapered into long lines an inch below the cheekbones of his tough-looking face...he was resting his forearms on the tabletop, and he wore a denim jacket that I could see was riding up on his solid shoulders...the man didn't even bother to raise his head as we all came in. To avoid him I tried admiring the mantelpiece on the far wall, which appeared almost as beautiful as the one in the other room, while Lonno and Georgie were moving over to stand at the hearth...Lonno propped an elbow up onto the mantelpiece's shelf...at the same moment the skinny man in the grey jersey began leaning in against Sammy's shoulder, and with a pang of envy I watched her wrap an arm around him...the skinny man smiled at me from inside her embrace with an enormous, doe-eyed enthusiasm that reminded me of Struan in Christchurch...it wasn't hard to think that he might be gay. 'This here is D.C.,' Sammy said to me. Next she nodded towards the burly-looking man sitting at the table. 'And that's Beats,' she added. Beats reacted by shifting round and peering up into my face for a few seconds... then silently he turned back again to his tea. I told everybody my name, but instead of anyone greeting me Lonno announced loudly, 'The cops, man. The fucking cops.' He shook his head and his jaw quivered. 'The fucking cops, man,' he went on, 'they're always waiting out there, eh, and Moondog's down to getting him.' Lonno lifted his arm off the mantelpiece and pointed at me. 'Fuck. What do you reckon, eh, those guys in the car, they're just too comfy sitting out there to walk on in?' I really didn't know how to interpret this…I heard D.C. producing an uneasy giggle, and Sammy merely sighed. 'Should be time for that smoke now, eh,' she said. 'Well, it's the dealer rolls,' Beats growled up from the dining-table. I watched Georgie begin moving all at once towards a half-open door at the rear of the room, still clutching the blue pack…he reached with his free hand to shove the door further open on its hinges and I could glimpse what looked like the flat's kitchen beyond it…then Georgie stopped, and stared round at me over his shoulder. 'Okay with you?' he asked.

'Okay,' I agreed. 'So who's the dealer?'

'You are, mate,' Lonno said. He let out a sudden guffaw…all the others began laughing at this too and saying how much it was really amazing…the question of the cops seemed to have vanished from their minds. Georgie waved for us to follow and headed into the kitchen…but before we could move, Beats rose with a scraping sound from his chair… he flicked some cigarette ash onto the table and started forwards in front of everyone else, as though exercising his rights…we shuffled slowly after him in a group. D.C. came up beside me and whispered in a worried tone, 'What's the story there with your eye, babe?'

'I was jumped by two men in a public toilet,' I said.

'Oh,' D.C. sighed, and nodded. The interior of the kitchen offered only a small space for the lot of us…we were pressed in next to a long grey Formica-topped bench with a dull stainless-steel sink…opposite was a fridge and a row of old cupboards with a few large coarse sacks in front, half open and bulging with potatoes, and in the far corner was an ancient gas stove…Beats had already positioned himself by the stove and despite the lack of room the others were getting as close to him as possible…I was stuck at the rear, staring over everybody's shoulders…I could see the stove had a low, stripped-down iron top with a blackened collection of burners, and Beats was running the fingertips of one hand across a burner as if to examine it. Sammy swivelled round and leaned over the sink…she reached out to check that each of the blinds on the windows was rolled completely down…Beats pushed the rest of us away from him a little and rattled open a nearby drawer below the bench…he kept his cigarette clenched between his teeth as he pulled a sheet of wax paper from the drawer and gave it to Lonno…Beats seemed all concentration… he began fossicking about further in the drawer while wisps of cigarette smoke drifted up across his fierce face. 'Yeah these'll do,' he barked at last, and the cigarette waggled on his lips as he spoke. I saw he'd hauled out a pair of table knives, and the metal on the blades of the knives was damaged and burnt black...Beats stepped back to the stove and opened up a gas-ring...next to him Georgie was lifting a small glass jar from the pack, cradling it in his palm...Beats lit the gas jet under the burner with the end of his cigarette, dropped the chewed-looking fag-end onto the hardwood floor and stamped it out...then he held both of the knives over the blue base of the flame. At once everybody started to scuffle forwards again...D.C. put an arm into my back and pushed me a little up beside Sammy, nearer the front...before me Georgie had the lid off the jar and was clutching a bit of thin grey wire...he dipped the wire delicately into the jar and began to smear a drop of its dark, syrupy contents onto one of Beats's knives. Lonno had the wax-paper sheet rolled into a funnel...I saw him lunge forward, gripping the funnel in his trembling fingers and cupping it over the knives on the stove...the paper was so close to the flame it looked ready to catch fire...Lonno didn't seem to care...Beats leaned in further to rub the knives into the heat, and off them came a slip of grey smoke...Lonno got down even closer and made a whooshing, sucking noise. 'Ever spotted hash-oil?' Sammy asked beside me.

'No,' I said.

Lonno's head jerked up and he dropped the funnel...it unrolled flat on the floor with a rustling sound...I watched him lurch past Beats and Georgie towards the sink while trying to hold his breath...his cheeks were bulged out, straining and struggling...all the effort to keep the smoke in his lungs was heightening the acne's colour under his jaw. 'You are going to love this, eh,' Beats said. I could see that he meant me as the one who was going to love it...he was glaring round at me from the stove, where he still stood half bent over the flame...his words felt a lot like an order... Lonno exhaled happily and took in a large gulp of air. 'So, what the fuck happened to your eye?' Beats growled in front of everybody.

'Two blokes tried to give me a hiding,' I said. 'I fought one guy off. But I hesitated with the second because he looked like my mother.'

Beats smirked a little, but I noticed he didn't say anything...D.C. had picked up the paper and remade the flimsy funnel...he handed it to me, and I stepped forward with the end of it pinched softly between my fingers... Georgie put another streak of oil on the knives. I tried to copy what Lonno had done...I got my face down low near the stove, and when some smoke came up from the knives I sucked through the funnel...the smoke was harsh against the back of my throat and in my lungs, but suddenly I understood what all the fuss was about...my head was becoming busy with everything, because everything appeared so dazzling and wonderful...I felt I'd absolutely joined up with the right sort of people, but I also felt that everything around me had receded far, far away...I thought of the Maoris in the car outside Masterton, and finally the whole deal just struck me as so absurdly amusing that I collapsed with laughter.

For a fuzzy, indefinite period we all of us sat in the living-room, flopped and weary, spreading ourselves over the armchairs and the sofa... people kept announcing that they felt mellow...we smoked cigarettes and listened to music from the stereo...once in a while somebody got up and fiddled with a record...there was a large, untidy row of LPs on the floor next to the sofa, which I hadn't noticed before, and I couldn't take my gaze off the ragged bits of inner sleeves and plastic covers poking up from the tops of the albums. So, I thought, this is mellow. I lay back with my bottom perched on the edge of one of the easy-chairs and stretched my legs...after a while I might have dozed, because suddenly I opened my eyes and noticed Beats, D.C. and Georgie were gone from the room... Sammy was still lying across the sofa nearby, with her feet voluptuously up on the armrest, and Lonno sat in an easy-chair engrossed in some sort of sleepy conversation with himself. But Lonno was becoming gradually more agitated, and his private conversation grew aggressive...he started to twitch, to fidget, and finally to wrench his neck and shoulders about on top of his narrow frame...all at once he stood up, and I watched him begin staggering around in the room...he was still grumbling and talking, but he couldn't find any balance and he floundered, bumping against the corners of the chairs...I straightened in my seat, and I could tell Sammy was worried too...Lonno was waving with his arms, groaning, as though working to push back some invisible people who were crowding him. In a moment Lonno turned, and he tumbled away from us out into the hallway...we could hear him colliding with the walls, over and over, as he shambled off along the passage...I wondered what Sammy might do, but she didn't move from the sofa...then a minute or two later Lonno blundered back into the room...his gaze had become alarmingly bright... immediately Sammy lowered her legs off the sofa and stood up. Lonno was shouting, but his words were incoherent and almost shaking themselves free from his mouth...Sammy put out her arms in Lonno's direction as if to suggest some sort of comfort, but Lonno paid no attention…he kept right on with his blustering…he started swinging both hands up near to his face and flicking his fingers…it was as if he was trying his utmost, and failing, to explain something difficult and deep…then suddenly he managed to break in on his own confusion and announced that a robber was out in the kitchen. 'Stealing the saucepans!' Lonno howled. At that same instant Beats appeared from the corridor and for an odd moment I wondered if he could be the robber Lonno meant. 'Stupid wanker!' Beats bawled at Lonno's back. Lonno ignored this, or maybe he just hadn't noticed… he'd bent down instead to stare at a cushioned panel on the backrest of an empty armchair…he was demanding that the cushion explain why it had no nose. I heard Beats yell to Sammy above the music, 'The stupid bastard's put a whole lot of pots on the stove. He's fucking lit all the gas-rings.' By now Lonno was haranguing the cushion at the top of his lungs. 'What do you think you're doing?' he hollered. 'What do you think you're doing there?' He had his chin pressed up against the edge of the chair… he poked at the fluffy panel with his finger. 'What is it? Eh? What is it?' he went on repeating. Beats and Sammy both took Lonno by the arms and shoulders…I stepped over to help…we struggled to lift him up, turn him round and sit him down in the chair that he was talking to…but Lonno didn't want to stay settled…he commenced flailing about at us from his seat. 'This is the datura, man. The fucking datura,' Beats bellowed above it all. Lonno began stamping on the floor so hard that the record skipped…I could hear somebody else coming in a rush down the staircase…I worked at getting a firm grip on Lonno's hands but he was thrashing about even more with each second. 'Hey, you stop that!' Sammy shrieked at him.

'What's datura?' I managed to ask.

Lonno was slapping up at my cheeks and weeping. 'What do you think you're doing?' he was wailing again between sobs. Sammy said to me, 'The boys boiled themselves up a batch in here a week ago. And this idiot, this one, eh, he had two glasses.' Sammy had got her palms flat on Lonno's wriggling chest with her fingers splayed out…I supposed she was hoping it would make him calmer. Next she added for me, 'He's hallucinating.' Over my shoulder I saw D.C. had entered the living-room from the hallway…he was standing in the centre of the room without a stitch of clothing on…in one hand he was clasping a long pink bath-towel, and his face looked flushed and thrilled…he started waving the bath-towel up and down like a veil over his lanky, hairless, stark-naked body. 'Pigs!'

D.C. screeched. 'Pigs! Pigs!' It occurred to me that perhaps he could be hallucinating too...D.C. was prancing past us all across the floor...at the window he flung back the curtains and exhibited himself to the street... Beats began shouting above the commotion for Georgie, wanting him to bloody well get his arse in here and help...but D.C. already had the side-window's lower sash pushed up...I watched him raise one skinny leg over the sill to climb out. 'Fucking pigs!' he yelled once more. 'Hey, get in here and do me, you pigs!' 'Stop him!' Sammy screamed close to my ear. I spied Georgie coming into the room at last and then saw D.C. start to fall outside through the open window...D.C.'s bottom and legs jerked upwards as he skidded from view, and he flopped down onto the porch somewhere with a dull smack...but in a second or so he got to his feet...he was still waving his towel up and around him...he seemed to be dancing about in the little garden. 'Oh wow,' Georgie said. I decided to abandon Lonno...I scurried across the room and tried to bend and slide myself through the window...as I clambered out onto the porch, banging my knees and elbows, I could see D.C. twirling round and round along the cracked front path...he was acting a lot like a pasty, nude ballerina, pirouetting near the gate while struggling to get up into pointe...in the police car, still parked on the other side of the street, nobody stirred. I dashed across to the gate for D.C. in a blind panic and almost knocked him into the mailbox...I grabbed at his neck and sweaty, slithering arms... for a few moments it was no good, until Georgie arrived just behind me... together we worked at pulling D.C. back up the small path to the house, but he screamed 'Pigs!' even louder into the street and battled to get away from us. Suddenly Beats appeared and he hauled one of D.C.'s legs into the air, so that D.C. let go of his towel and dropped with a loud wallop onto the paving...I heard him grunt from pain, and the impact took most of the fight out of him...the three of us picked him up and we began carrying him towards the porch...ahead of us as we approached, Sammy had leaned out of the window and she was begging us to be careful...but D.C. seemed to wilt and became cooperative, though we were all short of breath by the time we finally had him back inside...then we saw that Lonno was gone from the armchair where we'd deposited him. Sammy turned and dashed from the room...I wondered if it was always like this around here...within a minute she came back along the hall...she ran in wailing that the rear door out from the kitchen had been left wide open... there was no sign of Lonno anywhere. 'We have to find him!' she yelled.

317

'Don't worry. I'll help,' I volunteered.

But nobody paid me the slightest attention...the others were already leaving the living-room and heading towards the rear of the house...within an instant or two only D.C. and I were left...D.C. was lying exhausted and spread-eagled on the sofa...I decided to climb through the window once more and try combing the street for Lonno out along the front...by now the remains of the dope had mostly worn off and I felt ready for anything, especially if it involved pleasing Sammy. As soon as I got outside again, I saw the police car had vanished from across the road...at the mailbox I stood gazing along the street, first in one direction and then the other, feeling more than a little puzzled...I kept nursing a wishy-washy sort of desire that the cop car might turn up amongst the passing traffic...I considered going back and telling the others, but quickly abandoned the idea and jogged up the steep footpath beside the road for a bit. The glare of the hard light was shining on my face and the street seemed to get even busier with traffic as I trotted along...it needed only a few minutes of lumbering uphill to get me cruelly worn out...I was gulping for mouthfuls of air when I reached the top of the rise. There was a large dairy on the other side of the street under the shadow of a low veranda, and the sight of it made me think that part of my problem was hunger...immediately I crossed the road towards the shop...the dairy's doorway was completely open onto the footpath, and when I stepped across the threshold I felt the welcome cool of the store's shaded air...near the entrance was the serving area and I shuffled to a halt just in front of the counter. Behind the counter a very fat man stood lounging about, resting his elbows on the stained Formica edge of the countertop in the narrow space between a grey metal cash register and a rack of chewing gum...the man was fiddling absentmindedly with the cash register's drawer...he was getting on in years, with small eyes and a round button nose in his podgy face, and his white hair was cut short to the sides of his head...there were bits of salt-and-pepper stubble on his poorly shaved, jowly cheeks...the man stared at me as though he had much better things to do than offer me help, but eventually he asked in an irritated manner what I wanted. I stared back as nastily as I could...then I demanded a hot pie, a K-bar and a fucking milkshake...after a long moment of hesitation the man pushed himself away from the counter...he reached behind him to open the glass doors of a warmer, drew out a pie and put it into a bag...next he made a start on the milkshake and asked me over his shoulder what flavour that'd be…I told him, and when he had everything almost ready I took out my twenty-dollar note and tossed it onto the counter. But the man didn't touch the note…instead he stooped low to examine it as if he'd never seen one before and wasn't certain it was real. 'You got anything smaller?' he growled.

'Fuck no,' I said.

The man hesitated again and straightened himself up, tightening his big belly…I saw his eyes flick to the freshly made milkshake, still sitting by the machine…finally he scooped up the note, mumbled something about getting more change from his own wallet, and went off towards the rear of the shop. There were several stacks of newspapers at one side of the counter near me, and I gave the front pages a brief look-over as I waited…when the man returned, I supposed I might as well get a paper while the going was good…I slid a copy of the *Herald* off the top of a loose pile and said to include it…after all, I told myself, writers had to stay fully aware of the world, and even without Half-Arse I intended to manage things and write my masterpiece. By now I felt so hungry that I just tore the K-bar from its wrapper while still inside the shop…I'd almost finished chewing it to shreds and gulping it down when I got out onto the street at last…on the footpath near the front of the store I bent and spread my newspaper on the ground beside the gutter, smoothed it flat and knelt on it…the warmth from the pavement began coming up through the newsprint into my knees…I thought I'd eat the rest of my brunch at this nice spot by the edge of the road and plan my next move. I put the milkshake down, and gently I started to ease the pie out of its waxy brown bag…I took an explorative bite and wiped the pastry flakes from my lips while I leaned forwards to read the newspaper below me…the middle of the front page was creased from being folded and knelt on, but there next to my kneecap I could see a photo of several young and rather pretty women…something about them, a glimmer of something, appealed to my eye…they were posed as a group, two rows of them standing on a long, curved concrete staircase…near the centre of the group, smiling and supporting herself with one hand on her hip, stood somebody who looked like Gizi. I thought she resembled Gizi a lot, an awful, awful lot…I struggled to rearrange the parts of Gizi's face in my mind…then I squinted to see more closely and was sure…I was staring at her beautiful face in the paper, and it was impossible…for a moment Gizi's face stared back out at me with a life of its own, refusing to submit to my disbelief.

The photo was accompanied by an article about the Miss New Zealand contest...the article announced, in a tone breathless with excitement, that the beauty pageant proper was just about to start...the gala final was going to be in a week and would feature a full, comprehensive range of glamorous, sponsored eveningwear...my eyes flittered about the page, trying to take in everything at once...this year the pageant in its entirety was being held in Auckland...the contestants were all of them staying at the premier, five-star Sheraton Hotel. I put down the pie on the footpath... the oil from its pastry was on my fingers and I didn't want any to stain the precious pages...I wiped my palms across my jeans while I tried to concentrate wholly on the article...the first outing of the contestants was at the Sheraton early tomorrow evening, where the girls would gather and present a cheque to the manager of the children's ward at Greenlane...I hurried to read further, though the print kept on shivering before my eyes, until underneath the photo I saw Gizi's name quite clearly captioned...she was Miss Mount Victoria. A turmoil of serious thoughts and ideas surged up within me...I couldn't put any of them into words that were coherent, not even as words for myself...but a confusing, wretched sense of love overpowered me, and then I noticed that I'd omitted to read how Miss Mount Victoria had a manager...she was being managed and chaperoned by a Professor Bradley Bingham.

I spent a long, long time just roaming about the streets on my own...I was still, in theory, half-heartedly searching for Lonno, but mainly I was trying to come to terms with having seen Gizi's photo in the paper...I kept marching past letterboxes and hedges, through parks and even round a stretch of harbour, as if the shock of what I'd learned might be walked off, but all I could do was remember Gizi, picture her and talk to her in my mind...it seemed incredible how she still existed with her own separate life when I wasn't even thinking of her...now she, Gizi, was here in the same town as me, and why shouldn't she go ahead, after all, and actually win the Miss New Zealand contest?...but I couldn't for the life of me understand how she'd got into the pageant so quickly, and I couldn't understand what connection with it Prof Bingham might have. It wasn't until late in the afternoon that I returned to Parnell...I had to ask the way several times and reached the house feeling heavily distracted...I even forgot about the front door not working, and tried to knock on one of the door-panels while I stood on the porch...it was Lonno himself who pulled back the curtain at the window...at the sight of me outside he made a

320

flurry of beckoning signals and opened the window up. The moment he raised the sash a lot of sudden noise, mostly music and chatter, came from the living-room behind him...I could see plenty of other figures inside moving around...it looked like a party was going on...cheerfully Lonno began helping me over the windowsill, and I thought he was in fairly good condition for a man I'd last seen out of his mind. While I was still straddling the edge of the window frame, Lonno called to me above all the hoopla, 'They brought me home.' He laughed and pointed past me in the direction of the road...I glanced back over my shoulder and saw he meant the police car...it was parked again, waiting, on the other side of the street...when I got down into the room after a bit more effort, Lonno shut the window and drew the curtain firmly closed. There was a crush of people standing all around us, smoking, holding drinks and drifting about...they were everywhere that I could see and they looked a lot like students, only more grown-up and somehow tougher...amongst the crowd I could make out men with hard-bitten, bony faces and grinning women in clobber that looked as if it had been worn for days...but at that moment Lonno leaned forward near my shoulder, pressing his hands against the back of his hips, and I guessed he was trying to tell me something over the babble. I heard him say, 'Sammy kept asking what happened to you, eh.' But I felt too stunned by the crowd around me to react...I wondered where all these really cool though rather distant people could have come from at such short notice. 'Been asleep the whole afternoon,' Lonno was saying. He gripped my elbow and started leading me across the living-room...perhaps he sensed how lost I was feeling...we kept interrupting people on our way to wherever we were going and I kept apologising to them, and at the door to the hall we avoided a large purple splatter of wine spread on the floorboards next to a chair...Lonno was still attempting to explain something to me over the noise...it was about how he hadn't gone very far that morning...the police had swooped down within minutes and picked him up. 'They put me in the back seat of the bloody cop car and asked my name,' he announced into my ear. 'But I couldn't talk that well, see, because my speech was, like, slurred and stuff.' Lonno appeared delighted at having someone to tell his story to...as we entered the hallway, he turned round to me amid the press of people close about us... it was every bit as crowded here as in the living-room...Lonno fixed me with a look. 'They always kept asking what I was on,' he said. 'Over and over. The cops. "What are you on, son? What are you on?" Fuck. And I just kept saying that I was, you know, I was drunk. So they tried to roll my arms up and that, for needle marks, but I wouldn't let them, eh. "What are you on?" They kept hassling me about it. Man, I started to get that fucking paranoid—I thought, like, maybe they'd want to give me a blood test, eh. But in the end, they just dropped me back here again.' Lonno paused... he gazed around at the partygoers who were crammed so tightly with us into the narrow corridor, most of them trying to chat or to acknowledge each other while squeezing and shuffling on by...he seemed as much surprised by their presence as I was. 'The band's beginning to show up,' he declared at last. Lonno shrugged his shoulders...then he turned away for the living-room once more and I was on my own...I didn't know a soul, so I headed further down the passage into the dining-room...it was busy too, but Georgie and Sammy were there, standing near the very centre of the crowd...I thought they brightened briefly when I started threading my way over. They were both holding glasses of wine and were talking to a dark-haired girl who had her back to me and what looked like a man's oversized denim jacket wrapped around her shoulders...when I arrived at the edge of their conversation, Sammy began waving her glass near my face, almost sloshing the wine onto my T-shirt...from the dullness in her eyes I could tell she was drunk. 'Hey,' she said to me in a loud voice, 'a whole lot of us are flitting away from here out to the Art Extravaganza show. You know, flit, flit.' She drank from the wine glass and said, 'Happening over at the varsity tonight.' I nodded and made an effort to grin, hoping I was included...I'd never been to an art show before...in fact, I'd never flitted from one party to another before. Sammy added, 'And then there's Beats, eh, and that's about it.' With no further explanation she turned away and gazed around as though preoccupied...she was absorbed by the other guests near us in the room...the girl in the denim jacket smiled, and I saw a row of small blue stars tattooed in a line along the top of one of her gaunt cheeks. Georgie said almost as an interruption, 'Why don't you—yeah, you should be at this wingding.' But I wasn't sure whether he was really referring to me, and in any case I was now starting to feel peculiarly out of sorts...Sammy bent sideways to tell something to the girl in the man's jacket and seemed to miss her footing...she recovered by leaning against Georgie for support...I tried to look as if I had pressing business elsewhere, and wandered off. I made my way towards the front of the house once more and in the hall I almost collided with a couple of stocky men coming out of the living-room...both had dirty black hair that

322

fell to their shoulders and they wore thin, dishevelled beards...they were struggling, both of them, to carry wooden crates crammed with bottles of beer...one of the men lumbered past up the passage with his back stiff and his arms straining, not giving me a second glance, but the other put his burden down hard on the floor beside me...the man had an affable smile on his face, and even as he straightened up to catch his breath the smile still stayed on his features...I asked him who all these people at the party were. The man kneaded the muscles in his back and said, 'Oh, mainly hairdressers, record traders and such. Probably doing stuff in shops, eh. I'm not too sure.'

'Is the band here yet?' I asked.

The man opened his mouth again, but a sudden surge of music at high volume roared out at us from the living-room...the man shrugged and rolled his eyes at all the noise...then he bent once more, heaved up his crate and moved on. I stepped through the doorway into the living-room and at once saw an elderly lady who was wearing a flowing, faded orange caftan and who was twirling rapidly about, dancing in circles in the middle of the room's floor...the other partygoers were all getting discreetly out of her way...with a bit of trouble I edged along the back of the crowd, spied a cardboard box of wine perched on the edge of an armchair and picked it up to pour a drink into an empty coffee mug nearby...I tilted the box to encourage its flow, and after that I stood quietly for a while with my cup amid the hammering din of the music...at last the woman gave up on her whirling and I managed to have myself a second mug of hooch...the wine was starting to do its job of making me feel loose. I watched a man by the mantelpiece swinging a beer bottle from its neck in his fingers as he stared into the fireplace, silently mouthing the lyrics to the music... in a corner a tall, dark-haired fellow was holding a girl and kissing her, squeezing her cheek hard...I heard a voice behind me say distinctly, 'Five bottles, that's a Manawatu half dozen,' but when I turned round I couldn't discover where the voice had come from. Then I saw someone climbing through the bay window into the room...only his blond, balding head was in view past a gap in the curtains, but all at once the man paused and clasped the drapes up beneath his chin...he thrust his face out at us and bellowed 'Whoa!' into the party noise in the room, sticking his pink tongue out...I saw that he was Moondog, the man from the train station that morning. Moondog was looking enormously pleased with himself... he climbed down into the room, fiddled with the edge of the curtain to get it straight again and marched through the crowd towards me...he clapped me across the shoulder and insisted on shaking my hand, really pumping it hard, and despite the music he tried telling everyone near us about the backpack full of hash. 'Okay, I just knew you were a freak! I bloody knew you were a body-thrasher, eh, the second I saw you over by the station,' Moondog shouted at the other guests. He kept on shaking my hand, but finally he let it go and rubbed at the blotchy skin on his face... people were staring and I felt terribly proud...Moondog started sidling away from me through the crush of partygoers...I thought of following, but now several people in the living-room seemed keen to talk...someone gave me a cigarette and asked about my eye...even the music was turned down a notch. At length I got into conversation with a plump-faced girl who had an untidy mess of copper-dyed hair styled in a pixie cut...the girl was wearing a dowdy brown velveteen dress and stood rocking from side to side in an uneasy way as she spoke, flexing her shoulders...she told me that the Extravaganza was being hosted by the varsity's Fine Arts Department...she tried telling me the names of the Department's staff and asked if I knew them...I pretended to know only one or two...the girl said it was all happening out in the Stud Ass building, and I nodded my head sagely at her mention of the Stud Ass. 'And the thing is, everyone's supposed to, like, wear an outrageous costume, eh,' the girl explained. I waved the matter aside with a large gesture to indicate that I was quite au fait...instead, I began to steer the conversation subtly around to Sammy.

'So, has she got a boyfriend?' I asked.

'Dean, she's going out with Dean,' the girl said. The girl looked surprised that I hadn't been aware of this...she brushed the fringe of her hair back from her eyes and glanced around the room as though Dean might actually appear. After a moment she added, 'I mean anyway it's, you know, it's his band. Dean's on keyboards. So he's basically still off in Hamilton, I reckon.'

'What sort of music do they play?' I inquired.

'Oh, country rock mostly,' the girl said, 'but with a bit of jazz influence, progressive rock, everything really, you name it. Like gospel, old time, the whole deal.' She looked quite serious, so I raised my eyebrows and grinned to imply that it was all finally making sense...secretly, though, I was still thinking of Sammy...I couldn't prevent myself from feeling disappointed about her boyfriend...I'd felt so sure that Sammy would make an excellent helpmeet for a writer. I thought of getting another refill for my mug and drifted away, yet I found the chateau-cardboard wine was finished...instead a small fellow with wavy blond hair had pulled the plastic lining from the box and inflated it...he shouldered past me to a corner with the plastic bag and started half-heartedly stamping on it...after a few seconds the bag exploded and one or two people were annoyed at being splashed by flying specks of plonk. But at that instant Sammy was beside me amongst the crowd...it felt marvellously as though I'd just wished her up...she seized my hand and began leading me out of the living-room...I trotted along behind her, thinking that she didn't look half so drunk as I'd seen her before...I could hear her saying that it was high time to get me all dressed up for the Extravaganza, and I made a poor show of trying to act reluctant while she pulled me towards the stairs. We headed up the thinly carpeted steps, and on the landing I could see that the corridor and the rooms off it were just as busy with partygoers as the downstairs had been...Sammy drew me into a large, crowded master bedroom at the front of the house...inside it I found a lot of guests were already there and changing, all of them getting into clothes or taking things off in a tremendous hurry...some people seemed to have brought costumes with them, but a fancy wooden chest of drawers and a wardrobe had both been hauled open and ransacked for items...people kept throwing clothes across the wide double-bed and I saw discarded bits and pieces lying about on the bare floor by everyone's feet...several guests were queuing to admire themselves in the only full-length mirror, a huge, oblong glass in a chrome frame. Sammy gestured for me to wait and left me in the middle of the clutter while she wandered about, bending to pick things up and delving into the chest of drawers and wardrobe...after a minute or two she returned holding a pair of baggy white denim trousers...she ordered me to put the trousers on and promptly disappeared from the room...I peeled off my strides and felt a bit relieved that she wasn't there to watch me, though stumbling about to strip didn't feel all that odd with so many other people doing the same thing...I kicked my jeans into a corner and threw my filthy T-shirt after them for good measure...it seemed entirely possible that my clothes might become part of someone else's outfit. Then Sammy was back again, holding a frilly white shirt and a black dinner-jacket for me to try...the shirt looked suspiciously like a donation from Struan's mother...it felt strange and loose when I put it on, but I tucked the ends down far into my new pants...the jacket fitted well, and I decided that I approved of myself in its suave, wide lapels...Sammy produced a bottle of Old Spice which she tipped over my head, and with her large hands she used the contents to slick back my hair...the cologne dripped down my neck in places and made me shudder, and I started to reek of the sweet scent, but Sammy ignored the smell and patted my hair until it was stuck flat against my skin. Another girl came up, pulled a deep glass jar from a bag and began to smear sticky white greasepaint from the jar onto my face...I could see that she'd already had a go at many of the other people in the room...the girl was tall and serious-looking, and she stared at me with her long brows furrowed as she worked...the greasepaint felt thick on my cheeks, and the growing warmth of my skin beneath the makeup caused me to fidget, but the girl seemed too absorbed in her task to notice...she let me watch in an old powder-compact mirror while she carefully added black teardrop eyes and black lips to the gooey mix, pressing gently on the bruised spots where I'd been hit...the girl and Sammy consulted in whispers as they got the parts of my face sorted out. Georgie strolled in... from the corner of my eye, standing rigid while my makeup was applied, I could see he was wearing yellow jodhpurs and a blue T-shirt under a long afghan coat...Georgie spent some time squinting at himself before the full-length mirror...he ran his hands down the coat as if admiring it... then he came over and asked, 'All right?' in a superior tone. The makeup-girl gave me a curt nod that I was done, and I watched her paint Georgie's mouth green with some sort of theatrical lipstick from her bag...next she began to comb silver into Georgie's hair and moustache...from inside the cover of my greasepaint and clothes I felt curiously keyed up, and it was some minutes before I noticed that Sammy had gone. I turned away to look for her and wandered out into the corridor, and almost at once I saw D.C. trotting up the stairs towards me...he was dressed in nothing but his underwear, with a faded blue New Zealand flag draped as a shawl about his pasty, narrow shoulders...when D.C. saw me, he halted near the top of the stairs and twirled about, and I could tell that a quantity of glitter had been dumped over him from his forehead down to his ribs. 'Ta-dah!' he announced, and twirled once again.

'You're going like that?' I asked.

'Ain't no wallflower, babe,' D.C. said. He bounded up onto the landing and wrinkled his nose as he drew near, perhaps at the Old Spice in my hair...D.C. got beside me and slipped one skinny arm under mine. 'Come on. It's time to be popular,' he declared in his high voice. 'My public is

out there, eh. They're waiting for us, right. They're waiting.' D.C. giggled
and squirmed and arched his bare neck...he started to walk with me in
procession along the corridor, keeping our arms still linked together...he
smiled with the affected radiance of visiting royalty and waved about him
at the old plaster walls...I was beginning to think the Extravaganza might
be a scaled-up version of a drag party and half expected to find Frannie
and Trudy hiding somewhere in the bedrooms we were passing. D.C. led
me to the end of the corridor and we entered a room at the back of the
house in fine style...straightaway I saw that Sammy was there, sitting
nearby on the edge of a bed, and that she'd changed her clothes into what
looked like a gorgeous full skirt wedding-dress...the dress had sometime
been dyed a rich dark grey...Sammy had the small lace train drawn up
on the pillow beside her while she bent and peered into a hand mirror,
puffing out her cheeks from concentration as she applied eyeliner with a
long black brush to her lower lids...she paused and waved to us briefly,
and D.C. blew her an exaggerated kiss. Then without a word D.C. left me
and strode off across the room...but I just stayed put, finding it hard not
to stare at Sammy in her costume...the snug-fitting, satiny material did a
lot to reveal her exciting figure, and after a bit I thought it best to leave. I
went downstairs, and in the living-room I discovered a press of partygoers
all gathered together in a large bunch around the curtains...everyone,
the lot of them, was trying to get out through the narrow space of the
bay window and onto the porch...I heard car doors slamming outside
on the street, enthusiastic shouts and the roar of a revving engine, and
guessed the party must be breaking up...suddenly I also just wanted
to take off now, and I joined the back of the pushing, straining group...
after a few annoying minutes I was able to twist my way through the
window, knocking my legs on the sill, until at last I set myself down on
the porch outside. The early-evening light had deteriorated into a glare,
and I shaded my eyes...the sun had almost gone behind the cluster of
buildings across the street and the whole sky was a muddy wash of red
and violet streaks...the partygoers standing about in a loose mob before
me were already casting lengthy shadows...I made my way towards the
gate, and I saw the guests were collected everywhere in the garden or
were drifting before the house and along the footpath nearby...a number
of them had wandered onto the road holding cigarettes and clutching
cups or glasses...the passing traffic had to slow down for them and an
angry driver somewhere gave a shrill honk on his horn, but the guests

appeared too caught up in their own activities to care. Many of them, mostly the costume-dressed people, were getting in and out of a few cars which lined the kerb along the front of the house...I couldn't tell if the police were around to witness all these goings-on or not, but the energy of the party people seemed to infect me with an impulse to hurry or risk missing something vital...a little distance down the street was an old car of some type, a Hillman perhaps, which had its rear door open and a lot of guests already inside...without hesitating I scuttled over to it...a few other people joined me on the way and we tried cramming into the back of the car, pushing and shoving to get ourselves a bit of space, until still more people arrived and began climbing over the top of our legs...for some moments I was down under several bodies on the sticky vinyl seat cover, but I wriggled free despite a stray elbow in my ribs...I heard a voice whooping at us from off on the street. A girl in a badly torn, blue Indian sari appeared at the kerb...she tried to squash herself into the car against me and everybody else...she looked so cadaverously thin that I worried she might be sick or something, though she had plenty of strength for pushing...after a few instants the scrawny girl settled on the edge of my lap, and with one arm she slammed the door shut beside us... immediately there was a shudder throughout the whole car as the engine started. The car pulled away from the kerb and commenced toiling uphill, creaking miserably on its springs...I was surprised that the old bomb could move at all under our combined weight...I wanted to see who was driving, but the arch of the girl's bony back was jammed into my face... everybody around me swayed helplessly as the car negotiated the first corner with us all inside...I could feel each bump through my buttocks while we trundled along...as the seat warmed beneath me the smell of its vinyl grew rancid in my nostrils. Sometime later we halted, and at once people started opening the doors...I worked my face free of the material in the girl's sari but I could tell only that it was very dark now out on the street, with almost nothing to see past the door except the gutter, the grassy patch of a berm and a footpath...we all managed to tumble off the seats and out of the car...the sudden chill of the air woke us up and we shook off the stiffness in our arms and shoulders...we were standing around on the grass verge of a long, ordinary road of suburban houses...a lot of other cars, a whole convoy of them, had stopped in a row up ahead of us, and the passengers in their costumes were spilling out here and there into the darkness. I looked for anyone I might recognise, but with no success...a girl dressed a little like a pirate, in a red frock coat with gold buttons and epaulettes, walked over through the shadows and explained to me that one of our cars had gone and packed a sad...she seemed very concerned...a few normal vehicles drove past us out of the night, and I could tell the people inside were gawking at us through the windows. Soon I heard a lot of shouts and groans from the stalled car being push-started down the road...it didn't sound too good...but at last there also came the roar of an engine catching and revving, and everybody began cramming into the vehicles again...this time I was careful to get myself into another ride, one with more room and with a proper view out of a window. We set off and headed for what felt like ages along a very straight, very boring street...we paused only for traffic lights and occasionally to collect up stragglers in our drifting convoy...then all at once we went down some kind of turnoff and bumped over a set of awful judder bars, and I saw we were approaching something...it was a complex of large, elongated buildings that was still far away, and even from a distance their brilliantly floodlit walls and rows of gleaming windows stood out against the wide black spread of the sky. I nudged the ribcage of a long-limbed, sleepy-faced fellow who was sitting next to me...he was wearing a pair of overalls that was bulked up with polystyrene to look like a spaceman's suit, and a silver-covered cardboard helmet was cradled on his lap...I asked him if this could be the Stud Ass just ahead and his eyes widened as he looked at me in surprise. 'That's the airport,' he said. He pronounced the word 'airport' as if stating an obvious fact...he straightened his back against the seat and stared harder at me.

'It's not the Extravaganza?' I asked.

'No, mate,' he repeated, 'it's the airport.'

'Well, what the hell are we doing here?' I demanded.

'We're seeing that joker off,' the spaceman guy replied. 'The one who's leaving, eh. Beats.' The fellow twisted away from me on the seat as best he could, perhaps embarrassed at speaking to me any further...but we'd kept on getting nearer and my heart quickened as I gazed out again from the car's windows...I could distinguish it easily now, an airport, beginning to spread everywhere and surround us, with the white walls of hangers and warehouses dotted about, and the control tower, and then the long terminal buildings themselves still off before us...a dazzling bustle was going on in front of the terminal of flickering streetlamps, gorgeous lit-up shop displays and signs in neon colours...we passed through a busy intersection, and other cars, vans and taxis came by from confusing directions...next we entered a short, curving approach road with the main terminal buildings all lining one side, and I saw the yellow light from their upper windows was spilling down across their verandas onto the tarseal in front and on the covered parking area opposite. I'd never been to a real airport before...I rolled down the window beside me in a nervous hurry and stuck my head out to get a better sense of everything as our car lumbered closer...the cool air nipped at my painted cheeks...from somewhere I could hear a strong whine of large jet engines idling, and I could smell gasoline. Our group of vehicles pulled in at the near end of the terminal complex in the dark and we all piled out again... immediately we began walking in a loose collection on the footpath under a high, sloping white veranda, making for the main building...the names of airline companies were hanging on exotic signs under the veranda's roof and the lighting shone weirdly down onto our faces...suddenly I noticed Lonno, D.C. and Sammy up ahead...there they were, the three of them, straggling forwards together in a little knot amongst our crowd...I trotted over to catch them up. Lonno was nearest, at the back of the other two, walking with his shoulders slumped and not dressed in any costume, and he grinned at me when I fell into step with him...Sammy was right in front of me, still wearing her lovely grey dress although she appeared to have discarded the train, and D.C. was still in his obscene underwear and with the blue flag draped around his shoulders...I saw even Georgie was there...he was a little further ahead, marching in his afghan coat and talking to someone else...a set of doors was not far off with a red-lettered sign marked 'Departures,' and we were all wandering towards it.

'So where's Beats going?' I asked Lonno.

I hoped saying this would make me sound knowledgeable. But Lonno replied, 'Sydney. Where else?' He leaned towards me and added, 'The usual.' Lonno winked...I wanted to ask him what the usual really was...I wanted to ask him what on earth we were doing here in our costumes, but we'd reached the building's entrance. The automatic doors in front of us slid back, and then kept shuddering from attempts to close while we all came through in dribs and drabs...a couple of travellers came in with us, bent over and pushing their bags on rattling metal trolleys...we were making quite a bit of noise around them, a real hullabaloo, but they ignored us and trundled away to queue at a long row of check-in counters on the other side of the room...we crossed the cavernous terminal, and as we moved onwards I observed how spick and span everything looked... despite our costumes, no one at all paid us any attention...at the escalator we rode in a body up past an overhead sign that announced the international departure area. The broad concourse at the top, when we reached it, was crowded with bunches of passengers and well-wishers who were standing about and waiting...we joined them, and I could hear the excited emotions pent-up in their subdued talk and I thought how the sharp fluorescent lights in the high ceiling made everyone's faces look waxy and drawn... still no one paid even the slightest attention to our clothes...a woman nearby kept checking a small gold watch fastened to her plump wrist, and I spied a man with a half-unwrapped roll of lifesavers who was offering them around to his friends...in another group a tall man in a grey charcoal suit and with a stooped back and long arms was going about shaking people's hands. Next to me, Lonno started murmuring something and I caught the words 'duty free'...but it was getting late, and the stores lining the concourse looked closed, with steel-mesh grilles pulled over their display windows...a boarding announcement was being called, but the whole place had a distinct air of being shut down for the night. Someone spotted Beats...he was over on the far side of the crowd, and we hurried to approach him...I saw he was standing next to an empty row of vinyl-covered benches with the large black departures board nearby...Beats had several white plastic shopping bags clasped in his hands...he was shifting about, rubbing one foot against the back of the other leg, and he appeared pleased to see us as we arrived through the crowd. We gathered around him and everyone started saying at once how we all wished we could be going across to Sydney together, and D.C. took some of the plastic bags from Beats's hands...Beats was looking very smart, and the striped shirt and jeans he was wearing seemed brand-new...his sideburns were shaved back to the lobes of his ears and the new image made him look younger...he talked and answered our questions, but he kept glancing over towards a narrow green portal in the centre of one wall of the concourse...the portal was flanked by wide, frosted-glass panels which left everything beyond it misty and vague, and I saw there was a stencilled sign above that said: 'Departures all Flights'...a traveller went off through the portal and, past the murk of the glass, I could just manage to watch him being accosted by shadowy figures on the far side. D.C. had pulled a bottle of whisky from one of the shopping bags...he worked now at unscrewing the cap...he took a generous swig out of the top, slurping the

331

whisky into his mouth, and gasped after swallowing it...D.C. gave the bottle to somebody else for passing around, and we watched him try rummaging quickly through the other bags as if hoping to find more to drink. 'She's all real at Kings Cross!' someone was bellowing over and over. Then D.C. began striding up and down amongst the other neatly dressed, waiting passengers...he was marching across the lino in his underwear, and he hauled off his flag and stamped his feet...he shrieked gleeful, incomprehensible things at some people who were eyeing items behind the shop-grilles...a few of our group followed him, and I hurried to join them too...our party seemed to be starting up again here in the midst of the departure area. In front of us D.C. kept waving the flag with one arm and flapping the cumbersome shopping bags with the other, and we commenced trailing after him in a silly, teetering conga line...finally the rest of our gang pitched in and soon we were all cavorting through the crowd as a noisy column, each with our hands on the hips of the person before us...the travellers watched us with a sort of bemused tolerance...I was jumping around after somebody in front of me, chanting the same nonsense as everyone else, and we kicked our legs out and swayed in unison...I could smell Chemico coming up from the polish on the floor, although it was slowly giving way to the aromas of my own sweat and Old Spice...the beige tiles across the ceiling were shimmying, darting before my eyes. Some of the other travellers tried larking in our conga line along with us, but through the crowd I saw that Beats had stayed still in his place...he was only jiggling a little up and down on his toes, and it was remarkable just how much he didn't seem a part of things...I thought it was strange too, since we'd come out to the airport to see him off... suddenly all the yellow-lettered signs on the departures board began to click downwards in a flurry...the mechanical racket, happening holus-bolus, somehow carried with it intimations of importance and everybody broke off their prancing around...the Air New Zealand flight for Sydney was being announced, and it felt as if time was running out. Then we heard weird, hurried whooping sounds from somewhere and a man in a bulky grey-furred rabbit suit appeared, shouting and clutching something awkwardly between his gloved hands...he'd come from the top of the escalator and was dodging past other passengers and in amongst us...I couldn't help but admire how good his costume was, with its floppy ears, thick black whiskers painted on his cheeks, and a lot of sleek pale fur marking his underbelly...the man moved past me, red-faced with excitement and speaking in almost breathless sentences to people in our group, and everybody pressed around him in an expectant crush... someone said to me that the man had found two boarding passes downstairs, just there, just begging to be picked up...a fuss was already developing about going to Australia with Beats. I tried to push myself forwards into the crowd and squeezed a little between the shoulders and the forearms of others in front of me...I was ravenous for a ticket, and a desperate feeling of wanting not to miss out mounted again within my chest...I strained, craning my neck, and managed to see past a tall man in a top hat, even though he had bunches of frizzy red hair bushing out around his head which got into my face...D.C. was near the centre of the circle, arguing that he'd be the best at sneaking onto the plane...the rabbit-costumed man was holding up the boarding passes...he'd claimed one for himself, and he kept glancing around at everybody's faces as if to check that it was really all right. D.C. kept insisting he would fucking get on the airplane and go, no matter what...I glimpsed the veins standing out pink in his neck as his high voice rose...it was Sammy he was disputing with...I couldn't see her in the crowd, though I recognised the timbre of her voice...she was wailing that D.C. didn't even have a real change of clothes...but D.C. only acted even more resolved. 'Look, I'll send you a postcard, babe,' he finished up. I watched him bend forward, half out of sight, with the flag bunched loosely round his neck...he was flexing his skinny shoulder muscles and I guessed that, behind the man's head blocking my view, D.C. was starting to give Sammy some sort of hug...he seemed intoxicated with his own happiness...the final call was being announced, and our group began to break up and separate...D.C. passed close by me with his flag hastily rearranged across his shoulders...he kept his head up and didn't bother looking about, drifting with Beats and the rabbit man towards the green departures-portal. They gathered together among the other travellers who were leaving, and Beats slipped through the portal past the glass...D.C. ducked his head as he entered, followed by the rabbit man, and then they were gone...we stood in our places, uncertain what to do or what might happen next...I half expected the three of them to come back...it was hard to believe that D.C. wouldn't jump out from behind a pillar and lead us on a new triumphal march...but there was nothing else, and finally we began to turn away and make for downstairs in ones and twos. I spied Georgie walking alone, and made sure of getting into a car with him...the drive back into the city from the airport went slowly...the cars stopped all over the place, and people got in and out for reasons I couldn't understand...I just stayed put because Georgie did... the convoy broke up, but sometime much later we arrived back at the flat in Parnell. When our carload of people had been disgorged onto the footpath and I'd climbed with them through the window into the living-room, I saw that there were still plenty of partygoers about, still enjoying themselves...the big hooley hadn't ceased...but I was feeling exhausted, and I asked Georgie straight out where it was best in the house to crash... at first he turned away from me and stared off so hard at the mantelpiece that I thought he might be irritated by my question...but after a moment he swung round again and suggested using Jordan's room. 'The thing is, if someone's in bed there, he's, oh—he's in Hamilton,' Georgie said in a weary voice. 'That's for like, getting the van ready, you know what I mean?' I didn't know at all what he meant...I didn't even know who Jordan was...I just wondered where precisely Jordan's room could be, though Georgie already seemed too distracted by the other guests for me to badger him with any more questions. At last I trudged out of the living-room and up the staircase towards the bedrooms on the first floor...I tried asking a couple who were seated on the edge of the landing about Jordan and where he slept...but they were cuddling and paid me no attention...then I saw a narrow door nearby that I didn't know, at the very front of the flat, and cautiously I opened it. No one was inside...I was staring into a tiny room with a mattress in the centre of the floor and a half-open sleeping bag spread out across it...there really wasn't space for much else...some coloured candles and a sloping stack of worn-out paperbacks were the only furniture, all on the ground and shoved away in a corner...the room smelled heavily of stale beer...its bare brown walls were dank, close and more than a little confining, but I stepped in and pushed the door closed. Quickly I got down into the sleeping bag, still in my clothes, not even bothering to try and get them off...I zipped the sleeping bag up along the side and wondered if this could actually be Jordan's room...there was a lot of noise coming through the walls, and above me the ceiling looked startlingly high and distant, but I told myself that when I closed my eyes I could drift off from the sight of it...I started saying to myself, in a voice that was almost coming out of a dream, 'What a life I'm having. What a life I'm having'...but it was hard to concentrate even on anything as simple as my own words...it took no more than another moment to fall asleep.

I awoke from an inky blackness, and realised where I was and what had happened the night before...my eyes were half focused and a bad ache in my head failed to clear...after some seconds of lying very still, and next a full minute of doing nothing except easing onto my side, the sick sensation wasn't getting any better...my body kept aching with the effort of each breath and there was a foul-smelling sweat all over my skin...I found the damp, rustling nylon of the sleeping bag around me was smeared with greasepaint from my face...I spent a few minutes working to wipe the squishy bag clean, but I only made it all worse. I was glad that no one was there to watch me, but at the same time I wondered why it had to be like this...why couldn't I just be waking up after a night of passion with a beautiful woman?...why wasn't I already working on the pages of a brilliant novel?...I got to my feet in a series of unsteady movements and glanced about the narrow room...it felt a little as if it could be mid-morning, or perhaps a bit later...after some more pointless fumbling with the sleeping bag, I pulled open the bedroom door and at once sensed the house was unusually quiet. I started padding about along the corridor upstairs, hoping to find a few of the others...at first I tried just to peep round doorways discreetly, but soon I gave up and started making some noise, though each of the rooms upstairs appeared to be empty...in the master bedroom, where I'd got changed the day before, I found my jeans and T-shirt lying on the floor in a corner...I'd forgotten to take my money with me, but it was still in the back pocket of the jeans, untouched...I pulled off my costume and it was a relief to be able to put on my own clothes again. I discovered the bathroom, and there I stood over the sink and wiped away the remainder of the icky makeup... dragging my shirt up to my shoulders, I rubbed myself down with a wet towel as thoroughly as possible...I even managed to rinse most of the smelly gunge of aftershave out of my hair...the cold dripping water felt so good against the back of my neck and face that I drank some of it straight from the tap. My headache was waning by the time I clumped downstairs...I strolled along the empty hallway, still expecting to come across someone in the house...I kept calling out in a cheery manner, as if I'd just arrived, but there didn't seem to be anybody anywhere...there was only the forgotten mess from the party strewn about, bottles, glasses, dirty plates and cigarette-ends...on several parts of the floor I had to be careful where I put my feet. In the kitchen I thought maybe I could make myself some coffee, but I was interrupted by a sudden sound of heavy knocking out on the front door...I trotted through the house and hoped that some others in the flat might appear too, but I was still completely on my own...ignoring the front door like an expert, I went into the living-room and pushed up the window...there was a very tall teenager, with a long bent back and large hands, waiting before me on the porch. I could tell he was younger than I was, just an overgrown kid, despite his height...the kid had a messy bundle of dark spikey hair on top of his head that flopped into his eyes as he peered about...he had ugly blue tattoos running from his wrists along both arms, and the tatts went all the way up into the sleeves of the shabby grey T-shirt he was wearing...the kid saw me, moved a little away from the doorstep, and began rocking from side to side impatiently in the middle of the porch...he was twitching as he put his weight on one leg and then the other, but he kept his arms down and rubbed his fingers at the stitching on his jeans. 'Hey,' he grunted.

'Good morning,' I said.

The kid reacted by glancing back over his shoulder...at that moment I noticed an ancient red Zephyr was parked across the gate, with its big engine idling...the car was chock full of passengers staring out at me through the windows...I couldn't see the people in the car well, but they all looked much older and rougher than the kid before me on the porch. 'Hey, you got any gear?' the kid said. He'd turned to me again...he was leaning stiffly towards me with his arms still down at his sides. 'Gear,' he said, speaking carefully and in a low voice.

'Any what?' I asked at last.

The kid offered up a thin, nervous laugh...he glanced back over one shoulder again towards the waiting car. Next he said, 'Tents and shit.' He was staring at me hard...he'd balled his wide hands up tight into fists, and I could see pale patches along the knuckles where the blood was being forced away from his skin. He hissed at me, 'You fucking got any?' By now I had a suspicion that this was maybe about drugs.

'No,' I said. 'No, I'm sorry.'

'You sure, eh?' the kid asked. He took a brisk step towards me at the window, bent low and tried looking past me into the house...I watched him raise one arm and shade his eyes with his hand while he squinted into the dark of the living-room. He said doubtfully, 'Nothing in there?'

'Absolutely positive,' I said. 'Nobody's even here, eh.'

Immediately it occurred to me that I'd told him the wrong thing, but somehow this only helped the kid make up his mind...he swayed back from me, straightened and pivoted around on one foot...I watched

336

with relief as he stepped off the porch and strutted away down the path towards the gate as if his errand was finished. At the car the kid leaned over by the passenger window and said something to the people inside, and suddenly I felt anger coming out of the vehicle from them in waves... I wondered if I was going to end up facing the whole carload, everyone on the porch, determined to get into the flat...I looked further across the street and saw the police were gone...it was true, what I'd heard about the cops, that they were never there when you needed them...but the kid pulled open a rear door of the car and started elbowing his way in...the Zephyr sank a little on its back wheels as its engine gurgled, and it took off fast before the door was even closed. I hauled the living-room window shut and was careful to lock it tight...after that I went around the house, locking everything else...I even went upstairs and locked the first-floor windows into the bargain, and all the time I kept asking myself why no one seemed to be anywhere with me in the whole place. In the kitchen I made some coffee and carried it back towards the living-room once more...I selected the most comfortable-looking armchair in the room and sat down... after a while I thought of how a deserted flat might give me a good chance to get started on my novel...if I could only find a pen and some paper, I could get cracking right away...I got out of the armchair again and headed into the hall, feeling keyed up and ready to produce. But almost at once in the corridor I stopped by the flat's shiny grey telephone...it was attached to the passage wall, right in the centre at my shoulder height, with its long, tumbling spiral cord hanging down low...contact numbers had been scribbled at random over the brown-wrapper wallpaper around it and there was a thick, badly crumpled phone book lying in a heap on the floor beneath it...inside the book, tucked away somewhere, would have to be a number for the hotel with the Miss New Zealand contestants. I couldn't resist...I knelt and began thumbing through the coarse-grained pages for the Sheraton...it was possible, I thought, that this might not be such a good idea...my feelings about Gizi were so complicated that no one was likely to understand them...but I soon found the number, and immediately knew that I wasn't going to stop. I got up off my knees, clutching the bulky book and feeling my heart lurching in my chest...I reached for the phone's receiver and had to wedge it as best I could between my chin and shoulder while dialling...when the call was answered there was a hotel receptionist at the other end of the line, and I asked to speak to Professor Bradley Bingham...the receptionist kept wanting to know my name and what my call pertained to…I told her only that it pertained to Prof Bingham and me being real old mates…at last a peculiar, lengthy silence ensued down the line, but finally the receptionist announced that she was putting me through. I heard a buzzing sound, and then Prof Bingham's voice as he said tentatively, 'Andy.'

'Yeah, it's me,' I said.

I couldn't believe that I'd made this happen simply by dialling a number…but I was intensely aware that everything I cared about and had fretted over was going to be decided *now*, in the next few instants…I tried lowering the telephone book…it might be wise to free up my hands for holding the receiver…but the book slipped from my grip and dropped to the floor with a clatter amongst the dust by the skirting board.

'What are you—what the hell are you doing up here?' I managed to ask. 'Where's Gizi? Is she there? Is Dulcie there with her?'

'Oh, Dulcie's around,' Prof Bingham muttered. I'd forgotten how indistinctly he could talk…I jammed the receiver harder against my ear to listen to him. 'I think you should know, yeah,' he was murmuring, 'that I've just been giving out your name and description to the security guys. I guess it's all for the best really. I imagine you're more or less up to speed about Gizi's decision to break into some modelling?'

'But you weren't—' I objected.

Then I stalled in the midst of my own interruption…I wasn't up to speed.

I said, 'You were—you were just out on the West Coast.'

'Personal growth, that sort of thing. It's a mentor opportunity for yours truly, is what it is,' Prof Bingham was saying rapidly. He'd not been listening to me. He added, 'This modelling thing is a real common sideline for students, happens a lot. Take it from me, I should know.'

'But—' I started to say again.

Prof Bingham blocked me with a chuckle. 'Lucrative as all hell,' he said.

'You're not making any sense!' I shouted into the phone.

But there was no response to this except for an odd noise…Prof Bingham was muffling his receiver with his hand while he spoke to somebody else…I tried hard to hear who it might be but I could discern nothing beyond the swooshing sound of Prof Bingham's palm against the phone, and I felt painfully conscious of standing lost in a strange hallway, far from everyone…at last Prof Bingham removed his hand and he started

338

speaking to me once more in his quiet drawl. 'Andy,' he said, 'I'm afraid Gizi hasn't been entirely honest with you.'

'Is she there?' I asked.

'The point is,' Prof Bingham continued, ignoring my question, 'a while back Gizi went and entered herself in the local Miss Mount Victoria pageant. Yeah, hell of a thing—apparently it's not that hard to get into, and anyway, she won.' He chuckled once more. 'Well, you've seen her. She's kind of stunning to look at. But she didn't really want to go through with that stuff all the way to the nationals. So okey-dokey, since it was coming down to contest-time for choosing Miss Long White Cloud, she and Dulcie were planning to be a no-show, see. They were off on their way to Franz Josef when they hooked up with us. Dulcie told me the whole damn thing. So listen, what I did there, right there on my lonesome, was I persuaded Gizi to turn up for the big competition.' Prof Bingham halted, but in the silence that followed I was too surprised to protest...I didn't know about any of this, nothing, not so much as a hint...when finally I spoke, I couldn't even manage to raise my voice.

'Just like that?' I asked.

'Sure just like that,' Prof Bingham insisted. 'Flew up by charter from Grey yesterday, piece of cake. Now look, you of all people on God's little blue planet should be happy. Shit, we're going to be on television. If Gizi wins, she goes off to the Miss World in jolly old London. So I've made some calls to the right kind of guys. I've got a few Media Studies connections left that my bitch of a wife hasn't queered up. A smidgeon of this, a sprinkle of that, it's all pretty much legit. In modern life, buddy boy, it's not what you know, it's who you know. Trust me on this, I'm an educator.'

'I want to talk to Gizi,' I said over the top of Prof Bingham's idiotic mumbling.

Despite the man's patter, I wondered what he might still be keeping from me...I had no intention of trusting him on anything...vile, anxious thoughts were swirling around in my head.

'I want to talk to Gizi,' I said again.

'I mean, she's already got the sponsor and the entry money, see,' Prof Bingham was saying. He went on without a break or even a pause for breath, 'We're talking swimsuits, formal wear, we're saving the children, we're cuddling small spongy animals, it's the whole works. It's rickety-goddamn-boo. Hell, never mind if she loses, we'll still rustle up a photo-shoot contract. The fucking competition takes a week and it sure was a nick-of-time thing to get here, but these events are, you know, what do you call them—' Prof Bingham halted once more…after a few seconds it appeared obvious that he was genuinely waiting for my answer.

'I don't know,' I said at last.

Then I really could hear someone else in the room with Prof Bingham…it was definitely another person speaking some words, a phrase, softly and from a distance. 'Yeah, that's it, it's a "rort",' Prof Bingham announced to me down the phone and giggled. He said, 'But hey, in this country it's your language. I'm only trying to feel my way in.'

'Put Gizi on the line,' I interrupted.

'Oh, that wouldn't be fair to the rules of the contest,' Prof Bingham said. 'Look, I can't tell you any more, it's strictly on the hush-hush. I've signed all kinds of non-disclosure stuff.' Prof Bingham was acting unbearably smug…he sounded as if he knew his talk was made-up bullshit and felt pleased at how well it had turned out.

'I'm going to come and see Gizi,' I insisted.

'No, no, I don't think that would be a good idea. She needs to move on,' Prof Bingham said in a decisive tone. But he seemed to sense that I was going to object again and added, 'Look, honestly, the heart has its reasons and n'est-ce pas, but there's no call to go around upsetting her. I have to keep her focused before these finals, you hear what I'm saying? It's a big day. And there's not supposed to be any kind of boyfriends hanging about in any case. I'm the only guy she sees. You know, I am the motherfucking chaperone, for Christ's sake,' he finished up. Suddenly my suspicions raged inside me.

'Are you sleeping with her?' I asked.

As soon as the words were out of my mouth, I felt my own violent reaction to what I'd just said…I felt harsh, quivering chills running up and down my back. But Prof Bingham was only muttering, 'Gizi needs careful treatment, yeah. It has to be the total package, her cute side and that zip-a-dee-doo-dah wholesomeness deal. I mean, we've got to find her one of those huge stuffed pandas, I mean a really big fucker. It's all about going over well on TV. You savvy that.' But I savvied no such thing…before my eyes everything turned a lurid red.

'You better stick to Dulcie if you want to educate someone through her cunt!' I screamed down the phone. 'You leave Gizi alone! You just leave her the fuck alone! Or I'll fucking come down there and kill you!'

340

'Security, Andy, I warned you about this,' Prof Bingham said brightly. But I heard a new hard edge moving into his voice. 'You make an effort to understand here,' he said, speaking in a tone I scarcely recognised. 'Listen,' he added. 'Listen, she's over it. Be a big boy now. Jeepers-creepers, Andy, Freud was right—especially about you. She's over it.' He hung up...the phone went dead...there was no one left to argue with...at first I felt only disbelief, and I wanted to ring Prof Bingham right back and shout at him and threaten him again and this time make it work...but it was doubtful whether the hotel operator would let me through. I paced up and down across the dusty boards of the hallway...I was trying to force myself to remember everything Prof Bingham had said...but all I could think of, the sole object of importance that kept appearing to my eyes, was Gizi's pose in the newspaper...I felt a yearning for Gizi which was so strong that it broke down into an irritated, resentful impatience. I was still walking about angrily when I heard a peculiar noise, a sort of busy rattling sound, coming from the living-room...I went into the room and realised it was happening outside the house...something outside was scratching on the curtained window...at last I pulled back the drapes and found myself face-to-face with a sweaty, scarlet-cheeked man. The man was pressing his forehead up hard against the other side of the glass...he was bent over almost double, gritting his teeth and snorting...he was struggling furiously with the bottom of the window frame...I saw how his dirty, poorly crimped long hair was very blond and shook about his shoulders all the while...he was attempting to haul the lower sash up and open, and it wouldn't budge in his grip...the man glared at me with outrage in his eyes and stepped back to gesture wildly at the window's closed latch. I hesitated...I could see the man was dressed in a strange red-and-yellow silk robe which hung down to his ankles and looked a bit like some fancy bathroom get-up... he was shirtless beneath it, in just a pair of jeans, and the robe fell back and away from his shoulders to show off a well-built and smooth-skinned torso...I wondered if this could be a costume from the night before which he was still wearing for the Extravaganza...I thought that, what with the outfit and his shaggy blond hair, the man would look like quite a cool guy if he didn't act so uptight. I went on hesitating, but behind the man one or two other people were drifting up the pathway...then I noticed some cars were parked off at the kerb by the gate...the cars seemed to have just arrived, with their doors open or opening, and with even more people getting out...I unlocked the window and pushed its sash up.

'Excuse me, who are you?' I asked quickly.

The man's handsome, heavy-boned face was still flushed all over from his efforts...he stood staring at me with his mouth open...his bare barrel chest heaved as he took in a few deep breaths. 'I'm Dean,' he managed to growl. 'Who the fuck are you?' But Dean didn't bother waiting for a reply...he was already starting to climb up through the window, until with a single leg dangling inside he sat down all at once on the sill...he turned away from me, facing out towards the house's front path and gate again, and stared at the others who were coming...a scrawny, unhealthy-looking fellow holding a battered brown cardboard suitcase was stepping up next to him on the porch, and Dean said something to the man in a whisper. The man bent down low to peer in at me past Dean through the open window...he cocked his head, and I saw that the man's face was as pinched and wasted-looking as his body...he had badly cut, dark matted hair that was falling across the sallow skin on his sunken cheeks, and one of his earlobes was crammed with a line of discoloured silver studs... the man furrowed his brows and worked to gaze beyond me further into the dim room...next he stood up again, and shyly he handed Dean the suitcase...something, an intuition, made me certain that this new man was Jordan. With the suitcase in his grip, Dean stepped down into the living-room and marched straight past me as if I simply wasn't there, heading for the hall...he brushed back one side of his robe with his free hand as he went, like someone utterly confident in the power of his own presence...I turned from watching him and saw Jordan was manoeuvring his angular body with care through the window...there were others gathered waiting out on the porch and path, more and more of them, and it was a relief to notice Sammy and Georgie among the crowd...in a few minutes the living-room started to fill up with people...everyone was talking excitedly about the van. Dean returned from somewhere off in the hallway...he announced that it felt bloody good to be back...he stood in the centre of the living-room and rubbed his naked chest with satisfaction in front of the assembled group...he seemed convinced that this news was going to make everybody pleased...then he noticed me again and shuffled forwards to within a few feet of me...Dean made a point of staring at me slowly, up and down, and after a moment he asked if I played an instrument.

'Not my thing,' I said. 'I'm a writer.'

People were watching us...I realised that this was the first time I'd

342

told everybody in the flat about me being a fledgling author...up until then they'd all assumed I was a drug dealer. 'So, you mean that's like lyrics and stuff?' Dean was asking.

'No. Novels and stuff,' I said.

All around me no one appeared to show the slightest enthusiasm, though it was hard to imagine that they couldn't be interested.

'Only trouble is,' I said, 'I haven't ever written a word, eh, and I've really got no idea what to write about.'

My honesty struck me as refreshing, but Dean merely arched his neck and grunted...I decided I'd been wise to dislike him in advance. 'Well, nothing good's ever come out of a book,' Dean snapped, as if the matter was now closed. But he took a step nearer and went on talking anyway. 'You know what your problem is, mate,' he said, staring into my eyes, 'you want to find out something more about the fucking real world. Yeah, that's what you need a crash course all about. Bloody write down something real, eh.' Dean broke off and glanced solemnly around the room, as though to make sure that he'd mustered each and every last person's attention. 'Look at this,' he said suddenly, 'if you want to write yourself a bloody story.' Dean pulled up the left sleeve of his robe and raised his arm towards me, so that the robe's soft, glossy material bunched thinly along his bicep...on display for everyone to see was the inside of his exposed forearm, looking yellow and bruised...despite how close we were already standing, I leaned in and tried peering a little closer...Dean's forearm was lined with a lengthy series of blue-tinged puncture-marks, and there was an ugly, pus-filled lump up near his elbow...I could sense shock radiating from some of the others around me in the room...I made a supreme effort and kept myself gazing impassively at Dean's disgusting arm.

'That looks painful,' I managed to say at last.

'A wee mistake,' Dean said. His tone had a blunt pride to it that felt a bit forced...I supposed he was referring to the lump's pus-jammed mess, but it wouldn't really have been a stretch to imagine that he meant the whole arm...I straightened up, and Dean lowered his arm to his side. 'Now,' he said directly to me in a quiet voice, 'I want you to leave this room and get entirely away from a whole lot of stuff that doesn't concern you, boy, while we sort a few shit-serious things out.' 'No offence, eh,' Jordan chipped in from nearby. I turned and saw that Jordan was looking at me nervously, as if he'd dared speak when he shouldn't...then I spun round and hurried for the hallway, and there was an immediate and furious eruption of talk behind me...out in the corridor I realised my face was red with blushing...but as I reached the dining-room, I could still hear Georgie's voice...I turned again, and saw that he and Sammy had followed me along the passage. 'Listen—it's—oh bugger, I knew it,' Georgie was saying to her as they entered the dining-room. 'I knew it!' he repeated with vehemence. 'Well, he told me he got something for three hundred bucks,' Sammy replied quickly. 'That's what he said, and that's two and a half thou to flog off.' But Georgie was grumbling, 'I thought— oh, it can't be—fuck, it's just dope.' Georgie pulled a chair towards him from the dining-table with a swift, angry motion and sat down...Sammy and I then did the same and settled opposite him...I felt pleased to have the two of them there with me, but they continued with their conversation as if scarcely even registering my presence. 'He'll stick it up the chimney, that's what I reckon,' Sammy was saying to Georgie, 'and he'll just stockpile it for Nambassa.' But Georgie went on grumbling to himself about dope and finally Sammy appeared to lose patience...she pushed back her chair, took hold of the edge of the table and got to her feet once more...she glared at us both and growled that we were useless...next she stalked off into the kitchen, and I heard her start messing about with a clatter and bustle in the other room...a few moments later, she stuck her head out towards us through the kitchen doorway. 'Don't go lighting any fires,' she barked. I wanted to promise her that I wouldn't, but Georgie folded his arms and looked so glum that I thought it best to keep quiet... Sammy retreated into the kitchen and went back to whatever she was doing...there was the squeaky sound of a tap turning. From a distance I heard Sammy say clearly, 'You know, I wish D.C. would give us a ring, eh. Or Beats.'

'D.C. told us he'd send a postcard,' I called towards the kitchen, trying to get myself included.

But Sammy only muttered something inaudible in response...after a few minutes, several of the others from the front of the house came into the dining-room and joined us, and I supposed the shit-serious things had got themselves sorted out...by this stage everyone seemed to be making a big effort at being cheerful, and people were lighting cigarettes and making hearty jokes...more and more people kept coming through the doorway...a plump man wearing a loose green tank top, baggy shorts and a pair of jandals walked in, and the whole room welcomed him as though he was just the person we'd been waiting for. Sammy shuffled out of the

344

kitchen...she was smiling now and had a large number of steaming grey tea mugs gripped unsteadily in both hands...she was stooping to try and prevent them from spilling...the warm, milky smell of the tea spread around the room, and everybody appeared delighted and made space for Sammy while she advanced towards the dining-table. Georgie reached out when the cups were put onto the tabletop in front of him...he pushed one across to me...immediately I was so happy that, when a lot of people began jostling past me to grab for the remaining tea mugs, I didn't mind a bit. Lonno came in...he announced that Jim and Sharon had arrived...he sounded very satisfied and surveyed the entire scene before him with a broad grin on his face...from the far side of the house I could hear some music starting up on the stereo and the steady, hefty beat of the base came thumping through the walls...it felt a lot as if another party was developing. The mess of dirty plates and cigarette packets by my elbow didn't look so bad any longer, and nor did the fag-ends scuffed into streaks of ash on the floor...I turned a bit in my chair and watched a girl not far off who was breaking into a quirky little dance beside her group of friends...Georgie began to explain something to me over the growing hubbub, but it was only gossip about the wife of the man in shorts and jandals...Georgie told me the man's wife was pregnant, and she'd been going to the doctor and had some sort of problem or other with her blood pressure, but he wasn't too sure...in any case I wasn't really listening, or even touching the mug of tea cooling in front of me...that was because I was experiencing a fresh new burst of inspiration. My new inspiration was as clear and crisp as the one I'd had at the dinner-table in Palmy...the old one seemed such a long time ago that I'd almost forgotten how suddenly it had flooded my mind with a warm flow of ideas, but I understood now, all at once, what I could write about...the very thing was settled...it was even better than settled, it was perfect, and it occupied my whole head...I was going to write about television. I could remember how TV had come to us in Palmerston North...television had started up first in Wellington on WNTV1, at a time back when I was just a kid...but for a good while it was unavailable in Palmy because the ranges were still blocking the signal. An Australian man was living with his family in a house down the right-of-way behind us...his name was Joe Brighton... the Brightons had a TV set that they'd brought with them when they moved across from Sydney, and they couldn't bear all the waiting around over a problem from a few bloody hills...Joe Brighton decided that the answer was he'd build himself an aerial, and he told everyone in the neighbourhood about the job...he'd build a fifty-foot tower in his back yard and he'd put the TV antenna on top...that'd be a pretty decent aerial, he reckoned, but the only thing was he'd need a spot of help. Thinking back, I could easily recall some useful details, like the rattle of the metal pipes that Joe Brighton bought for constructing his tower...they were delivered by a truck down the right-of-way beside our house one morning, clanking on the truck's tray and waking everyone up...there were several large piles of them, the silvery pipes, spread out in heaps in the Brightons' back yard...the Brightons' long back lawn ran down to some gum trees at the edge of the local golf course, so there was plenty of space...I even had a thin picture in my mind of men from the surrounding houses, gathered on the grass by the early afternoon of the appointed day and looking ready to get stuck in. I could imagine my father at our kitchen doorstep...I had the feeling that actually he wasn't too keen...he was giving my mother a quick kiss on the cheek and saying that he'd better go and do his bit, before slowly he disappeared off down the drive...but that same afternoon all of us neighbourhood kids sloped over to the Brightons' house without ever being asked...we didn't want to miss the excitement, and we trailed about here and there in the back yard...we avoided the places in the grass that had prickles and were secretly thrilled when told to get out of the way. Finally we collected under the washing-line, where we were allowed to watch...we saw the men hoisting the heavy pipes up from the stacks onto their shoulders...the men had to jiggle to get a proper grip round the metal with their strong, sunburned arms...they were swearing, and hollow mechanical noises rang everywhere...they carried the pipes about and laid them in rows along the brown summer lawn. Joe Brighton was across the yard and at work, bent down on one knee to brace himself...he was welding everything together with an acetylene torch, and an assistant kept the gas cylinders propped up behind him and turned on...Joe Brighton was wearing gloves and goggles, and blue sparks jumped about near his face...meanwhile our mothers appeared, bringing tea and plates full of cakes and snacks...a few of the women waved their arms to shoo us around, and we were warned on no account ever to gaze at the welding's harsh blue flame. At last the tower was ready to be hauled up with ropes... there was a lot of shouting, and no end of complaints and giving directions and getting people into position...the men pulled on the ropes, heaving in rows on cue...the bloody thing weighed a ton...we heard the awful sound

346

of the metal groaning under stress as it rose up, and then the whole structure fell back across a hard patch of ground to our cries of dismay. But finally, towards the end of the afternoon, the long gangling tower was up high and straight...it kept wobbling dangerously until it was held fast with wires...the wires were pegged all around the base, and in the breeze they rippled and creaked...I thought the aerial looked like a scaly, silvery metal fish gobbling upwards, trying with its snout to escape through a net...I was never really sure why I thought so, because in my mind now it didn't resemble a fish at all, but back then I'd been very young. By this time the daylight was almost gone and we were hungry...we ate saveloys with tomato sauce in the gloom of the long shadows...somebody put on the rear lights of the house to help us see...when the saveloys and the remaining slices of cake and the chippies and biscuits were finished off, we crammed into the Brightons' living-room, everyone, the entire neighbourhood, to watch television. In the severely limited space before the set we little kids had to sit or squat hunched low at the front...the taller people had to scoot by themselves all the way to the back of the crowd...we peeped over each other's shoulders, grown-ups and children, and some grainy pictures started to flicker across the tiny screen. A few months later the new transmitter opened at Aokautere, and the new signal was so powerful that we didn't even need an aerial...a skinny strip of plastic wire down one side of the house did the trick...after that, we kids spent most of our evenings in the neighbouring homes that had TVs, camped out in other people's living-rooms, watching everything...but gradually the novelty wore off as each family saved up and bought a set. In my mind the story felt bright with its own heat...I tried to push myself and build it up further by thinking of a title, but all I could manage for a silly, giggly instant was *The Charterhouse of Palmy*...at last I decided that *Strange Fish* would sound more like literature...I wasn't sure if *Strange Fish* would be a novel, but it was exciting to imagine the bulk of the thing already written...I could see it making the light of day in print, its title running in big bold letters across the cover...all that was necessary was to open the book, press back the crisp, fresh pages and find the words. An impulse rose within me to tell Sammy that I'd just written my first masterpiece...I looked about for her among the others in the dining-room, but Sammy had disappeared and no one else around me seemed to realise they were witnessing a major artistic event...I supposed I'd better find somewhere, and soon, to do my actual writing...all at once I was tired of these people constricting me, so I got up and elbowed my way through the party's hoi polloi to the front of the house...in the living-room amidst the noise and activity no one seemed to have the slightest interest in what might be hidden up the chimney...no one knew anything of the story gradually losing its lustre in my head. I hesitated, and even considered trying to find a quiet pozzie upstairs, but after a moment I climbed out of the window and onto the empty porch...the police car was back in position on the opposite side of the road...I offered a friendly wave to the car, which looked a bit lost on its own there by the kerb...I tried to make out the stern faces of the officers inside it, but with no success, and then turned away and walked off down the street.

Getting into town took such a lot of time that I asked myself if there might be a shorter route somewhere, and at length it felt best just to follow my nose...after a while I stopped at a dairy to buy an exercise book and a biro, and by that stage I had no idea where I was...I crossed a park with a ring of tall, wrinkled palm trees around a white stone fountain at the centre, and at the far end the traffic noise of the city sounded a lot nearer and more hopeful...I continued towards the hum of cars but came onto a narrow asphalt path that went down a steep slope, winding its way past a row of ancient pohutukawas planted on the hillside...the long, low-slung branches and knotty elbows of the trees leaned out and made me stoop as I walked...beneath my feet the path was buckled and uneven where the roots were forcing up the earth. On the roadway at the bottom I tried asking people how to get to the nearest public library...an elderly man told me that it was only a few blocks distant...I started in the direction he'd indicated, but then I thought that, probably, a busy public library was no place to exercise my talents...I wanted to explode and write like billyo...I'd need to be completely alone to compose...it was always so easy for art to get sidetracked, and if I didn't leap in right now my masterpiece might just never happen. I walked on further and found a main sort of street in front of me that appeared to give off a moody feel of bustle and determination...it was lined by very high, flat-roofed office buildings, some with the names of famous companies on signs above them, and with verandas and shops along the ground floors...it had a lot of cars and foot traffic, all passing me in a whooshing muddle...I joined a group of people that were halted at an intersection...on the other side of the road, past the traffic lights and in amongst the jumbled buildings, was a massive movie theatre in the old art-deco style...the theatre stood facing the street on one corner, rising up to the height of several storeys, with its long columns of windows covered in some sort of intricate, damaged beige latticework and with a large square clock set into the very top of its facade. The other people around me left the footpath when the green pedestrian light came on and they began crossing the street in a body, but I stayed waiting at the kerb…I let my eyes wander all over the frontage of the cinema building…its veranda, running along two streets, met on the corner with a peculiar upward curl which displayed a half-peeled-off hoarding just above the empty entrance area…below were some glass main doors that had worn handrails, rows of faded posters in rusting frames that were bolted to the walls, and a black sandwich board with matinee prices on it in yellow chalk…the whole rinky-dink edifice looked sad and forlorn…but then I had yet another brilliant idea. I got across the road quickly, before the lights could change against me…at the theatre I pushed back one of the heavy glass doors and went inside…the door swung shut and I was standing in a foyer that was bare of customers, while the noises out on the street had all but disappeared…around me the air was stale and the worn red carpet under my feet smelled musty, but I took my bearings, shuffled further in and kept as far as possible from the ticket booth in one corner…behind its window I could see an old biddy was sitting, slumped half away from the counter with her long, wrinkled neck bent and her head down…she was making a slow, sputtering sound with her lips that might just have been a snore. I went on slinking across the carpet…all the dim lighting around me showed up only the faded lower walls, but the foyer looked to be a garish, golden-coloured mess of over-fancy decor and the place felt pleasant and almost familiar…it was much like the Regent in Palmerston North. Still the snoring old dear slumped in her ticket booth did nothing to stop me…I passed a snack bar with no one behind the counter…a scribbled-on piece of cardboard Sellotaped to the display-case offered me ice-cream in a tub or a cone…I was approaching a huge, carved staircase at the far end of the foyer…the stairs were roped off from use and the broken steps rose upwards into total darkness, but I turned instead at a poorly-lit overhead sign and wandered down a side-corridor for the toilets. The gents was also deserted when I walked in…I saw the old-fashioned lighting up in the low ceiling was good, but everything around me, the line of sinks, the stainless-steel urinal and the row of stalls, appeared clammy with damp… instinctively I held my new exercise book and biro clutched safe to my chest...I checked each of the grimy, tiled stalls, chose the tidiest one, got in and then locked the door. I sat on the plastic toilet seat in my jeans... the seat was badly fixed and slid a little under me...it felt cold and hard, but the discomfort was nothing and I balanced the exercise book open across my knees...now at last, I thought in triumph, after such a lot of delay I was ready to begin my writing. A bit of muffled sound rumbled somewhere above my head, which had to be from whatever movie was screening...it would have been nice, I supposed, to have brought along an ice-cream...I stared for a few seconds at the door shut so close in front of my face...it was covered with obscene writing in various colours...it had scrawled, scratchy pictures of crude penises and vaginas...I forced myself to ignore them and to concentrate. After a minute or so, I wrote the title of my story into the exercise book...next I tried to think of the first sentence to put down...I was a little disconcerted at the number of variations available, and it seemed important to get all of them in equally... for a while I thought of my favourite television programme from when I'd first started going round to watch TV each evening at the Brightons' house...the show was called *Stingray*, with Troy Tempest, and it was made using only marionettes...Troy and his string-controlled friends defended the world against the evil Aquaphibians. I knew that the puppets on the screen weren't real, but at the time I'd thought all the details in the programme must actually exist somewhere...as a result there must be complete, detailed lives for all of the characters...they might be puppets, but the characters had to be living in a whole world of their own of which I could glimpse only excerpts...I'd never considered there could be any other way for the story to happen...Commander Shore might instruct Troy Tempest to search through area-code 45-blue, but that meant the show's makers must have segmented the entire earth's surface into a real grid, with real maps and data...anything else would have been too obvious, too cheap, to be so convincing. I gave up thinking about *Stingray* and waited for my head to clear...slowly I wrote a few sentences on the unsteady page, putting down whatever came to mind...back during my moment of razzle-dazzle inspiration, I'd imagined my story all finished... reconstructing it was going to be hard, but I told myself not to worry too much...I was just warming up at becoming an extraordinary person...I was still auditioning for immortality. I searched my mind and wrote on until I'd almost reached the bottom of the page, but then I sat, stymied, and chewed at the hard plastic end of the pen...this was beginning to fee

350

a lot like homework…I decided it would be best, probably, to read through what I'd composed, but when I ran my eyes over the words they were strange and disappointing…they were words, and didn't convey any experience of Joe Brighton and the men and the antenna tower…they didn't even properly match my memory…they were just words. I wondered how I was going to get the tower into the story so that it didn't seem like any kind of flimflam…it occurred to me that this might not even be possible…I felt a sense of panic rising at the base of my throat…then I heard the noise of somebody else coming into the toilets. There were two voices, whispering not far away, somewhere just beyond my stall…it was an odd thing to be sitting down in a toilet with my pants up and a book propped open on my knees, and I felt more than a little guilty…I had no idea how to explain myself and worried that at any instant I might have to…the door of a nearby stall creaked open and was shut again with a dull bang…there was some shushing and an excited giggle…one of the voices was a woman's. I heard some hurried pushing and bumping from the pair moving about, and they were both breathing heavily…after a moment or so the woman commenced moaning…my cheeks reddened with a mixture of pleasure and shame, and I wondered if other authors faced these types of problems when they got into a new novel…there were a number of intense slobbering noises, alarmingly close, and then the shock of something colliding with a wall near me as the woman began whimpering 'Fuck me, fuck me!' over and over again…I didn't think it would be a good thing to get caught like this…my cock was already becoming excited, and that didn't feel like a good thing either. I held my breath and decided to take a chance on leaving…I stood up quietly, and by the time I'd got out of the stall into the washbasin area the loose lock on the door to the couple's own stall was quivering and rattling…suddenly the entire door itself began to thump hard and I could see it smacking against its frame to an accelerating rhythm…at least the whole feverish racket gave me a minute to rinse my hands in a sink before going.

I wandered the streets outside for a bit…I thought of Mrs Macalister and made sure I got something to eat, but at last I couldn't help myself and started walking for the Sheraton…several times I asked myself angrily just what in the world I wanted by going there, though I didn't seem to have any sort of answer…to find the way I had to approach and quiz random people, but pretty much everyone I questioned appeared to keep pointing off in the same direction…for a long while I went on padding uphill beside a broad road with the whining sound of cars rushing past over the rough seal...my exercise book stayed gripped in one sweaty hand with my fingers staining the cover, but I marched on until finally I saw the hotel's round logo at the top of a tall building in the near distance and picked up my pace. When I got to the hotel, I saw it was a swanky affair...it was a shiny steel-and-glass tower, with a short, curved cement driveway that swept up to a covered entrance area at its base...there were shrub-filled ornamental gardens, green and bushy, planted in the narrow space along the hotel's frontage next to the ground-floor windows...I started up the drive, and the wide white veranda out from the forecourt soon extended itself over me...under the shadows of the veranda was a line of waiting cars, each of which looked expensive, with a number of taxis idling amongst them ready for hire. As I came up the drive and drew closer, I noticed some sort of doorman in a uniform who was loitering to one side of the revolving door at the entrance...his red, braided topcoat looked heavy for the warm weather, and he stood with his hands clasped lazily in front of his stomach...I wondered if maybe he'd try and stop me...the man couldn't possibly mistake me for a guest and perhaps he'd even been alerted to keep a watch out for someone suspicious...my clothes were filthy, and all of a sudden I was painfully aware of them and how my left eye was still black and easy to discern. I spied a middle-aged couple just up ahead, climbing out of a taxi...the man, overfed and with a florid face, was saying something pointed to the woman in a kind of good-natured argument as the taxi driver went trotting round to the boot to fetch their suitcases...I proceeded up alongside the doorman but he didn't move at all, or perhaps gave me only the merest nod...I passed him and pushed my way in through the swishing, revolving doors, and an instant later I was safe in the broad open space of the lobby...then I paused, and sensed my newfound luck beginning to drain away again. The lobby was immaculately decorated and my battered sandshoes looked dreadful on the soft, patterned grey carpet...my T-shirt and jeans were all wrong too...they were in stark contrast to what I could see around me, the sombre timber-panelled walls, some heavily upholstered red chairs, the discreet entrances off to corridors and the shiny lift area with its metal doors...behind a high row of check-in counters across the room a youngish woman stood dressed in navy-blue business attire, and she was watching my movements...I wished that I was better turned out, or at least carrying Half-Arse instead of a scungy exercise book...I was

352

only now aware of soft soothing background music coming from somewhere up above my head, and it wasn't doing its job of soothing me at all. The woman at the check-in was using one small hand to adjust her gold-rimmed glasses, not dropping her gaze from me, while she leaned towards a doorway behind her and tugged at the sleeve of a fellow in an official-looking blazer...I swivelled hard on one foot, leaving an indent in the spongy Axminster, and turned away across the lobby...I put a serious expression on my face and strode like a man in a hurry past a lot of people toting suitcases...there was some crowd noise coming from the direction of a nearby corridor and so I headed for it, marching into the corridor as if that noise was somewhere I should definitely be...nobody came after me from the check-in area. Several moments later I'd passed down to the far end of the passage, and on rounding the corner I at once discovered a large, loosely packed group of people...they were milling about by the open entrance-doors of what appeared to be a hotel banquet hall...there was quite a racket coming from the heavily-amplified sound of a public address system within...the people in the doorway were standing at the very back of whatever was going on inside, and they were having trouble seeing...most were craning their necks and trying to gaze over the tightly-jammed throng standing in the hall further in front of them. I stood on tiptoe and got a peek at the banquet hall's interior...there was little I could see except a very large, densely packed room...a dull chill wafted towards me from the ceiling fans, drifting over the tops of people's heads and ruffling their hair...a tall, flustered-looking man came wriggling out through the crammed-up doorway, trying at the same time to wrestle a film cartridge from the back of an open camera...the man freed himself from the assembled spectators and hurried past me...he was still struggling with the camera's mechanism, and when he saw I was watching he confided 'Bloody thing' to me with an odd, satisfied snarl. I began to work at pushing a path for myself into the room...the going was slow, but a sudden intuition entered my mind that the universe was guiding me... this absolutely had to be the right place at the Sheraton for what I was seeking...I started using my elbows and shoulders and murmured polite excuses...it was much too noisy with excited chatter from the sound system for anyone to hear me, but I just went on pushing and apologising. Soon I could see across to the far side of the long hall...it meant peering past a jumble of the necks and heads of other people in amidst the smell of perspiring bodies, but I kept wedging myself forwards...up front above the crowd I could make out a short man, facing everyone, who was clad in a tight brown-plaid leisure suit…he had bushy, curly hair and a moustache, and he kept shouting for all he was worth into a silvery, hand-held microphone…the man was standing in partial view on top of one corner of some sort of makeshift stage…it was a wide but very narrow strip of wooden platform, extending back only a few feet, which was set up before a pleated blue curtain that covered the entire rear of the room. The man was making jerky, expansive gestures with one arm and his steady flow of banter kept on booming through the sound system above…I supposed that probably he was a master of ceremonies…I forced my way still nearer, threading into gaps between people, and saw the words 'Miss New Zealand' printed across a large white cardboard sign pinned to the back curtain…then I saw there were also other persons up on the stage, the contestants, all standing well apart from the man and gathered in one corner at the far side…suddenly I felt as excited and nervous as everyone else. The crowd was a bit thinner now near the front of the room, and I found it easier to move and see things…I watched three markedly overdressed girls in the process of heading self-consciously across the stage towards the MC…two of them were wearing loose, roll-necked tops under long suede jackets, with elaborately ruffled skirts, and one was in a pink paisley jumpsuit…the girls were each walking in high heels…they swung their legs but stepped warily across the constricted space available on the stage, and I wondered if the real contest was not to fall off the platform. 'Look at them, ladies and gentlemen, a big hand,' the MC announced more clearly now. 'They're like hokey pokey ice cream, these girls, ladies and gentlemen, you just want to scoop them up and lick them down.' The MC laughed with a nasal snort at his own ugly joke. 'A big hand,' he repeated. 'Come on, folks. Let's welcome these ladies. Aren't they lovely, eh? The only thing that's wrong with them is they've still got their clothes on.' People around me were actually starting to laugh at this rubbish, and I felt sorry that the contestants had to suffer it…the three girls had stopped near the centre of the stage, almost in unison, and turned sideways on to the crowd…next all of three them posed with their hips cocked and their hands on the edges of their buttocks…only one had made up her mind to smile…some flashbulbs went off from somewhere in front of me and the room broke into scattered, distracted applause while the MC offered up an oily smirk but didn't even pause from his gabbling. At the far end of the stage I could see the remainder of the

354

contestants were still waiting their turns...they were bunched up into an untidy group and I thought that Gizi had to be there, someplace amongst them...one more girl detached herself from the group and sauntered, pouting, across the platform towards the centre...the MC began introducing her, but mostly he went on acting pleased with his own performance...I saw that down on the floor nearby two hefty-looking security men were standing in the tight, navy-blue buttoned-up jackets of their uniforms, with neckties around their bulging collars and peaked caps balanced on their heads. The girls who were still waiting at the far edge of the stage stayed jammed together in their narrow cluster, glancing at each other nervously, while some were trying to whisper remarks into each other's ears...but there was one girl a bit off to the side on the platform, very dressed up and wearing a bulky, ankle-length brown fur coat which she held wrapped shut in front of her with her hands thrust into the pockets...she was in jeans and black leather boots, and she was standing up straight in the long coat with her feet planted solidly apart...a black Spanish hat with a red band was on the girl's head, and her hair was tied up and pinned beneath it...the hat made the girl look exotic, and I felt she surely must be Gizi and pushed closer. For a horrid second I still couldn't tell if it was really her, but then she tightened her lips, compressing them hard against her closed mouth in a way I'd seen Gizi do before, and I was certain...my heart felt as though it might burst inside my chest from aching...immediately I was desperate to catch her attention...the sound system gave a loud squawk of feedback...it spilled out across the air and jolted the entire room, but the MC put on a smug grin and looked about at us, acting as if it was all part of the show...he pretended to adjust one of the wide lapels on his jacket before continuing.

'Gizi,' I said hesitantly. 'Gizi.'

I wasn't certain if she'd heard me up there on the platform...Gizi seemed all composure...a strong calm was arranged on every feature of her beautiful face...she appeared to be gazing in my direction with a questioning, superior look...the MC had brought one of the girls from centre-stage over beside him and was attempting to interview her...his words were interrupted by a quick, blinding flurry of flash photos.

'Gizi!' I shouted. 'Gizi!'

A few people around me were shifting in irritation...I didn't care...I thought I'd better try calling out her name some more and a lot louder, but I could see Gizi turning herself a little towards me, aware of my presence...

355

she was keeping her hands still pushed well down into the pockets of her coat…she half lowered her head and fixed me with mocking eyes, and then I didn't want to call her name any longer…she seemed to gaze right through me as if I just wasn't there, and for a moment it even felt as if my whole self, Andrew Murray Ingle, might not exist anymore in the world. But the ugly spell was broken by Prof Bingham's bald head coming into view…he was nearby on my left side, with his fat body jiggling about in the crowd…I saw that he was starting to raise his arms…he had them up in the air and kept pointing down over people at me with both hands… the sleeves of his jacket were riding back along his short, plump wrists, and he stared at me and looked away several times, jerking his neck and nodding…at first I supposed it was some kind of greeting, but soon I realised he was signalling as hard as he could to the security men. One of the guards had begun shoving his way towards me through the throng… it was difficult for the guard to manoeuvre with his cumbersome frame, and I saw him even ducking his head a little so that his cap wouldn't block anybody's view…I should have tried to go at once, but I already felt too crushed inside to worry much about whatever might happen next.

'Gizi!' I bawled as loudly as I could, to the girl that I'd loved back in Greymouth.

The security guard was already up close to me…he caught hold of my arm and, with a violent wrench to my shoulder, hauled me sideways until I almost fell on him…the guard dragged me off in his direction amongst the crowd…I stumbled along as compliantly as possible, but my feet kept leaving the floor in the tight space…the guard paid no attention and went on dragging me behind him willy-nilly. People were struggling to get themselves out of our path, but my mind was mostly elsewhere…all I could think of was how Gizi had ignored me…the guard hauled me through the crowd towards one side of the room…there was the covered-up counter of a serving area before us, and I could recognise the jutting shapes of beer taps beneath the spread of a white cotton sheet as the guard shoved me past…a narrow emergency exit was in the wall beside us, with a crash bar for a quick passage out, and the guard pressed the crash bar down with a slap…he rammed me forwards through the doorway as soon as a space opened up. My shoulder hit the doorframe hard as I went on by, but now we were standing outside amid low piles of torn paper-rubbish bags in a small service alley…the exit door fell shut again, and suddenly the PA system sounded muffled and far off…I watched the guard brush

356

down his rumpled tie with the palm of his free hand…with the other hand he was still firmly gripping my arm…he had dark, tired rings below his eyes…I could see where the stiff white collar of his shirt was chafing his thick neck. 'Stay the fuck away from the girls, you perv,' he hissed at me. I nodded my head vigorously at this…it was meant to indicate that I didn't want any kind of trouble and I certainly didn't want to be any sort of perv…but the guard pressed my back up against the rough, concrete-covered wall of the alley…he let go of my arm and took a moment to brace himself with his legs well apart…next he paused to hitch up his belt and then merely waited, squaring his shoulders, but I knew he was going to hit me and even I could tell it would be a thoroughly good idea…I didn't see much point in trying to negotiate an exemption. After another moment or so the guard laid into me with an efficient jab to the stomach and a clip to the temple…the second blow, coming at me stale and a bit lackadaisical, was still enough to knock me right off my feet…it hurt most where it connected with my old bruises…I started picking myself up from the asphalt, and the side of a rubbish bag proved handy for support…I reckoned that I was getting used to this. I straightened myself up as far as I dared…the guard didn't look as if he intended to hit me again, but in case I was wrong I began tottering away…all the while the guard yelled at my back that I better get the fuck off out of things and never show my fucking face round here again. The alley led onto the street near the front of the hotel, and I saw that the sky had clouded over and the sun was beginning to go down…my shadow, cast by the swill of low light onto the uneven cracks on the footpath, was deep and long…my hands were empty and this was somehow odd, until I guessed all at once that I must have dropped the exercise book behind me. It came as a shock…I struggled to remember the last time I'd been holding the book…that time was probably back somewhere in the banquet hall…but on second thoughts it didn't really seem like much of a loss…there was nowhere left to go and get the fuck off out of things to, nowhere except Parnell, and so I made my way in the likely direction of the flat, still feeling leaden and disappointed.

The sun had long since set, leaving everything on the roads to darkness and the fuzzy glow of streetlamps, when finally I approached the flat…I stepped up onto the dim, familiar front porch with a sense of relief…the lower sash of the window nearby was open, with just the drapes closed…from inside I could hear the stereo was on but turned well down, and there was a distinct buzz of urgent talk. I reached in through the window and pulled back the curtain...the brightness of the living-room lights hurt my eyes and it was no great surprise to find the place busy with people and activity, but suddenly I felt very tired...I was in the wrong sort of mood for this, though I commenced climbing up over the windowsill...bits of me still ached, and not always where I expected...but as I got both feet down onto the floor of the room, everywhere about me the atmosphere appeared to be somehow strained. I stood quiet, waiting for a moment and surveying the crowd of guests...then the curtain was tugged aside behind me again and other people were trying to get in, so I shuffled out of their way...I could sense now that the whole house, not just the living-room, was chock-a-block with partygoers and that a peculiar vibe was definitely coming from the people all around me...I passed a chubby-faced, bearded man wearing a woollen hat, who held out a half-full wine glass towards me...he was standing with one arm resting up along the mantelpiece while leaning his back comfortably against the wall...the glass in his hand looked like his own and I tried to refuse it, but he nodded in a cheerful fashion down in the direction of the floor, where several long-necked flagons of wine were lined up in a row. The man started speaking to me about the cops and the flat and the whole afternoon stuff...he was talking in a confident way, as if I was already in the know...I tried pretending I was, but couldn't keep things up for long...even so, when the man understood that I knew nothing, it only made him all the keener to talk. He said two uniformed cops, that very afternoon, had walked up the pathway of the flat...they were bold as you please...they'd just clambered in through the open window with no warning...they'd stepped right into the midst of a hectic party, and it was quite a sight...for what seemed a long, long time the cops had waited in the living-room, with stupefied freaks and heads and fuckwits all staring at them, these two cops, standing together in their nicely starched uniforms...then the pair of them quietly put on their caps. I listened to the man telling me this, but other people at my elbow were interrupting with their own versions of the story...suddenly I understood at last that all the conversations in the room were on exactly this same topic...somebody took over explaining how one cop had simply walked up to Jordan in the frightened crowd and ordered him, by name, to come outside...someone else said that Jordan followed the cop away like a little lost lamb...but the other cop had marched off into the house, strolling forwards along the corridor with

358

nothing but silence and a stunned paralysis everywhere around him...he went through to the kitchen, keeping his head up and not seeming to look about, until finally he spotted Dean, who was standing next to the sink with a cigarette in one hand. The cop announced, 'You know me, don't you.' He stepped closer. Dean struggled to whisper back, 'I don't think so.' The policeman put a large, steady hand up onto Dean's shoulder... after a moment he led Dean out through the back door of the kitchen, and they went down past the side of the house to the front path...Jordan was waiting with the other cop, and there was a patrol car at the gate...the policemen took them both away...I kept nodding my head at everything that was said, while the story was starting to be repeated by others around me. 'Anyhow, Deano's back,' the chubby man in the woollen hat said near my face. 'Already.' He gestured in the direction of the crowded hallway. 'Been there, done that,' he laughed. I grinned as though I was in on the joke, then headed off for the corridor and slipped further into the house...I was still clutching my borrowed wine glass...the dining-room, when I got to it, was so jam-packed that I had to squeeze past bodies and ingratiate myself just to get in, but Moondog and Georgie were there among the swell of people...Moondog's sunburned face looked drawn and showed that he was preoccupied. Dean was holding court...I shifted to find a better view and saw he was sitting, half reclining, on a chair by the table... he had his back propped against the support of the wooden wainscot...he kept one foot up and resting on the knee of his other leg, as if he needed a lot of valuable space to relax...Dean seemed in the midst of a monologue...his silken robe was pulled open from his bare chest and his head lolled casually as he talked. 'Yeah, they reckoned they could get a warrant inside of ten minutes, eh,' he was saying. 'Bring in all the drug dogs and that.' Dean spread out one of this hands on the table and examined the back of it while he continued speaking, but I thought his bored manner appeared a bit affected. He said, 'So anyway, you know, I just refused. I wouldn't give them permission, eh. And the lot of them, they all wanted to hear about the van. "How'd you pay for it?" kind of thing. "How'd you get it?" Stuff like that, just going on and on about it. "Where'd you get the money? You selling morphine?" Like I say—' Dean raised his hand to show three fingers and glanced around him '—three fellows, the whole bunch of guys in plain clothes. Yous get plenty of smokes in the interview room while you're waiting them out, eh.' Dean smiled...he turned his attention to picking his fingernails. Someone behind me piped up and asked, 'I thought they kept wanting to know if you and Jordan were addicts.' 'Yeah, well I'm not,' Dean snapped. 'All right?' For a moment I felt the atmosphere in the dining-room had become brittle, but Dean seemed to settle down again...he shrugged. He added, 'The cops, man, they were just all over the show. No lawyer, nothing. And bloody Jordan wasn't anywhere, eh. Maybe he had a separate interview or something, I don't know. But like, what they were really interested in was the van. And it was—they got me to roll up my arms.' Dean smirked. He said, 'Told them I was a diabetic, eh.' It was growing uncomfortably hot in the dining-room, and I started to leave, wedging myself out through the crush of bodies...in the hallway I overheard someone at the foot of the stairs, a tall moustachioed man, saying just how amazing the entire business was. As I sidled past, he added in a tone of authority, 'The cops, they just, like, knew everything about the layout of this place, eh. Bloody everything.' He half closed his eyes while he went on speaking. 'Like, they even told Dean who was sleeping in what rooms.' I drifted upstairs... from two or three other conversations I learned that several more cops had come into the flat soon after Dean and Jordan were taken away...the cops marched about acting angry and officious, and no one was allowed to leave the house...two of the cops had tramped around the bedrooms in big clunky policeman's boots...they'd poked their noses into everything without asking even the slightest permission, found an empty pipe and removed it in a plastic evidence bag...I heard the whole boring search had taken them over an hour, and the cops got more and more heavy as nothing special turned up, but I supposed none of them had ever considered checking in the chimney. A woman told me that Jim and Sharon had hidden themselves away inside a wardrobe, though finally they got so tired with waiting that they'd started pashing each other up... everybody appeared delighted at how hopeless the police were...a man leaning against an upstairs corridor wall kept scuffing the back of his shoes on the skirting board and saying that the cops had told Dean to get the hell out of Auckland...they'd told Dean they were sick of tailing him. '"We're sick of it, sick of tailing you!"' the man repeated with glee. Then the word came round that Jordan was back...somebody said he'd just arrived and had come in through the living-room window...at once a few of us went downstairs to find out what was going on...we stopped and told others, and soon we made up a large group...but I didn't want to be too obvious, and so when I got to the living-room I merely poked my head past the doorway from the hall. I saw Jordan in the centre of the room, standing with his hands thrust hard into the front pockets of his jeans and his shoulders bent low…gathered about him already was a crowd of people, and one or two of them were pressing him with questions…but Jordan was only insisting that he hadn't said anything to any police at the station…I noticed his face was puffy and close to tears…he kept gazing down in a grim manner at his shoes. 'Don't use the phone!' he wailed suddenly. He stole a shy glance around him and added, 'Look, they said that they're going to get us, eh. The phone, it'll—fuck, it'll be bugged.' But no one seemed frightened…Jordan was far too late returning to us… we didn't care anymore about why he'd been taken to the station or what had happened…people started to move off almost as quickly as they'd appeared, and slowly we left him alone. In the hallway the man who I'd seen kicking the skirting board upstairs came into view again dragging a chair and clutching a cardboard box full of red light bulbs under one arm…he began to get up onto the chair in front of us all and unscrew the bulb in the hall's ceiling…the frail chair shivered beneath him every time he stretched up onto his toes…he screwed in a new bulb, and immediately somebody at the end of the corridor played at turning on and off the light in a series of clicks…but the man only gathered up his stuff and shuffled away, not uttering a word…before long each of the rooms on the ground floor was washed in a dim red glow. The volume from the stereo increased and filled the place…we'd all become loose and even super-relaxed…it was as if the bust's total failure had managed to guarantee our safety, and I was really beginning to feel sorry that I'd missed it. 'Get the hell out of Auckland,' people chortled together like a mantra. Georgie started to haul his drum kit inside piece by piece from the van, carrying the parts up along the outside of the house and then in through the back door and all the way down to the living-room…several people joined him, trying to help…when it was done, I wandered into the living-room and watched Georgie assembling the clanking pieces of the kit on the floor…he was kneeling awkwardly and had a frown of great intent across his face as he managed the fiddly bolts and screws in the weak light…even before he'd finished tightening each of the lugs and knobs, a few of the guests started to bash at the kit with his sticks…most of us retreated from the room, but the dull, enthusiastic boom of Georgie's drums reached everywhere around the flat. In the dining-room I had to step past a man who was holding a big brown paper-bag open just in front of him…the bag was crammed with dope, and the man kept lifting it up near his nose and staring with delight into its contents...another man in khaki overalls and badly stained white gumboots was stalking about between the dining-room and the kitchen asking for cigarette papers. 'Let's go get stoned!' he was shouting. Within a few short minutes there were joints circulating... the smokes seemed to make the lot of us feel very active...a noisy group went dancing on the road outside the flat, and we heard them jumping and cavorting on the tarseal to the sound of their own screams and howls...a man waving a large, drooping grey branch torn from a tree appeared in the house, shaking it everyplace he walked...later I sloped off with some of the others to get fish and chips from a takeaway bar...the party kept going until well into the night. But at last the collective energy in the flat began to drain away...the dope in the bag was used up...the drum kit was abandoned and forgotten, and the long stone among the partygoers wore off...people were vanishing into the darkness outside... the remainder were nestling in comfortable spots to wait for the dawn. On the first floor I found Jordan's room was occupied...I picked my way down the staircase again, past a man who'd simply crashed on the steps as if settled for the duration and who was struggling and muttering in his sleep...then in the living-room, amidst all the guests, I spied an empty easy-chair that somebody must have vacated...it was over next to the stereo and there was music playing rather loud, but still I could scarcely believe my luck. I sat on the chair and stretched myself out with my arms spread wide...now everything was hunky dory and almost at once I dropped away into a half-doze, despite the noise...occasionally I was made aware of partygoers using the window to leave...each time they disturbed me, I wondered what kind of strange hour in the early morning it could be. But when finally I did come to, it took me several moments just to understand what had happened and that I was in a room full of people fast asleep...it was still night-time...the lights with their dreamy ruby glow were still on above me...someone lying on the floor, completely out of it, had his head up close to my feet...the needle on the stereo's stylus was scratching round and round at the end of a record. I could see Jordan's skinny frame slinking across the room from the doorway...he was not up in his bedroom, if he'd ever been there...instead he was stepping along softly and skirting the edge of the drum kit...Jordan squatted down in a crouch before the fireplace and then wriggled himself further and further forwards into the hearth. Even in the low rosy light

Jordan's features were pale…his face looked squeezed and intense with effort…his knees were splayed apart in an ungainly fashion, pressed up against the hearth tiles…one shoulder he had jammed up under the mantelpiece and he was twisting with his arm deep inside the chimney…I realised some others around me were awake and also watching…at last Jordan dragged down a bundle wrapped in a sooty cloth, and grunted from satisfaction. Still grunting, making little childish spurts of noise, Jordan moved round to rest with his back to the fireplace, jiggling in a delicate way on his haunches…he began to work at untying the rough bundle in front of him like a man who had no time to waste…he seemed to be the only one in the room who didn't understand that people were staring, but then perhaps he didn't care…the ends of the cloth fell apart and a length of discoloured rubber hose dropped out across the floor, but Jordan paid it no particular mind…his whole gaze was fixed on several small glass vials and a battered tin box…I guessed the jars must hold morphine and tried to crane my neck to see them a bit better. Jordan picked up the vials with one hand and arranged them in a neat row along the edge of the cloth, adjusting them despite all his hurry with a sort of loving attention…at last he prised open the top of the box and took out a syringe with a needle already attached…I saw that by now several other guests around me were beginning to leave the room…but Jordan ignored us and squinted hard as he commenced inserting the needle into the soft top of one of the vials…nobody tried to stop him, and he looked far too fierce to question. I wanted to stand up and go, but what Jordan was doing was fascinating…then suddenly I got to my feet anyway, and found myself awake and starting to move…I stepped round the sides of the room and out into the hall…there was a lot of furtive activity amongst people in the corridor, and I sensed our feelings of bewilderment had already spread everywhere over the flat…I went to the dining-room and stood for a while with a few partygoers who were gathered in a corner…more people came in with foggy, exhausted faces, and everyone was hissing at each other in anxious whispers. Finally I rubbed my eyes and made for the kitchen, but the door between it and the dining-room was closed tight…the door was only a thin, ledged-and-braced thing, and so I leaned myself against its flimsy boards and pushed…nothing budged…there was some kind of heavy object lodged on the other side…I pushed a lot harder, and whatever was blocking me moved until the door slid back a little…as I wormed through the gap I almost fell over a shapeless sack of potatoes still lying in my path. Sammy was sitting alone on the hardwood floor of the kitchen, down next to a cupboard under the sink, and in the red light I could see her knees were drawn up close to her chin...her large hands were raised and clasped over her face, and the tangled ringlets of her golden hair were falling down around her fingers...I thought how beautiful her hair looked, hanging loose and stained a little by the red glow...but Sammy's breathing was short and she was crying. After a moment she removed her hands and glanced up at me...she seemed from the whole expression on her face to be imploring me for comfort...I pushed the awkward door closed once more, and for good measure I even managed to shove the grimy potato sack back up against it with my foot...then I sat on the floor beside Sammy, stretching my legs out a bit, and put my arm around her...I didn't know what to say to her, but she leaned her head on my shoulder, where it felt marvellously substantial and fleshy, and she continued crying...there was no hint of movement from anyplace in the rest of the house and I thought it best to let her go on with her tears. 'They've had all this stuff,' Sammy whimpered at last, speaking somewhere down into my armpit. 'This stuff they're getting.' I still didn't know what to say that might help...I just knew that she felt warm beside me and I was sad for her...Sammy wept some more, and I wondered once again about her relationship with Dean...did she love him?...did she feel she couldn't live without him?...I knew that I could live without him, and it was a pity it didn't count. A few minutes later the slow rhythm of Sammy's crying appeared to have stopped...without thinking much, I gave her a small kiss...she kissed me gently back...it seemed like a good idea to give her another, but this other kiss felt rather different...it grew longer and more and more mutually intense, and by the end of it I was lying on top of Sammy across the narrow kitchen floor, with one shoulder pushed hard against the fridge. We had our hands all over each other...I started reaching up under Sammy's loose cotton shirt...she wasn't wearing a bra, and I touched and then cupped her breasts...they felt heavy and a little slippery, and I felt her ribs alongside them moving beneath her skin...it occurred to me that it was only yesterday or so when I'd first caught sight of Sammy...I stretched my neck and manoeuvred to kiss her plump lips once more, but she turned her head quickly away. 'Don't,' she whispered. 'Don't. I'm sorry.' My feelings were in a hubble-bubble of commotion and I needed a few seconds to take in exactly what she meant...but I admitted, with disappointment, that she meant we had to stop…only the dead weight of a sack of spuds, after all, was separating us from a room filled with people…Sammy was gazing up at me from under my chest…she had her chin pressed down into her neck. 'I've got toothache,' she mumbled, 'and kisses, yeah, they just make the pain hurt worse.' I hadn't moved while Sammy spoke…I'd kept my hands still clasped tight to her sides, but now beneath me I felt how she was beginning to shift about…she was putting her fingers in under my T-shirt…she was rubbing herself close against me, wriggling with her whole body, and she began smiling up through the curls of her hair, which lay mussed across her cheeks. 'Promise no kisses,' she murmured. I felt a deep thrill of anticipation.

'No problem,' I whispered back.

I pulled up Sammy's shirt, just as I'd always wanted to…I put my face down onto her massive breasts where they were spread out on her chest and looking pink in the light…Sammy moaned happily as I nuzzled and sucked at them…things seemed to be going rather well…after a while I kissed my way along Sammy's voluptuous midriff, over the muscles in her stomach, and headed past her little navel to the top of her jeans…she made no objection at all when I unbuttoned the waistband on her jeans and lowered the zipper. I peeled away the fly and slid my lips under the edge of Sammy's panties…she arched her back appreciatively…it was hairy and musky against my nose and lips in there, and I liked it…I tried not to let myself think about anyone else maybe interrupting us, shoving their way through the kitchen door and barging in, as I'd done…instead I drew down Sammy's jeans and underwear below her knees, and then put my head between her legs and looked around…within an instant or two I found something I remembered from all my reading of *The Little Red Schoolbook*. So, I thought, this is a clitoris. I puckered up and gave the spot an experimental peck…Sammy jumped under me as if she'd been stung by an electric shock…it was such a wonderful reaction that I went straight on kissing at the little bump…things seemed to be going a lot better than rather well…soon Sammy started to thrash about…she gripped her thighs tight round the sides of my face, raising her knees as I bent in further. Sammy's legs were rubbing against me until my cheeks were sore, and it was tough work keeping my lips on target…I stayed pressed as close as I could and at last Sammy grabbed my head with both hands…she tore hard at my hair…it hurt my scalp, and I paused and looked up…perhaps she meant somebody was opening the kitchen door. 'Don't stop now!' Sammy yelped. I didn't...I kept on going...but soon Sammy let out a series of huge, wrenching sighs and went limp...I collapsed as well, feeling as if I'd been in a wrestling match. 'You sweet man, you,' I heard Sammy murmuring. She slid herself apart from me, and then drew her panties and jeans most of the way up her legs with a deft heave...she shifted and squirmed slightly to get everything pulled up over her bottom...after a moment I watched her struggle at closing the waistband. 'Don't tell Dean,' she whispered as her fingers worked at the button in the waistband's fastener. I nodded my head...Sammy finished doing herself up and got to her feet, standing right above me...she spent another few moments adjusting her clothes...finally she stepped over to the kitchen door and dragged it open with a grunt. From my place down on the floor beside the fridge, I heard Sammy call something cheery past the threshold to the people in the other room...she shuffled forwards and left me, and I found myself genuinely hoping she felt better...Sammy was careful to pull the door shut behind her as she went out...I wasn't sure what to do next, but I didn't much care now if anyone wandered in or not...the wooden planks under me had developed a new and comfortable feel...I stretched, closed my eyes and after a minute fell sleep without the merest trouble.

I woke up later, still lying sprawled on the solid kitchen floor...sharp sunlight from the windows was shining all over me as though it were being tipped into the room out of a bucket...my back was stiff...I was aware of somebody beating Georgie's drums at the far end of the house, and the rhythm, throbbing through the floorboards, sounded brisk and businesslike...I flexed my shoulders against the wooden planks beneath me and heard some faint, brief strums coming on an electric guitar, together with the drumbeats...perhaps the noise had brought me round. Slowly, a little tentatively, I stood up and started to massage the sore muscles above the edges of my hips...I rubbed at my neck and pondered what time of the morning it might be...a second guitar was distinctly starting up, and some sort of keyboard music was working its way into the tune...it sounded as if maybe the whole of the band had something doing, a practice session...it felt marvellous to me that they could manage to dredge up the energy. I leaned on the kitchen bench, gazing out through the window...some yellow and pink towels in the back yard were draped dry and motionless on a saggy rope clothesline...I let myself imagine how the sky above the washing looked like the kind of flat and wide blue space you saw at the back of a painting...the rough dry grass everywhere around the yard was glimmering with gold in the fresh tints of sunlight...there was even an early monarch butterfly perched on the edge of a bush, warming its red wings, and it seemed that all the bad feeling of the previous evening had gone. Unmistakeably now, one of the guitars was starting up on some sort of introduction...next I heard the rest of the band joining in, louder though still far away...I turned, roused myself and began to walk through the house towards the loping rhythms of the song...the notes of the music were intriguing, familiar...gradually I recognised them as 'The Weight,' and was delighted that I knew it...it was a pity there was nobody in the dining-room or the hallway to share this with as I passed through. Even the living-room was almost empty when I walked in...only Georgie was there, sitting at his drum kit...he'd dragged it over to the bay window and had it set up facing outside, and he was playing his drums in the sun-rinsed space of the bay for all he was worth...the steady boom and bash of the bass and snare crashed off the walls of the room all around us, and the sounds were mixed with more music coming from somewhere out in front of the house. I approached Georgie across the room and nodded my head, still not sure if he was even aware of my presence...before him, Georgie had the window sashes pushed up and open, and he was staring out while he played, jiggling on his seat with his back very straight...he kept his elbows up high at each beat and seemed lost, close to dreaming, as he measured off each bar...I stepped nearer and watched him prodding the bass-drum pedal with his foot, and after a moment of hesitation I started to twist sideways and wedge myself past a cymbal on a stand to get a look outside...Georgie hit the cymbal nonchalantly at the end of a roll. I could see the porch before me was crammed with equipment and busy...the rest of the band had set itself up there and by the corner of the house...they were playing to an impromptu audience that was gathered in the narrow space remaining over the path, the grass and garden at the front of the flat...most of the people listening were sitting about on a number of large mattresses and immediately I wanted to join them...I got around past Georgie's kit and struggled to work my legs up and out through the window. Everyone was staring at me as I stepped down into the rear of the band, but I didn't care because it was tricky work...I was distracted by an extravagance of wrapped wires and band-equipment lying all across the porch...the stuff was spread out in a treacherous fashion everywhere that I tried to put my feet…I had to stop myself from bumping into a precarious stack of untidy black amplifiers, or from falling against some speakers next to them which were facing off to the road. Finally I straightened up and was standing outside, and nearby at the centre of the clutter I beheld Dean… he was stooped at a keyboard with his robe trailing back about him, glaring at me and trying to sing into a mike arranged on a long pole…I started to get the pleasant feeling that I was really disturbing him. I commenced fumbling over the porch towards the audience…it felt easiest just to cross in front of the band, since I was pretty much one of the musos now in any case…I saw two guitarists were a little away to one side of Dean, both playing with their shirts off in the sun…they were skinny, and the lean muscles of their arms were flexed where they gripped at the necks of their guitars…the taller of them had long, lank hair that drifted down almost to his pickup…another man stood behind them with a saxophone at the ready swinging from a tight wire cord round his neck. I glanced again at the mattresses, which nearly everyone before me was sitting on…the mattresses were misshapen and tucked into pink-and-striped covers, and I supposed they'd been hauled out from the bedrooms and simply dropped down onto the garden from upstairs…there were a lot of people on them, and everybody was sitting and squatting anywhere they could manage…most people were smoking, and they were balancing bottles upright close to their feet in the unkempt grass…still more visitors were standing around at the gate or leaning over the fence. I picked a path towards Lonno, who was sitting on a mattress nearby that had a free corner of it sticking out a little beside him…briefly I turned back and noticed Dean shooting me a superior look, even while he went on moaning his vocals…I supposed he hadn't much liked being upstaged, but the rest of the band seemed relaxed and I thought they sounded good…I squatted down next to Lonno on the spare corner of the spongy bedding, and my buttocks could feel the warmth from the sunshine coming up through the kapok…Lonno nodded solemnly at me…he was smoking, and he took out a packet and passed me a cigarette. 'Okay, good,' he growled. 'Now we can bloody get some coffee. Some of us have been waiting for you, eh.' Lonno chuckled. Then he added, 'Sammy was, like, not letting anyone go into the kitchen at all while you were asleep.' Lonno offered me his lighter and I lit the cigarette he'd given me…I handed the lighter back, and the music swept over my thoughts while the sun satisfyingly burned my skin…I felt at peace, so very much at peace that it seemed impossible to

believe in the existence of any kind of trouble anywhere in the world...
glancing behind me, I saw the number of passers-by collected at the gate
had grown...the police car was gone from over the road, and that was a
pity, I decided, because they were really missing something. The band
reached the end of a chorus...suddenly Georgie's drum-beats stopped
coming from inside the house...the band tried going on without him, but
there was no cue for the rhythm and the tune dwindled and died...Dean
started thumping a fist against his keyboard...there was a short wail of
feedback through the amplifiers. 'What the fuck's going on?' Dean
shouted near his microphone. Georgie stuck his head out from the lower
half of the window...his eyes were sparkling with embarrassment. 'Wow,'
he said, and giggled. He added, 'I reckoned we'd finished, eh. I guessed
it was, you know, the song was—you know, over.' Georgie popped his
head quickly back inside...we heard him smack his sticks together,
calling 'three, four,' and he recommenced his drumming...no one else
from the band joined in. Finally, 'The Weight' straggled together again
from the top...by the time the band reached the rising harmonies at the
end of the first chorus I found a podgy man had come up and halted just
behind Lonno and me...he began half crouching down at our backs,
forcing himself a bit into the limited space available...he wore a green
card-dealer's visor wrapped across his forehead and it flopped above his
face as he moved...but something about the sight of the man nagged at
my memory, until I recognised him as the fellow whose wife was pregnant,
the woman with the blood-pressure problems...I twisted round as best I
could towards him and asked after her condition. 'Oh, she's good,' the
man murmured. He smiled and nodded, as if happy at the mere idea of
what he'd just said. Next he added, 'All systems go.' I wasn't certain if this
meant his wife would give birth soon or not, so I thought perhaps I'd
better ask about that too...but the man was busy slipping something into
Lonno's hand...he pointed at me. 'Yous both have one of these,' he said.
Suddenly the man glanced around him in a hurry, and I saw that already
he was getting to his feet again...I watched him start to move away,
heading for the gate by tiptoeing among the people on the mattresses...a
moment later Lonno opened his hand close to my side and let me take a
peek at what he was holding...two small squares of pastel-blue paper
were nestled on his palm. 'Acid,' he whispered. He passed me one...I took
the little square between my thumb and forefinger...then Lonno also
stood up abruptly, stretched in a rather odd, self-conscious manner and

began to walk off. For a few seconds I stared at the tiny bit of paper between my fingers…it was amazing, I thought…I felt convinced it was amazing even though nothing had actually happened yet…but I realised I wasn't exactly sure what to do with the acid, and I was even less sure what the acid would do with me…I looked around for advice about maybe swallowing it, but everyone else was watching the band…in the end, I put the mysterious square of paper into my pocket. I sat in the sun and finished my smoke instead…there was plenty of wine around, and I managed to have a glass or two with some other people, but at last I got up from my spot and wandered along the outside of the house towards the back door and the kitchen…on the way the narrow passage between the fence and the dining-room was in shade and it felt pleasantly cool after all the heat in the front garden, so that my head grew clearer…when I pushed open the back door into the kitchen, I found Moondog and Jordan together inside…they were standing not far off in a corner and were half bent over, intently examining some sort of wide, badly blackened saucepan on top of the hissing stove. I could see that both Moondog and Jordan were focusing their attention hard on something cooking in the pan…the same look of anxiety was attached to each of their faces as they peered forwards over the rim…I noticed that after last night Jordan seemed especially tired, though otherwise he appeared normal enough… he kept craning his stringy neck to get himself further over the top of the saucepan…but Moondog raised his head and saw me, and he beamed energetically. 'Well, well, well,' he said. 'Sleeping bloody beauty. You know, it was only a few minutes ago we were talking about you.'

'About me?' I asked, and moved closer.

But Moondog returned his attention to the saucepan…he took its handle and jiggled the whole pot a little on the flame…an oily smell of liquid wax came up into the air across the kitchen…Moondog stepped back, and I saw the edge of one of his jandals brush against something, a row of fat green cylinders down by his feet…there were six of them, and I realised they were large green candles, up-ended and placed neatly along the floor near the wall. 'What about it? How'd you like to fly over to Sydney today?' Moondog was asking. As if anticipating my surprise, he added quickly, 'See the thing is, mate, we need someone to do us a favour eh. It's for the Ozzie run this afternoon—you know, like what Beats went on a couple of nights ago. You want yourself a free trip?' Moondog looked at me and cocked his head to one side in a comical way, but I could tell he was watching very carefully for my reaction.

'I don't know,' I replied. 'It's just that—I've never been overseas before.' I considered this point further for a moment and said, 'I don't have a passport.'

'Yeah, no problem. You don't really need one, except just in case,' Moondog announced, and grinned. Without taking his eyes off me he raised the saucepan by its handle from the stove...making small gentle circles, he started swirling around the molten material at the bottom of the pan, and next I heard the gas jet give a fierce little gulp as he turned it off. 'See, we'll lend you Jordan's passport, eh,' Moondog said. 'You're about roughly the same height, and you've both got dark hair.' 'Yeah, dark hair,' Jordan agreed, a bit too hastily for my liking. He added, with the tone of someone summing up, 'We look pretty much near to the same, more or less.' I was horrified at the mere idea of looking anything like him at all...but then after an instant of reflection I supposed it was just about possible...I wondered if the pair of them here were improvising all this, and I tried hard not to let my muddled feelings show too much on my face. Moondog crouched down, still with the pan swaying in his hand, and he began deftly dribbling warm wax into the hollowed dimple at the bottom of one of the candles...I watched while he filled the hole until the candle's base was sealed level and smooth...he wriggled slightly on his haunches and moved to fill another...Moondog never stopped grinning as he worked, and he looked up to fix his gaze on me again for a time before finally going back to fussing with the saucepan. 'Just don't shave off your beard,' he muttered almost to himself. I touched my chin...it had produced a couple of days of growth once more...in fact, it felt as if the bristles were coming out quite well with a nice, even spread...I went on rubbing at my face and leaned over to take in more closely what Moondog was doing.

After a while I asked, 'Is that hash inside there?'

I gestured to indicate the darkish smudges in the green colour near the centre of each of the candles, just as Moondog finished sealing the last one...I thought that, if I was right about the hash, there was an awful lot of it. 'You go and take all this stuff over there, eh, and in the airport you only tell them it's presents,' Jordan said quietly beside me. I needed a moment to understand what he meant...then I glanced at Moondog's face for confirmation...he was peering down close at his handiwork to see if the wax was completely flush across the candle-bottoms, but I could tell that, even without looking at me directly, he was still registering every detail of my behaviour...in the silence that followed I made a thing out of gazing at the up-ended candles too...they were bulky and decorative, almost innocent-looking, and their colour was dull and rich, a bit like a thick pea soup...there were a few dribbled white streaks that ran prettily along their sides.

'I don't have a proper travel-bag for this,' I said at last. 'It wouldn't—'

'I'll lend you my backpack,' Jordan cut in. Something about his eagerness made me turn towards him and study his face...I wondered whether his passport photo showed all the ugly studs that were stuck into his ear.

'So why not you?' I asked him. 'Why aren't you going to head over to Oz?'

'Because I've got to go to Hamilton again tomorrow,' Jordan snapped. 'With Dean. All right?' 'Sammy's going as well,' Moondog announced in what sounded a lot like a shrewd tone. He was still crouched in his position on the floor.

I asked, 'To Hamilton?'

'No, to Oz,' Moondog said firmly. He started to blow a little on the candles...but the wax was already good and dry, and looked solid. 'Yeah, and there's a couple of hundred bucks in it for yous,' Jordan said. My mind had begun to race, thinking about Australia and Sammy, although I knew this was utter foolishness...but I remained hopelessly dumb in the face of any kind of temptation.

'Why is Sammy going?' I asked.

Moondog raised his head, and I watched his eyes flicker in calculation as he gazed up at me. 'She's worried about D.C.,' he said slowly. 'I told her not to sweat it. But anyway, she reckons she'd go over with you and get a line on what happened.' He smiled sardonically. Next he added, 'I hope it's not too much of a hassle for you, eh.' 'Yeah,' Jordan piped up. He said, 'She had a bit of a barney with Dean about it.' They stopped talking and waited for my response...I thought that now the whole business was there in front of me, or at any rate as much of it as they were ever going to let me see...I didn't really know if I should believe them both or not...but one thing in all this was certain, I'd never been to Sydney before.

'What time's the flight?' I asked.

The flight was in just a few hours...Moondog sent me upstairs to star getting ready...he said that I should at least scrounge myself up a clean

T-shirt...I hunted about and after a bit I found one, a pastel red shirt, wrinkled and half folded, hanging on a rail in the bathroom...it was a little large, but it was dry and cleanish and would probably do. Since I was there, I decided to have me a quick wash into the bargain...the bottom of the bathroom's old white enamel tub was covered with some sort of buttery yellow stain, but it looked all right to go ahead, and I spotted the remnant of a cake of soap on the lino...I bent and ran some water from the ancient, squeaky taps...I got undressed and sat in the bath while it went on filling up with water...the muffled noise of the concert out front was coming through a louver window just above my head and the whole show sounded in full swing...contentedly I patted my hand against the tub's rim to the rhythm of the music. My mind drifted to ideas of being in Sydney together with Sammy...I could see myself at a table in a small but cosy flat, with my novel coming along while Sammy was busying about nearby...I smelled the invigorating aroma of eucalyptus wafting in from the gum trees outside and heard a fly buzzing somewhere on a sun-warmed windowpane...I'd become a young writer to watch...I thought of how, after my productive day's writing, Sammy and I would go out in the evening and paint the town red...on the morning of the next day we'd wake up in each other's arms to the blunt Ozzie sunlight, lie about amongst the bedclothes and fuck, and everything would be perfect and lovely. When finally I got back downstairs from the bath, Moondog and Jordan were waiting for me in the dining-room...I saw they'd stowed the candles away in the bottom of an old orange backpack, and they'd even thrown in some random clothes and a towel as well...I glanced into the pack at the jumble of stuff and supposed it all appeared about right...but Moondog looked in a hurry to get me gone, and his face was blotching up as he tried to restrain his nerves...he started saying that a ticket for the flight was waiting at the airport and it was already booked in Jordan's name...he said there was no problem because what I needed to do was just ask for it at the check-in counters when I got to the departure terminal. While Moondog was explaining all this Jordan pulled something from his back pocket...he held a bent, battered navy-blue booklet out towards me...I could tell it was his passport, but before I could take it from him he peeled open the first page with his photo on view inside...even at a distance I saw that the picture was of someone surprisingly respectable... the photo didn't look much like the real Jordan, but then it didn't look so much like me either. Jordan stepped closer and held the passport's page with its picture up beside my face...he stared at it self-consciously. 'Yeah, that black eye'll help,' Jordan said at last. He dropped the passport into the open top of the backpack...I leaned over and tightened up the drawstring and pulled down the flap...the pack smelled of canvas, and I noticed the metal frame was broken along one side and had been bound up with wire...it didn't seem as if anyone was going to send me out of the house with their most precious possessions...I knelt down to work at adjusting the shoulder straps, and at the same time half-ignored some complicated information Moondog was trying to give me...it was something about finding the airport bus in town. 'Look, you really need to go, because now is the flaming hour,' he said. He appeared more anxious to be rid of me than he was in clarifying his instructions, so I figured I'd better simply check things with people a bit further along the line. Moondog added, 'Try heading your way out from the kitchen. It's probably best, eh, in case the cops are parked at the front again. There's this gap in the back fence—in a spot over near the corner, right? Just nip through and you can get yourself down the driveway on the other side.'

'What about Sammy?' I asked.

'Sammy's going to meet you at the airport,' Moondog said. I stood up and he gave me a small wad of cash...the money felt pleasantly thick in my fingers, and it took quite a bit of stuffing to push into my pocket...then he handed over a piece of paper with a long telephone number written in the middle. 'Ring this when you make it to Oz and arrange a pickup,' he said carefully. Moondog looked very serious now and he was focusing on me hard...the furrows across his high forehead were set in deep red lines under the skin...I watched his eyes searching my face again, as if questioning whether he could rely on me...I glanced across at Jordan, but he didn't want to meet my gaze. 'If you find yourself bloody getting into strife, get rid of that paper straight away,' Moondog said.

'Okey-dokey,' I said.

I hoisted up Jordan's backpack...it was rather heavy on my shoulders, and I was aware of things shifting inside...I shook the pack up and down a couple of times till it felt settled and right. Suddenly Moondog seemed to hesitate...I worried that he might be about to stop me, to change his mind, and so I turned with no more than a curt nod of goodbye and headed into the kitchen...it was a relief that neither he nor Jordan followed me and in a moment I was marching out of the back door...I congratulated myself that at least I'd got the first part of the plan off pat. Outside, ducked past the clothesline and soon spied a small collection of long, rotten palings lying spread on the ground near a far corner of the yard's decrepit wooden fence...there was a hole where the palings had fallen, or perhaps been prised away and abandoned...I bent and manoeuvred through the narrow open space in the fence, not bothering to take off the pack, and on the other side my feet went into the soft, loamy dirt of a sparsely planted flowerbed...I straightened up and saw I was in somebody else's back yard...a bit of rough lawn was just in front of me and also the end of a house that was only half painted in a thin brown finish...further off nearby was an empty carport and one edge of a long, scoria-covered driveway. Casually I picked my way out of the flowerbed and across the lawn, scraping the dirt from my shoes onto the grass as I went, and soon I commenced walking down the crunchy pink gravel on the driveway for the road...I was passing close to the side of what appeared to be an old railway cottage, one that was in the process of being maintained or done up...little of this felt like anything Moondog had described, as far as I could remember it...but nobody happened to notice me from any of the cottage's windows...I strolled out of the front drive past the letterbox and onto a tiny, featureless street, and I guessed that at a pinch I could now pretend to be the owner of the place behind me. After going a block or so I cut back to the main road...I kept on plodding downhill, thinking how I was playing it by ear already, though perhaps this was actually the best idea...I told myself that whatever was likely to turn up, it felt better, it felt great, just to be off once more and heading somewhere...a few minutes later I crossed beneath the railway bridge and stopped at a dairy to get a new exercise book for my novel...if I had a chance, I could maybe write something on the plane, and this time round I'd be rewriting...rewriting was where artists became professionals. My thoughts skipped along, and my ideas about a really grouse, immortal masterpiece occupied me far more than the steady pace of my own feet...in my mind I became involved with organising the illustration for the novel's cover...I started selecting endorsements for the blurb...I considered the general torrent of rapturous reviews, the fuss and hokum of promotion...when I finally got round to paperback editions I wasn't paying proper attention to where I was going, but it wouldn't have helped much anyway...I had no clue at all about where the airport bus or any other kind of bus might be. Eventually I crossed a broad intersection at some lights...it felt as if I'd been here before and I decided that I must be getting close to town...but instead of heading down a slope as I'd half expected, I discovered I was toiling up a narrow street with the asphalt on the footpath loose beneath the soles of my shoes...soon I was walking beside a long white picket fence that strained to hold back a grassy mess of scrub and bushes behind it...a lot of cars were parked up on both sides of the road around me, some with their wheels over the low kerb, and I had the impression that people had been feeding the meters to let the vehicles stay put there the whole day. But when I crested the slope, I found a tall, flat hotel tower was located not far off on the other side of the street...it was set well back from the buildings nearby, taking up lots of space along the road, and it looked like the sort of ritzy pile where international travellers chose to stop...I stared up at the tower's columns of windows and watched them shimmering with reflected light against the blue sunlit sky...I continued approaching on my side of the road until I was almost opposite the tower...there was a nicely trimmed lawn extending across the front of the building from the forecourt, with a neat row of dull grey birch trees grouped in the lawn's centre...past all the trees a white mini-van was waiting, off in a narrow turning-bay, and I could make out the words 'Airport Shuttle-Bus' boldly stencilled in large blue letters on the van's side. I headed out between a couple of parked cars into the road and crossed the street... when I reached the far kerb, I marched quickly up the hotel drive towards the turning-bay, giving everything the once-over...there was no doorman out front in the shade of the covered entrance area...in fact the whole of the building appeared deserted and quiet...apart from a dog whining somewhere I could have heard a pin drop...the only person around I could see was a driver sitting at the wheel of the van, a fellow dressed in a loose white shirt. I got closer and saw more clearly through the van's front windscreen that the driver was a portly, middle-aged Maori man with puffy face and heavy-lidded eyes...his skin looked so dark and velvet that it had almost a purplish tinge...the driver had his side-window down with an arm up on the edge and his solid elbow stuck out, and he seemed very comfortable...he was having a cigarette which he held in a delicate fashion between his large fingers, drawing on it gently as if he wanted to savour the taste.

'Excuse me,' I called, still from some distance off.

The driver shifted a little in his seat...he began watching my approach with a hard stare set on his features, but I ignored it...I came up beside his open window and tried glancing past him through into the back of the

376

van...there were no passengers anywhere within that I could see.

'Excuse me, you couldn't give me a lift out to the airport, could you?' I asked.

'So, you a guest in the hotel, eh mate?' the driver replied. He went on examining me, and his disdainful look suggested he already knew the answer...I noticed he had a tiny grey pencil moustache which waggled on the end of his upper lip as he spoke.

'No, I'm not really staying with you guys, sort of style,' I confessed. 'Sorry about that,' I added.

Suddenly the driver started to laugh...it came up from his big belly in a friendly-sounding giggle. 'Well, you *are* polite,' he muttered at last. He took a strong drag on his cigarette, and amid a cloud of exhaled smoke he added, 'Good enough for me. Hop in, eh.' I didn't trouble myself with feigning any kind of restraint...I just slid open the door at the side of the van, mumbled some thanks and climbed up as fast as I could into the empty space in the rear...even before choosing myself a seat from the three rows available I shoved the door shut behind me...it gave off a long rattling thud as it rolled back into place...then, bent half over under the roof, I shuffled forwards and lowered myself into a seat at the very front, right behind the driver...by now I was feeling well content. The driver did nothing for a few minutes but continue to enjoy his smoke and rub with his free hand under the loose collar of his open-necked shirt...finally he leaned far out of the van's window with the stub of his cigarette in his fingers and tossed the fag-end gently across the asphalt driveway onto the grass...he drew himself back in and started the engine, but he let it idle, still not in any hurry... the base of my badly upholstered seat commenced shuddering from the vibrations of the motor...I guessed it was now time for the shuttle to leave, but there weren't any other passengers coming out of the hotel to join us. 'Handy thing you happened along in the end, eh,' the driver said over his shoulder after a minute more. I saw him check his watch, but still he did nothing else...after a while he spoke up again above the lazy rumble of the engine. 'Where you flying off to?' he asked.

'Sydney,' I said. Next I added, 'I've got myself a job delivering a consignment of illegal drugs.'

The driver laughed in his falsetto giggle once again and finished up with a grunting cough. 'Yeah, good one,' he said. He reached out and put the van into gear...within a moment we began to creep forwards along the driveway for the road, almost a little reluctantly...when the front wheels dipped into the gutter, the driver halted us and glanced round at me in my seat. 'Hey, you want a smoke?' he asked.

'Is it tobacco?' I asked back.

The driver laughed even harder. 'Good one,' he said. He pulled a badly crushed cigarette packet out from a shelf near the dashboard and held it raised up over his shoulder, waving the packet in my direction...I took a smoke from it and thought how we were getting on famously...after that, we drove off down to Mangere...this was the second occasion I'd been driven to the airport in nearly as many days and I was beginning to think that perhaps I'd seen and done all there was in Auckland...but at least it was interesting to take in some of the local sights during the daytime hours. At last the driver headed into the long turnoff that I remembered going down on my previous trip to the airport, and this time I could see there was flat green farmland around us with the fence-lines set far back from the road...there was little traffic except for our van, and I gazed at straggles of sheep in the distance, fattening themselves serenely in the paddocks...we cruised down the length of the dull, straight road and finally passed a few warehouses, a car park and a cluster of signposts on a pole...I saw we'd reached the edge of the International Terminal. The driver dropped me off at the wide, ornately curving veranda I'd been standing under two nights earlier...I got out, made extra sure that my pack was in good order and slung it onto my shoulders...then I opened the passenger door and thanked the driver again for his kindness...we shook hands while he wished me luck...when I shut the door and walked away, felt like somebody parting from an old friend. Inside the airport building, thought the place hadn't changed at all since I'd last seen it...the long row of intimidating-looking check-in counters was still there, but with a hand sign propped against one counter that said something about tickets... went up to the counter, peeled the bulky backpack off my shoulders once more and deposited it at my feet...after everything that had been going on, simply to pause and take in a breath or two seemed nice. Across from me stood an overweight woman who was wearing a white shirt and a new black business dress, and who was preoccupied with writing down lists numbers on a page in a ring-binder...I saw there was a thin silver chain hanging near the edge of her collar, and I supposed it might have hung lot lower on a person whose neck wasn't quite so large...after a while the woman closed the ring-binder and asked how she could help...I told her that a ticket was all set someplace around here and ready for me to colle

'Right. And under what name would it be?' the woman asked in a deep voice which suddenly made me think of Mrs McCreedy.

'You know, that's a good question,' I said.

Laboriously I untied the pack on the floor in front of the counter and pulled out the passport…I straightened up, managed to get the first page open and peered into it.

'Jordan Sanders,' I read aloud.

'Right. Just one moment, Mr Sanders,' the woman said in a frigid tone. She turned and marched away along the counters, and I started to wonder if something bad could be about to happen, but a few minutes later she was back with my ticket tucked into a little, glossy white-paper folder…the woman directed me to another check-in counter, though when I picked up my pack I decided on rambling a bit through the terminal instead…it was still pretty much on the early side for the flight. Upstairs on the first floor I wandered into a small cafeteria and had something to eat, and afterwards I went searching for Sammy…she was nowhere about, but I hoped that maybe I'd just bump into her in the building, because the whole place felt fairly quiet…at last I tried looking for her up on the observation deck but found it almost deserted…the observation deck was a lengthy, narrow room in which the only furniture was a single line of hard blue plastic benches spread close to the windows, and I selected one of the benches to sit on and have a break. Through the thick glass window panels I gazed outside at the level vista of the runway, long and grey and with coloured markings, while the planes left the ground and landed…there appeared to be a lot of aircraft, a real collection of them ranging from tiny up to very large, and I spied what seemed a jumbo in the near distance coming in and banking for its approach…I'd never seen a jumbo jet before…it swung lower and lower…I thought it looked more like a building arriving out of the sky than a plane…the jet reached the runway, briefly hovered, and set all its wheels down on the tarmac with a tremendous bang that seemed to menace everything around it. I shifted on the bench and felt nervously about in my pocket for my ticket…the ticket was there still, together with the money and the crumpled note containing the telephone number in Sydney…but up against the lining I also found the tiny square with the LSD. For a few seconds I fiddled to get the square of acid between my fingers, then took it out and stared at the odd, forgotten bit of paper…I wondered how it would taste…I sniffed it for any strange signs, put it against my lower lip and swallowed…it tasted like nothing at all.

After that I sat for a good while longer, nodding to anyone who happened to walk past, until finally I was restless and bored with sitting and I bent to open the backpack by my feet...I thought it best to double-check on how things were, but things weren't really all that great...in the bottom of the bag one of the candles was beginning to leak...I pulled it out, held it up to the light and saw there was a definite hairline crack along the edge of the seal...down in the pack a streak of hash-oil had smeared itself on the exercise book that was going to become my revised and famous novel. It occurred to me that Moondog probably wouldn't want a drop of the hash-oil wasted....I began hunting about the observation deck, thinking perhaps there might be something which would repair the leak, and eventually far over in one of the corners I discovered a cylindrical metal rubbish bin which had a crinkled wad of chewing gum attached to the rim...the gum struck me as just the job...it was still damp in my fingers when I prised it from the bin's chrome plating and carried it away to my seat on the bench...it spread nicely across the crack in the wax, and I was pretty confident it wouldn't come off...I wrapped the restored candle tight in a towel and put the bundle back in place in the bag, rather proud of my own repair work under pressure. Now at last it felt like the real hour for departure, and so I glanced around the room for a clock until I spotted one on the wall near the emergency stairs...to my surprise I could see that my final chance to check in was passing by at just this very instant...without a moment to lose I grabbed the pack, hurried for the emergency exit and scuttled pell-mell down its steps, my footfalls echoing in a sort of ringing panic inside the empty stairwell...but on the ground floor, on impulse, I dashed all the way up to the automatic entrance-doors still flailing with the pack in my hands...the doors opened for somebody else, somebody who was coming in, and I sneaked outside through the gap and at once a confusion of engine noise and human activity hit me on all fronts from under a bright sky...the difference from the terminal interior was stark. On the road before me there were cars halted or pulling to a stop everywhere along the kerb, and from many of them passengers were alighting...there was the high-pitched shriek of a jet performing take-off somewhere behind me...but there was no Sammy, and I felt that I'd got something straight in my head at last...she wasn't going to be with me on the trip. I stood amid the barely manageable bustle of other people and wondered if Sammy had ever really been planning to turn up...I wondered if perhaps Dean had stopped her...perhaps D.C. had phoned at the vital moment and they'd had their talk…on the edges of my mind a few further perhapses began to crystallise, though they only seemed more and more unlikely…this was all such a change from the kind of sendoff Beats had been given. I decided to try checking my bag in anyway…I re-entered the terminal and crossed the lino to the long row of passenger counters, and for the first time I noticed a large red 'Departures' sign that was set far up above the check-in area…by now I'd become resolved on going to Sydney…there was an empty counter where nobody was queuing and I hauled my backpack up onto it…I knew I should be waiting at almost any of the other places, behind other flyers in the proper lines…but that just felt too much like trouble and I was in a desperate rush. Fortunately one of the baggage handlers, a woman in a smart pale-blue airlines uniform, detached herself from the staff who were dealing with the customers nearby and approached me…she took my ticket without uttering a word…next she wrapped a tag on my pack and dropped it onto a conveyor belt behind her, still without saying a word, not even a hint that I was late and behaving badly…I was grateful…I thanked her in an apologetic way while she patiently arranged my seat number and scribbled on some forms. When finally I received my boarding pass, I was beginning to feel strange and light-headed…the woman standing opposite me at the counter was young, and most of her was hidden in the stiff and enveloping folds of her uniform, but I could see she had wide, attractive cheekbones and a long neck…I could also see that the blue-and-white scarf pinned at the front of her jacket was very large and hung very low, and had an interesting sort of sweep to it…the narrow-brimmed hat perched on the woman's head made her look unusually tall…at that moment the woman smiled at me with a new and pleasant air…it was a smile that came right out at me over the counter, and I grinned back, quite a bit more broadly than I'd meant to. 'Is there anything else?' she asked.

'I don't know,' I said.

I was thinking how intense the blue of her uniform had become.

'*Is* there anything?' I tried to ask in response.

We stood together for what seemed a long, long while…I just couldn't stop grinning at this astoundingly attractive woman who was standing behind the counter in a hat which went almost to the ceiling…it was hard believe how much I was captivated by her company. 'May I suggest you the departures area upstairs, sir?' the attractive woman said, resuming r patient manner.

'That's a good idea,' I said. 'That's a really, really good idea,' I added.

I smiled broadly once more…everything in my mind had become formed somehow, the totality of it, in ways that were very complicated to consider…but I applied myself, and in the end I spoke mostly by instinct.

'Are those guys calling my flight?' I asked.

'They've been calling it for a few minutes, sir,' the woman replied. I nodded, since this type of reply felt more and more comprehensible the more I took it in, and I turned and walked away…but after a short period of walking I stopped and squeezed my eyes tight shut…when I opened them again, the room was nearly a complete white in its glittering brightness… as everything came back into proper focus, I realised I was standing still by the escalators…by now though, they were the most amazingly hypnotic escalators I'd ever seen in my entire life, and the whole jaw-dropping idea of taking a ride on one without needing to walk felt incredible…up, the slinky metal steps kept going, up, up, up. Then I noticed a down escalator arriving right there in front of me too, and for a time the breathless choice of going either up or down was more than I could manage…but finally I remembered with glee that the down escalator was useless because the escalator was stopping, right there, on the ground floor…I stepped onto the smoothly sliding up-belt and glanced about me with an air of triumph while I rose…my eyes went in large sweeps over the whole place, but there was no last-minute sign of Sammy to be made out anywhere… wondered if, like me, my backpack could also manage finding its way to the plane on its own at this last minute, but when I reached the first floor just sashayed across the concourse feeling easy in my mind…it was good not to worry. There were plenty of people around, but I ignored them… made directly for the elaborate green portal labelled 'Departures'…it came up fast, all by itself, and I headed on through…on the other side an angry-looking official man wearing a fuzzy grey suit and a tie was seated at a table in front of me and talking non-stop…he kept demanding over and over to see my boarding pass and asking whether I had a passport. luckily the exact same things happened to be there, between my finger so I thought it best to give them to him. 'Mr Sanders,' the man snapped 'You'll have to shake a leg if you want to get to your gate, eh. Your plane leaving at any moment.' I tried to register what the man had just told me but it was hard to concentrate on his words…I was too busy examining the gang of white mice that were frolicking across every inch of his tabletop

'Okey-dokey,' I said.

The man swivelled in his swivelling chair...he was calling to yet another pretty woman in a blue uniform...I watched her approach, and next I heard the man barking a gate number at her in a very negative fashion. 'This way, sir,' the woman said to me. Her tone was urgent...she gestured with one long outstretched arm while she started striding off ahead...I worked at following the pretty young woman...we were hauling arse...I liked her an awful lot for just how confident she seemed...she'd determined that I was the right person and she was taking me to the right place. Back over her shoulder the woman called to me, 'You'll really need to rush, sir, if you mean to catch your flight.' Unfortunately the heavy carpet beneath my feet was dissolving into sticky treacle, but I still managed quite a good job of keeping up...I felt the patterns on the carpet were beautiful and endlessly intricate...they were branches in a dense forest from some wonderful fairy story...it must have been a tale that someone had neglected to tell me, because for the life of me I couldn't remember how it might turn out...I admired the spectacular threads of the manifold branches...I admired the rapid way they extended and receded under the soft drumming of my shoes...they were scurrying to go everywhere and nowhere all at the same time. So, this is acid, I thought. To my surprise we reached the gate almost within an instant, but had no chance to ponder this...the woman directed me through, using a professional sort of fluster...she pushed my documents into my hand and I headed out carefully onto the echoing airbridge...I was fascinated by the curved white wall of the actual plane as I approached, and by the long spreading lines of rivets on its fuselage...a stewardess, waiting at an exquisitely low doorway that displayed soft, rounded corners, asked me if I had any cabin baggage.

'Nothing,' I said, and she let me past.

Inside the plane, it took me quite a while to find my seat...there appeared to be so many to choose from...the aircraft was mostly full with people already sitting down, but I didn't want to let that detail limit me...a stewardess at the front of the plane took my boarding pass, and she led me firmly back along the aisle and far through the cabin...it turned out my seat was near the wing, beside a white window moulded in plastic. I shuffled past the knees of a pair of people who occupied the seats next mine and sat down in my own spot...immediately I examined the tray set into the seatback in front of me and fiddled with its latch...I picked up the loose straps of my safety belt and buckled it across my lap, getting it

tight, then unbuckled and buckled it a few times more, just to make s
that the thing was really on...at last I reclined my back and should
into the spongy, welcoming cushions of my seat and grinned at my c
folly...the passengers next to me had showed no interest in what I w
doing, but for a little bit I gazed steadily into their nondescript face
we all of us understood exactly why we were here. Outside, through
window, the wing was amazing...it stretched wide and flat and lean acr
the tarmac...it went way on stretching, all by itself, up into the dazzl
clear blue of the sky...around me the whole long cabin was throbb
with music and voices and with the colours of a thousand pictures...
sounds and colours seemed to flow easily in and out of me, and I was
going to have any more trouble now selecting the first thing that ca
into my mind. I thought of all that had happened to me and what I co
write about...I thought of Gizi, and how glad I was to have met he
soon she'd have her moment in the spotlight, just as everyone shou
but that life would be unconnected to mine, something new made fr
something I couldn't understand...the idea left me with a stab of h
in my heart, followed by a surge of joy so powerful that I could scarc
breathe...everything seemed to be behind me now, but I told myself t
was only an illusion...then suddenly I thought that, on balance, th
must be a God, and that He is on the side of the young and does not l
us to get old. With a jiggle the plane started to move...we were mov
backwards...I gasped, and was completely thrilled by it...I had no id
that planes could be made to travel backwards...but then, I'd never be
on an airplane before. We bumbled along over the runway...the inter
of the cabin was shaking gently around us...it was all systems go...af
a while I imagined that, when we took off at last, I'd be flying upward i
the boundless spaces in my own wild head.